P9-CRC-826

14 DAYS

GAYLORD M

WOLF
IN THE
SHADOWS

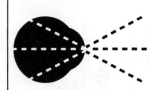

This Large Print Book carries the
Seal of Approval of N.A.V.H.

WOLF IN THE SHADOWS

MARCIA MULLER

Thorndike Press • Thorndike, Maine

Thorndike Large Print® Cloak & Dagger Series edition published in 1993 by arrangement with Warner Books, Inc.

The tree indicium is a trademark of Thorndike Press.

Set in 16 pt. News Plantin by Barbara Ingerson.

Printed in the United States on acid-free, high-opacity paper. ⊚

Library of Congress Cataloging in Publication Data

Muller, Marcia.
    Wolf in the shadows / Marcia Muller.
       p.   cm.
    ISBN 0-7862-0087-1 (alk. paper : lg. print)
    1. McCone, Sharon (Fictitious character) — Fiction.
2. Private investigators — California — San Francisco —
Fiction. 3. Women detectives — California — San Francisco —
Fiction. 4. Large type books. I. Title.
    [PS3563.U397W64   1993b]
    813'.54—dc20   93-37404

*For Anne-Marie d'Hyevre and
Michael Dowdall*

Many thanks to Liz Alexander, Lewis Berger, Sacramento County Deputy District Attorney Janice Hayes, Betty Lamb, DeEtte Turner, Collin Wilcox, and an anonymous officer of the U.S. Border Patrol. Your generous volunteering of your time, expertise, and insights is greatly appreciated.

And special thanks to my in-house editor and husband, Bill Pronzini.

Part
One

Part
One

Thursday, June 10

The mesa was the most desolate place I'd ever seen.

I climbed out of the Scout and followed my guide across rock-strewn ground where nothing but mesquite and spiny cholla cactus grew. The morning was overcast, the air saturated with salt-laden moisture — spitty weather, we used to call it. The wind blew sharp and icy off the flat gray sea.

Ahead of us where the ground dropped off to distant ranchland stood the tumbledown adobe hut. My guide, Andrés, stopped several yards from it and waited for me to join him. "There is where it happened," he said in a hushed voice.

I looked at the hut, felt nothing. It was simply a relic of a bygone time, crumbling now into the earth that had formed it. I started toward it, then glanced back at my companion. He stood, arms folded, staring resolutely at the Pacific. Su-

11

perstitious, I thought, and kept going.

The hut had no roof, and two of the walls leaned in on each other at abnormal angles. I stepped through an opening where a door once had been onto a packed dirt floor. Loose bricks were scattered underfoot, and trash drifted in the corners; fire had blackened the pale clay.

I still didn't feel anything. No more loss or grief, no sense of horror — none of the emotional shock waves that surge through me at the scene of a violent death, even though the death that had happened here should have touched me more deeply than any.

What's **wrong** *with you? I asked myself. You can't have used up all your tears in one night.*

For a few minutes I stood still, looking for something — anything — and willing my emotions to come alive. But there was nothing here, so I turned and went back outside. I felt a tug at the leg of my jeans and glanced down: a little tree, dead now. Poor thing hadn't stood a chance in this inhospitable ground. A few crumpled papers were caught in its brittle branches; I brushed them away. *Rest in peace.*

One of the scraps caught my eye, and I picked it up and smoothed it out: *U.S. Department of Justice, Immigration and Naturalization Service, Notice and Request for Deposition.* The form the border patrol issues to illegal aliens when they pick them up, carelessly discarded here because it didn't matter anyway. *One trip over the border fence and through the wild canyons — infested with rattlers, scorpions, and bandits — had been aborted, but that made no difference. Soon the illegal — in this case, the form showed, one Maria Torres — would be back, and others would follow in a never-ending stream. I let the paper drift from my fingers.*

Then I walked away from the hut where so much had come to an end and stood at the very edge of the headland. To my right lay the distant towers of San Diego and, closer in, the vast Tijuana riverbed. The river itself had long ago been diverted from its original course; it meandered westward, its waters made toxic by Mexico's raw sewage. Straight ahead was its destination, the leaden gray Pacific. And to my left, Baja California. A border patrol helicopter flapped overhead.

I turned and faced south. Cars moved on the toll road leading away from the border; beyond it sprawled the pastel houses and iron and red-tiled roofs of Tijuana. The famed bullring — like a giant satellite TV dish that could service all of Baja — stood alone at the edge of town. I stared at the black steel-paneled boundary fence that lay across the ridge of rugged hills, and thought of satin funeral ribbons.

For a long time I stood there, thoughts and impressions trickling randomly through my mind.

I recalled the words "You keep what you can use, throw the rest away." And then the sluggish flow began to rush in an unstemmable torrent toward the obvious conclusion. When I finally began to feel, the emotions were not the ones I'd anticipated. I turned and ran back to where Andrés still contemplated the sea.

I'd come here this morning on a pilgrimage, thinking that everything was over, finished. Now I realized my search was only beginning.

One

Monday, June 7

"Hey, where're you going in such a hurry? I need to talk with you."

Hank Zahn's hand gripped my shoulder as I tried to squeeze by him on the front stairs of All Souls Legal Cooperative's main building. He jerked me to such an abrupt halt that I nearly lost my footing on the fog-damp step.

"Sorry," my boss added, steadying me with his other hand and whacking me on the elbow with his briefcase.

"Let go of me," I said through gritted teeth, "before we both fall down and end up in matching leg casts."

Hank did as I told him, running his free hand over his wiry gray-brown hair. "Sorry," he repeated.

"Just see that it doesn't happen again." I kept going, hoping to make a getaway while he was still befuddled.

"Wait!" he called.

15

I sighed and turned. "What?"

"I need to talk with you before the partners' meeting at three."

It was close to noon now. "What about?"

Hank's eyes grew evasive behind his thick horn-rimmed glasses. "Oh, some things to do with the reorganization."

So they'd finally coined a term for it — reorganization. It referred, I supposed, to the mixed bag of changes that had gone into effect during All Souls's transition from a small neighborhood law cooperative to one of northern California's largest legal-services plans. At any given time during the past year you could have found at least one employee reeling from some change in job status or description, and now it appeared it was to be the turn of their chief investigator. From the look in Hank's eyes, I wasn't going to like what I heard. Still, I had my priorities. . . .

"Hank," I said, "I'm working a case, and I've got to take off."

"I really need to —"

"I'll try to get back to you before three."

"If not . . ." He paused, looking downright guilty now.

"Yes?"

"The partners would like you to attend the meeting."

Bad sign. Very bad. What the hell was this?

16

Surely they didn't plan to *fire* me? There had been a number of dismissals lately, and Lord knew I'd played fast and loose any number of times with what few rules All Souls had, but I was a good investigator, and they damn well knew it.

I frowned, but before I could say anything, Hank fled up the steps. "Be there," he called back to me.

I watched him go inside, his shoulders hunched under the burden of his guilty knowledge, then shrugged and headed downhill, where my old red MG was sandwiched between the corner and a fireplug.

All the way to Oakland Airport I fretted. I'd just come off an investigation that had turned into a flat-out case of obsession, and I'd expected to give such behavior a rest for a while, but here I was tying myself into emotional knots a day and a half later. From All Souls in San Francisco's Bernal Heights district to Treasure Island in the middle of the Bay Bridge, I obsessed about my job. From Treasure Island to the airport, I obsessed about Hy.

Hy — Heino — Ripinsky. Gentleman sheep rancher and director of an environmental foundation in the Mono County town of Vernon on the shore of Tufa Lake. Multitalented:

17

airplane pilot, book collector, naturalist, sometime diplomat, sometime protester for worthy causes. Long rap sheet to go with the latter. Multilingual: English, Spanish, Russian, and French, speaking all with unaccented fluency. Tall, lanky, hawk-nosed, with shaggy dark-blond hair and a droopy mustache. Given to rugged outdoorsman's clothing, but also at home in formal fund-raising attire. A gentle, passionate man, but a man whom I'd also heard described as dangerous, perhaps violent.

And he did have his darker side. Tragedy in his background: one wife, Julie Spaulding, who had, as he put it, saved him from hell and later died of a debilitating disease. Julie, who had understood his self-destructive urges and wisely established the Spaulding Foundation to occupy his lonely hours. Mystery in his background, too: a nine-year hole, years away from Tufa Lake about which rumors abounded. Rumors, from employment by the CIA to a prison term — and none, I was convinced, that came close to the true story.

Hy refused to tell me the truth, even after we became lovers late in March. The barrier of silence had driven me to set up a case file containing what fragmentary information about his past I'd been able to gather. A file that I'd destroyed only a little over a week ago, convinced I had no right or need to pry into what he seemed determined to conceal, and had set up once again just this morning when I learned from his assistant at the foundation that Hy had apparently staged a deliberate and well-thought-out disappearance.

At first tracking him down had seemed like an adventure, perhaps a response to a subtle challenge on his part. But after an hour of thought, I began to wonder if the disappearance was deliberate after all. Hy didn't play games, not that kind. Now tracking him down seemed imperative. Now I was afraid for him.

Oakland Airport was nearly socked in by fog, and the wind gusted across its north field, where the general aviation terminal was located. A couple of corporate jets were fueling up, but otherwise there was little activity. I skirted the terminal building to the small aircraft tie-downs.

The wind made the Cessnas and Beechcrafts and Pipers strain at the chains that tethered them; their wings creaked and shivered, looking deceptively fragile. I moved quickly among them until I spotted Hy's Citabria Decathlon in the tie-down where he'd parked it last Wednesday morning. Even if it hadn't been in the same place, I would have known it instantly by the blue silhouette of a gull that seemed to soar against the white background and the identification number, 77289. It was a small, high-winged plane — tandem two-seater, and aerobatic. Hy had once proudly informed me that it could fly upside down, but so far, thank God, he hadn't treated *me* to that experience.

As I approached the Citabria, I felt deflated, a little shaky, even. I supposed that in the back of my mind I'd hoped to find it gone, learn that Hy was on his way back to Tufa Lake, and be able to stop worrying. But seeing it here brought the gravity of the situation home to me, and now I was sure that Hy's disappearance wasn't a playful challenge to my investigatory abilities.

When we'd climbed out of the plane last Wednesday morning, back from a Memorial Day weekend vacation in the White Mountains, he'd said he planned to refuel and immediately continue on to San Diego, where one of his many unnamed old buddies had a business proposition to make him. True to form, Hy hadn't given me a hint as to what the proposition might be or where to reach him, had merely said he'd fill me in if it worked out. Probably I should have become concerned for him sooner, because he hadn't called me. One thing — practically the only thing — I could depend on Hy for was to keep in touch.

"Can I help you with something, ma'am?" One of the linemen, bundled against the cold in a down jacket, appeared around the tail of the Citabria. Hy often claimed that a pilot could instantly identify an airport by looking at a picture of the line personnel — in Burbank, for example, they all resembled movie actors — and I had to admit that this one, with his unshorn hair and single earring, had a touch of nearby Berkeley about him.

"This plane," I said, resting my hand on the Citabria's wing, "has it been moved since last Wednesday?"

The man shook his head, then looked more closely at me. "You were the passenger, I remember."

"Right."

"Well, it's been here all along. The people at the counter in the terminal are getting a little curious; fellow said he'd only be tied down overnight, and it's coming up on a week now. He doesn't show pretty soon, they'll have to do some checking."

"He said he'd be staying here in the area?"

"Guess so."

I couldn't believe Hy had lied to me about his destination. That wasn't his style; rather than lie, he'd simply employ silence. "Did he mention where?"

"Not to me. In fact, at first he wasn't going

to stay at all. Said he was going to make a phone call, then fuel up. But when he came back outside, he told me his plans had changed and got his gear."

"And went where? Did somebody pick him up?"

The lineman shrugged. "Didn't notice."

"Well, thanks for your help." I dug in my bag and gave him one of my cards. "If he comes back or calls in, anything like that, will you get in touch with me?"

His eyes widened slightly, the way some people's do when they realize they've been talking to a private investigator. "Sure. You might want to check with Sandy at the desk inside. She probably knows more about this."

"I'll do that." I gave the Citabria a last glance and headed for the terminal.

Sandy had curly auburn hair and a friendly freckled face, and reminded me a little of my assistant, Rae Kelleher. When I explained what I was after, she pulled the card Hy had filled out and let me see it. All it gave was his name, address, and the plane's registration number. He'd also told her that he only intended to tie down overnight and had asked that they have the Citabria refueled.

"The lineman told me that Mr. Ripinsky originally came inside to make a phone call," I said, handing the card back to her.

She nodded and motioned toward the pay phones. "He did that before he checked in with me."

I myself had made a brief call before driving back to the city; Hy must have come in very soon afterward. "Did you notice if it was local or long-distance?"

"Long-distance. He came over and asked me for change for the phone, but I couldn't spare any, so he said he'd use his credit card."

"Did he make just the one call?"

"No, two. And he wrote something down, maybe directions."

"And then he checked in with you?"

"Yes. Afterward he went outside, and a little while later I saw him talking with Jerry, one of the linemen who was just going off shift. I got the impression they know each other pretty well. Does Mr. Ripinsky fly in here a lot?"

"Fairly often. Is Jerry working today?"

She shook her head. "He's on vacation — visiting his folks in the Midwest, I think. Won't be back till next week."

Dead end for now — dammit.

"Jerry gave him a ride," Sandy added. "Probably to the main terminal."

"What makes you think they went there?"

"Because Jerry's seeing a waitress at the snack bar there and he usually goes over and has breakfast when he gets off."

"You're a good observer."

"Well, I had a good subject." She winked at me. "Mr. Ripinsky's a very attractive man."

I could think of only two reasons Hy could have had for going to the main terminal: to catch a connecting flight to a city that was far enough outside the Citabria's range to make flying himself there a hassle, or to rent a car. And since he'd told both the lineman and Sandy that he only planned to tie down overnight, the latter was the more likely. It was close enough to the time of day when he would have arrived at the terminal that I reasoned the car-rental clerks would be the same ones who were on duty that morning; I started at Hertz and worked my way along the counters, showing the photo of Hy that I kept in my wallet. At a small cut-rate firm called Econocar — trust Hy not to squander on inessentials — I got lucky.

The young black man with a high pillbox haircut recognized Hy immediately. "Yeah, he rented from us," he said. "It was a slow morning, and I remember him because he was carrying a bunch of expired credit cards. Had a hell of a time finding one that wasn't. He joked about it, said he couldn't be bothered with cutting them up and signing the new ones." He shrugged skeptically.

"In his case, it's the truth. Do you recall how long he planned to keep the car, or if he returned it?"

"No."

"Can you find out?"

He hesitated, frowning. "I'm not sure I can get that kind of information, or if I should be giving it out."

I flipped from Hy's picture to my identification. "It's a missing-person case. His plane's tied down at North Field, and they need to free the space."

"Well, if it's airport business . . . The cars're tracked individually by vehicle number, so I should be able to pull it up." He turned to his computer and typed, peered at the screen, typed some more. After a couple of minutes he said, "He kept the car for four days. Was returned on Saturday to SFO."

"What kind of car was it?"

"Ninety-two Toyota Cressida. Blue." The clerk smiled. "He asked me what the hell Cressida meant. I didn't know. Then he goes, 'How can I risk my life on the freeways in something called that — especially when I don't even know what it means?' "

I smiled, too. Hy's interest in — and knowledge of — cars stopped around the year his ancient Morgan had been manufactured. "And

25

that's all the information you can access?"

"Yeah. Anything else you'll have to check with our people at SFO."

"You know the name of the supervisor down there?"

"Dave Fry. He's at the car-return area, not the counter in the terminal."

"Thanks for your trouble."

"Don't mention it. Good luck finding the guy."

Before I left the terminal I went to the snack bar and asked for the waitress who was seeing a North Field lineman named Jerry. The woman behind the counter pointed out a petite blonde named Katie who was juggling four plates with skill worthy of a magician, and said she'd send her to me when she was free. While I waited I nursed a cup of coffee.

The sight of my I.D. turned Katie's blue eyes a shade wary. Yes, she said, Jerry had come in for breakfast last Wednesday morning. "What's he done?" she asked.

"Nothing that I'm interested in. Did he mention giving somebody a ride over here from General Aviation?"

She frowned. "I don't . . . Wait — the guy with the Citabria?"

"That's the one."

"Yeah, he did mention it. The guy's not

26

really a friend of his, but they talk when he flies in here. Jerry wants one of those Citabrias real bad, and the guy . . . What's his name?"

"Hy Ripinsky."

"Right, how could I forget that one? Well, Hy told Jerry he'd let him know if he heard about a used one for sale cheap." She shivered. "I sort of hope he doesn't. Those planes scare me to death."

"Did Jerry say why Hy needed the ride or where he was going?"

"Just that he'd only landed to drop off his girlfriend and refuel, but then he'd made a phone call and found out that the plans had gotten switched around on him. He was pissed because if he'd made the call a few minutes earlier, he could've caught a ride into the city with his girlfriend instead of having to rent a car. What's going on, anyway? Is this Hy in some kind of trouble?"

"Some kind." I gave her a conspiratorial smile. "I'm the girlfriend."

For a moment Katie looked dismayed; then she laughed. "I know how that goes," she said. "If I was a detective, I'd've gotten the goods on Jerry months ago."

I thanked her and left the terminal, trying to sort out what had happened last Wednesday morning. Hy was sorry he hadn't been able to ride into the city with me; that meant he'd felt no need to conceal whatever he planned to do there. Maybe that would make tracing his movements easier.

Dave Fry, manager of the Econocar lot on the frontage road near SFO, looked like a very depressed individual. I could see why. His desk in the office shack was heaped with unprocessed paperwork; the windswept lot was full of unrented cars; the terminal shuttle bus stood idle. I saw only one other employee, a young Asian man who sat on the step of the bus, looking as down in the dumps as his boss. When I showed Fry my identification, he sighed and shrugged — obviously expecting some kind of trouble and resigned to it.

"That car was returned after office hours on Saturday," he told me. "What they do, they drop the keys and paperwork in the lockbox outside, and we bill their credit cards."

"May I see the paperwork?"

Fry looked at the desk in front of him, mouth turning down. "Someplace here," he muttered, pushing a couple of piles around, then lifting another and peering under it as if he hoped a pair of helping hands might reach out to him. After a few moments of fumbling, he worked a folder free of the stack; it had a yellow Post-it note stuck to its flap. "Hey, that's right," he said. "The car you're asking about is the one that came in damaged."

"Damaged how?"

Fry examined the envelope. "Dented right front quarter panel and busted headlight." He held it out to me.

I took it and examined the Post-it note. The message on it said to bill all charges for repairs to American Express, and the writing wasn't Hy's. His was more like printing — bold and sprawling. This was fine script that reminded me of Hank Zahn's nearly illegible scribbling.

Quickly I looked inside at the contract, where the credit card had been imprinted. It had Hy's name on it and also that of the Spaulding Foundation. I took my notebook from my bag and scribbled down the credit-card number and expiration date, then handed the folder back to Fry. "There's no one at all on duty here after hours?" I asked. "Not even a security guard?"

He motioned through the window at the lot. "Lady, does our volume of business suggest that we could afford a guard?"

He had a point. "Is the car still here on the lot?"

"Yeah. It's not going into the shop till to-morrow."

"May I have a look at it?"

Fry's eyes narrowed. "The car wasn't

used . . . well, like in a crime?"

"Not to my knowledge. This is just a routine skip trace." Didn't I wish.

He nodded. "Then I don't see any reason you shouldn't take a look. Space thirty-four, back against the fence. Hasn't been moved since it was returned. You'll have to find it yourself; I can't leave the office."

I went outside and crossed the lot. The Cressida was pulled in, nose against the fence, badly dented and very dirty. I ran my finger over the damaged quarter panel, and it came away with a coating of fine gray-black dust, like ash. I went around and slipped into the driver's seat. It was drawn up so that a much shorter person than Hy — or than I, for that matter — could drive it.

The shaky feeling I'd experienced when I first saw the Citabria in the tie-down at the airport returned. Questions flooded my mind: How had the car gotten damaged? Why hadn't Hy returned it himself? Who had? I didn't speculate on the answers, merely turned my attention to a systematic search.

Nothing in the glove compartment but the owner's manual. Nothing in the ashtray. A couple of Styrofoam cups that had contained coffee on the passenger's side floor. Some loose change caught in the crack between the seat back and bottom. And shoved down beside

30

the seat, a map. I pulled it out and unfolded it.

It was a Triple A road map of the area south of San Jose where Highway 101 cuts through Santa Clara and San Benito counties on the way to Salinas. A smaller area was circled in red felt-tip on the portion that had been folded out, and in the margin Hy's hand had written, "Ravenswood Road."

Ravenswood Road. Something familiar about that. Where . . . ?

I closed my eyes, pictured the stretch of highway; I'd driven it any number of times over any number of years, en route from San Francisco to my parents' home in San Diego. You bypassed Morgan Hill and Gilroy on the freeway, and then the road narrowed and was open to cross traffic. There was that stretch — I couldn't remember whether it was before or after the turnoffs for Hollister and San Juan Bautista — where the north- and southbound lanes were divided by a big stand of eucalyptus. If you were driving north, you saw a turnout with boulders covered with graffiti on the left, and on the right a sign for Ravenswood Road. A scenic place, and isolated. Nothing much there that I could remember. Why . . . ?

I folded the map and stuck it in my bag, then pulled the trunk release and went to look inside. Nothing. I went over the front seat and the backseat once more, then hurried to the office. Fry still stood behind his desk, staring dejectedly at his mounds of paperwork. I gave him my card, asked him to call me if he heard from the renter of the damaged car. As I ran to my MG, I tried to estimate the amount of time it would take to reach Ravenswood Road. It was quarter to three now —

Dammit! I'd forgotten about the partners' meeting at All Souls. Command appearance, and I was reasonably sure I'd be in big trouble if I failed to show. I'd have to return to the city for it, then double back, and brave San Jose in rush-hour traffic. At least it stayed light until eight or eight-thirty this time of year, so I'd be able to see whatever there was to see down there — if anything.

I pointed the MG toward the entrance to northbound 101.

TWO

When I hurried into the foyer of All Souls's big Victorian in Bernal Heights, I saw that the sliding doors to the parlor, where the partners held their weekly meetings, were closed. Ted Smalley, our office manager, looked up from his computer and said, *"Aspice quod felis attraxit."*

I sighed. "And that means . . . ?"

"Look what the cat dragged in."

During the past weekend Ted had come across a gem of a book by one Henry Beard entitled *Latin for Even More Occasions.* Ted, who is an odd combination of Renaissance man and efficiency expert, read and memorized the entire volume and was now planning to search the stores for all the other Beard titles, as well as seriously considering signing up for a refresher course in the dead — well, apparently not so dead — language. Recently I'd been worried about him because he'd seemed depressed — not an unusual emotional state for a gay person who had lost at least a dozen friends to AIDS during the past year — and I welcomed this improvement in his spirits. But if he was going to greet me every morning with such expressions as *Expergiscere et coffeam olface* (Wake up and smell the coffee), I wasn't altogether certain how long I could endure this bizarre new enthusiasm.

I motioned at the closed doors. "I take it they're annoyed with me for being late."

Ted shrugged.

"Should I go in?"

"Hank said they'd send for you. If you ever showed up." He went back to his computer.

Terrific, I thought. The summons to the meeting had sounded ominous from the first, and now I was out of favor for being late. Bad initial impression, and if I went in there preoccupied with Hy's situation, I was likely to compound it. What I needed was to put Hy out of my mind for the moment. Perhaps some diverting conversation — and not in Latin — would help.

Instead of going up to my office, I went down the hall to the cubbyhole under the stairs that belonged to my assistant, Rae Kelleher. She sat at her desk, one foot tucked up in the chair, the other scuffing rhythmically against the floor as she spoke on the phone. I squeezed past her and curled in the armchair — my former ratty armchair that she'd slipcovered in blue and white — and waited while she finished a conversation relating to one of the background investigations she was working. The office, a converted closet that the building's former owner had the gall to call a den, was overly warm and stuffy; I glanced at the ficus plant Rae nurtured under an ultraviolet bulb and saw its leaves were dusty and drooping from lack of water. Rae herself seemed similarly uncared for; her curly auburn hair needed washing, and her jeans and sweater looked as if she'd slept in them. It didn't surprise me; she'd had a big disappointment the week before. Her current love, jewelry chain owner Willie Whelan, had demanded she sign a prenuptial agreement before he'd present her with a diamond engagement ring, and Rae had flown into a rage at his remarks on her inability to wisely handle her own finances. Since then she'd handled her hurt with alternating fits of fury and dejection. This must be a dejected period, because when she hung up the phone and swiveled toward me, I saw her eyes were red.

"You all right?" I asked.

"Oh . . ." She waggled an outstretched hand from side to side.

"Another fight with Willie?"

"Look, I can't talk about him, I'd just start

crying again. What's with you?"

I'd come here for diversion, so I wasn't about to explain the Hy situation. "I've been summoned to the partners' meeting."

"Uh-oh. How come?"

"Don't know, but Hank acted mighty shifty when he asked me to be there."

"Weird." She screwed up her freckled face in thought. "I've been hearing a word around here lately — 'reorganization.' "

"Yes, Hank said that's what they want to talk about."

"Well, it sounds to me like a euphemism for demotions or layoffs. This place is getting too corporate, if you know what I mean."

"I do. And I hate to sound like I'm wallowing in nostalgia, but I miss the good old days." In the old days All Souls had possessed a certain laid-back ambience as well as an excitement about the challenge we were presenting to the legal establishment. Now we *were* establishment. We'd incorporated; we'd bought the Victorian and spiffed it up with its first paint job in decades; we'd rented two additional houses across the park out front for our support staff; we had an 800-number hotline for clients; we had marketing people to sell the membership plan to large northern California employers.

But those were only surface changes. Others

36

went much deeper, and the fact that I was currently sweating over attending a meeting of the partners told me just how deep. The partners: my friends.

Hank Zahn, senior partner and sole remaining co-founder of All Souls, was my oldest and closest male friend. He was one of several people I'd shared a house with in Berkeley while getting my degree in sociology. His wife, Anne-Marie Altman, another founder of the co-op, had left to become head counsel for a coalition of environmental organizations — including the foundation Hy ran — but she remained my closest woman friend.

Jack Stuart, our criminal specialist, wouldn't be at today's meeting because he'd left town this morning to sort through some painful feelings about the case he and I had just concluded. But Larry Koslowski, our corporate specialist, would be present. Larry, our resident health nut whose good intentions and peculiar culinary concoctions had nearly poisoned me on any number of occasions. And then there was Pam Ogata, the tax attorney who had filled Anne-Marie's shoes — a Japanese-Hawaiian whose exquisitely decorated quarters on the second floor spoke of her homesickness for the islands. Pam, with whom I'd shared many an expedition to flea markets, thrift stores, and antique shops.

How on earth could I shrink from a meeting with such friends? Of course, there *were* two relatively unknown quantities. . . .

Rae asked, "Shar, what do you think of Mike Tobias?"

It was as if she'd overheard my thoughts. Mike Tobias was one of the unknowns — a newish partner. His background — a childhood spent in the drug- and crime-plagued Sunnydale projects and a stint as a social worker before attending Hastings College of the Law — had made him a tireless crusader and perfectly suited him for working with our needier, less empowered clients.

"I'm not sure," I told Rae. "I like him, and I certainly admire him, but I don't really know him."

"The reason I ask is that this corporate stuff became more pronounced about the time Mike made partner."

"Well, the incorporation and the new partners all happened at the same time. That was when Gloria came on board, too." Gloria Escobar devoted her attention to equal-opportunity and civil-rights cases. I knew even less about her than I did about Mike, because she seldom socialized with any of us.

That was another difference from the old days: back then I could count on knowing all my colleagues well. Many of them had lived in free rooms that the co-op provided to offset the low salaries a poverty law firm offered. All employees were welcome to attend the frequent potlucks, parties, and poker games. Today everyone was adequately compensated, and the few who remained in communal living quarters — Ted, Pam, Larry, Jack, and Rae — paid fair-market rent. A number of the newer associates and employees led personal lives that were strictly segregated from their work lives, and while the potlucks, parties, and poker games continued, they catered to an ever-diminishing core contingent.

Rae said, "Mike and Gloria seem like good people, but I can't warm up to either of them. I get the feeling that anything not strictly relating to work is off limits, and you've got to admit that neither of them has a sense of humor."

"They're crusaders, Rae. People with missions often don't see much to laugh at."

"Well, if I couldn't laugh at stuff, I'd go totally insane. Even this thing with Willie has its funny side, if you think about it."

I agreed — both about the thing with Willie and the need for laughter. If I lost my ability to laugh at life's snares and pitfalls — to say nothing of my own foibles and pomposities — I'd end up in the bin within weeks.

Ted stuck his head through the doorway.

"They're ready for you, Shar."

"Thanks." I got up and followed him, smoothing my long red sweater over my jeans and feeling ridiculously like a little kid being called to the principal's office.

As I slid open the parlor door, Ted whispered, *"Noli nothis permittere te terere."*

I glanced back at him. "What?"

"Don't let the bastards get you down."

They were all there, seated in various attitudes and degrees of repose. Hank was sprawled on the piano bench, leaning back, elbows propped on the keyboard cover. Pam, always more comfortable on the floor, had her back to the ash-clogged fireplace. Larry slouched in the overstuffed armchair, his feet propped on its hassock. He had a big pottery bowl in his lap and was fishing walnuts from a sack and shelling them into it. Mike anchored one end of the maroon sofa, Gloria the other.

I shut the door and looked around for a place to sit. The only one was between Mike and Gloria, but being hemmed in by the two partners I was least comfortable with would put me at a psychological disadvantage. Finally I went over and plopped down next to Hank, poking him in the ribs to make him move over.

"Sorry I was late," I said. "I got hung up on a case I'm working."

Hank held his ground, poked me back, then

sighed and relinquished the center of the bench. Larry tossed me a walnut. Pam smiled and said, "Better late than never."

Pam loves to utter aphorisms in a manner that makes them sound like arcane bits of Asian wisdom. I said, "That's deep, Pam. Maybe you should get Ted to translate it into Latin."

She made a face at me. I glanced at Gloria and Mike; neither looked amused. Gloria's eyes were impatient, Mike's somewhat annoyed.

Well, no wonder, I thought, recalling the conversation Rae and I had just had. To them the law and its trappings — even All Souls's shamelessly casual partners' meetings — were a serious matter.

Both Gloria and Mike had struggled to achieve what Hank, Pam, and Larry took for granted. While I knew only the outlines of Mike's earlier years and nothing at all of Gloria's, I was certain neither had enjoyed the slightest privilege or luxury. In contrast, Hank had been raised in an affluent Peninsula suburb and hadn't worked a day until he graduated from law school. Pam's childhood had been spent on a Lanai pineapple plantation; private schools, both there and on the mainland, had prepared her for law school at the University of Chicago, where the worst hardship she'd endured was snow. And Larry — he'd been a rabble-rouser all his life, bummed around Europe for a couple of years after college, then skated through Yale Law. It was a wonder any of them had developed so much as a shred of social consciousness, but in some way they had. I supposed that the assurance and feelings of entitlement instilled in them by their upbringing had enabled them to simultaneously take the law seriously and engage in antics such as poking and joking and walnut-tossing. Just as the lack of said assurance and feelings of entitlement made such antics seem inappropriate, if not downright offensive, to Gloria and Mike.

In an odd way I empathized with them all, because my own experience bridged the gap. My father had been a chief petty officer in the navy, underpaid and often out to sea. In his absence, my mother's hands were too full raising five problematical kids to supplement the family income. True, we owned our own big rambling home on a large lot on one of San Diego's finger canyons, but there were years when we depended on the largess of my uncle Ed, a commercial fisherman who brought us catch after catch of rock cod and sea bass and halibut. To this day I will not willingly eat fish.

In my family, high-school graduation was

supposed to be the cutoff date for financial support, and unlike a couple of my freeloading siblings, I'd taken the rule seriously. I went to work in retail security, lived at home, paid room and board, and tried to save toward an apartment of my own. Given my spendthrift tendencies, I suppose I'd still be living there and saving toward the apartment if my supervisor at the department store hadn't encouraged me to go to college. That, plus incredibly high SAT scores and a small scholarship, had gotten me to Berkeley. But even then college hadn't exactly been a carefree interlude — not when I was working nights and weekends as a security guard.

Maybe, I thought now, I'd forgotten where I'd come from. Lost sight of who and what I really was. Maybe because I'd achieved more than I'd expected to — a certain professional reputation, a newly remodeled home of my own, a comfortable life-style — maybe I'd lost my ability to relate to people like Gloria and Mike, people who deserved far more credit for their accomplishments than I for mine.

The thought unsettled me. I wasn't like that — at least not in the self-image I valued.

Hank glanced at me. Whatever expression I wore seemed to sober him. He said to the others, "Okay, let's come to order again — if possible." To me he added, "We asked you

43

to attend the meeting to discuss a promotion."

A promotion. They weren't going to lay me off, or even demote me. They wanted to give me a better job.

So why had Hank acted so goddamn shifty earlier? Why did he now fail to meet my eyes? Why was Pam staring down at the rug, her face hidden by her shiny wings of black hair? Why did Larry's waxed handlebar mustache twitch as he burrowed through his bag of walnuts? Only Gloria and Mike looked at me — expectantly, as if they wanted to share my pleasure.

"What kind of promotion?" I asked, trying not to sound suspicious.

Hank cleared his throat before speaking. "As you know, with the growth of the firm, the investigative caseload has become extremely heavy."

I nodded.

"We want you to hire more investigators. Two, to begin with. You and I can go over the salary budget later. In essence, this creates a department, which you'll head up." He paused, seeming to search for words. So far this was all good news; why was he having such a hard time delivering it?

"With the increase in responsibility, of course, will come an appropriate salary increase for you, plus other perks," he added.

"Does that mean you'll pay for my car phone?" I asked the question jokingly, but it was one of the perks I'd insist on. Over the weekend I'd had reason to become enraged with All Souls's stinginess when it came to equipment I considered essential; that morning I'd informed Ted that I was buying a phone, and if they wouldn't pay for it, I'd foot the bill myself.

Hank's smile was strained. "I'm sure that can be arranged. Now, in addition to an increase in the investigative caseload, you've probably noticed that we've come to rely more heavily on our paralegal researchers."

Something in the way he stressed the word "now" put me on my guard. I waited.

Hank took off his glasses and began twirling them by one earpiece — a telltale sign of discomfort. "As you know, the use of paralegals eliminates time-consuming tasks for attorneys, provides more efficient service to our clients, and produces a higher profit margin."

"Christ, Hank," Larry said, "you sound as if you're quoting from the *California Paralegal's Guide*."

Hank silenced him with a glare. I glanced at Pam; she was smiling at the rug now, her normally pale face pink with suppressed laughter. Hank glared at her too, even though she couldn't see him, then put his glasses back

45

on and regarded me apologetically. "Sorry if I sounded like I was talking down to you. I was trying to make the basis for our decision clear."

"Why don't you just tell me the decision, and if I need clarification, I'll ask for it."

He looked around, as if he hoped someone else would take over. No one volunteered. Finally he said, "We've decided to make investigative services and paralegal research one department, with you as its administrator."

I frowned, unable to assimilate what I was hearing. Supervising a staff of investigators was one thing, but what did I know of paralegal work? "I'm flattered," I said, "but the two don't strike me as compatible. Besides, I'm not sure I know what most of our paralegals *do*."

Gloria leaned forward, dark eyes intense, carmine-tipped fingers shaping her words. "A paralegal researches case law, Sharon. She or he interviews clients, writes memoranda and briefs, prepares exhibits for trial, drafts interrogatories, indexes documents for trial — handles anything, short of practicing law, that makes the attorney's work simpler."

"I understand the basic job description," I said, "but it seems to me that, since the paralegals work closely with the attorneys they're assigned to, they'd be better off reporting directly to them."

"Currently they do, and they'll continue to, but we need to ensure that the work flows smoothly. That's where you and the new research department come in. As administrator, you'll log in cases and keep tabs on every phase of the research, so none of the steps is neglected. Plus supervise your own investigators, of course." Gloria's bright lips — the exact shade as her fingernails — curved into a smile, as if she'd given me a particularly nice present and was anticipating enthusiastic thanks.

Now it was becoming clear why Hank was nervous about this discussion. Why Pam and Larry wouldn't look at me. Why only the two partners who scarcely knew me thought I should be thrilled with this promotion. I said, "That sounds like a very time-consuming process. Given how frequently I have to be out of the office on my own investigations, I don't think it's feasible."

Mike frowned, bushy black eyebrows meeting in a straight line. From his quick glance at Hank, I revised my earlier assessment of the situation; he and Gloria had also known I wouldn't like their plan. "Sharon," he said, "that's why we're giving you the go-ahead to hire more investigators. They'll free up your time for administrative duties."

Yes, now it was all very clear. "You want

to confine me to a desk job," I said flatly.

Mike drew back a bit, still frowning, lower teeth nibbling at his neatly clipped mustache. Then he went into his sincere mode: eyes wide and guileless, speech patterns turning folksy, tone warm and intimate. "Big step up for you. Big increase in pay. But hey, we forgot to mention the incentive plan!" He actually clapped his hand against his high forehead in an imitation of the guy who could have had a V-8.

I wasn't falling for any sincerity act. Looking from Pam to Larry to Hank, I asked, "You all approved of this? Jack, too?"

Hank's shoulders hunched defensively; I'd seldom seen him look so miserable. Pam's fingers tightened on her blue-jeaned thighs. Larry practically stuck his head into the shopping bag full of walnuts.

Finally Gloria said, "One of the incentives we've talked about is to bring you in on the profit-sharing plan. I don't know if you're aware of it, but profits were up fourteen percent last quarter."

I was silent, my emotions in a turmoil. On the one hand, I was appalled at the prospect of a desk job, but on the other, I wondered what was wrong with me. Substantial salary increase, profit sharing — the American dream. So why did I feel so confused and resistant?

"Sharon," Pam said, her delicate features strained, "you may not think so now, but you'd make a terrific administrator. You could turn the new research department into the mainstay of the corporation."

Research department. Such a dry sound. Research was an activity carried on in musty archives: slow, methodical, analytical — and boring.

I shook my head in confusion, fighting off a sense of betrayal and trying to imagine the scenario they'd presented me. Supervising a larger staff of investigators, even relatively untrained ones, would be easy. I'd hire bright people, teach them what they needed to know. Even dealing with the paralegals would pose no real problem; during my tenure at All Souls I'd read a fair amount of law and picked up even more informally. What I couldn't envision was me behind a desk forty hours a week.

I said, "I still think it's a mistake to combine the two activities."

Mike replied somewhat tartly, "It's not up to you to critique our organizational chart."

"But she might have a point," Larry said thoughtfully. "We should at least hear her out."

"Larry, the matter's already settled."

"But, Mike, she's saying exactly what we

expected she would."

"Of course she is — and you know why, given where she's coming from."

Quickly Hank held up a hand. "Let's not argue."

"Just where *am* I coming from?"

Hank made a dismissing motion. "I don't think we need to get into —"

Pam's voice cut through his words. "We've always been up-front here. We might as well get into it."

"Get into *what?*" I demanded.

Hank sighed heavily. "I asked you to meet with me beforehand. But no, you couldn't be bothered. Too busy. Off working a case."

"Which is precisely the problem," Gloria added.

I faced her. "The problem?"

"Yes, problem." She nodded emphatically, long curls bobbing. "You're a good investigator, Sharon. But you lack discipline. The Benedict case is a good example."

The Benedict case was the one I'd just wrapped up. "What about it?"

"Did you receive authorization to work on it?"

"Not initially. Hank was on vacation —"

"Did you request it from anyone else?"

"I've always reported to Hank. And when he came back, he gave me the go-ahead."

"Only after you were in over your head."

"Jack requested —"

"He had no right, and both of you knew it. It was Jack's personal crusade, and by giving in to him, you neglected your other duties."

Mike added, "That's not an isolated instance, either. That business up at Tufa Lake is another."

Outraged, I turned to Hank. "You loaned me out on the case. The California Coalition for Environmental Preservation reimbursed the firm for my time."

Mike said, "He only loaned you because Anne-Marie's his wife and their chief counsel and she requested you. He didn't go through channels, get approval from the rest of us. This new organizational plan will prevent abuses like that."

Surprisingly, Hank nodded. "Mike's right — I admit it. We've talked — and fought — this through at our meetings. Back when All Souls was a small cooperative, I could bend the rules, but as it grew I just kept doing that, to our detriment. We all have to learn to adapt."

His words rendered me speechless. His words, and the truth of them.

After a moment Gloria moved her hands together in a gesture that apologized for the dissension. Mike leaned forward, elbows on knees, soft eyes begging for understanding. Larry looked hangdog, Pam hopeful. Hank reached over and squeezed my hand.

These people are not out to get you, I told myself. They're good people, dedicated people, and they have the best interests of the co-op at heart. But, damn, they're asking too much!

Hank said, "So what do you think, Shar?"

I remained silent.

Gloria added, "All Souls needs you."

"I'm not sure you need me in that particular capacity."

Larry said, "Everything changes, Shar. Maybe you should change, too."

Pam added, "There's a lot of energy being generated by the reorganization. We want you to be a part of it."

Mike said, "I know Jack would tell you the same if he were here."

So they were all committed to this new plan. It was take-it-or-leave-it time.

I thought of the future if I accepted this promotion. Tried to look at it in a positive light. A desk job, supervising a staff of investigators and paralegals. Log sheets, meetings, mediating disputes . . . Ugh! But balance all that against the satisfaction of watching the department and the co-op grow and prosper. Balance that against the satisfaction of prospering personally. A higher salary, car phone, profit sharing. I could pay off the second mortgage I'd taken out to finish remodeling my house, buy good furniture, bank a portion of my take-home pay. Maybe I'd even be able to start taking flying lessons again. I'd had a few lessons years ago, and Hy had been teaching me informally, but I needed to log time with a licensed flight instructor. And a desk job would give me the time for that; there would be no more evenings wasted freezing my ass off on stakeouts, no more weekends wasted chasing down elusive witnesses. I'd put in my eight hours five days a week and have a life as well.

It would also mean stultifying boredom and a hell of a lot of clock-watching. It would mean surrendering the freedom I loved.

But face it, McCone, I told myself, if you don't agree to their offer, it'll mean starting over. It'll mean giving up All Souls, the closest thing to a family you've got anymore.

They weren't going to get off cheaply, though. I would really stick it to them. "What about a pension plan?" I asked. "You partners have one."

They exchanged surprised glances. "I'm sure that could be arranged," Hank said.

"And this salary increase — just what are we talking here?"

"At least one-third over what you're making now."

I did some mental arithmetic. "Double would be more attractive."

"The point is negotiable. So what do you say?"

"I'll have to think on it."

"But what's your initial feeling?"

It sucks, I thought. Aloud I added, "I don't want to leave All Souls, so I'll give your offer very serious thought."

Again the partners exchanged glances. Relief was the primary component this time, tinged with incredulity in the eyes of the three who knew me well.

Hank asked, "When may we expect your answer?"

"Give me till close of business on Wednesday."

"Fair enough. In the meantime, if you have any questions —"

"I know where to find you." I smiled wryly at him, got up, and moved toward the door. Behind me I could feel an easing of the collective tension. I stepped into the hall, shut the door, and started toward the stairs.

On my way past Ted's desk I asked,

"What's the Latin for 'between a rock and a hard place'?"

"Sorry," he said, eyeing me sympathetically, "the book doesn't say."

Three

Before the partners' meeting I'd needed something to take my mind off Hy; now I needed to think of him to keep myself from brooding. I sat down behind my desk in the window bay at the front of the second floor, swiveled around, and stared moodily at the houses across the little park. After a while I turned back to the desk, pulled the phone toward me, and dialed the number of the Spaulding Foundation.

Kate Malloy, Hy's executive assistant, answered. "You've heard from him!" she exclaimed when she heard my voice.

"No, I haven't, but after I talked with you this morning, I got concerned and did some checking." Briefly I told her what I'd found out. "Kate, the phone-company credit card Hy used to make those calls from the airport — would it be his personal card or the foundation's?"

"He usually uses the foundation's and reimburses us for personal charges later. I doubt

56

he even has one for his home phone — you know Hy and plastic."

"Will you give me the four-digit code, please?"

She told me, then repeated it. "You're going to find out who he called?"

"I'm going to try. I gather he uses this American Express card in the same way." I read her the number I'd copied off the rental-car contract.

"That's right."

"Will you do me a favor and call American Express? I'd like to know if Hy used the card for anything after he rented that car."

"Sure. You sound as worried as I've been ever since I found out the plane's still at Oakland."

"I am. I don't like the fact that the car was damaged and dropped off by someone other than Hy. While I've got you on the line, will you also give me the name and number of his accountant?"

"Barry Ashford, here in Vernon. I'll check the phone book." While she paged through it, she asked, "Why do you want to talk with Barry?"

"This morning you mentioned that Hy left instructions with him to pay all bills as they come in, and he also paid his ranch hands two months in advance. I want to know if he gave any explanation."

"Good idea. Here's the number." She read it off to me. "Sharon, do you want me to go out to the ranch and talk with the guys? Maybe he mentioned his plans to one of them."

"If you would, I'd appreciate it. But I'll bet he didn't tell them a thing. There're times when being the strong silent type isn't a virtue — and this is one."

After I hung up, I checked my watch. Five to five. Quickly I looked up the number of the general aviation terminal at Oakland Airport and dialed. Sandy was about to go home, but willing to take a moment to check the number of the pay phone from which Hy had made his calls. Next I found Pacific Bell's toll-free customer-service number in the directory; after listening to a recorded voice drone out a long list of options that seemed to encompass everything except talking with a human being, I finally reached a service representative.

I identified myself as Kate Malloy of the Spaulding Foundation. "On the morning of Wednesday, the second, one of our employees made some credit-card calls from Oakland Airport. We haven't received our bill yet, and I need to find out the time and charges as well as the numbers called."

"I'm sorry, ma'am, but there's no way I

can access that information. The employee should have asked that the time and charges be reported at the conclusion of the calls."

"Who *can* access that information?"

"You might talk with one of the supervisors in the billing office, but it's closed now."

I looked at my watch again. Five straight up. "Thanks for your trouble."

There had to be a quicker way to find out what I wanted than waiting until the billing office opened in the morning. I thought for a moment, then dialed my friend Adah Joslyn's extension at the SFPD homicide detail. Adah was out, the inspector who answered told me, as was her partner, Bart Wallace. No one knew when they'd be back. For a moment I considered calling my former lover, Greg Marcus, now a captain on Narcotics, and asking him to expedite an inquiry to Pacific Bell — but only for a moment. Greg operated pretty much by the book, and before he'd make the request, he'd want to know exactly why I needed the information, an explanation I wasn't prepared to give him.

As I sat drumming my fingers on the base of the phone, a memory nudged at me. I muttered, "What did I do with that card?" Grabbing my Rolodex, I thumbed to the *P*'s. Nothing where Pacific Bell would be filed. I could have sworn I'd kept it, though. Phone company, perhaps? No. Telephone? No again. Sexy-guy-I-met-at-a-party? Hardly.

Informant — phone company. Aha!

His name was Ron Chan, and I'd met him at a Christmas party at my neighbors' house. We'd hit it off instantly and spent most of the evening together. Before I left, he gave me his card — he was a mid-level manager in Pacific Bell's marketing division — and said he'd be glad to help me with information they normally didn't give out, providing I didn't misuse it. I hadn't needed any favors since then, and I hadn't pursued the invitation that his writing his home number on the back of the card implied.

Now I pulled the card out and turned it over. The home number was a 648 prefix, the same as All Souls's. It was too early for Chan to have returned from his downtown office, so I slipped the card into the pocket of my jeans; I'd try him later. Then I dialed Barry Ashford's number in Vernon, got no answer, and put the paper I'd jotted it down on with the card.

My purse was still downstairs in Rae's office, where I'd left it before the partners' meeting. I'd grab it and head out for Ravenswood Road in San Benito County.

Once I was past Daly City and out of the

fog belt, the early evening turned hot and sunny. Traffic was slow all the way down the Peninsula and came to a near standstill in San Jose. Many years of dealing with northern California's varied climate zones have conditioned me to keep a couple of changes of clothing in the car, and as I breathed exhaust fumes I thought longingly of the tank top and shorts in the trunk. But joining one of the long lines of exiting cars on the shoulder in order to get to a gas station and change seemed like more trouble than it was worth, and even if I could easily have reached my overnight bag, I've never thought much of disrobing in front of the curious eyes of dozens of fellow motorists. In the end I just kept pulling my sweater away from my sticky back and chest, and turned the blowers on the MG's vents to max.

Then San Jose — sprawling tracts and office parks where orange groves once stood — was behind me. The highway paralleled railroad tracks for a while, fruit stands heaped with early-summer produce lining either side. A newish section of freeway bypassed Morgan Hill and Gilroy — farm towns turned bedroom communities — and narrowed in the lower reaches of Santa Clara County. At the first turnoff for Hollister, I thought of a tragic case of mine that had its roots in that area, and felt a brief touch of regret.

The stand of eucalyptus and boulders was farther south than I remembered. By the time I got to it, it was well past seven-thirty. I made a U-turn at the first opportunity and drove north in the slow lane. Ravenswood Road branched off to the east about a hundred yards beyond where the rocky wooded area began.

I pulled onto the shoulder and stopped, not making the turn just yet. Across the pavement to my left the graffiti-splashed boulders and towering trees were cloaked in shadow. Only an occasional car sped by, its air currents making the little MG shudder. I looked to the east; mellow evening light spread over the flatland that the secondary road bisected on its way toward distant craggy hills. This was farm country — fields of tender green crops and uniformly tilled soil, occasionally interrupted by clusters of utilitarian buildings where combines and tractors stood idle.

Hy, I thought, why did you come here? Where did Ravenswood Road take you?

After a moment I turned the MG and started east. The pavement was poorly maintained, cracked and potholed. I kept my speed down, searching for anything that would provide an indication of where Hy had been headed. The road ran relatively straight for about five miles, then took a sharp southward bend and dead-ended in seven-tenths of a mile at a pasture fence. The field beyond the fence lay fallow, deserted except for some sort of rodent that scurried into its burrow as I stopped the car. I got out and looked around.

Nothing here except for a distant two-story gray house and barn. A single barren tree that looked as if it had been split by lightning stood in the foreground. Nothing moved over there, nothing made a sound; not even a dog barked in warning of my intrusion. The place looked as dead as the tree. I could see no access to the property; in order to get to it, I supposed, one would have to take another county road out of Hollister or Salinas.

This, then, had not been Hy's destination. Logic told me so, but I also knew it on a deeper, more elemental level. From the day Hy and I met, there had been an odd emotional connection between us. At first I'd resisted it, this tie to a man who wouldn't permit me to know him, from whom I also felt compelled to keep secrets. But as last winter wore on — even though we remained separated by our mutual stubborn silence and the frozen Sierra Nevada — I'd felt the pull more and more strongly.

Of course, the roses had been a constant reminder. Every Tuesday morning a single perfect rose arrived at my office, by Hy's arrangement with a neighborhood florist. Yellow roses: pink was too sentimental, red too traditional for me, he claimed. On one of those Tuesdays, when the tug of longing was particularly strong and the snow was melting on the mountain passes, I'd gotten into the MG and driven back to Tufa Lake and we'd become lovers. After that, the roses were an exotic tangerine — a tangerine, Hy said, that was the exact color of our passion.

Now, standing there beside the pasture fence in the gathering dusk and silence, I strained to feel a connection to Hy. Tried hard, but fell far short. Nothing.

No, I decided, he had not come to this lonely place, not ever. If he had, I would have known. It was that simple.

I was about to turn north on 101 when the clearing in among the boulders and eucalyptus caught my attention. I waited for a semi to rumble past, then accelerated across the highway. The clearing was fairly large — about twenty feet in diameter — and tire-marked. Farther back, in a circle of stones near the base of a huge tree, were the remains of a campfire. I shut the MG's engine off, got out, and went over there.

An odd place for a campfire, I thought, and a dangerous one. Dry eucalyptus ignite easily and can turn a spark into a conflagration in a matter of minutes — witness the tragic fire that destroyed twenty-five lives and hundreds of homes in the East Bay hills close to two years ago. But people seldom learn from such examples and will camp or picnic anywhere — gas stations, parking lots, the middle of shopping malls. This place, even though they'd be sucking up exhaust fumes with their hot dogs, was more scenic than most.

I went up to the improvised fire ring and peered around into the deepening darkness. The picnickers — many groups of them — had been careless; trash covered the ground amid the boulders. I glanced down, saw that the circle of stones had been broken and scattered; there were tire tracks through the cinders and ashes.

Ashes. I thought of the damaged rental car, the fine ashlike dust coating its exterior.

The tracks pointed toward the boulders where the trash was strewn. I went that way, taking my small flashlight from my bag and shining its beam over the ground and rocks and tree trunks. One of the boulders had a prominent white scar some two feet off the ground. I shone the light closer and saw blue paint scrapings on the pale stone. Squatting down, I shone the flash on the ground. Broken glass that looked as if it might have come from a headlight lay scattered there.

So this was where Hy had come — and where the car had gotten damaged. But why? And how?

I felt in my bag for one of the envelopes I keep there, then scooped up some of the glass fragments and placed them inside. Took another out and used my Swiss Army knife to scrape some of the blue paint into it. Then I stuck the envelopes in the bag's flap pocket and stood, began going through the trash on the ground item by item.

Potato-chip bags and fast-food containers; paper plates and plastic forks; used condoms and beer cans; candy wrappers and Styrofoam cups; pop bottles and soiled disposable diapers. God, people could be pigs! At least Hy, devoted environmentalist that he was, had tossed his cups on the floor of the rental car. If they *were* Hy's . . .

The accumulated garbage disgusted me, but I determinedly waded through it. Newspapers and plastic bags; gum wrappers and matchbooks and cigarette butts; assorted scraps of paper.

Including one bearing Hy's bold handwriting: "RKI mobile unit — 777-3209."

Car phone. Whose? RKI. What — a person or a company? Mobile unit — it sounded more like a company.

I kept searching, but found nothing more that I could link to Hy. Finally I gave up and went back to the car.

So what had happened here? I wondered. Hy must have had good reason to search this place out. What? A meeting with someone? Perhaps. For sure something to do with RKI, whatever or whoever that was. Somehow he'd managed to drive the rental car through the fire ring and ram the boulder. How hard? Enough to injure himself? Maybe. Enough to kill himself? Doubtful. And why? I couldn't begin to guess.

It was full dark now. Vehicles, including a Highway Patrol car, sped past on 101, but none of their occupants seemed to notice me. A good meeting place, then, one where a parked car would attract minimal attention. Meeting place for what, though?

Finally I started the MG, flipped on its headlights, and drove north toward San Francisco. But at the first opportunity I pulled off into a gas station and placed a call to Ron Chan, my contact at Pacific Bell. He was home, pleased to hear from me, and willing to check out the numbers Hy had called, provided I'd have lunch with him next week. I promised I would, and Chan said that he knew a night supervisor at the phone company who owed him a favor. He'd get back to me later tonight or first thing in the morning. Next I tried Hy's accountant, Barry Ashford, but again got no answer. Then I continued back to the city.

It was nearly eleven when I arrived at my brown-shingled earthquake cottage near the Glen Park district. I hadn't left the porch light on this morning because I didn't expect to return after dark, and on the steps I stumbled over something. An indignant yowl arose. "Sorry, Ralphie," I said and opened the door for my tabby cat. He streaked inside, still scolding.

A sheet of paper had been slipped under the door — an estimate from a contractor for reshingling the cottage's facade. Nearly two weeks ago it had been sprayed with some ugly graffiti — a consequence of my involvement in the case that the All Souls partners now labeled Jack Stuart's personal crusade — and I was eager to have the work done. As I went down the hall to my informal sitting room I glanced over the figures. They looked reasonable; I'd give the contractor the go-ahead.

The light was blinking on my answering machine. Ignoring Ralph's loud pleas for food — augmented now by those of his calico sister, Alice — I played the tape. Ron Chan: Hy had called a La Jolla number first, then one here in the city. Both belonged to Renshaw and

Kessell International. Chan also gave the addresses. No additional calls had been billed to the credit card to date.

Renshaw and Kessell International. RKI. It sounded vaguely familiar.

I picked up the receiver and called the San Francisco number. A recorded voice said, "You have reached the offices of Renshaw and Kessell International. Our hours are from nine to five, Monday through Friday. If this is an emergency call, please enter your security code and press one. Stay on the line. A representative will be with you."

Emergency? Security code? I listened to the taped message replay, then hung up. Who were these people? None of the references I had here in my home office would tell, unless I wanted to stay up all night reading the Yellow Pages. I'd have to wait until morning when I visited their offices on Green Street.

But damn, the name sounded familiar! Why?

Four

Tuesday, June 8

When I woke at ten after seven the next morning, my subconscious had dredged up what Renshaw and Kessell International was — and the knowledge made me damned uneasy. Confused, too. I couldn't see why Hy would be mixed up with them, unless . . . But if that was true, it would mean I'd severely misjudged him. It would mean that I, who thought I instinctively understood him, had rejected what casual acquaintances had assumed all along.

It was too early to confirm anything. For a while I lay under my quilts, hemmed in by the cats. Then I threw off the quilts — and the cats — showered, dressed in jeans and a sweater, and took a brisk walk down Church Street to a corner store where I bought a copy of this morning's *Chronicle* and a whole-wheat bagel.

Mr. Abdur, the store's owner, smiled and

told me the fog had put roses on my cheeks. He was young — well, about my age — and one of the new breed of neighborhood grocer who had come to realize that pleasantries, rather than surliness, would bring the customer back. Since taking a vigorous walk to buy the paper was part of an ambitious new morning routine I was trying — without great success — to adopt, I was pleased to have located a shopkeeper who wouldn't snarl at me and spoil my day.

When I got home, it was still too early to call anyone to confirm what I'd remembered about Renshaw and Kessell, so I toasted the bagel and had it with the first of my customary three cups of coffee. I supposed I should eliminate caffeine if I planned to lead a virtuous life from now on, but I knew I wasn't going to give it up — just as I suspected that my good intentions would soon go the way of most New Year's resolutions. That was okay, though; my vices are so few — caffeine, white wine, chocolate, and an addiction to late-night grade-B movies — that relinquishing any would practically turn me into a saint.

There was nothing much of interest in the paper; it even felt thin. The comics weren't funny, the crossword and the Jumble were all too easy; in desperation I even read the business section, but the lead article on the un-

expected withdrawal of an initial public offering of Phoenix Labs stock failed to stir me.
Finally it was nine o'clock, time to make my
call.

I dialed the number of one of the city's
larger security firms and asked to speak to
Bob Stern, my former boss. Bob, who has
changed companies about once every nine
months since I worked for him, saved me from
a hideous life by firing me several years ago,
and has spent most of the intervening time
trying to hire me back for whatever outfit he's
hooked up with at the moment. I have a certain reputation in investigative circles here in
the city, and while the consensus is that I'd
be impossible to work with, a number of people would like to give it a whirl.

"So what is it, Sharon?" Bob asked. "You
ready to come back to me?"

"No way."

"You're not going to lure another of my
promising new operatives away, are you?" Rae
had worked briefly for Bob at one of his former
gigs, before he sensed she'd be fully as difficult
as I and recommended her for the job at All
Souls.

"Not today." But as I spoke I reminded myself that soon I might have to call on Bob for
referrals, should I say yes to All Souls's offer.
Quickly I put the troublesome thought out of

my mind and said, "I'm after information. What can you tell me about Renshaw and Kessell International?"

"RKI? Shit, Sharon, don't tell me you're thinking of hiring on with that bunch!"

"Why is it you always suspect me of looking to change jobs? I've been with All Souls ever since you tossed me out on the streets."

"Those bleeding hearts aren't good enough for you. Come back to me. I promise —"

"RKI, Bob."

"Right. You know Ackerman and Palumbo? Paul Chamberlain? The big guys in the international security consulting field?"

So I'd remembered correctly. "Yes."

"Well, RKI's right up there with them, but that's where the resemblance stops. A and P are mainly former spooks. At PC you got the guys with law or accounting degrees and nice suits. RKI uses both, but it's the other types that make them flashy — and dangerous."

"Other types."

"Yeah, people whose past you really don't want to know too much about. People who don't play by anybody's rules. They're what makes RKI so effective in certain kinds of situations. Firms that're desperate or very vulnerable use them. Insurance companies — well, they're leery."

It sounded like a place where Hy would feel

right at home. "So who're the principals there? What're their backgrounds?"

"Strictly off-the-wall. Take Gage Renshaw. DEA, years back. Was tapped for a very select and low-profile task force called Centac in the mid-seventies. Then in eighty-five Centac was disbanded. Renshaw was in Thailand; he disappeared. Three years later he resurfaced, came back to the States, apparently affluent. Set up the RKI shop in La Jolla in partnership with his old pal Dan Kessell."

"So La Jolla is where they're headquartered?"

"With offices in major U.S. and foreign cities."

"That's pretty impressive growth in not much more than five years."

"Well, I wouldn't guarantee that some of the offices aren't just mail drops, but it looks impressive as hell."

"This Dan Kessell," I said, "what about him?"

"Kessell's background is harder to pin down. Special Forces in 'Nam, that much I know. Renshaw's their front man — gives interviews to the *Wall Street Journal*; you've seen that kind of stuff. Kessell stays out of the public eye."

"And he's an old friend of Renshaw's from where?"

74

"They went to high school together in Fresno, of all damn places."

Fresno. Maybe that was the connection. Hy had been born in Fresno; his father had operated a crop-dusting service there. But his parents had divorced when he was twelve, and he'd been raised on his stepfather's sheep ranch — the ranch he'd inherited, where he now lived — near Tufa Lake. "Bob," I asked, "have you ever heard the name Hy Ripinsky mentioned in connection with Renshaw or Kessell?"

He considered. "No, I'd remember if I had."

"What about if you wanted to get close to these people without them knowing what you were after? How would you go about it?"

"Very carefully."

"But how?"

"Sharon, just what *are* you after?" Now Bob's tone was concerned.

"I have reason to believe that a friend of mine got mixed up with RKI and may have gotten hurt."

"So you're riding to the rescue."

"Uh-huh."

"When're you going to learn?"

"Probably never."

"Sharon, you may think you're hot stuff because you've gotten your picture in the local

75

papers so many times that now you have to work to keep it out, but you're not in RKI's league. These people have been around — everyplace. They're tough and they're dangerous."

"That doesn't tell me what I need to know."

He sighed. "I'm trying to tell you to leave them alone."

"Can't."

A silence. "All right, then, I'll give you this advice: you want to find out about your friend, you level with them. No subterfuge is going to get you what you need to know. Make an appointment with Gage Renshaw, and just come out and ask what happened."

It sounded good to me; I've always preferred the straightforward approach.

After I hung up, I sat on my sofa with my feet propped on the coffee table and thought for a while. The international security consulting business is an outgrowth of the rise of terrorism against employees and executives of U.S. companies both at home and abroad. The firms provide such services as risk analysis, security program design, preventative and defensive training for personnel, guards and escorts. That's the part they talk about in *Wall Street Journal* interviews.

The activities they don't like to talk about are what they call contingency services: crisis-management plans for extortions or kidnappings; ransom negotiation and delivery; hostage recovery. Insurance companies that write large anti-terrorist policies specify which of the security firms is to be called in, along with the FBI, in the event of a kidnapping. When Bob said that the insurance carriers were leery of RKI, it meant that their methods were unorthodox, that they would often bypass the step of bringing in the federal authorities. Their tactics in paying ransoms and recovering hostages would be riskier than those of the other firms; they would probably have a high success rate, but when one of their negotiations went badly, it would result in a tragedy.

What was Hy *doing* with these people?

He'd told me an old buddy in San Diego had a business proposition to talk over with him. An old buddy from his childhood in Fresno? Or an old buddy from that nine-year hole in his life? Either way, it had to be someone from RKI, probably Dan Kessell or Gage Renshaw. And my former boss was right: the best way to find out was to ask.

I went to the phone and dialed the La Jolla number that I'd copied from my answering-machine tape the night before. A woman answered. I asked for Gage Renshaw. He was out of town. What about Dan Kessell? He was unavailable at the moment. Could I perhaps reach Mr. Renshaw in San Francisco? I could try; did I have the number there? Yes, I did, and thank you.

I dialed the San Francisco number. A man answered. Again I asked for Gage Renshaw. He took my name and put me on hold. Thirty seconds later he was back, asking what the call pertained to.

"Hy Ripinsky," I said.

There was a slight pause. "One moment, please."

The next voice that came on the line was strong and resonant — and very guarded. "Gage Renshaw here. What can I do for you, Ms. McCone?"

"I'd like to schedule an appointment to talk with you about Hy Ripinsky."

"Ripinsky . . . ?" In spite of his attempt to imply lack of recognition, I caught an undertone of interest.

"Mr. Renshaw, you know him."

". . . Yes. What's your connection with him?"

"Friend."

"I see."

"I'd like to meet with you."

There was an odd sound on the line; Renshaw was probably recording the call. "All right, Ms. McCone, I have a light schedule

78

today. Can you be here by ten-thirty?"

"Certainly."

"And you have our address?"

"Yes."

"Then I'll see you within the hour."

I set down the receiver and went into the bathroom, where I dabbed on a minimum of makeup and twisted my hair into a knot, which I secured with a tortoiseshell comb. Then I regarded my jeans and sweater in the full-length mirror, saw the frown lines between my eyebrows, and laughed wryly. One thing for sure, nobody at RKI would care about the inelegance of my wardrobe. They, and I, had more vital matters to concern us.

The block of Green Street that I wanted was just off the Embarcadero between Battery and Front. From its foot I could see the piers across the wide shoreline boulevard; behind me rose the sheer rocky cliff of Telegraph Hill. The area contains an interesting mix of buildings and businesses: manufacturers' showrooms and reclaimed warehouses; trendy restaurants and antique shops; television stations and that venerable San Francisco used-furniture institution, Busvan for Bargains. I squeezed the MG into a mostly illegal parking space on Front and walked to RKI's address. It was one of the smaller renovated warehouses — old brickwork and high arched windows, augmented by new skylights and iron trim. Liquid amber saplings grew in brick-faced planters on the sidewalk, and a plate-glass window afforded a view of the building's rather stark lobby. A man with a movie star's profile, wearing a plain gray business suit, greeted me at the reception desk; his keenly assessing gaze told me he was a guard, and a bulge under his jacket indicated he was armed. He checked a clipboard for my name, gave me a plastic-coated visitor's badge, and directed me up a curving wrought-iron staircase to his right.

There was a fire door at the top of the staircase. I pushed through it and immediately confronted another guard station, staffed by a woman this time. Careful people, Renshaw and Kessell. Careful to the point of paranoia.

The woman also checked a list when I gave my name, then buzzed someone on her intercom. While I waited, I looked around. Three rows of cubicles covered in a gray carpetlike material, offices around the perimeter. No plants, artwork, or chairs where visitors could sit. In about a minute a youngish man emerged from the aisle to my left, introduced himself as Mr. Renshaw's assistant, and asked that I follow him.

The cubicles we passed were occupied by

men and women performing routine tasks. They stared at computer screens, typed, studied reports, spoke on the phone. In spite of the activity, the area was very quiet; when I commented on it, my escort said, "White noise — it keeps one person's conversation from interfering with another's."

High-tech people, too, I thought. A bland, sterile workplace like this would depress the hell out of me. I pictured my own office at All Souls — the small Victorian fireplace, the bay window, my salmon-pink chaise longue and Oriental rug, the Tiffany lamp and other mementos of past cases — and offered a silent prayer that the co-op would never blunder this far into the twenty-first century. If that happened, it would be no place for a person like me.

Renshaw's assistant stopped in front of a corner office and motioned for me to enter, then departed without a word. A man in a rumpled brown suit sat on top of the metal desk in front of the arched window, feet flat on a chair, talking on the phone. He was tall and thin, almost emaciated. Narrow face with an Abe Lincoln brow; longish black hair with a startling white streak that curled over his forehead; dark-framed glasses that couldn't hide the keen intelligence in his eyes.

"We'll talk more later," he said into the

mouthpiece. Then he hung up and regarded me thoughtfully, as if he was memorizing every detail of my appearance.

I stood just inside the door, letting him have a good look. After a moment he nodded, his image of me apparently filed in some mental data bank. He said, "Sit down and tell me what it is you want."

I came all the way into the office and took a chair in front of the desk. Gage Renshaw remained atop it, hunched, elbows propped on his bony knees.

"Hy Ripinsky had an appointment with someone in your La Jolla office last Wednesday," I began.

Renshaw didn't respond, just watched me attentively.

"He called there from Oakland Airport, was told there had been a change of plans, and came here instead."

Still no response.

"At some point after that, he drove his rental car to a place off Highway One-oh-one in San Benito County, near Ravenswood Road. He had an accident there, dented the car and broke a headlight by running into a boulder. On Saturday night the car was dropped off at SFO by someone other than Ripinsky."

Renshaw's reaction to that was so minute I almost missed it — a slight tightening of the lines around his eyes. "Go on."

"Ripinsky's plane is still tied down at Oakland Airport. No one at his office has heard from him since he left Tufa Lake. What happened to him? And where is he now?"

"Why are you looking for him?"

I hadn't decided how to play this part of it yet. To buy time, I said, "My reasons are private and have nothing to do with your firm."

Renshaw got off the desk and walked around behind it. He straightened a pile of folders in its center, looked at his watch, pushed the lock of white hair off his forehead. Buying some time of his own. "Up to now," he finally said, "you've been very direct, Ms. McCone."

"As I told you, my reasons are private and unrelated to RKI."

"Maybe, maybe not." He leaned forward on the desk, palms flat against its surface, the white lock of hair flopping down again. "I do wonder what a private investigator employed by a local legal-services plan wants with Ripinsky." To my surprised look he added, "Yes, I recognized your name and had you checked out. It's a policy of ours. What I discovered muddies an already muddy situation."

"What situation?"

He shook his head. "You really can't expect me to level with you if you're not willing to return the favor."

And even if I did, he might not. I thought quickly, trying to decide how much to tell him.

Renshaw waited. When I didn't speak, he straightened and began to pace, long arms clasped behind him. "Ms. McCone, I've already given you more time than I intended. What's your interest in Ripinsky?"

Something in the way he said Hy's name put me on my guard. I saw a tightening of his mouth, a telltale whiteness of the skin. This man was angry at Hy — very angry. I thought of how Bob Stern had described the people at RKI: "They're tough and they're dangerous."

"All right," I said, attempting to feed into his anger, "Ripinsky and I were involved in a business deal. I can't go into the details. He cheated me, and I want to find him."

Renshaw glanced sharply at me. Again I sensed he was taking a mental photograph, filing it for future recall. After a moment he crossed to the desk and resumed his former position. "I'm glad to hear we're on the same side," he said in a confiding tone. "But I'll need to know more about this business deal."

"I can't tell you any more. There are other investors involved, and they value confidentiality."

For a moment he was silent, pulling at the knot of his frayed green tie. Gage Renshaw didn't believe my story of the business deal any more than I believed his abrupt shift to the role of confidant. I met his eyes, saw they were amused, felt my lips twitch in the beginning of a smile.

Renshaw smiled, too. "Well, here we are, Ms. McCone — two stubborn bullshitters at a standoff. You want Ripinsky, and I'll admit I want him, too. Same objective. Motive? Maybe the same, but probably not. What are we to do?"

I couldn't level, not with this man. My motives — concern, caring, something like love — weren't within his frame of reference. Oh, he'd heard of them, all right, maybe even experienced them a time or two, but in this situation they simply didn't apply.

"Your move, Ms. McCone."

Again I met his eyes; they were no longer amused. I said, "All I can tell you is that when I find Ripinsky, there'll be nothing good in store for him."

"Either you're telling the truth or you're a very good actress. For your sake, I hope it's the former."

"Why?"

Behind the sheen of his glasses his eyes went hard and icy. The skin around his mouth paled. "Because," he said, "if you have any affection for Ripinsky, you're going to be badly hurt. When I find him, I intend to kill him."

Five

Now I had to call upon all my acting skills. With an effort, I kept my voice level as I asked, "What did Ripinsky do to you?"

Renshaw shook his head. "That's confidential — like your business dealings with him."

I thought for a moment. "All right," I said, "I'll tell you what I think happened. You or your partner hired Ripinsky, possibly to deal with a situation that required his specific talents. Ripinsky screwed up or double-crossed you. You say you want to find him, so you probably don't have any more of a clue to his whereabouts than I do. That's why you agreed to see me; you thought I might give you a lead."

Renshaw regarded me with narrowed eyes.

"That's where I can help you," I added. "If you tell me what went down, I can find him. You see, Ripinsky and I used to be lovers; I know how he thinks." Two lies there, McCone.

Renshaw raised his eyebrows in disbelief.

"You were lovers, and now you're willing to turn him over to me?"

I shrugged. "Situations change. People change."

"That's cold, Ms. McCone."

"You were a friend of Ripinsky once?"

He nodded.

"Well, then, you ought to understand. Why should I feel any differently than you, now that it's over?"

That gave him pause. He got up, began pacing again. I watched him carefully. This man wanted to kill Hy; if I were to prevent that, I'd need to know him.

"Ms. McCone," he said after a bit, "I understand you're a good investigator, and I suppose you have the inside track if what you say about your former relationship with Ripinsky is true. But I still doubt you can find him when our operatives haven't been able to locate him since Sunday night."

Sunday night — not Saturday, when the rental car had been dropped off. "We've reached a stalemate, then."

He faced me, hands on hips. "You realize I don't believe a word of your story — the business deal, the other investors who require confidentiality, Ripinsky cheating you. I'm not sure I even believe what seems more logical — that he dumped you and you're attempting to use me to get back at him. All of this seems like a smoke screen for some private agenda that I'm not going to try to guess at."

"My motives don't matter. What does is that I can be bought to do what your operatives so far haven't managed."

Renshaw didn't respond, but his eyes moved swiftly — calculating. He cocked his head as if listening to some internal debate. Then he nodded, said, "Okay, come with me," and started for the door.

I got up and followed. "Where're we going?"

"Downstairs. There's a lot of material I need to familiarize you with. Afterward we'll discuss your price."

Five minutes later I was seated in the front row of a projection room off the building's lobby. Renshaw pressed a switch on a console between us; the lights dimmed. He pushed another button, and a man's picture appeared on the screen.

"Timothy Mourning," Renshaw said. "CEO and chairman of the board of Phoenix Labs."

Phoenix Labs. Where had I . . . ? Oh, yes — the company whose initial public offering of stock had abruptly been canceled; I'd tried to read the article about it in the business section this morning, and damned near fallen asleep. I studied the man's face. He was young for a CEO and board chairman, perhaps in his mid-thirties. On the plump side and mustached, he had a slightly receding hairline topped by a wild mop of dark blond curls. I was willing to bet that in high school his classmates had labeled him a nerd; now, while many of them remembered those brief years as their only time of glory, Mourning was head of a corporation. His unabashed grin and the gleam behind his wire-rimmed glasses told me he possessed both a sharp intellect and a zest for living.

Renshaw pressed the button, and the picture changed. "Diane Mourning," he said. "Tim's wife of eighteen years, and chief financial officer of the labs."

Diane Mourning's face was thin, with high cheekbones, an aquiline nose, and wide-set hazel eyes. Her shoulder-length blond hair also curled, but in a more disciplined fashion than her husband's. Unlike Timothy, she apparently considered posing for a photograph a serious matter: she stared uncompromisingly at the camera, her small mouth set in a firm, straight line. Not much humor there, I thought, and wondered how they got along.

Again Renshaw changed slides, to a sprawling one-story stucco building surrounded by a chain-link fence topped by barbed wire. Open fields lay on either side, and an oak-dotted hillside rose in the background. A guard shack sat next to the gate, and a sign on it said: Phoenix Labs, Inc.

"The company's facility in Novato," Renshaw explained. "Basic utilitarian plant, but someday there'll be an office tower next to it. Phoenix is one of the hot firms in the biotech industry. You know anything about biotech?"

"Not a great deal."

"I'll give you a background file; you read up on it. Basically it's the wave of the future — genetic engineering, disease prevention and cure. Real growth industry here in the Bay Area. Nine months ago Phoenix announced they were developing a drug called Enterferon-One that can retard the growth of the HIV virus. They've planned an IPO of stock to finance the final stages of development."

"I read in the *Chronicle* that the IPO was withdrawn. Why?"

In answer, a new picture appeared: a narrow road with wild vegetation on either side; a red Mazda sports car sat nose down in the right-hand ditch.

Renshaw said, "This is where Timothy

Mourning was kidnapped. At approximately seven-ten A.M., Tuesday, June first. On the road leading from his home outside Novato."

So Phoenix Labs was an RKI client. "Was there anti-terrorism policy on Mourning?"

"No. He was extremely wary of that kind of coverage."

"Why?"

"Because, much as the existence of such policies is supposed to be confidential, leaks occur. And a leak is a direct invitation to violent fringe groups. Mourning believes in good security and contingency planning rather than insurance. Doesn't like insurance much, isn't even covered by keyman or any other kind of life policy. Apparently, though, he operated on the mistaken assumption that nothing could ever happen to him, because he ignored the advice we gave him."

"And that was . . . ?"

"Standard: Vary your route to work. Vary your routines. Do not stop your car to help anyone, no matter what the circumstances. If stopped, do not unlock your doors or open your windows. Use your car phone to summon help. Granted, he couldn't vary his route to work; he lives on an isolated road — Crazy Horse — and there's only the one outlet. But he could have changed the time he left home, if he wasn't such a stubborn creature of habit.

As for the rest . . ."

Renshaw switched slides. A close-up shot of the car appeared, the driver's-side door wide open. "We assume he was forced into the ditch. He either got out of the car on his own or was driving with the door unlocked and taken out forcibly." Another slide, the car's interior, phone still in its cradle. "Either he didn't go for the phone or had no time to use it."

"When was the kidnapping discovered, and by whom?" I asked.

"Diane Mourning left the house at seven twenty-three. At least one of them varied the routine. She found the car and called us."

"Why not the police?"

"Our agreement with the client is that they call us first. If we feel it's in their best interests, we notify the authorities. As you probably know, there's no statute on the books that requires citizens to report kidnapping or extortion attempts."

"And did you feel it was in Mourning's best interests to report it?"

"No. Initially there was some speculation that Mourning might have staged his own disappearance, and no ransom demand was made that day or on the following two. From the first, though, we proceeded on the assumption that it was an actual kidnapping. There had been threats from lunatic-fringe animal-rights groups against the labs and the Mournings personally."

"Why?"

"Because the production of the new drug, Enterferon-One, requires the extraction of a substance from the cartilage of dolphins. A group called Terramarine has made several bomb threats, and both Mournings, plus other key employees, have received written and telephoned death threats."

"All from the same group?"

"That isn't clear. But from there it was only a short step to a kidnapping."

"I assume you brought Ripinsky in because of the environmentalist angle."

"Ironically, no. I'd contacted him several weeks before that about joining the firm. We need someone of his abilities. He and I were to meet in La Jolla on Wednesday; I was prepared to offer him an ownership percentage if that's what it would take. But by then the Mourning kidnapping had gone down, and I was already here in the city. I brought Ripinsky in on it, figuring he could help us deal with the environmentalists, if necessary. It was also in the back of my mind that giving him a taste of the old action might persuade him to come on board."

I wished I could ask about the "old action"

— where he'd known Hy, what they'd been involved in, why Renshaw wanted him to join RKI. But I couldn't do that without undermining my claim that I knew him so well I could easily find him.

"All right," I said, "what happened then?"

"We waited until the kidnappers finally made contact on June fourth. Still no way to tell if they were Terramarine or one of the other nut groups. The contact woman spoke with a Hispanic accent; Ripinsky thought she might be a Mexican national. They wanted two million in small unmarked bills. You know how much that weighs, how cumbersome it is?"

"Very, I imagine."

"Some two hundred and ninety pounds, enough to fill a couple of trunks. We tried to talk them into a wire transfer to a Swiss or Bahamian bank account. No dice. They know governments and foreign banks cooperate against extortion attempts. They wanted cash, and they were very nervous. We did get them to send proof that the victim was still alive." Another slide appeared on the screen: Timothy Mourning, holding a copy of the June 4 *New York Times*.

Renshaw went on, "Finally Kessell — Dan Kessell, my partner — hit on the idea of an irrevocable international letter of credit drawn on Phoenix's bank account here to whatever foreign company they specified. And they went for it. Apparently they knew somebody they could trust at a firm, Colores Internacional in Mexico City."

"You checked them out, of course."

"Yeah. Fairly good-sized operation, makes silk flowers, crap like that. Privately held by a member of one of Mexico's wealthy families, Emanuel Fontes. Fontes is an environmentalist, has donated to a number of causes, particularly ones having to do with the protection of marine mammals."

"Dolphins. Interesting."

"What's even more interesting is that Fontes's brother, Gilbert, owns a large tuna-fishing fleet headquartered in Ensenada. Diametrically opposed viewpoints there, and bad blood between them."

"Bad enough blood to make Emanuel an extremist?"

"We've kicked the thought around."

"Have you tried to get the Mexican authorities to lean on him, find out if he's connected with any of the fringe groups?"

Renshaw looked at me as if I'd taken leave of my senses. "Down there, where you never know who's involved in what? No, we backed off and set it up. The objective was to get the victim back alive; then we'd let the au-

96

thorities go after the kidnappers — that is, if we didn't take care of them first." He smiled grimly. "Ripinsky was to make the drop; we hoped he might be able to identify somebody. They went through the usual nonsense: go to this phone booth, wait for another call. Finally they named the location — that turnoff in San Benito County."

"What happened down there, do you know?"

"I know. And that was the first time I had a funny feeling about Ripinsky. According to him, there was another car in the turnoff when he arrived. Its driver panicked, forced him into the boulder, and took off. Ripinsky waited, but nobody else ever showed."

"But you don't believe that."

"At the time I did, but like I said, I had a funny feeling. Anyway, Ripinsky came back here and we waited some more. Didn't take the kidnappers long to reestablish contact. They wanted to move the drop south, said Ripinsky should check into a place on Hotel Circle in San Diego and they'd call him on Sunday. That gave us real cause for concern."

"Why?"

"Because it indicated they might've taken Mourning into Mexico. If they reneged on setting him free once they had the L.C., there'd be no way we could recover him by force.

In most foreign countries, we work either with or around the authorities, but not down there. After last year's U.S. Supreme Court ruling that it's okay to snatch criminals from foreign jurisdictions to stand trial here, Mexico quit cooperating completely. The political situation's just too damned volatile for us to go in on our own. Company policy says we don't set foot south of the border."

"I see. So Ripinsky flew to San Diego that night?"

"Uh-huh. One of our operatives dropped him off at SFO and returned his rental car."

"He had the letter of credit with him?"

"Damn right he did."

"Did he contact your people in La Jolla?"

"He did not. Too risky, in case the kidnappers had him under surveillance. We know he checked into the motel, the Bali Kai, and on Sunday he sent a message through a woman friend of mine on Point Loma, saying the drop was set for eleven P.M. And that's the last we ever heard. Ripinsky checked out of the motel with the two-million-dollar L.C. and vanished. His rental car didn't even turn up."

I masked my surge of concern by asking, "Has the L.C. been drawn upon?"

"No. We're monitoring Phoenix's bank account minute by minute."

"Any chance Ripinsky met with foul play

before he could make the drop?"

"That's possible, but not too damn likely. Ripinsky can take care of himself. The assumption I'm acting on is that he made a deal with the kidnappers — or was in collusion with them from the first."

"You mean since before you brought him in on the case? How could he have known Phoenix was your client?"

"Because among the materials on the firm that I sent him several weeks ago was a complete, confidential client list. Sheer stupidity on my part. I ignored what you pointed out earlier: situations change, people change."

Renshaw paused, his face pale and drawn. "Because of my stupidity, Timothy Mourning is probably rotting in a ditch somewhere with a bullet in his brain, while Ripinsky's sitting back and waiting until he thinks it's safe to draw on Phoenix's two-million-dollar L.C." His eyes glittered against the darkness that surrounded us. "Ripinsky's going to pay for this."

I looked away, glad he couldn't see me all that well. Stared at the slide of Mourning holding the June 4 *Times*. The laughter was gone from his face, leaving it a rigid mask of fear. The gleam in his bespectacled eyes had been replaced by a sheen of horror. Timothy Mourning had known he was going to die.

But not because of Hy's actions. Imperfect as my understanding of him was, I knew he would never have colluded with the kidnappers or cut a deal. Would never have caused this innocent man's death. On the surface, the circumstantial evidence against him looked bad, but if I dug deep, I knew I'd uncover a different set of facts. And I would dig. Gage Renshaw was not going to make Hy pay for something he'd had no part in.

Renshaw asked, "Are you still with us, Ms. McCone?"

I hardened my expression as the lights came up. Turned to him and said firmly, "Yes, I am."

"Then let's discuss your price."

Six

The bargain I struck with Gage Renshaw would have been lucrative — had I any intention of honoring it. In fact, it shocked me to learn just how much money could be made, providing you worked for a certain type of people. The outrageous figure Renshaw agreed to pay when I delivered information about Hy's whereabouts told me that for years I'd been shortchanged by even more than I'd suspected; in fact, made me feel like a mere novice in a field where only hours before, I'd considered myself a consummate pro. If you threw in expenses, which Renshaw also agreed to pay, for a single job I would have earned only slightly less than my yearly salary at All Souls.

Yes, there was a lot of money to be made in investigation — providing you wanted to work for a firm like RKI. Providing you were willing to bend the rules as they did. Providing your sleep wasn't susceptible to guilt- and horror-induced nightmares.

101

None of those circumstances applied in my case, though. I pocketed the advance check Renshaw had the business office issue me for expenses, took down directions to the Mourning home outside Novato, and agreed to meet him there at four. Diane Mourning, he said, had been adamantly against calling in the authorities, but that hadn't prevented her from taking RKI to task for mishandling the situation. Perhaps talking with me would assure her they still were making every effort. Since I'd hoped to speak with the victim's wife anyway, the drive up there seemed worthwhile.

My business with Renshaw concluded, I stopped at RKI's bank and cashed the check. Then I went to a nearby branch of Bank of America and deposited most of it in my account, holding out some for incidentals. Finally I returned to my office to finish some paperwork and talk with Rae.

The co-op was quiet; Ted slumped in his desk chair, staring at his computer screen. I reached into my box for my message slips and said, "*Amo, amas, amat.*" It was the only conjugation I remembered from my high-school Latin classes.

He continued staring at the screen, ignoring me.

I asked, "What's the Latin phrase for today?"

"*Tete futae* and the horse you rode in on."

Stung by his uncharacteristic grouchiness, I said, "The same to you," and went upstairs.

Now, what was that about? I wondered as I dumped my bag and jacket on my chaise longue. He'd been perfectly cheerful when I left the night before. Maybe the stress and uncertainty of this reorganization was taking its toll on him, too.

For about half an hour I took care of my messages and dictated a couple of reports. Then I called Hy's accountant, Barry Ashford. Ashford said he had a standing arrangement with Hy to take care of his bills when he went out of town for extended periods. "Goes back to the days right after Julie died when he was getting busted for doing stupid things at environmental protests," he said. "I should've explained that to Kate; obviously she's made this out to be a bigger deal than it is."

"Did Hy say how long he'd be away?"

"No, but he told me he'd probably be back before anything needed to be paid. In case he wasn't, though, he wanted to alert me."

It sounded as if he'd been keeping an open mind about Renshaw's offer. If things looked good in La Jolla, he'd stay longer; if not, he'd simply return home. "Did Hy mention why he was going away?"

"Hy? Are you kidding?"

I thanked Ashford and hung up, glad I hadn't talked with him yesterday. The accountant's casual attitude toward Hy's unexplained absence might have lulled me into a false sense of security, convinced me there was no need to continue looking.

Next I called Kate Malloy. She said she'd been out to Hy's ranch and spoken with the hands. "Not much there. Hy didn't tell them anything, and the reason he paid them for two months is that one man needed an advance because his wife's having a baby. Hy just figured it was easier to pay them all the same amount."

"What about American Express? Were you able to find anything out?"

"Yes. He used the card twice after he rented the car in Oakland: for a ticket to San Diego on USAir on Saturday night, and at the Bali Kai Motor Inn there. No additional charges since Sunday, but they may just be slow coming in."

It fit neatly with the story Renshaw had told me. "Thanks, Kate," I said. "I've got a line on Hy, and I'm going to San Diego tonight. I'll check in when I know something." Then I ended the call before she could press me for details.

I swiveled around and slumped in my chair, staring unseeingly out the window. In addition to supporting Renshaw's story, the facts also supported what I instinctively knew. If Hy had already been in collusion with Timothy Mourning's kidnappers when he left Tufa Lake, he would have made provisions for a lengthy absence, probably liquidated his assets. But Hy's departure, prompted by a call from me that precipitated our trip to the Great Whites, had been strictly spur-of-the-moment.

And afterward, when Renshaw contended he'd gone over to the kidnappers' side? Well, I still had no proof he hadn't except my faith that he was incapable of such an act. And that was solid enough proof for me.

I thought for a while more before I buzzed Rae's office and asked her to come upstairs. She didn't look much more convivial than Ted, and she'd continued to allow her appearance to go to hell. Her hair stuck out in greasy little curlicues, her sweater had holes in it, and her jeans were ripped at the knees. She saw me glance at them and thrust out her jaw as if to say, "You want to make something of it?"

"Have a seat," I told her. "I need to ask a favor."

"I heard about your promotion." She looked at my chaise longue and apparently decided that moving the jacket, briefcase, purse, camera bag, stack of files, and bag of Hershey's Kisses was too much trouble. Flopping on the floor in front of it, she added, "Congratulations."

"Thanks — I think."

"Your rose came. Since you weren't here to deal with it, I stuck it in a water glass in the bathroom. Couldn't bear to put it in your bud vase; that was so dirty I've got it soaking in the sink." She glared at me, as if she'd narrowly prevented me from neglecting a child.

I ignored the glare, said humbly, "Thank you, Rae."

"Just see you take care of it. I'm not your gal Friday, you know." Then she perked up some. "I suppose this promotion means you'll be getting a raise. Maybe we should celebrate. You want to go down to the Remedy?"

The Remedy Lounge is All Souls's favorite tavern, on Mission Street. We hang out there a fair amount, but we don't usually head downhill at a little after two in the afternoon. "Now?" I asked.

Rae shrugged, looking hurt.

What the hell, I thought. Maybe if I bought her a beer she'd stop sulking long enough for me to ask my favor. "Why not?" I said. "Let's go."

"Forget it — it was just an excuse to get plastered. I've got to watch that. Don't want to turn into a stereotype."

"Stereotype?"

"The Irish sot, and the scorned woman."

"Willie still being difficult?"

"Still. Bastard's not budging on the prenup. God, as if I wanted his money! I'm not even sure I want *him* anymore. He's no prize, you know. The man used to be a *criminal*."

Poor Rae. I was sorry she was hurting, but relieved she wasn't about to become the third — or was it the fourth? — Mrs. Willie Whelan. The man had a big heart, but he'd yet to prove he could stick to the straight and narrow; when I met him, he was a successful dealer in stolen goods, and proud of it. Should his discount-jewelry chain — empire, he called it — collapse, he might revert to type, and then where would Rae be?

I said, "Instead of a drink, have some of those Hershey's Kisses."

"Kisses are what got me into this mess in the first place," she said sullenly. But she reached for the bag and proceeded to litter the rug with little paper pull tabs and foil wrappers while I told her about Hy's disappearance, Gage Renshaw's threat to kill him, and the job I'd pretended to take on in order to save him.

As Rae listened, her eyes got wider and she stopped bothering to lick the smears of chocolate from the corners of her mouth. "God, Shar," she said when I finished, "don't those RKI guys *scare* you?"

"I'm more scared of what may have happened to Hy, and what Renshaw will do if he finds him."

"Can you even investigate a kidnapping, though? I mean isn't it like a homicide? The cops can get you for messing around in a murder case. And RKI didn't even report this."

"Strangely enough, there's nothing on the books that compels them to report it or prohibits me from investigating." Frequently when I'm bored, I dip into the volumes in All Souls's law library, my favorite being the one containing the California Penal Code. Over the years I've gleaned many fascinating facts — for example, that it's illegal to trap or kill birds in public cemeteries. "A specific provision in the Penal Code's section on kidnapping states that nothing prohibits a person from offering to rescue an individual who's been kidnapped, either by force or by payment of ransom."

Rae looked impressed. So far as I know, she hasn't opened any book more weighty than a shop-and-fuck novel since graduating from Berkeley.

"Anyway," I went on, "I'm going to Novato to talk with the kidnap victim's wife in about an hour, and then I'm leaving for San Diego. And that's where I need your help."

"You mean you want me to cover for you here? You know I will. But if the partners find out . . ." She shrugged. "There's that new rule against us taking outside employment. This could screw up your promotion."

"I'm not sure that would be such a bad thing."

"Why —"

"I don't have time to talk about that now. I can't even think about it. Will you cover?"

"Sure. But I think you'd better have a good excuse for not showing up at work, like sickness."

"I don't like to lie."

"Neither do I, Shar, but we're going to have to. I'm putting my job on the line, too, you know."

"Then I can't ask you to —"

"No, I don't mind. This is important." She paused, her freckled face tense with concentration. "Maybe a summer cold . . . No, a female complaint is better. The women'll understand, and the men — for all their so-called sophistication — will be afraid to ask questions. But make sure I know where to reach you, and for God's sake, leave your answering machine on."

"Okay." Then I thought of Ralph and Alice.

"Can I also ask you to feed my cats?"

"Sure. Just don't let Ted find out. The way he takes on over the care and feeding of those beasts, you'd think he was a doting uncle."

"Well, he *was* responsible for me having them." I tossed her my extra house key. "You can also have my rose." Then I glanced at my watch. "We better get started going over our caseload. I'm caught up, and you should be able to handle what comes in. And when this is all over, I promise you'll be handsomely rewarded."

Rae grinned evilly. "Just bring me the head of Willie Whelan."

I had made my travel arrangements and was about to leave the office when I heard a knock on the doorframe. Gloria Escobar, looking hesitant. "Do you have a minute?" she asked.

I checked my watch. Quarter to three, and I figured I'd need the extra fifteen minutes I'd allowed for the trip to Novato, in case traffic jammed on the Golden Gate or at the bottleneck at San Rafael. "Barely."

"This won't take long." She came in and perched on the edge of the chaise longue, rearranging my jacket and bag carefully, then smoothing her gray gabardine skirt over her thighs. Gloria's clothing was always understated, bordering on the drab; her only concession to style was her bright lipstick, nail polish, and smoky eye shadow; her only undisciplined feature was her irrepressible dark curls.

I waited, wondering if this was to be a rehash of the critical comments she'd made about me at the partners' meeting.

She cleared her throat, more ill at ease than I'd ever seen her. "I want to apologize for my remarks yesterday. They were uncalled for."

"Well, my response to the promotion wasn't all that gracious, either. You people caught me by surprise."

"Have you thought about it?"

"Some, but not enough to make a decision."

She hesitated, seemed to be making a decision of her own. Her eyes moved around the room, resting on the rubber plant in the far corner. When they returned to me she said, "Perhaps it would help you make up your mind if I told you why I feel so strongly about you accepting it. To do that, I'll have to explain where I'm coming from."

Her phrasing brought my guard up. I'd never once heard Gloria use the words "where I'm coming from," but I had heard Mike Tobias utter them on any number of occasions. To me they suggested that the two had gotten together and scripted a sales pitch.

"Sharon?" she said. "Please hear me out."

"All right." Mentally I subtracted the extra fifteen minutes of travel time to Novato.

"My mother was born in Tijuana," she began. "Very poor. My father deserted her when my sister was four and she was pregnant with me. She decided to make the trip north across the border; there was an aunt who had married a Mexican-American who would help. One night she took my sister and waited on the hill above the canyons. When it was time, they crossed with the others who were there."

I knew the hill — a ridge of them, actually. When I was a child, friends of my parents had a small ranch on Monument Road, in the unincorporated area of San Diego County, within sight of the border. During our visits there, I'd see the people patiently waiting on the hills. By daylight a festive mood prevailed: they would picnic and barbecue, and the children would play. But at dusk everything became curiously quiet. Even on the hottest nights, they would then don layer upon layer of clothing — whatever they were able to bring with them. And at dark their figures became indistinct as they continued to wait for the moment when *la migra* — their name for the U.S. Border Patrol — was looking the other way. Then they would move out, disappearing into the untamed canyons — canyons with names like Deadman's and Smuggler's Gulch — eluding rattlesnakes, scorpions, and bandits.

They were called *pollos* — chickens — by their predators. I'd seen them running along the drainage ditches beside Monument and Dairy Mart roads, fleeing alongside the San Diego Freeway — now eluding not only *la migra* and the American variety of bandit but also, I was told, crooked Tijuana policemen who had crossed to prey on their own people. The *pollos* came from diverse backgrounds and places, but they had in common three things: they were poor, desperate, and very, very frightened.

Gloria went on, "My mother was attacked by bandits in Smuggler's Gulch. She wasn't raped, but they took what little money she had. All she was able to save was the address of the safe house in San Diego where she was to wait until my aunt could come for her. She walked there from the border, seven months pregnant, carrying my sister."

But that was fifteen miles, give or take. I tried to imagine the journey, but couldn't.

Gloria said, "I was born two months later in a migrant workers' shack in Salinas, where my aunt's family was working the lettuce harvest. The doctor was Hispanic; he assisted at births for free. My mother was ashamed to take his charity, but she knew he'd issue a birth certificate proving I was born on American soil. Three years later the INS caught up with her, and she and my sister were deported. I stayed behind with my aunt. You see, I was an American citizen."

As she spoke, I'd waited for some display of emotion that would contradict the flat, staged quality of her recital. All I got now was a faint bitter smile. Was she that tightly controlled? Given the history she was relating, she should have been angry. And why was she telling this story to me, anyway?

In the same passionless tone she went on, "My mother died a few years later in Tijuana. I barely remember her. To this day my sister hates me, even though I've repeatedly tried to help her. I don't blame her; I was the one who got to stay."

Now I spotted a slight tremor at the corners of her lips; her eyes clouded. The story was true, but something was lost in the telling. Perhaps she'd used this personal history to fuel her passion to succeed so many times that it no longer had the power to stir her.

I started to speak, but Gloria held up her hand, silencing me. "I know this doesn't seem relevant to your accepting or declining the promotion, but please let me go on."

I nodded, too interested in both the story and her motives for telling it to worry about lost travel time.

"My aunt made sure I went to school, even though we lived in a series of shacks from the Canadian border to Riverside County. When I was fifteen we were able to settle near Marysville, and there was a teacher in the high school who decided I should go to college and arranged a scholarship to the University of Oregon at Eugene. I did well, applied to law school there, and got another scholarship. Then in my senior year I fell in love — or so I thought. He was an Anglo, his family had money. When they found out I was pregnant, they shipped him off to Europe for a year. Didn't want a 'wetback,' as they called me, for a daughter-in-law."

I made an involuntary sound of sympathy. Gloria's eyes hardened and she resumed speaking, more swiftly now.

"I had the baby, a daughter named Teresa, after my mother. I moved into a women's cooperative in Eugene, where we all helped each other care for our kids while attending school. For a while after graduation I worked for the ACLU, then for a small progressive firm in Portland. They're the people who told me about the job here; they knew it was what I needed to be doing."

She looked back at me, gaze level, lips pulled into a straight, controlled line. "Teresa's ten now. Gets straight As. She's beautiful. She's also the reason I'm committed to what I do. No one is going to hold my daughter back because of their own narrow prejudices. No one is going to make her feel the humiliation I suffered almost every day of my childhood and young adulthood."

I waited for her to go on. When she didn't speak, I said, "So that's where you're coming from."

"Yes." She paused, watching me. Anger moved beneath the level surface of her gaze now. "I've given up a lot, Sharon, to work in behalf of people who are in danger of losing their rights. Other than Teresa, I don't have much of a personal life. I live and breathe the law eighteen hours a day; the other six I dream it. That's why I came on so strong with you yesterday — and why I think you should accept this promotion. Right now All Souls is in a critical transition period. We need our people to make sacrifices, to give up their own concerns and make this co-op a truly viable institution. All Souls has been good to you. Why can't you return the kindness?"

Abruptly I stood and turned my back to her, staring out the window while gathering my thoughts and trying to assemble them within a logical framework that she, as a woman of reason, would understand.

"A great deal of what you say makes sense," I finally told her. "And what you're working for — it's so people can be free to live their dreams. Am I correct?"

"Yes."

"That's good. That's what we all should do, isn't it? And even though you've sacrificed your personal life, aren't you in fact living your dream?"

"Of course."

"Then I'm happy for you. But what about *my* dream?"

"Your dream?" She sounded surprised, as if it had never occurred to her that people like me — who were more or less mainstream Americans, who had more or less not had to struggle — could possibly entertain a dream.

"Yes, Gloria, I have one. And in essence you're asking me to give up my dream for yours."

"But mine is —"

"Better? More worthy because you've experienced hardship and discrimination?" Now I was the one who felt angry.

"No, no." She held out her hands placatingly. "I guess I assumed that because you work here, your dream is the same as mine."

"Possibly it is. At least in the abstract." I got my emotions under control and sat back down. "You've been honest with me," I said, even though I wasn't sure her motives were all that pure, "so now I'm going to return the favor and tell you something that I don't tell many people because, frankly, it makes me feel silly when I put it into words. After I graduated from college I had a lot of time on my hands because I couldn't get a job that didn't involve guarding office buildings in the dead of night. And I became addicted to detective novels. I'd devour them, one or two a shift, and there'd still be time left over, so I'd dream. And what I'd dream about was going out into the night, strong and unafraid, on a mission to right wrongs. I wanted to make things right, just as you did.

"Fortunately for you and me, we got to realize those dreams. You right wrongs through the legal system; I do it by getting at the truth and trying to salvage a bad situation. Maybe my method doesn't have as sweeping an effect as yours, but it makes the best use of my abilities. Makes a much better use of them than if I were logging in cases and making sure paralegals do their jobs. I'm a damned good investigator, and if you ask anybody who's been around here awhile, you'll find that I've pulled this co-op out of a bad spot more than just a time or two. So don't talk to me about how I'm not returning what All Souls has given me, because I have, over and over."

Gloria was silent, staring at the rubber plant again. After a moment she said, "You have an answer for everything, don't you? And you've had it so easy. You can't possibly understand."

"How do you know I've had it so easy? You don't know anything about me — haven't even bothered to ask. I haven't experienced as much hardship as you, but my life hasn't been so wonderful, either. Especially not when it comes to prejudice. You may have noticed, although you've never remarked on it, that I have Indian blood — I'm one-eighth Shoshone. Bigots don't like half-breeds — or eighth-breeds."

She studied my face now, her expression puzzled, and I realized that she'd been so caught up with her own minority status that she'd ignored what should have been obvious.

I glanced at my watch and stood. "Gloria, I've given you all the time I can. I'll consider the promotion, but strictly on its own merits. But let me ask you this: whose idea was it for you to approach me this way?"

". . . What do you mean?"

"You're not a woman who easily shares the

details of her personal history. Was it you or Mike who decided this was a good way to play on my emotions?"

"I would never —"

"Sure you would. You're an excellent attorney. So is Mike. Nothing wrong with working on the emotions of a jury, so why not mine?"

She stood, too. "You're right, Sharon. Why not? You do what you have to."

"That's not the way we operate at All Souls."

"We. Meaning the old guard. The privileged. The ones who feel they can ignore the rules."

Maybe she had a point. We, the old guard, might have subtly excluded her, Mike, and any number of other new personnel. "I think we should talk more about that," I said. "When we have some free time, why don't we get together?"

She shrugged and moved toward the door, but before she stepped into the hall, she turned. "Maybe you don't know All Souls as well as you think you do, Sharon. You asked about who came up with the scheme to work on your emotions? Well, it was all of us — the partners. And maybe it wasn't the best of schemes, but it was well intentioned. None of us want to see you leave."

120

As her footsteps tapped angrily down the hall, my spirits took a swift downward spiral. I *didn't* know All Souls anymore. Didn't know my old friends, the partners.

Seven

When I finally found Crazy Horse Road it was already four-ten. True to form, traffic had jammed at San Rafael, and then I'd missed a couple of turns coming out of downtown Novato. By now I felt irritable and concerned about catching a flight to San Diego in time to accomplish what I needed to do tonight.

The road was narrow, winding through the countryside near the Indian Tree Open Space Preserve. I saw few houses, mainly mailboxes standing in groups at the ends of private drives. The land rose on either side of the pavement, covered with oak and tangled vegetation; an occasional red-tailed hawk swooped by, and a road sign warned of deer. After two-point-six miles I came to the steep pillar-flanked driveway that Gage Renshaw had described to me; when I identified myself through the security talk box, the gates swung open and I followed the winding blacktop up the hill.

The Mourning house was of redwood and

rustic stone, built so the lower story spilled down the slope. Several vehicles crowded the parking area at the top of the drive: a beat-up green Ford, two matching gray-and-maroon vans, which I assumed were RKI's mobile units, and a BMW in an odd teal blue with a car phone antenna mounted on its trunk. I maneuvered the MG between the vans and got out. Stone steps led alongside the garage to a second gate; again I spoke into a talk box and was admitted. The house's entrance was off a patio with a small swimming pool; as I passed the pool, I saw a dead mouse floating at the deep end; the container plants on the patio's retaining wall were wilted and browning.

The door of the house opened, and an armed guard in a gray uniform stepped outside and scrutinized me. Gage Renshaw appeared seconds later. "It's okay," he said to the guard. To me he added, "You're late."

"Sorry." I didn't offer any excuse; he didn't want to hear one.

Renshaw motioned me into an entry area whose hardwood floor was partly covered by a blue Chinese rug. Directly behind it, across a mahogany table that held a single jade bowl, lay a living room with tall windows that looked out into the branches of the oak trees on the downward slope. I caught a motion to my left and glanced over there; in an adjacent formal dining room sat two men dressed in the same type of gray suit as the guard in the lobby of RKI's building had worn. The table was covered with telephone monitoring devices; the men were smoking and looking bored.

Renshaw said, "We've still got our communications technicians here, in case the kidnappers make contact again."

"There's been nothing since we last spoke?"

"No."

"And the letter of credit still hasn't been drawn on?"

He shook his head. "Come into the living room. Mrs. Mourning'll be with us shortly." He preceded me and flopped into a leather chair, propping his feet on its hassock and clawing at his tie. It was badly frayed around the knot, as if it took a similar beating with each wearing.

I sat down in a matching chair, feeling the buttery softness of the leather. "Nice house," I commented.

Renshaw shrugged and glanced around; it was clear he hadn't before given the house a thought.

"I'm going to San Diego after I leave here," I told him. "Will you give me the name and number of your woman friend who served as your contact with Ripinsky?"

"Alicia Ferris. As in the wheel." He closed his eyes briefly, dredged up the number, and repeated it to me. "You plan to contact our people in La Jolla?"

"No — for the same reason Ripinsky didn't."

He nodded. "You might need them in an emergency, though. Kessell's back down there now, so go directly to him. You'll need a code number to get through after hours; I'll have one assigned and phone it in to you. Where'll you be staying?"

"The Bali Kai."

"Any lead you might pick up there'll be damned cold by now. Besides, our people have already checked with the motel and taken a look at Ripinsky's charges. Room, bar, restaurant, and the one local call to Alicia."

"And you say he rented a car down there?"

"Yeah — Avis. Hasn't been returned yet. We got the license number off the motel registration."

"What is the number?"

He took a notebook from his inside suit coat pocket and read it to me. "Gold Honda Accord, this year's model."

I wrote down the number and description. Renshaw asked, "You know San Diego?"

I'd been prepared for the question. "Not so well anymore. I grew up there, but my parents have divorced, and the rest of the family's scattered, too."

"You must have friends there."

"Not really. I doubt if I'd recognize most of them if I ran into them on the street. But don't worry; I won't have any trouble getting reacquainted with the territory."

"Well, anything you need — Ah, here's Mrs. Mourning now." He stood as she entered the room.

Diane Mourning looked smaller and thinner than in the slide I'd seen — possibly an illusion fostered by her slim-legged black jeans and loose T-shirt. Her blond curls had been trimmed to chin length since the picture was taken, and new lines of strain pulled around her eyes and mouth. She nodded to me, motioned for Renshaw to sit, and curled into a corner of the sofa, drawing her bare feet up. The pose was not relaxed, however; she seemed coiled tight, ready to spring.

"Gage tells me he's hired you to look into the mismanagement of our ransom delivery," she said.

If her choice of words bothered Renshaw, he didn't betray it. I said, "I plan to fly to San Diego tonight and begin an investigation into the whereabouts of your husband, the letter of credit, and the man who was to make the drop."

"You mean the whereabouts of my husband's *body*."

"We have no proof he's dead."

Diane Mourning brushed the statement aside with a flick of her hand. "The kidnappers have the L.C. They must, because there've been no further demands from them. Do you really think they'd let Timothy live?"

"We also have no proof that they have the letter of credit."

"Then why haven't we heard from them?"

"Protracted silences are a common tactic with kidnappers; it's their way of working on your nerves."

"Well, they're doing a damned good job of it. I hate this, I hate the waiting. I can't make any assumptions. I don't know how to proceed."

"Proceed with what?"

Abruptly she uncoiled her body and placed her feet flat on the floor, leaning toward me. "How much has Gage told you about the situation here? The professional, as opposed to the personal?"

"Not a great deal. I know that the new drug Phoenix Labs is developing has angered animal-rights activists, and that you suspect a radical group of having kidnapped your husband. I know that you've withdrawn your initial public offering of stock."

127

Renshaw said, "I've given Sharon a file on the biotech industry."

Diane Mourning didn't bother to look at him. "Forget the file. Most of it will be superfluous. I can tell you all you'll ever need to know."

I glanced at Renshaw. He slouched in the chair, seemingly as relaxed as before, but his fingers were laced together as they would have been if he were strangling someone.

"Our industry is a relatively new one," Diane Mourning began. "Ten or twelve years ago there were only two biotech companies whose stock was offered publicly, now there are around two hundred and fifty, with a combined market value of over forty billion dollars. Most people still think of us as genetic engineers, but that's only one of a whole range of avant-garde techniques — including rational drug design, which Phoenix Labs employs. Is this clear so far?"

"So far," I said, not thrilled with her patronizing tone.

"Financing has always been a problem for the industry. We're on a ten-year product cycle — meaning that's how long it takes on the average to bring a drug to market. This doesn't mesh with the stock market's quarterly profit cycle; investors are wary of firms that don't produce those regular dividends.

At Phoenix we've been fortunate; a couple of major venture capitalists got interested in us early on and helped to privately raise most of the fifty million we needed for the initial phases of development. Now we're beginning on the final phase, and those sources have dried up, so we need to raise an additional fifty million."

"Okay, I understand the financial problems involved, but what about the environmental — or animal-rights — issue?"

"The drug we're developing, Enterferon-One, belongs to a group called tat inhibitors. They have the potential to destroy the HIV virus's ability to reproduce. We're about two years away from knowing conclusively whether it works on humans, and the next phase is very critical. It's also controversial because of the requirements for the experimentation. You see, the production of Enterferon-One relies on the use of a substance called Delphol, which is extracted from the cartilage of dolphins. And that's what's got the animal-rights advocates up in arms."

"They oppose your slaughtering dolphins."

"Animals before people." Mourning shrugged one shoulder contemptuously. "Personally, I think it's more important to prevent people from dying of AIDS. But, frankly, all this flap is so unnecessary. We don't intend to harvest Delphol from dolphins except for experimentation; the amount needed for one treatment would require too many to be cost-effective, and besides, dolphins are protected under the Marine Mammal Act of 'seventy-two. What we do intend is to synthesize the substance, and one of our scientists has already come up with the basic process. All we need now is the funds to proceed with testing. But try to tell that to these fringe groups. They don't *want* to listen."

"But now you've withdrawn the stock offering."

"Yes, at exactly the time when we should be moving ahead rapidly. Do you follow the stock market, Ms. McCone?"

"No." I've seldom had enough surplus cash to care what the stock market is doing, but I doubt I'd follow it closely, anyway. Paper profits don't confuse so much as bore me.

"In nineteen ninety-one, biotech IPOs raised over a billion dollars. Analysts were worried by the boom; the companies showed very little in current earnings, but dazzled investors with promises of huge future profits. Dazzle lasts only so long before disillusionment sets in, and many of the stock issues were by marginal firms to begin with. Last year the speculative bubble burst. Recently there's been a slight rally, but no one's certain if it'll hold or if the market will go into another blow-off stage."

"And now you've been forced to hold off because of the kidnapping."

"No one is going to invest in a firm whose future leadership is in serious jeopardy."

"Is that why you've been so adamant about not bringing in the police or the FBI? Because of the potential for adverse publicity?"

"Partly out of a fear of publicity and partly because I thought we had a security firm that knew what it was doing." She shot an icy glance at Renshaw.

Renshaw didn't respond, but now his fingertips tapped on the arm of his chair.

I asked, "And you still don't want to call in the authorities?"

"No. Timothy's dead — I'm certain of it — and the authorities can't change that. Besides, if they were called in, they'd take over and hamper your investigation. Gage tells me you have inside information that may enable you to locate Mr. Ripinsky and recover our missing L.C. The two million dollars that we can't put our hands on will make our financial position unattractive to potential investors — to say nothing of precarious for us."

"The L.C. hasn't been drawn on. Why can't you put your hands on the money?"

"Because when an irrevocable L.C. is issued, the bank puts a lock on the funds, like an escrow account in a real-estate transaction. When the terms of the L.C. are met by the recipient, the funds are released, but until then neither party can touch them."

"What were the terms?"

"Merely upon presentation of the L.C."

I said to Renshaw, "I'd like a copy of the L.C."

"I'll fax one to you in San Diego."

I looked back at Diane Mourning, studying her more carefully. Was she actually as cold as she came across, or had she put her emotions on hold? Was she focused on the financial issue to the exclusion of the larger, human issue, or had she used it to divert her attention from the probability that her husband had suffered a horrible death?

Mourning was also studying me, her gaze skimming over my face as if she were speed-reading it. After a moment she leaned forward, cupping her hands in front of her; her fingernails were bitten to the quick and made her look vulnerable, but I wondered if the cause of the biting had been fear for her husband or for her company.

"I know what you're thinking," she said to me. "I know how I must sound. Timothy's kidnapping is a personal tragedy, but there's nothing I can do about it. All I can do is prevent it from becoming a tragedy for the labs as well. In a way, that's the only thing I *can* do for Timothy — protect the company he built. I can't let all his years of sacrifice go for nothing."

Renshaw snorted derisively.

Mourning turned to him, suddenly furious. "What the hell is that supposed to mean, Gage?"

"Pardon me for saying so, but you and Tim live a little high to support this self-sacrificial rhetoric. You may have given up the condo in the city and the beach house, but this place isn't exactly chopped liver."

"For your information, this house, along with everything in it, is borrowed from one of our venture capitalists who chooses to live elsewhere. The cars? They're leased by the company. If you want you can examine the labels in my clothes — they came from the Emporium. Frankly, Gage, we lost everything when the speculative bubble burst. We don't have a pot to pee in."

He held up his hands in a placating gesture.

Quickly I said, "Let's talk about the kidnappers for a moment. You're reasonably convinced they were members of a radical animal-rights group?"

She nodded, but not before she gave Renshaw a last hard look. "Eco-terrorists,

133

your Mr. Ripinsky called them — before he took off with our letter of credit."

"It couldn't have been someone using the environmental issue as a cover? A disgruntled employee, for instance?"

"As far as I know, our people are happy. For the most part they're young, very challenged, and learning as they go. There's a critical shortage of skilled workers for the biotech industry in the Bay Area, so Phoenix has hired and trained promising college graduates."

"What about personal enemies?"

"I've been over all this with Gage. Timothy and I have none."

"Well, that about does it." I checked my watch. "It's time I got back to the city."

Renshaw stood, looking glad to get out of there. "She'll report to me periodically, Diane, and I'll keep you informed."

Mourning nodded, still angry. Her nod to me was only a shade more cordial. As we left the room, she curled in a corner of the couch again — poised to strike, should she find a suitable target.

Eight

Renshaw said, "She's full of shit, you know."

We were in the driveway of the Mourning house, leaning against his car — a green Ford that was as disreputable as his tie. I said, "People have different ways of handling their grief."

"I'm not talking about whether she's hurting or not. That's her business. But this crap about Tim being self-sacrificing . . . I knew Mourning fairly well. The guy loved to spend. They didn't lose their money when the biotech market went flat; Tim piddled it away on boats, cars, an expensive wine cellar."

"So maybe Diane's trying to sanitize his memory."

Renshaw brushed his white forelock off his brow and glared at me. "You know, you have a very naive streak."

"I call it an open mind."

"Whatever."

"I want to ask you about something you mentioned earlier today. There was some speculation before the kidnappers made contact that Mourning planned his disappearance?"

"Right."

"On whose part?"

"Mine. Kessell's."

"Why?"

He looked around before speaking in a lowered voice. "Mourning is one of those people who always have to be on the cutting edge. You know the type: If this was the old days, he'd be an explorer on the western frontier. If it was the sixties, he'd be beating down the door to get into the space program. In the eighties, there was biotech — tailor-made for Tim. But biotech's practically establishment now; as Diane said, the bubble's burst, and Tim's looking at years and years of hard work. From talks I had with him, I got the feeling he was ready to move on to some other frontier, but I didn't get the feeling he'd be taking Diane with him."

"The marriage was in trouble?"

"They didn't spend a lot of time together, they didn't have much in common, and Tim always spoke of 'I,' rather than 'we.' "

"You think he might have set the kidnapping up?"

"It's a possibility, one way he could get away with plenty of cash."

"But you saw the photo the kidnappers sent — Mourning was one terrified man, and he wasn't acting, either."

"So something went wrong. His co-conspirators turned on him."

"That doesn't explain Ripinsky being missing. Or the L.C. not being drawn on."

"I tell you Ripinsky's got it and is holding off, figuring we'll eventually ease up on our surveillance and he can slip it through."

"You really think he's that stupid?"

Renshaw folded his arms across his chest and stared up at the trees for a moment. "If I look at it logically, no, but . . . You strike me as someone who works on instinct. Your impressions of the people you're dealing with meld with the facts you're presented. Sometimes your conclusions aren't strictly logical, but they feel right. And nine times out of ten they turn out to *be* right."

"And the tenth time they're wrong because you've shaped them to fit what you want to believe."

"Playing devil's advocate, are we? Well, this is *not* the tenth time. Mourning's dead, Ripinsky's got the L.C., and you're going to find him for me."

So much for instinct, I thought.

Renshaw asked, "When did you say you plan to fly down to San Diego?"

"I've got a reservation on USAir's eight o'clock flight. If I don't make it, there's another every hour."

"Well, I'll fax you a copy of the L.C. in time so you get it when you check into the Bali Kai. You renting a car down there?"

"Avis."

"Have a safe flight. Success." He gave me a mock-military salute and went back to the house.

As I started the MG I smiled wryly. God, Renshaw could be transparent. He didn't fully trust me, and I was willing to bet that he was on the phone right now, arranging for surveillance on me all the way from my house to San Diego's Hotel Circle.

Well, that was okay. When I wanted to shake them, I knew how to do it.

I was packing my weekend bag when the doorbell rang. At first I ignored it, but when it rang again I realized it was obvious I was home because my car sat in the driveway. Dammit, I thought, I'll never make my flight at this rate! Then I went to answer it.

Mike Tobias, clutching a fistful of pink carnations. Now, what on earth? Surely Rae hadn't already begun to spread the rumor I'd come down sick.

"A present," Mike said, "to make up for

138

my remarks at the meeting yesterday." He thrust the flowers into my hands.

First Gloria, now him. Part of the same scheme that had brought her to my office earlier, or a contingency plan because she had failed to win me over? Who would they decide to send next? Not Hank — he couldn't fool me, and they knew it. Larry, to soothe me with herbal tea? Pam, to enlist me in the name of sisterhood? Why not summon Jack Stuart back from whatever wilderness he'd fled to to lick his wounds? Surely he was carrying around enough psychic pain to make my heart bleed.

I didn't have time to waste on this nonsense, though, so I decided to play into Mike's scenario and get rid of him. "Mike, thanks. You didn't have to do this."

"Yes, I did. I treated you shabbily. Please say you'll accept the promotion; All Souls wouldn't be the same without you."

Gloria's failure notwithstanding, they were holding to the take-it-or-leave-it policy. "As I told you all at the partners' meeting, I'll consider the offer very seriously." It was obvious he was waiting for an invitation to come inside, so I added, "Look, we'll talk more, but right now I've got somebody . . ." and motioned at the hall behind me.

"Oh, sorry. Didn't mean to interrupt your evening. Anyway, you keep thinking on it."

"I will, Mike. And thanks again for the flowers."

He nodded and went down the steps, stuffing his hands deep in the pockets of his 49ers jacket.

I took the carnations to the kitchen and put them in a vase, taped a note to it telling Rae to take them home and enjoy them. Then I hurried to the bedroom and finished packing my bag and a big oversized purse that I seldom used. It was seven-oh-seven. Maybe, just maybe, I'd make my eight o'clock flight.

The flight was crowded, and my bag didn't want to go into the overhead bin. Finally I squeezed it between two others that were well over the regulation size for carryons, nearly falling into the laps of the two people who occupied the window and center seats next to mine. Mumbling my apologies, I sat down. I leaned back, closed my eyes, and let the familiar predeparture bustle lull me.

I'd seen no evidence of surveillance on me at the airport, but that didn't mean much. RKI's people would be good, very difficult to spot. Or the surveillance might not begin until San Diego. Renshaw didn't trust me, but he'd probably assume I'd play straight with them until I had a concrete lead to Hy. His people would keep their distance until I made a move.

God, I thought, the world that people like Renshaw operated in was a strange one — full of paranoia, suspicion, distrust. I'd come up against a fair amount of duplicity in my own world, but in his it seemed the accepted norm. Could he ever distinguish his friends from his enemies? Probably not; this afternoon he and his own client had been at each other's throats. Was he ever able to let down his guard and confide in anyone? Perhaps his partner, Dan Kessell, but nobody else. And this was the world that Hy had connections to, somewhere in that nine-year void. . . .

It occurred to me now that my former boss, Bob Stern, could very well have been right: I might be playing with people who were out of my league. If I made a mistake, it could prove fatal. But I had no choice — had I?

No, not if I cared for Hy. And I did care — more than I'd allowed myself to admit. Hard to commit your deepest feelings to a man who wouldn't entrust you with knowledge of his past. Hard to give of yourself when you feared you'd receive nothing in return. Yet here I was — how had Bob put it? — riding to the rescue. No turning back now.

The plane lifted off, then began its southward turn over the Pacific. I reached under the seat in front of me and pulled the file on the biotech industry that Renshaw had given me from my oversized purse. Leafed through it until I found a copy of an *Image* magazine profile on the Mournings, and began to read.

They were originally from the Midwest — she, Wisconsin; he, Minnesota. They'd met and married while students at the University of Wisconsin, then come to the Bay Area; she'd entered Stanford's prestigious M.B.A. program, he'd gone to work as a biochemist at Syntex, the pharmaceuticals giant. There had been lean times, when she was still in school and he and a partner left Syntex to tinker with biotechnology. There had been in-between times, when she trained in finance under a high-powered San Francisco venture capitalist — later one of the major investors in Phoenix Labs — and he began to get the infant firm off the ground. There had been glitzy, high-flying times, when — so the article implied — they had dipped into the venture capital for personal use; they'd owned a condo on Russian Hill, a beach house down south, a half ownership in a boutique winery in Alexander Valley. And there had been lots and lots of lovers.

Both Mournings had been frank with the reporter about their earlier extramarital escapades. Too frank, I thought, and not just because I was a private person where such matters were concerned. The reporter seemed to share my view; it came across in the sneering undertone of his prose. Neither Diane nor Tim would have noticed that, I was sure. They struck me as narcissistic, extroverted, certain that nothing they did could possibly be wrong or even in bad taste. A touch of the sociopathic personality to this couple: if it feels good, I do it; if you don't like it or if I hurt you, tough. As I held out my cup to the flight attendant for more coffee, I felt vaguely uncomfortable. I set the cup down, rubbed my hands together as if brushing off dirt; touching the copy of the article had made them feel unclean.

There were other puff pieces: *Fortune* magazine had named Timothy Mourning one of a hundred bright young individuals who had made a difference; Diane Mourning had been profiled in the *Wall Street Journal*; they'd both been interviewed by *People*. The color photo in *People* showed them posed on the balcony of the Russian Hill condo they'd occupied until fourteen months ago, a typical trite cityscape in the background. Diane wore a black caftan that was as severe as her facial expression, an elaborate hammered-silver and turquoise necklace gleaming against the dark fabric. Tim wore jeans, a sweater, and the grin of a kid who is being photographed by the small-town paper for raising the biggest pumpkin at the county fair. Again I marveled at what an unlikely pair they were.

The flight attendants came along, collecting cups and glasses. The plane began its steep descent directly over the city of San Diego to Lindbergh Field. I leaned forward, looked across my seatmates to the window, and saw the lights of home.

Home? No — former home. Years and years since I'd lived here. The landscape had changed: high-rises, the Coronado Bridge, tracts that spread as far northeast as Escondido. The north county was now referred to as "north city"; the South Bay bore more resemblance to Tijuana than to San Diego proper. I'd heard the spirit of the city had changed, too — warped by the pressures of too much growth, too much crime, too many immigrants from Mexico. Racial prejudice, both covert and overt, was evident in the statements and actions of many residents. People in the north locked their doors and security gates against Hispanics; people in the south struggled to survive crime, overcrowding, and a swelling drug problem.

Still, the city had been my home for nearly twenty years. There would be landmarks to guide me. And alien and dangerous as the territory might seem on this particular evening, I knew I could make my way across it to familiar, safe ground.

Brer Rabbit was born and bred in a brier patch; when predators threatened, he lay low there. Later on tonight I'd find a brier patch of my own.

Nine

As soon as I saw the Bali Kai, I remembered it from prom night. Pseudo-Polynesian was all the rage back then, and for those of us who considered ourselves the high school's smart set, nothing would do but to commandeer a wing of rooms for our post-prom party. Parents objected, were cajoled, and gave in. Tuxes and limos were rented; formal dresses and corsages were bought. Actually, what went on in the wee hours of that morning was pretty innocent. Oh, three girls got drunk and threw up, and two couples had sex for the first time, but most of us just drank a little and necked a lot, gobbled up the warmed-over hors d'oeuvres that passed for exotic South Seas fare, and stifled yawns as we waited for the glorious, interminable night to be over.

The intervening years had not been kind to the Bali Kai. The tiki heads that guarded the lobby entrance were cracked and weathered; the bamboo and fake thatching merely looked silly; even the palms flanking the reception desk seemed to suffer from a fungal ailment.

Renshaw's fax of the letter of credit had arrived, and at its top he'd written and circled a four-digit number, presumably my emergency security code. I stuffed it into my purse, showed the desk clerk my identification, and asked if the night manager or security officer was available. He checked, said both were on break but should be back within the half hour. I told him I'd come back later.

Carrying the map of the motel grounds that the clerk had given me, I went out to my rental car — a tan compact of some indeterminate breed, whose lethally fast automatic seat belt had serious potential to decapitate its driver. The map, on which the clerk had drawn an intricate series of circles and arrows showing how to get to my room, only served to confuse me. After studying it both upside down and sideways, I slipped it into my purse and set off unaided.

The Bali Kai was one of a long string of establishments on the south side of Hotel Circle. It sprawled between the frontage road paralleling Interstate 8 and the cliff face rising to the Mission Hills district where I grew up. Next door to it was an even larger motel where my brother Joey, a man of many trades, had been working as a bartender a couple of summers ago when I'd paid my annual duty visit to my family. Beyond that was an Italian restaurant; I made a mental note of its name.

Finally I found my room in one of the far-flung wings, carried my bag inside, and went straight to the phone. Alicia Ferris, Renshaw's friend who had acted as Hy's local contact, was at home and expecting my call. When I asked about her conversations with Hy, she said they'd spoken only the one time, around nine on Sunday evening.

"Can you repeat what he said — the exact words, if possible?" I asked.

"Well, it was something like 'This is Ripinsky. Tell Renshaw it's a go for eleven. I'll be in touch afterward.' And then he thanked me and hung up."

"How did he sound? Tense? Anxious?"

"Neither. I'd say controlled. He had a job to do, and that was it."

I sighed. Not much to go on.

"Ms. McCone," Ferris said, "you should give me your room number there at the motel, in case I need to reach you."

"One thirty-three." I glanced at the key that lay next to the phone for confirmation.

"Good. Feel free to call me if you need anything at all."

As I hung up, I contemplated Ferris's request for the room number. It was possible

148

she was simply trying to be helpful, but she wouldn't need the number to reach me by phone. Perhaps Renshaw was using her in his surveillance, was planning to have his people search my room when I went out. For all I knew, Ferris was one of their operatives. But why ask such an obvious question that might tip me? Why not just get the room number from the desk clerk? Of course, the clerk might mention to me that someone had asked —

Whoa, I told myself. I was starting to think in as fully paranoid a fashion as anyone at RKI. Then I reminded myself that paranoia has its uses. Even though I hadn't spotted anyone maintaining surveillance on me at any point during my journey, I had that feeling of being covertly watched.

I took the motel map from my bag and familiarized myself with its layout. Then I dredged up my memories of the place next door, where Joey had worked. The bar stretched between the lobby and swimming-pool area, with an entrance at either end, and as I recalled, the ladies' room ran beside it, also with two entrances. Beyond the pool enclosure was a maze of paths leading through the gardens, among which the wings of guest rooms were set. Dark gardens, spreading from the main building to the cliff face, with parking lots on either side . . .

It might work.

I removed the phone book from the night-stand drawer and looked up the number for Reliable Cab Company — a firm whose reputation fit its name, if my mother, who dislikes driving and does as little as possible, was to be believed. I reached for the receiver, then pulled my hand away. Paranoia striking again. It wasn't possible RKI could have bugged the line in the minutes since I'd given Alicia Ferris the room number, but how could I be certain that their operatives didn't have an in with someone on the staff? Ferris's question could be a smoke screen; they might have known for hours what room was assigned me. When dealing with people like them, it was better to err on the side of extreme caution.

I copied the cab company's number down and put the slip of paper in my pocket. Then I got started on the room. Opened my travel bag and hung some things in the closet. Draped a robe over a chair and scattered toiletries on the bathroom vanity. Then I added a rolled-up T-shirt and some extra underwear to the oversized purse, gave the room a final once-over, and headed back to the main lobby.

A man in western wear sat reading a newspaper in one of the rattan chairs, and two women in shorts were studying brochures in front of the tourist information rack. All three looked at me as I crossed to the reception desk, but that didn't necessarily mean anything; there was little enough to look at here at eleven-thirty on a sultry Tuesday evening.

Mr. Perkins, the night manager, was barely out of his teens, and the sight of my I.D. made him nervous. He withdrew to his office to call his daytime counterpart about their policy on opening guest records to investigators. While he was in there, I placed ten dollars on the counter, and the desk clerk brought the information up on his computer screen.

Hy had checked in shortly after midnight on Sunday; he'd had breakfast from room service at nine, and there was a coffee-shop charge at four-thirty and a bar charge at eight. The only phone charge was for the one call to Alicia Ferris's number at nine. His room key and credit-card authorization had been retrieved from the express checkout box on Monday morning. I asked the clerk if the room had been occupied since then; he checked and told me it was currently in use.

Mr. Perkins emerged from his office and said he'd been unable to contact the day manager. Perhaps I could speak with him when he came on in the morning? I said I would, waited until he disappeared again, and asked the clerk if the security man had come back from his break yet. He hadn't, but the clerk thought he might be in the coffee shop. His name was Ken Griffith; I should look for a balding heavyset man in a tan uniform.

As I crossed to the coffee shop, one of the women by the tourist information rack gave me a curious look. The man in western wear kept his eyes on his newspaper.

Ken Griffith was the coffee shop's sole customer. He sat in a rear booth, picking through the remains of a salad, and when I showed him my I.D., he invited me to join him. I scanned the menu, thinking I should eat something, but the offerings — Pago Pago Burger, Tahitian Fruit Salad, Castaway's Low Calorie Plate — looked singularly unappetizing in the unnaturally bright color photos. Griffith applauded my abstinence; even the Chinese Chicken Salad he usually had, he said, sucked.

I took the picture of Hy from my bag and passed it across the table. "This man was a guest here on Sunday. Do you remember him?"

Griffith scrutinized the photo with trained eyes — former cop's eyes, I was willing to bet. "Yeah, I remember him. Paid particular attention to him, as a matter of fact."

"Why?"

"He's got a way about him. Quiet, but he could be trouble."

"*Did* you have any trouble with him?"

Griffith shook his head. "Shows you never can tell. Why're you looking for him?"

"Routine skip trace. How many times did you see him?"

"Twice. When he checked in and late Sunday afternoon, maybe quarter to five, when he was driving out of the parking lot."

"You notice which way he went?"

"Left, like he might be picking up the freeway west."

"And that's the last you saw of him?"

"Right." Griffith looked at his watch; he'd be wanting to get back to work soon.

I glanced around the coffee shop at the two waitresses who were clearing tables. "Tell me, are the waitresses on shift now the same ones who would have been working around four-thirty on Sunday?"

"Probably." He turned and called to the woman nearest us, "Hey, Emma, your shift's four to midnight, right?"

"Yeah."

"You want to come over here a minute? Lady's got a question."

Emma set down the tray she was loading and moved toward the booth, wiping her hands on her apron. She was well over retirement age, very thin, and walked as if her joints ached. Griffith got up and gave her his place. "You set awhile. I got to get going." To me he added, "You need anything else, the desk clerk'll know where to find me."

Emma heaved a weary sigh as she sank onto the banquette. "What do you want to ask me, honey?"

I handed her the by now well-thumbed photo of Hy. "Did you see this man in here on Sunday afternoon?"

She squinted at it, then nodded. "He was one of my first customers. Kind of quiet. Good tipper."

"Did he say anything? Ask you anything?"

"Well, as a matter of fact, he did. When I brought the check he asked how long it would take him to drive to Imperial Beach. That's where I live, so I could tell him practically to the minute. Then he asked if I knew where the Holiday Market is down there. I told him right on the main street — Palm Avenue. I kind of wondered what he'd want with a place like that."

"What sort of place is it?"

"Mexican hangout. Open twenty-four hours. There're always at least a dozen Mexes there, loitering in the parking lot." She glanced toward the kitchen door, anxious lines puckering her forehead. "Honey, I got to get back to clearing those tables. The boss's looking."

"Thanks for your time, Emma." I fished a bill from my wallet and passed it across the table to her.

"Thank *you*."

I got up and moved toward the lobby door, fitting what Emma and Griffith had told me into my mental picture of Hy's movements on Sunday. At four-thirty, more or less, he'd asked about the Holiday Market in Imperial Beach, one of the communities in the South Bay, between downtown San Diego and the border. At around quarter to five he'd driven out of the parking lot, possibly headed that way. But at nine he'd been back in his room here to make the call to Alicia Ferris telling her the drop was set for eleven. What had been the purpose of the trip to Imperial Beach? An intermediate contact with the kidnappers? Part of what Renshaw called the "usual nonsense"? Very possibly. But why send him all the way down there, to a place where he would be conspicuous? So the kidnappers could be sure who they were dealing with, or so someone could make an identification of him?

As I crossed the lobby toward the cocktail lounge, I noticed that the man in western wear was the only person left there. He'd swiveled his chair slightly, giving himself a good view of the coffee-shop entrance. I looked directly at him as I passed; he seemed aware of me, but kept his eyes on his newspaper.

That made me suspect he was part of a surveillance team. According to the motel map, the coffee shop had an entrance from the parking lot, as did the bar. If Renshaw's people had done their homework — and I was sure they had — they'd have someone outside as well.

Getting out of here was going to be more difficult than I'd anticipated. Still, I knew the territory. . . .

The interior of the bar had a steamy, tropical feel — probably because the air conditioning wasn't functioning properly. A waterfall flowing over lava rock into a pool that contained two bloated koi further added to the humidity. The decorator had been heavy-handed with fishnets and seashells, stands of fake bamboo and plastic bird-of-paradise plants, capiz-shell tables, and rattan chairs. Thus inspired, he or she seemed to have gone berserk: a replica of an outrigger canoe outlined with winking blue and green lights, hung from the ceiling; more tikis supported the thatched roof of the bar; the ashtrays were shaped like giant garish pineapples. I half expected to see a conga line of bare-breasted hula dancers wend its way from the rest rooms. I slipped onto a stool and ordered a glass of white wine from a tropical-shirted bartender whose shoulders bore the burden of an enormous plastic-flower lei.

He brought the wine and set it down with a sour look at a quartet of noisy tourists drinking fruit-garnished concoctions and talking about their visit to Sea World. I fished my I.D. and Hy's picture from my bag and laid them on the bar next to a twenty.

The bartender noted all three, cocked his head, and waited.

"Sunday night," I said, "around eight. This man was in here?"

He nodded.

"You serve him?"

"One beer. He nursed it, maybe forty-five minutes."

"You talk with him?"

"He's not the kind who chats up the bartender."

"What else?"

"He asked for change for the cigarette machine, bought some, and left."

But Hy didn't smoke. So far as I knew, he never had. "You're sure he bought cigarettes?"

"Winstons." He motioned to the bar's left. The machine was the only thing in here that the decorator hadn't managed to trick up.

The tourists called for another round. The bartender excused himself, muttering under his breath. I sipped wine, glanced through the door to the lobby; the man in western wear hadn't moved. Quickly I reviewed my options and decided how to handle this.

When the bartender came back, I asked, "Is there anything else you can tell me?"

"That's it. He was a nice, quiet customer — and from me, that's praise." Another sour look at the tourists and he began fixing their drinks.

It wasn't much information for twenty dollars, I thought, but left the bill on the bar next to my half-full glass of wine. Then I moved toward the hallway leading to the rest rooms and stopped at the pay phone. After a brief call to Reliable Cab Company, I stepped through the parking-lot exit.

The air was still sultry at half past midnight — unusual for San Diego in June. Soft halos from security lamps relieved the darkness. I saw no one on foot or in any of the cars. Moving casually, I turned toward the wing where my room was. Held down my pace and regulated it, listening for a counter rhythm. For a moment I heard nothing but the slap of my own shoes; then I heard others, like a soft echo of mine.

I kept walking slowly, went as far as the door to my room, then hesitated, feigning indecision. Began walking again, toward the motel next door. The footsteps — at some indeterminate point behind me — stuttered. Then they came on regularly again, their sound deflected faintly off the surrounding buildings. I gave no sign I was aware of them, just moved in my ambling out-for-a-stroll pace toward the next motel's main entrance. The footsteps stopped; my tail was allowing me some distance.

Big mistake. Once inside the lobby, I put on speed. Slipped around a tall planter and ducked my head, moving even faster. The bar and ladies' room entrances were exactly where I remembered them.

I pushed through the swinging door of the rest room, heart pounding now. On my way past the mirrors I caught a startled look from a woman who was combing her hair. Caught a glimpse of myself, too: grim, intense, focused.

Out the other swinging door and into the pool area. Darkness there except for the bright aquamarine rectangle. No hesitation now — a jog to the right, up some steps, through the gate in the enclosure, and into the gardens.

White crushed-shell paths winding through the shrubbery. Small lights bordering them, and a soft glow from some of the guest-room windows. I chose a path, plunged off it, ran along its side, out of range of the lights.

No point in listening for a pursuer; I couldn't have heard one. No point in looking back; it would only slow me.

Gardenias there — sweet, decaying fragrance. Something else, a bitter-smelling plant. Around a hedge, and then the lights of Paoli's Restaurant shining bright across the parking lot.

The lot was at a lower level, bordered by a four-foot-high retaining wall. I crouched on top of it, jumped, feet hitting the concrete and pain shooting up my legs. Ignoring it, I ran for the shelter of the cars and dodged through them.

At the last row of cars, I stopped, leaning against one. Glanced back at last.

No one.

I scanned the front of the restaurant. And saw Reliable Cab number 1102, waiting just where I'd asked for it to be. I hefted my bag and began running toward it.

Sist'r Rabbit was on the way to her brier patch.

Ten

The house lay dark and silent, burdened by age, neglect, and — to a person who knew its recent history — disappointment. I pulled the key that had been mine since high school from the lock, shut the door behind me, and dropped my heavy purse on the floor.

Heat was trapped in there, mustiness, too. Out of habit, I moved down the hall toward the kitchen. The floorboards creaked, the joists sighed. Other settling noises formed a chorus of complaint.

When I switched on the kitchen light, the enormity of the changes overwhelmed me. No cheerful flowered dishes in the glass-fronted cupboards; no bright pottery bowls and red canisters on the counters. Those things had all gone to Ma's new kitchen in the Rancho Bernardo home she shared with her new love, Melvin Hunt. The room smelled wrong — of cleanser rather than hearty cooking.

I crossed to the sink, peered out the window at the dark rectangle of garage. I hadn't expected anything, but it still seemed strange not to see lights, not to hear the whine of power tools, a baseball game on the radio, Pa's reedy voice raised in one of his dirty ditties. But Pa had been traveling around the country in his new camper for three months now — traveling, I suspected, with a new woman friend. Funny none of us had dared ask about that; was Pa really such a private person that he'd have resented his grown sons and daughters inquiring into his new life?

I turned my back to the window, leaning against the sink, shutting my eyes and listening. Traffic noises — had there been any at this hour — were muted here at the far end of the cul-de-sac, but even so, the house had never been so quiet. There was no laughter, no bickering, no shouts and taunts and sudden bursts of song. The voices of my parents, us five kids, our friends and relatives, even the most recent grandchildren, had been stilled. All that spoke to me were memories.

What was I *doing* here?

Well, for one thing, this house was the best refuge I knew from RKI's surveillance. For many years Pa — now there was a true paranoid — had insisted on an unlisted phone number. Since the divorce, the property wasn't even in his name on the tax rolls; in order to divide their community property with

Ma, he'd been forced to sell, and he'd struck a bargain with the only family member who had any real money, my sister Charlene's husband, country-music star Ricky Savage. A few years back when everybody else had given up on Ricky being anything but a backup musician in a second-rate band, Pa had loaned him the money to cut one final demo record. Ricky had hit it big with "Cobwebs in the Attic of My Mind," and since then he'd looked for a suitable way to pay Pa back for his confidence in him. The divorce crisis was made to order: Ricky bought the house and signed an agreement saying Pa could live there as long as he wanted; the property was now listed in the name of a corporation Charlene and Ricky had formed for tax purposes.

Conceivably RKI could find me here, but it would take them longer than I intended to stay.

After catching the cab at Paoli's Restaurant, I'd had the driver take me to the Westgate Hotel downtown. I entered by a side door, crossed the lobby, and at the main entrance hailed a second cab. That one took me to the Hilton at Mission Bay, where I waited half an hour, then took another cab here. Three different cab companies, three different pickup points, and none of the drivers had seen me catch my next ride.

Now that I was here, transportation would pose no problem. During my most recent conversation with my brother John, who lived in nearby Lemon Grove, he mentioned that he'd stored his four-wheel-drive International Scout in Pa's garage. The problem of having too many vehicles and too much junk in one's garage should be called McCone's Syndrome, and John freely admitted to suffering from it. I was welcome, he told me, to use the Scout the next time I visited Pa. Again a tendency toward paranoia, which my big brother also freely admitted to having inherited from Pa, was working in my favor: should RKI go looking for any relatives of mine in the area, they wouldn't find John; his home, telephone, and vehicles were all under the name of his house-painting company, Mr. Paint.

Now I pushed away from the sink, took the garage keys from the drawer where they were kept, and went outside. The garage stood at the far end of the property, beyond a bedroom wing that extended from the original house. The house, I reflected as I made my way through the dark backyard, had always possessed a peculiar chameleonlike quality. It had gone from being a small two-bedroom rancher on a large lot to a sprawling five-bedroom architectural horror that ate up the land on either side of the original structure. Baths had been added; the kitchen had been moved twice; a family room had been added, then turned into a bedroom, and a second family room had been built behind it. Rooms changed function and occupant so fast that you needed a chart to keep track of them, and in the end both the floor plan and the exterior only dimly resembled what the builder had intended.

The normal family would have been driven crazy by the constant upheaval, but since a state of good mental health hadn't prevailed in the first place, the McCones blithely accepted chaos as the status quo. So what, Ma claimed, if you absentmindedly went to what used to be the kitchen for a midnight snack and instead found yourself in your older brother's room, surrounded by a dozen pubescent boys leering at your shorty pajamas? Frequent change, my seafaring father claimed, was a good character-building experience.

Was it any wonder I'd chafed every moment my earthquake cottage was under renovation?

I was crossing the patio that stretched between the family room and the fence at the finger canyon's edge when I stopped suddenly, alerted to something unfamiliar. I looked around, didn't see anything at first. What . . . ? Oh, no — Pa had filled in and paved over the swimming pool!

Of course, it had never functioned as a real

pool, had been defective when Ma and Pa bought the house, and a sonic boom from a jet out of NAS Miramar had finished it. But for years it had made a splendid vegetable garden, well drained and full of rich earth we'd had trucked in to cover the rubble. Now — where once tomatoes, eggplants, corn, melons, and a riot of beans, peas, and zucchini had grown — there was nothing but concrete. I stood dumbfounded, my foot scuffing at the recently poured white surface.

What next? I thought.

I continued on to the garage and opened its side door with some trepidation. But there was nothing bizarre inside, just Pa's covered cabinetmaking equipment and a full range of symptoms of McCone's Syndrome, crammed from floor to rafters. John's red Scout was nosed into the last empty space. I went over there and slipped inside, discovering the keys were in the ignition and the registration and insurance card in the glove compartment. In a plastic recycling bin bolted down in the rear carrying space were flares, a first-aid kit, Thomas Brothers guides, and a jug of drinking water. Three sleeping bags were wedged into the wheel wells. I checked the gas, oil, and battery and found them in good working order.

How unlike John, I thought. I knew that

in recent years my big, brawling brother —
who had seen the inside of as many jail cells
as Hy — had undergone a startling metamorphosis into responsible business owner and
part-time single father, but I never could think
of him in his new form. To me he'd remained
the incorrigible who'd begun his impious career by being expelled from Catholic school
at age nine and more or less culminated it by
blowing up his wife's empty car the night she
announced she was leaving him. Now, apparently, I would have to recast that image.

Back in the house, the kitchen clock showed
three-ten. That couldn't be! I checked my
watch. Oh, yes, it could, and I wasn't a bit
sleepy. Also, I had another task to accomplish.

For as long as I could remember, Pa had
kept his .45 Smith & Wesson revolver in a
lockbox under a pile of old towels on the top
shelf of the linen closet. I went there and
dragged it down. Finding the key to the box
was no problem; Pa thought he'd secreted it
ingeniously, but he hadn't counted on having
a budding detective in the family. Since I was
fifteen I'd known it was taped to the bottom
of his nightstand drawer. I got it, took the
gun out, checked its condition. Then, in yet
a third hiding place under the kitchen sink,
I found ammunition. I loaded the gun and
placed it in my bag.

By now I was more awake than ever. Finally I went to the kitchen, found a bottle of wine in the fridge, and with glass in hand began to prowl through the house, checking doors and windows. Dust in the dining room. No furniture in the living room — that had gone to Rancho Bernardo with Ma. The bedrooms, even Pa's, contained so few traces of their former occupants that they might as well have been motel rooms. Mine made me particularly sad, even though the things I cared about from my childhood were now stored in my garage in San Francisco. So sad, in fact, that I knew I couldn't sleep there. I pulled the quilts and pillows off the bed, shut the door, and dragged them down the hall to the couch in the family room.

The family room was too tidy. No toys on the floor, no books and magazines scattered about, the TV set rolled back into one corner. I opened the sliding door to let some of the trapped heat escape, then took my wine out to the single lounge chair on the patio.

Had the house been so bereft of life in December? I wondered. Or was it merely Pa's absence that made the difference? I thought back to Christmas Day, when I'd met here with John, his boys, Charlene, Ricky, and the aptly named little Savages. We'd all cooked dinner for Pa, and the occasion had been cheerful, even festive. But in retrospect, I decided everyone — including Pa — had worked hard to ignore an underlying depression. Unlike the mood at Ma's Christmas Eve buffet, when with considerable relief I'd been able to let go the last of my reservations about her new relationship with Melvin Hunt.

I slipped down farther on the lounge, still not sleepy. The tops of the tall eucalyptus in the canyon blew lazily, outlined against a cloud-streaked sky. Something rustled in the underbrush beyond the fence and, farther off, I heard a coyote cry. By day, with sunlight silvering the eucalyptus and pepper trees and accentuating the brilliant colors of the wild plumbago and bougainvillea that grew among the yucca and prickly pear and greasewood, the canyon was beautiful and enticing. As children we'd played there, descending the stone steps that Pa had built into the steep downslope; the remains of our treehouse still perched in one of the sturdier live oaks. But I'd never liked the canyon at night, particularly after our favorite black cat disappeared into it. Then it was rendered wild and strange by the setting sun. Then all that moved down there were the hunters and the hunted.

The coyote howled again — closer. In spite of the night's warmth, a chill slid down my backbone. I closed my eyes, tried to picture

Hy's face. All I saw was Gage Renshaw's, and his expression when he said he intended to kill him. Hy seemed very far away, even though tonight I'd gone to places where he'd been only some forty-eight hours before, talked with people who had talked with him. Tomorrow I had to move faster, close the gap between us. . . .

Something screamed farther up the canyon — a small animal taken by a larger one. I came alert, knowing there would be little sleep for me tonight. Momentarily I was safe here, but people already were looking for me. One false step and they'd snap me up as sure as the coyote snaps up its prey.

Eleven

The Holiday Market was a drive-by hiring hall.

Dozens of men gathered in its weedy parking lot — drinking coffee from Styrofoam cups, talking idly, smoking. All were Hispanic and most, I was sure, had not long been on this side of the border. As they waited, hunched against the dawn chill, hands shoved into jacket pockets, their eyes expectantly watched the arrival of each truck.

The trucks that pulled into the lot belonged to any type of firm that used unskilled laborers, but the majority were building contractors. Each driver followed a prescribed ritual: get out of the truck, stroll into the market, return a couple of minutes later with coffee, then begin negotiating.

And if the police or the INS came by? Just stopping for a jolt of the old caffeine on the way to the job site, officer. Hiring illegals?

Christ, no, I wouldn't do that, and these un-documented workers aren't worth shit, any-way. Besides, this lot is posted. You see that sign — No Loitering, *Prohibido el Pararse*. Hell, everybody knows that's the local lingo for "Don't be picking up your cheap labor here."

That morning no INS sweeps interfered with the hiring process. I sat across the street behind the wheel of the Scout, watching the contractors strike their bargains and the work-ers pile onto the trucks. They would receive far less than the union wage for their day's work, and benefits were unheard of, but they were the lucky ones. Those who were left be-hind — many too sick or strung out for a con-tractor to take a chance on — would go hungry tonight.

After a while I got out of the Scout and locked it. It was overcast here by the beach, and even though the temperature hovered in the high fifties, I felt a deep bone-chill from the fog-damp air. It was a little after six; when sleep hadn't come to me by five, I'd given up, taken a shower, and driven down here to the South Bay. Traffic was light on Palm Avenue; I waited for a break, then crossed to the market. The knots of would-be workers drew back as I passed, eyes darkening with fear that I might be *la migra* and resentment that I was neither a potential employer nor one of them.

The building was cement block, a garish green with orange trim, and its dirty windows were heavily barred. I noted a pay phone a few feet from the entrance and went over there to have a look. The Plexiglas around it had been shattered, the directory was torn apart, and the receiver dangled free. The vandalism didn't look recent, so I assumed Hy's purpose in coming here hadn't been to wait for a call from the kidnappers.

Inside, the store was that peculiar combination of ordinary small supermarket and bodega that you find in southern California towns where mainstream blue-collar workers and military families live in uneasy proximity to recently arrived Hispanics. Tortillas crowded the bread; strands of chorizo were looped above the meat counter. Beans, rice, and a variety of peppers were staples, but the same was true of Hamburger Helper, canned tuna, and Idaho potatoes. Beer, candy bars, chips, and cigarettes seemed to outnumber all other items.

The market was empty except for a young mother with an infant and two toddlers who was getting started early on her day. I went directly to the counter and showed my I.D. to the heavyset Hispanic man at the cash register. He glanced at it, then stared at my face, his expression hard and immobile. When I held up Hy's picture and asked if he'd seen him on Sunday evening, he shrugged and turned away, muttering, *"No tengo inglés."*

The hell you don't, I thought, noting that he had the *Union-Tribune* open to the sports page. But I went along with it, summoning up what Spanish that working in San Francisco's Mission district had helped me retain from high school. *"En domingo, está aquí?"*

He looked at me as if I were speaking an alien tongue.

I repeated the question.

He shrugged, feigning bewilderment.

"Look," I said, motioning at the newspaper, "I know you speak English. This has nothing to do with you or what's going on in the parking lot. I just want to know if you saw this man here on Sunday evening."

"No tengo inglés."

I took a twenty from my bag, placed it on the counter, and pushed it toward him.

He looked at it, shook his head, and pushed it back toward me.

Serious resistance here. Because of the illegal hiring — or something else entirely? Something to do with Hy's visit?

I added another twenty, looked inquiringly at him.

174

He shook his head and turned away.

I pocketed both bills and went back outside. Most of the men were gone from the lot now, and those who remained had fixed, desperate expressions, eyes following every truck that moved by on Palm Avenue. For a moment I considered trying to question them, but quickly decided against it. *No tengo inglés* — and besides, none of them would have been here on a Sunday. I passed them by, and all the way back to the Scout, I could feel their anxious, hungry gazes follow me.

Taking a different route back to San Diego, I drove west on Palm Avenue, past fast-food restaurants and liquor stores and bars that mainly catered to the military, then followed the Silver Strand to Coronado. The Glorietta Bay area was much more built up than I remembered it; one of the more startling changes was that the Casa del Rey Hotel, where one of my most — literally — painful cases had begun at a private investigators' conference, had been torn down to make way for yet another condo complex. Thank God that the developers so far hadn't gotten up the nerve to attempt to supplant the venerable Hotel del Coronado, which now stood alone in its Victorian splendor.

As I drove across the soaring expanse of

bridge from Coronado to San Diego, I turned serious attention to the dead end at the Holiday Market. The proprietor's reaction to my question about Hy had been extreme; there was no way I would get him to talk. But was there another avenue of approach? I needed an in, someone he would be inclined to trust. . . .

Well, one solution to the problem was obvious to me, but it would mean violating a cardinal rule: when there's a possibility of danger, never involve, even to the smallest degree, family members or other people you care about.

Now I assessed the danger. I'd shaken RKI's operatives, I was certain. There had been no one waiting outside my father's house this morning, no one tailing me. I'd be taking a calculated risk, but the odds were on my side. Anyway, what could RKI really do? Torture my husky, six-foot-four, streetwise brother into revealing my whereabouts?

I looped onto the San Diego Freeway north, then caught 94 west toward Lemon Grove.

Visiting John's neighborhood in Lemon Grove is like taking a trip back in time. The streets are without sidewalks and hilly, the lots irregular, the small dwellings highly diverse. People keep chickens, goats, ducks, and horses; packs of wild dogs roam free. Ethnically, the residents are as diverse as the architecture and, so far as I know, live in relative amicability. Even what my brother calls the "car collections" in some yards are overgrown with vines and wildflowers.

John's house sat atop a knoll a few blocks over the line from San Diego's Encanto district. Its driveway was unpaved and rutted, winding among yucca trees that grew in profusion on the downslope. The small stucco house had a red tile roof and a fresh coat of — appropriately — lemon-yellow paint; a bench — stolen from a downtown bus stop in one of John and Joey's last thieving rampages — sat under a mulberry tree, and on it were two beer cans. I smiled, picturing my brother relaxing there as he surveyed his domain.

I pulled the Scout up next to a shiny new Mr. Paint truck and got out. Behind the house, by one of two oversized garages, stood numerous plastic paint buckets, apparently washed and set out to dry. The sun was just breaking through the cloud cover as I walked toward the house and heard music — sixties rock, the only thing John will listen to. A good sign that my brother was at home and probably in the mood for an early visitor.

As I stepped up to the front door, hand

poised to knock, the music abruptly broke off; from a loudspeaker perched somewhere in the trees behind me, John's voice said, "Sharon McCone, who told you you could steal my Scout?" Then the screen door flew open, and I was enveloped in a bear hug.

When he released me and I recovered my breath, I stepped back and looked him over. In appearance John and I are as different as can be: he has blond hair, and his features betray the Irish side of the family; I'm a genetic throwback to my great-grandmother, Mary McCone, a Shoshone woman who joined my great-grandfather Robert on his westward journey. But John and I have always been closer to each other than to any of our other siblings, and now I was pleased to see that he looked both healthy and — judging from his leather vest and cowboy shirt and new polished western boots — prosperous.

"Pretty snappy duds," I commented. "What's with the speaker?"

"Rowdy neighbors moved in downhill. When they get too loud, I turn the thing on and issue warnings with a heavy biblical flavor. Scares the shit out of them to think God's paying such close attention." He held the screen door open, and I ducked under his arm, smiling.

I hadn't remembered the little living room

as a claustrophobic's worst nightmare, but that was how it seemed today. John's office had expanded along the entire left-hand wall, and his sound system took up the one opposite. The couch was pushed dangerously close to a fireplace that angled alongside the glass door to the patio, and the rest of the floor was covered by stacks of cardboard cartons. John had only bought the house right before the Christmas holidays, but this was carrying on the post-move chaos far too long.

"What's all this?" I nudged the closest box with my toes.

John glanced into it. "Ma's dishes. You know, the ones with the ugly apples?"

"How could I forget them? But why are they here? I thought she gave those to you when you got married and Karen kept them."

He tried to step around me, couldn't find footing, and finally lifted me and set me on a stool in front of the breakfast bar. "She did. This is Karen's stuff. I'm storing it for her."

"Why?"

"She's getting married again and going off to Italy with the guy while he's on a year's sabbatical. He's some kind of professor at State. She sold her house, he gave up his apartment, and when they get back they're going to buy a new place, so in the meantime I'm stuck with everything." John went behind the bar and held up the coffee pot, raising an eye-brow in question.

I nodded yes. "How do you feel about that?" I asked, then realized I sounded ridiculously like a therapist.

"Being stuck with the stuff? It's a pain in the ass. Her getting married? I think it's great." He poured a mug of coffee and set it in front of me. "My spousal support payments stop, and I get the boys for a whole year while she's over there. Plus he's a nice guy, the kids like him, and Karen's so happy she's practically turned into a human being."

"Well, you've come a long way since the days when you wouldn't call her anything but 'that bitch.' " I raised the mug in a toast.

"Yeah, I guess I have." He looked away from me, gaze turned inward, but he glanced back just in time to see me gag on the strong coffee. "Shar, you don't look so good. And what're you doing here at seven-thirty in the morning, anyway?"

I set the mug down, pushed it away. "I don't look good because I haven't had any sleep in forty-eight hours. And the reason I'm here is a long story."

He waited. When I didn't go on, he said, "So you want to tell me about it?"

"Yes, and to ask a favor. But don't you have to go to work soon?"

"I *am* at work." He drew himself up with mock dignity. "You're looking at a white-collar type. I turned the on-site supervision over to my foremen, and now I stay home and run the business end."

"But I thought you liked being out on the job sites."

"I do, and I'll probably go back to it after Karen returns from Italy and we're sharing custody again. But in two weeks I'll be a full-time papa, and I need to be here for the boys."

My big brother was certainly a transformed man. If it hadn't been for the general disorder in the house and the loudspeaker in the trees, I'd have sworn that an alien had taken up residence in his body.

"So what's going on?" he asked. "You in trouble?"

"Not exactly."

"Well, you're looking worse by the minute. Let me get you some breakfast."

"I don't want —"

"Just a glass of milk and some toast." When I started to protest some more, he made a shooing gesture. "Go on, the sun's burned off the fog now; we'll talk on the patio. I'll be with you in about three minutes."

I slid off the stool, picked my way through the cartons to the patio door, and stepped out into the warming morning. A small tiled

Jacuzzi took up one corner of the patio; I approached it cautiously, alert for alligators. At Christmastime it had contained a primordial stew that promised either to give rise to a strange new species or to effect a cure for any number of previously untreatable diseases. There was no telling what might live there now. But surprise — the water was clear and smelled faintly of chlorine.

So why did that depress me? I wondered as I flopped on a lounge chair. My brother's life was on track, and it *depressed* me? Too much evidence of change in too few hours, I supposed. I hadn't been prepared for it, so now I was resisting.

Then my spirits took a further downhill slide as I remembered other changes, and that I'd promised to give All Souls an answer about the promotion by close of business today. No way I could cope with that — not in my present state. Maybe I should call Rae and ask her to pass on a message that as a result of my alleged illness I required more time. . . .

John delivered the milk and toast, sat on the edge of the Jacuzzi, and watched me like a prison guard until I'd drunk every drop, polished off every crumb. When he took the plate and glass away, his smug expression reminded me of my mother's when she'd duped one of us into swallowing some particularly odious medicine. And I had to admit I felt better, just as I'd always felt better after Ma's ministrations.

John came back and sat on the Jacuzzi wall again. "Now," he said, and waited.

"Before I go into it, let me ask you: do you ever hire illegals?"

"Well, sure. There's not a small contractor in the county who doesn't. I've done it personally, and as far as I know, my foremen still do."

"Don't you consider that exploitation?" It was off the subject, but I wasn't tracking too well and, anyway, it interested me.

"No," he said flatly. "At least they're eating, and cheap labor makes it possible for me to stay in business."

"But what about their rights?"

"What rights? They're here illegally."

"In case you don't know, there's been a series of court decisions that in essence say that once undocumented immigrants are in the country, they have the protection of our laws."

"Yeah, well, isn't that always the way? Protect the guy who's here illegally at the expense of the one who was born here. Protect the criminal's rights at the expense of the victim's. I'm getting damned sick of it."

"I understand why you're —"

"No, you don't, Shar. You're not a small

businessman who's struggling to give his kids a decent life. And I know what you're going to say to that: the illegals are trying to give their kids a decent life, too." He paused. "Hell, you know I feel for them. We're all getting fucked by the people who run things. And I'm not claiming I'm running a charity here, but the guys who hire on with me get treated good and can at least put food in their families' mouths. A square meal's a damn sight more nourishing than some rich politician's yap about rights."

"You have a point there."

"You bet I do." His eyes narrowed. "Why the questions about the illegals? You on an immigration case?"

"I'm not on any case at all, at least not officially." And then I began to tell him about it. Soon the words were spilling out so fast I could barely catch my breath, fast and with too much emotion — an odd mix of anger and fear and determination.

John didn't say a word the whole time, but his face grew grim. "So that's why the questions," he commented when I finished. "The Holiday Market."

"You know the place?"

He nodded. "In the past year we've been doing a lot of jobs in the South Bay. Cops run the illegals off from the Holiday now and then, and they go down the street to the parking lot of a taco stand. When the cops run them off of there, they're back at the market."

"John, I've got to find out if Hy went there, and what happened. Is there any way you can get the guy who runs the place to talk with me? Or do you know anybody he might trust?"

He considered. "Two of my foremen, Al and Pete, are Hispanics, and I know they've done a lot of hiring there. Maybe one of them. I'll ask."

"Would you?"

"Of course." He frowned, pulling at his lower lip — a childhood habit when he was worried. "But look, kid, aren't you getting in over your head?"

Kid. Years ago he called me that. When had he stopped? Somewhere around the time I shot and killed a man. With surprise I realized it had taken him all these years to accept it and acknowledge that deep down I was still his baby sister.

Truthfully I replied, "Maybe I am, but I've got no choice."

"This Ripinsky guy means that much to you?"

"Yes. It's . . . an odd relationship. I don't know exactly how to explain it. But he's the only person — with the exception of Ma, maybe — who's ever understood who and what I am and not judged me because of it."

"*Ma?*" John stared at me as if I'd taken leave of my senses.

"Yes, Ma. She said some things to me last fall when she was visiting that made me realize she knows me better in some ways than I do myself. Maybe knows all of us better than we think."

"What did she say?"

"Oh . . . that there's a side of me that's kind of . . . wild, is how she put it, that isn't going to fit into any of the convenient little niches that society uses to confine people."

"You know, that's interesting, because she said something to me, too, around the same time. What she told me was that under all the craziness I was really conventional as hell and just waiting for the time to come along when I wouldn't be too embarrassed to let it show."

"*You?*"

He grinned. "Well, look at us. Who's the one who showed up here at the crack of dawn looking like something the dog dug up? Who's the one who made the other eat breakfast?"

"True. God, if she saw those things in us, I wonder what she saw in Charlene and Joey and Patsy?"

"We ought to ask them."

I leaned my head back, suddenly feeling it was too much trouble to keep my eyes open.

"Hey, stay awake for a few more minutes," John ordered. "Can I borrow this Ripinsky's picture?"

"Sure, but what —"

"I'll have some copies made at the one-hour photo, and if Al and Pete think they can do something for you, I'll give them the pictures and have them ask around. In the meantime, you get some sleep."

"What?" I sat up. "I've got to —"

"You *don't* got to. Until one of them comes up with something, there's nothing you can do. So give me the picture, go in the boys' room, and sack out."

I had to admit the idea appealed. "You'll wake me up as soon as you know something?"

"I'll wake you up. Go!"

"You promise?"

"Yes! I swear to God, you remind me of my kids."

"I swear to God, you remind me of Ma."

"Well, everybody needs some mothering now and then, kid. Everybody."

Twelve

When I woke in the narrow kid's bed, afternoon sunlight had made the small room unbearably hot and stuffy. I lay there for a moment, groggy and filmed with sweat. The phone rang somewhere and was abruptly cut off by the answering machine; I heard my brother's recorded voice intone something about having reached Mr. Paint, and a woman left a mostly garbled message.

Finally I got up and opened the one window. Outside was a high-fenced area full of tall plants — John's dope garden. Solid evidence that my brother hadn't been taken over by an alien, after all. But what did he do with the plants when the boys stayed here? Surely he didn't allow them to gaze at a marijuana farm through their bedroom window. Or did he? Well, that was his business; where the boys were concerned, at least, John seemed to know what he was doing.

I wandered out to the kitchen; the only noise was the faucet dripping. The mentality of the drought years persisted among San Franciscans; I went over and tightened the knob until it stopped. In the fridge I found a can of ginger ale vastly outnumbered by six-packs and drank it thirstily while contemplating the problem of how to get in touch with Rae. By the clock on the stove, it was one thirty-nine; she'd probably be at her desk. Trouble was, I couldn't be sure the All Souls line didn't have a tap on it. By now RKI's operatives would be mounting a full-scale search for me.

Finally I went to the phone on John's desk and dialed All Souls. Pitched my voice higher than normal when Ted answered and said I was calling for Tony Nolan, the client for whom Rae was performing a number of background checks. Rae came on the line and immediately recognized my voice.

"Shar —" she began.

I cut her off. "No, I don't need to talk with Ms. McCone. I need to talk with you. I've found the remedy to the problem, and I want to discuss it in fifteen minutes."

Rae was silent.

"I have the *remedy,* do you understand?"

"Yes, I do." She sounded grave, even grim. "I'll be there early, if possible."

I hung up before she could say anything else.

Eyes on the clock of the VCR, I paced

around the living room, went to the patio door and opened it to let in some of the afternoon breeze. One of the neighbors' ducks had wandered in and was contemplating the Jacuzzi with more than normal interest, so I shooed it away. Then I went back inside and snooped idly into cartons as the minutes ticked by. One was full of photograph albums, and I pulled the topmost out and flipped through its pages. A Christmas picture caught my attention: John, Karen, Johnny, Billy, and little Kimmy, who had died of leukemia when she was two. They sat on a couch, the kids on their parents' laps, everyone smiling, their eyes shining from the glow of the tree — mercifully unaware of all the bad, sad days to come. I'd often wondered how things might have turned out for John and Karen if Kimmy hadn't died. . . .

Time to call Rae. I looked up the number of the Remedy Lounge in my address book, dialed, and identified myself to owner and bartender Brian O'Flanagan.

"No," he said formally, "you need to call the office number for that. Do you have it?"

If Brian had installed Rae in his office, which was also his home at the back of the bar, it would mean she'd been followed there. An RKI operative might be within earshot of this conversation. "Is it listed with Information?"

"That's right." I detected a note of relief in Brian's voice as he said good-bye.

This didn't sound good, not good at all. Neither Rae nor Brian was the sort to imagine things. I called Information, got the number, and dialed. Rae answered in the middle of the first ring.

"Shar?" Her voice shook slightly.

"It's me. What's going on?"

"Plenty — all of it bad. Gage Renshaw was at All Souls this morning asking if we'd heard from you. God, he's got mean, cold eyes."

"You talked with him?"

"Yeah, Ted had me come up front and deal with him. I went into the song and dance about you being sick, but he didn't buy it. And at noon when I went over to your house to feed the cats, somebody followed me. I shook him, but when I got to your place, they had somebody on it, too."

I felt a touch of panic — a flashback to when my house had been vandalized two weeks before. "Is everything all right there?"

"Except for Ralph puking on the couch, I think so. But, Shar, now somebody else has followed me here."

"I thought as much. Is he outside in the bar?"

"A couple of minutes ago when Brian came back here, he was. I spotted him coming down

Precita and speeded up, so Brian managed to get me into the office without him seeing, but he knows I came in here. I'll sneak out the back way when we're done." She hesitated. "Shar, what the hell's going on?"

"I gave them the slip last night and they're trying to find me, that's all. I'm perfectly safe now, but I don't think it's a good idea for you to know where. Listen, I don't like to keep asking favors, but I need another."

"Sure."

"Tell Hank that I'm too sick to make a decision on the promotion yet."

"Oh, Shar!" Her wail made me hold the receiver away from my ear. "That's the other awful thing. He knows. They all know."

"Know what? That I'm not sick?"

"Worse, even. When I told Renshaw you were sick he said, 'Don't give me that. She went to San Diego on a job for us last night.' And of course Hank and Mike Tobias chose that moment to walk through the foyer."

Well, that did it, I thought glumly. "They say anything to you?"

"Not Mike, and Hank didn't say anything at the time. But later on, he called me into his office. You know how he never reads you the riot act but you always feel like he has, anyway? Well, he said he was very disappointed in both of us — me for lying, and you for asking me to lie. And he *was,* Shar. You should have seen him."

How well I knew Hank's disappointed looks. "Go on."

"He asked me what was happening, and I said I couldn't talk about it. He said he'd respect that, but when I was ready to tell him, he'd be there."

"Then you'd better tell him."

"But —"

"No, go ahead and tell him. I don't want you taking the blame for me. Besides, I've screwed myself where All Souls is concerned, so it doesn't matter."

"What about the promotion?"

"I assume it's no longer an issue. But you might tell him . . ."

"What?"

My anger had begun to rise: At the unfairness of the partners, who were trying to force me into a job they knew I didn't want. At the new order they'd created at the co-op, which had made me feel I couldn't go to Hank and ask him to allow me the time to deal with this crisis. At their petty new regulation against employees accepting outside jobs, which had made me ask Rae to lie. I wanted to give Rae a particularly unkind, wounding message to pass on to Hank.

"Shar?"

See what you made me do? The childish phrase suddenly popped into my head. A convenient way to blame everyone else for your own mistakes. Lord knew I'd often employed it, but I wasn't a child anymore. *I* had neglected to explain my problem to Hank. *I* had asked Rae to lie. *I* had screwed myself out of my job. No circumstance or person had forced me to do any of those things.

"Rae," I said, "tell Hank I'm sorry. And tell him I'll explain when I get back, for the sake of our friendship. You're not to worry about being blamed for your part in this, either. I got you into it, and I'll set things right."

"I'm not sure I care. Without you here, this won't be a good place to work anymore."

"Don't say that." I heard an engine noise outside. Parted the curtains beside the desk and saw John coming up the driveway on his motorcycle. "We'll talk more about it when I get back. I've got to go now."

"But where can I reach —"

"Rae, it's not safe. I'll try to get in touch tomorrow. You take care." I hung up and went to greet John.

"So you're awake," he said, coming inside and leaving the door open to create a cross breeze. "Here," he added and tossed me a manila envelope.

"What's this?"

"Extra copies of your boyfriend's picture."

"Thanks. I'll pay you back — and for a couple of phone calls I made. Did you find out anything?"

He went to the fridge and got a beer. "Pete did. He's got some family connection to Vic, the guy that owns Holiday Market. The reason Vic was so uptight with you this morning is that the place serves as a sort of information center for illegals — you know, if they're trying to find somebody or a safe house or a ride north. Whatever they need, Vic helps them get it."

"Drugs?"

He shook his head. "Not to hear Pete tell it. He says the Holiday's there to help his people, not to bring them down."

"So what about Hy?"

John leaned against the back of the couch, sipping beer. "He went in there around five-fifteen on Sunday, bought some coffee, then went back outside and hung around for about half an hour. Talked to two women, that's all."

"Did this Vic know the women?"

"One he'd never seen before and could barely describe. Just said she was short with short dark hair. Hispanic. The other — Ana Orozco — he knows, and he called her and asked if she'd talk with you. She will, but it'll cost."

I'd expected to pay for information, would do so gladly if it would lead me to Hy. But I was running short of cash. "How much?"

"Seventy-three bucks."

"That's a lot. Why such an odd amount?"

"Because she's got two hundred and twenty-two bucks, and the abortion clinic charges two ninety-five. That's why they know her at the store; she crossed the border on Sunday and came around asking about clinics."

"I thought Mexico was where you *go* for abortions. At least that was what they said in high school."

John shook his head, eyes solemn. "Even then, abortion was illegal in Mexico, and there's been a big crackdown on the clinics. The wife of a buddy of mine works at a clinic in the Hillcrest district near U.C. Med Center; she claims that after the early sixties the only abortions you could buy in Tijuana were from cab drivers with rusty knives and pliers. I'm not sure I believe that, but I do know that the methods they use down there aren't real good for a woman's health. And they're expensive."

"So now Mexican doctors are telling their patients to go to San Diego."

"Yeah. Gina, my friend's wife, says that about a quarter of all the procedures they per-

196

form at her clinic are on Mexican nationals."

We were getting far afield from the business at hand. I asked, "Does Pete think this woman is on the level? Or could it be she doesn't know anything but sees this as a quick way to raise the money?"

John shrugged. "Pete trusts Vic, but he doesn't know the woman."

"Well, it's the only lead I've got, so I better follow up on it. Can you stake me to some cash?"

"I'll put it on your tab."

"Where is the woman?"

"National City."

"And her address?"

He hesitated, taking his time finishing his beer. "I'll take you there."

"No, just give me the address. This is something I have to handle by —"

"No, it's not." He straightened, went to the desk, and rummaged in a cashbox. "It's a rough area down there, and you shouldn't —"

"Exactly what do you think I've been doing all these years? Traveling with a bodyguard?"

"Obviously you haven't. In those years, you've been stabbed, almost drowned, and shot in the ass. Christ knows what else has happened that you haven't told me about."

"John, I can take care of —"

"All right — you can. But why make things

harder on yourself than you have to?"

"I'm thinking of you. This is a potentially dangerous situation, and I'm not just talking about muggers. It's not your problem, and I don't want to involve —"

"I'm already involved."

"No, you're not."

He spread his arms wide in exasperation. "Look, do you want me to get down on my knees and beg you to take me? All right, I will." Dropping to one knee, he raised his hands in supplication. "Dear sister, please take me with you."

"This is ridiculous. Get up!" I tugged at his arm.

He stayed where he was, grinning idiotically.

For a moment I considered telling him I had Pa's .45 in my bag, but my use of firearms had erected a barrier between us in the past — had erected a barrier between me and other people I cared about, too. "Oh, hell!" I exclaimed. I supposed I *could* take him along, have him watch for a possible tail as I drove. But some ground rules would have to be set right now. "All right," I told him, "you can come. But you can*not* go inside with me when I talk to the woman. You will do exactly what I tell you. And you will navigate while I drive."

"It's my Scout."

"You've been drinking."

"One beer."

"One's enough. You want to come or not?"

He thrust out his jaw belligerently. I was reminded of him at ten, pouting because Ma had swatted him for trying to climb into the polar bear pit at the zoo.

"You want to come or not?" I repeated.

He got off his knees. "You know, you've turned into a bully."

"Are you going to obey the rules and do exactly what I tell you?"

"Since when do you make the rules, anyway?"

I just looked at him.

"All right, dammit, I'll obey them! Somebody's got to protect you from yourself."

Thirteen

Before we left, I asked John if Karen, who is roughly my size, had stored any clothing in the cartons. He told me to take a look, and in one I found a treasure trove of jeans and shirts and T's and sweaters — perhaps not suitable for a new bride on her way to a romantic sojourn in Italy, but perfect replacements for the things I had on, which by now were barely presentable. I changed and went outside to find John in the driver's seat of the Scout. It took a fair amount of wheedling and, finally, threatening to move him over, but eventually we set off for the South Bay with me at the wheel.

National City is sailor town, a blue-collar town, an immigrant town, home to light-manufacturing plants, warehousing operations, trailer parks, and the famed mile of car dealerships. Ana Orozco's address was an old-fashioned apartment court on F Avenue, a couple of blocks off Highland. The narrow street was roughly paved and without sidewalks, overhung by very old pepper trees and dead-ending at the freeway. Most of the buildings were California bungalows built in the 1920s, and the apartments — one-story stucco, U-shaped, with cracked-concrete center sidewalks cluttered with toys and tricycles — were about the same vintage. I left John in the Scout, after making him promise he wouldn't stir unless he heard bloodcurdling screams in a voice clearly recognizable as mine, and made my way through the obstacle course to apartment number six.

It took Orozco a while to answer the door. When it opened, the eyes that scrutinized me across the security chain were red-rimmed and underscored by dark half-circles. I told her who I was, showed her the seventy-three dollars, and she let me inside a linoleum-floored, cheaply furnished room whose drapes were pulled against the hot afternoon sun. Orozco motioned at the shabby sofa, then curled her small body into an equally shabby chair, pulling a blanket around her and shivering in spite of the trapped heat. She was no more than eighteen.

I put the money on the coffee table and asked, "Do you speak English?"

She nodded.

"Are you okay? You don't look well."

"I will be okay soon." Her eyes strayed to the money.

"Will you be able to get an appointment at the clinic right away?"

She didn't reply, and for a moment I thought she hadn't understood. Then she fumbled alongside the chair's cushion for a tissue, and I saw she was crying.

"Ms. Orozco . . . Ana," I said.

She held up her hand. "No, I am okay. It is . . . I know that what I will do is wrong. Are you *católica?*"

"Yes." At least, I'd been raised Catholic.

"Then you must know how I feel," she said. "I did not believe in . . . this thing before I knew I was to have the child. I am not married. The boy went away when I told him. In September I am to go to the university in Mexico City, but . . ." She broke off, staring bleakly at me, then added, "I know I will feel bad about this for all my life. But I want to have children someday and give them more than what I have had. I do not want them to suffer for my mistake."

"I understand."

She went on, though — trying to convince herself she'd chosen the right course of action, I supposed. "My sister, years ago she went to a doctor in Santa Rosalía, where we are from. He did something that is not illegal in

202

Mexico, with a . . . you call it an IUD. It brought on the bleeding, but nothing else. *Tres meses* after, she had the *malparto* — the miscarriage — and almost died from the *infección*. Now she cannot have children. I do not want that for myself."

"You were right to come here for a safe procedure. I'm glad I can help you."

"You say that, and you are *católica?*"

"You've obviously given this serious thought. And we can only live according to our own conscience."

"Yes. And then we must answer *a Dios*. I hope he will forgive me." Then she seemed to remind herself of the purpose of my visit. "Now, what is it you wish to ask me?"

I handed her Hy's picture. She looked at it, nodded. "This man I remember. My friend who lets me stay here, he took me from the border to the store. He said the man there will tell me where is a good clinic. He" — her finger tapped the photo — "came to me before I could go inside and asked me if I am named Ann. I said yes. Ann, Ana." She shrugged.

"Go on."

"Then he asked me, 'Where am I to meet . . .' I think the name was Brockowitz. Could that be?"

"It could."

203

"I did not answer. He took my arm." She demonstrated, grabbing her left forearm with her right hand and yanking at it. " 'Come on,' he said, 'I am tired of waiting.' He hurt me."

Not like Hy to be rough with a woman — unless he thought he was dealing with an enemy, a kidnapper's contact woman. "What happened then?"

"I became afraid. He looked at my face. He said, 'You are not Ann Navarro?' I said no. He let go and said he was sorry to frighten me. I ran into the store."

"He didn't try to follow you?"

"No. He called after me, again saying he was sorry."

"Was he there when you went back outside?"

"No."

"And how long were you in the store?"

"Ten minutes? Maybe longer. There were people, and the man there could not talk at first." She paused, fingers pleating the tattered blanket. "This man — he is your enemy?"

"No, a friend."

"A good friend?"

"Very."

"Then I will tell you. If you said enemy, I would not tell you this, because I know there is goodness, *la dulzura* — gentleness — in him.

I saw it in his eyes when he let go my arm. The friend who lives here? He saw the man also. And that night he saw him again."

"Where?"

She shook her head. "I do not remember. But if you like, I will ask him."

"I'd like to talk with him myself. When will he be coming home?"

"I think not until very late. He is working, and then he will go to a bar not far from here, called the Tradewinds. I will call him there and then he will call you."

I hesitated. Ana seemed sincere, but I had to protect myself. "No, I'll just go there. What's your friend's name?"

"Luis Abrego. He has a *mostacho*." Her fingers illustrated its length and curve. "Very long hair." Hands at shoulder level. "And the skin, very dark."

"Thank you. I'll talk with him."

"Thank *you*." She rose and gently touched the bills on the coffee table. "This money will make many things possible."

When I got back to the Scout, I found John slumped in his seat, morosely watching a couple of kids who were sifting through the trash in a can in front of one of the nearby houses. "Christ," he said as I got in, "one of them ate some moldy bread he found there. All I could think of is how I'd feel if my boys were that hungry."

"Well, they've never been and, God willing, won't ever be."

"No. But these shouldn't be, either." He straightened up. "You find out anything?"

I told him what Ana Orozco had told me. "It's a little after four now," I concluded, "so I have time to run you home before I go to the Tradewinds and talk with Luis Abrego."

John folded his arms and set his jaw. "I told you before, you're not running around down here without me."

"John, what do you think I've been doing —"

"All these years — I know. So humor me."

I sighed. John took it for assent and perked right up. "Brockowitz," he said. "Weird name."

"Definitely not Hispanic, which knocks a hole in the theory that Mourning's kidnappers were Mexican nationals. Of course it could be an assumed name, or someone fronting for the kidnappers. On the other hand, we have only what Hy told Gage Renshaw about the accent of the contact woman to back up that theory, anyway. Hy's very good with languages, but I wonder if a telephone voice is really enough to base an assumption like that on. But then there's this other name — Ann Navarro. Probably Hispanic, except the first name's anglicized, so who knows? Ana was definite about it being Ann. I'm pretty sure she's on the level, but I'd feel a lot better if I knew something about this Luis Abrego before I —" I broke off because John was staring at me, mouth agape. "What?"

"You talk things over with yourself like that a lot?"

"A fair amount, but usually just inside my head. With you here, though . . . well, you're sort of like the cat."

"What? I'm what?"

"When one of the cats is around, I think aloud. Doesn't seem so silly if there's something to listen."

"Some*thing*."

"Or someone. Look, do you want to make yourself useful?"

"I'm not sure, since the cat comment."

"Well, do it anyway. Call Pete and ask him to check with the guy at the Holiday Market. I want to know if it's okay for me to tell Abrego he — what's his name?"

"Vic."

"If it's okay to tell Abrego that Vic sent me, just in case saying Ana sent me doesn't work. And also have Pete ask Vic if he knows anything about Abrego, Navarro, or Brockowitz. Got that?"

"Yes, boss." John unfolded his long frame

from the Scout. "I saw a convenience store with an intact pay phone right around the corner. Will you be okay if I leave you alone here?"

"I'll fend off any muggers by running them over."

As soon as he was out of sight, though, I began to feel uneasy — that particular brand of unease that makes me suspect somebody's watching me. I glanced in the rearview mirror, checked out both side mirrors. No one in any of the parked vehicles, no one in any of the overgrown little yards. Just the waving branches of the pepper trees. The ragged kids had vanished. The feeling persisted, however, and I slipped down in the seat. Even on a bright summer afternoon, this shabby little dead-end street had pockets of shadow — pockets where a watcher could hide.

Don't get overimaginative, I cautioned myself. RKI hadn't known where I was at nearly two o'clock when one of their operatives tailed Rae downhill to the Remedy. It was doubtful they'd been able to trace me through John this fast, given that his identity was hidden behind that of Mr. Paint. I'd covered my trail perfectly.

Hadn't I?

When John opened the passenger-side door,

I jerked violently. "Scared?" he asked in mocking tones.

"Shut up. What did you find out?"

"Okay to use Vic's name. Neither he nor Pete knows anything about Brockowitz or Navarro. Abrego — he's sort of a coyote."

"You mean one of those people who move illegals across the border?"

"That's why I said 'sort of.' He picks them up at the border, takes them where they want to go. He's a roofer by day, belongs to an organization called Libertad and works for them at night. The way Pete tells it, those guys're like an underground railroad. He says Abrego is completely honest, charges only what he needs to keep going."

"Why is it that Pete makes everybody sound like a saint?"

John shrugged, annoyed. "Why is it that you're so cynical?"

"If you'd seen what I've seen —"

"All these years. Yeah, yeah."

"John!"

"Shit, let's not fight, okay?"

I didn't reply. Then I told myself it was silly to get angry over nothing. "Thanks for making the call."

"*De nada.*"

"I didn't mean to put your friend down."

"I didn't mean to put you down. I just don't

understand why you can't see some goodness in these people. After all, you're the one who was championing the rights of illegals this morning."

It was a good point. Maybe I was more fond of championing minority rights in the abstract than in the concrete. And if so, that bothered me a great deal. I said, "I guess I've become conditioned not to accept anything until proven."

"Conditioned by what?"

I sighed. "Let's not get into all that now. When this is over, I'll try to explain. By then I'll owe you an explanation."

"You'll owe me a damn sight more. You're already in to me for breakfast, a couple of phone calls, the use of the Scout, and two hundred bucks. Plus when Karen gets back I'm gonna have to explain why her clothes have disappeared. And she's one scary lady."

I smiled, looking at the clock on the dash. "Well, it's five now. What do you say we try to find the Tradewinds?"

He grinned. "No problem. I looked it up in the phone book. It's three blocks north on Highland."

It was fortunate he had looked it up — even though his foresight had made him smug beyond endurance — because the Tradewinds was the least prepossessing building on an undistinguished strip of fast-food restaurants and small commercial establishments. Wood frame with no windows and only an unlit neon sign with the name and a wind-tossed palm tree — that was all. I parked down the block and told John to wait for me. This time he got out of the Scout. "No way!"

I got out too and glared at him across the hood. "I thought we'd established some rules here."

He crossed his arms and glared back. "No National City bars for you without me."

"This is ridiculous!"

"Say another word and I'll cause a scene."

Already he was causing a scene. A couple of sailors some ten yards down the sidewalk had paused to watch. I said furiously, "Why the hell do you have to be so obstreperous?"

"What's that, your new word for the week?"

"Dammit, you son of —"

"Don't say that about Ma. Hey, look — those nice sailors are coming to your rescue."

I looked. The two — who were all of twenty and probably had never gone up against a serious bar brawler like my big brother — had started toward us. I grabbed John's arm and said loudly, "Come on, darling." Then I muttered, "I'll get you for this."

"That's what you've been threatening ever

since Joey and I rolled you up in the rug."

"Don't mention that." As far as I was concerned, it was a particularly dark event in our personal history. "I will allow you to go in there with me," I added grimly, "because I don't want you to have to punch out those poor sailors. But you are to sit at the bar and leave me alone. Do not follow me, do not say one word, or so help me —"

"Yeah, yeah."

As soon as we entered, I realized Tradewinds was a misnomer. Not the slightest current of air moved in there, and when I drew a breath my lungs filled with cigarette smoke. The darkness blinded me for a moment. Then I saw neon beer signs and an illuminated backbar stocked with every brand of liquor known to mankind. A babble of Spanish rose to my ears as I waited for my eyes to adjust enough to distinguish the customers. John tensed, put his hand on my shoulder, and tried to pull me back outside.

"Holy shit," he muttered.

The people at the bar and tables were mostly men, and all Hispanic. As we stood there, they stopped talking and turned to look at us. Dark eyes glittered, and faces grew hard and hostile.

I tensed, but said to John, "It's okay," and scanned the room. At the far end of the bar sat a lone man with a long, drooping mustache, hair to his shoulders, and skin so dark he could have passed for black. Luis Abrego. I started down there, felt John close in behind me. "Go have a beer," I told him.

"No way."

"I mean it!"

"I'm looking to protect myself, not you. They probably won't knife a woman, and besides, you know self-defense."

"All right, come on. But if you say one word —"

"You'll feed me to the mean-looking guy by the cigarette machine."

"Right."

As we approached, Luis Abrego swiveled on his stool and got up to greet us. Soft, liquid eyes appraised us; then the mouth under the limp mustache spread into a grin. "You're the lady Ana called about," he said to me. "She wanted to make sure I waited for you."

John made a sound like air escaping from a tire.

"Mr. Abrego," I said.

"Luis." He extended his hand and we shook.

"I'm Sharon, and this is my . . . associate, John. Can we talk?"

"Sure. Lemme get you a couple of beers. Take that booth over there." He pointed.

The other customers had looked away and

resumed their conversations by now. As we got settled in the booth, I said, "Still want me to protect you, big brother?"

"Fuck off, little sister."

Abrego came to the booth, three bottles of Miller's clutched between his hands. He passed them around, then sat across from us. "Hey, Ana told me you paid her the money she needed. She shouldn't've asked for it. I told her I was gonna have it tonight, if this . . . job that I'm waiting to hear about goes okay, but would she listen? No, she's too proud to take my money."

I said, "I didn't mind paying her. She helped me, and I'm glad I could do something in return."

"Yeah, she's a doll, that Ana." His face grew glum, and he looked down at the table. "Bad break for her. She's nice and smart as they come, going to college in the fall, even. Sort of a relative of mine — everybody from Santa Rosalía's family somewhere along the line. I'd like to kill the bastard knocked her up, you know?"

"She'll be okay now."

"Maybe." He looked up, eyes uncertain. "I don't know, though. I think there's something wrong with her. You see how sick she looks?"

I nodded.

John said, "I know somebody at the

Woman's Place Clinic in Hillcrest. I think they charge less than two ninety-five for the . . . procedure, and they'll check her over for other problems. I'll write down my friend's name and number; you tell Ana to call her. Gina'll make sure she gets good care."

Abrego brightened and fished a finger-smudged piece of paper from his shirt pocket. John took it and wrote. As he passed it back, I squeezed his arm, but he just shrugged and looked away, embarrassed.

"So," Abrego said to me, "you want to know about the guy who came up to Ana in the Holiday Market parking lot."

"She told me you saw him again that night."

He nodded. "It was down near the border on Monument Road. I was . . . you know what I do?"

"You help people get where they need to go."

"Right. I had a pickup scheduled for Sunday night. Maybe around eleven, maybe later. What I do, I sit in my car across from the old dairy — sometimes most of the night — waiting for them and hoping they'll make it through the canyons okay. Anyway, I noticed this guy because he was an Anglo, and you don't see too many down there at night unless they're *la migra*."

"What was he doing?"

"Just sitting on a pile of broken-up concrete by the road that goes up to the mesa."

"You're sure it was this man?" I showed him Hy's picture.

"Yeah, that's the one, same one who bothered Ana. I watched him pretty careful. He was just sitting there on the concrete with a lit cigarette, but he wasn't smoking it. He'd knock the ash off, and as soon as it burned down, he'd light another. Some kind of signal, I guess."

That explained the pack of cigarettes Hy had bought at the Bali Kai bar. "And then?"

"A Jeep came by, maybe about fifteen minutes later. The guy got in, and it drove up on the mesa."

"This mesa — what's on it?"

"Not much. Rocks and dirt. A burned-out adobe. You need a four-wheel drive to get up there. Sometimes tourists go look at the view, but *la migra* warns 'em off. It's dangerous even during the day — too close to the canyons."

I considered that. "It's a strange place for a meeting, if the border patrol watches it."

Abrego smiled. "Hell, they can't watch it at night; they're too busy chasing my people in and out of those canyons. You gotta remember, they only got around thirty guys working a shift, and they cover the whole county, including the border checkpoints and the airports. I'll tell you, though, your friend and whoever else was in that Jeep were taking their lives in their hands going up there. Bad stuff goes down all over the place at night. Real bad stuff."

The words chilled me. I asked, "Luis, did you see the Jeep come down again?"

"No. My people made it through maybe five minutes later." He shook his head, pulled heavily at his beer, emotion clouding his eyes. "People made it through," he repeated, "and then I lost 'em."

"What happened?"

"Damned San Onofre checkpoint — you know, the border control station near Oceanside?"

I nodded. It was where many illegals attempting to travel north on Interstate 5 were stopped.

"The way we work it," Abrego said, "we drop our passengers off before we get to the checkpoint. Tell 'em to run across the freeway when it's clear and go around the station in the brush. No way *la migra* can patrol that whole area. These people we're moving, they're tired, scared, their judgment isn't so good. My organization, we know they're gonna head north anyway, so we try to help 'em have a safe trip. But some of 'em just don't make it across the freeway."

Beside me, John grunted.

Abrego gripped his beer bottle, looking down, shaking his head. "About two hundred and fifty people been killed up there, run down because they couldn't tell how fast the cars were going. A couple of years ago they posted signs — down here by the port of entry, too. 'Caution,' and a picture of a family running." He looked up, eyes bleak. "You know what's so funny about that? A lot of our people can't read. They don't know 'caution' — in English or in Spanish. They look at those signs and they think they mean it's a safe place to cross." He bit his lip, raised his beer bottle, drank again. "I explain it real careful to my people, so that wasn't the problem last night. These people were from a little village. They never seen cars going that fast before. They . . . just . . . couldn't judge the speed."

I reached over and touched his hand. "Luis, I'm sorry."

"Yeah, thanks." He wiped his nose with his hand. "So about this guy . . . Ana says he's your friend."

"Yes."

"Well, even though I didn't see him come off the mesa, I think I can help you."

"Oh?"

"Guy I know. Name's Marty Salazar. He's

slime. He's such slime I want to kill the bastard, just wipe him off the face of the earth — you know? But I've got something on him, so he'll talk to you."

"And you think he knows something about my friend?"

"Yeah, I sure do." Abrego nodded, face grim. "Marty followed the Jeep up there."

Fourteen

Abrego excused himself and went to make some phone calls, and John and I waited in the booth. After a moment John said, "Interesting guy."

I nodded.

Fifteen seconds or more passed. He asked, "So what do you think?"

I shrugged.

"You're awful quiet. Worried?"

"Uh-huh."

"What, you think Abrego's not on the level?"

"No, I'm pretty sure he is."

"This Salazar character, then. You're —"

"Let's just drop it for now, okay?"

He frowned, but backed off.

In truth, I was very worried — so much so that I couldn't voice my concerns. Something had gone wrong on that mesa, I was certain, and I couldn't shake the sense that something was about to go wrong again. Even though I was closer to finding Hy than at any time since this thing began, I'd never felt so distanced.

Abrego came back to the booth. Salazar would see us, he said, but not until ten-thirty. "You can meet me here at ten, and I'll take you to him."

"I thought you were waiting to hear about a job," I said.

"That?" He moved a hand, pushing it away. "I gave it to another member of my organization."

"I don't want to keep you from —"

"You're not. I didn't want to make the trip, not after Sunday night. It was only for Ana I was doing it. But since you gave her the money, I don't have to." He paused, looking indecisive. After a moment he sat down and said, "I gotta tell you — Marty Salazar's not a guy you or anybody else want to go see alone. But with me and what I got on him . . . well, he's gonna act like a real gentleman."

"Tell me about Salazar. You called him slime."

"Too good a word for him, really. Salazar's got his fingers into everything down here and in Tijuana — drugs, girls, porn, fake documentation, you name it. He'll buy and sell anything or anybody for the right price. Do anything, too. He slithers around like a rattler looking to strike, and when he sees his

221

chance . . ." Abrego's hand flashed out and grabbed my wrist in an apt imitation of a snake.

"You think he'll tell me what went down on the mesa?" I asked.

Abrego considered. "He'll tell you something. Part of it'll be true, part'll be lies. You keep what you can use, throw the rest away."

I nodded, then looked at my watch. "Thanks for setting it up, Luis. I'll meet you here at ten, then."

"I'll be outside. Gray Dodge, kinda beat up. You'll follow me."

When we got back to the Scout, John asked, "What do you want to do now?"

"I don't know. What do you want to do?"

"I don't know. You hungry?"

"Not really."

"Ought to eat — and we've got a lot of time to kill."

"We," I muttered, too worn down to fight it.

"I know what. Take the freeway north. There's a good burger place on Harbor Drive; they make them big and cheap."

One thing about my brother — he'll never become a food snob.

When we left what could loosely be termed

a restaurant, it wasn't yet eight. The big, cheap burger sat in my stomach like a lump of clay. "Now what?" John asked. "Any ideas?"

"No."

"You got to stop worrying."

"Well, that's not likely to happen, is it? And now that I think of it, there *is* something I want to do: go for a walk on the beach."

"Now? Why?"

"I still head for water when I'm upset."

"Okay, then we'll walk on the beach. Which one?"

"Doesn't matter."

In the end we cut over to Ocean Beach at Point Loma, where John used to hang out before he married, trying to pick up girls. The area is typical southern California beach community: shabby apartment buildings and bungalows — some stucco, some wood or shingled, all weathered by salt and the elements. We parked and walked across the sand toward the water, skirting a bunch of teenagers who were playing volleyball. The tide was out, and I wandered along the wet, hard-packed sand, gradually pulling ahead of John. After I passed the first lifeguard tower, he lagged behind, apparently sensing my need to be left alone. I unbound my hair and let the cool breeze play with it, took in great gulps of fresh air.

And tried once again for a connection to Hy. Tried and failed, as I had the other times.

After a bit I quickened my pace and moved briskly in an attempt to shake my foreboding. All that did was get the adrenaline pumping, but not in a good way, and I cast suspicious glances at persons I encountered. I'd intended to walk all the way to the O.B. Pier, but finally I turned and ran back to where John sat on the sand, leaning against the guard tower.

"Let's get out of here," I told him.

He checked his watch. "Might as well head back down to National City. If we're early, we can just sit till Luis shows up."

Back at the Scout, I found my nerves were so shot that I was afraid I'd be a menace behind the wheel, so I asked John if he wanted to drive. He climbed in and took over — master of his own vehicle once more. I sighed, wondering why I'd bothered to fight him in the first place. As in all the minor skirmishes of his life, circumstances had conspired to give him exactly what he'd wanted in the first place.

The address Abrego led us to was on Island Avenue in downtown San Diego. Although it is only five blocks and scant minutes from Broadway, the street might as well be on another planet. On Broadway you have distinctive and sometimes outlandish architecture, such as that of the new Emerald Shapery Center, which is designed to look like cut green crystals. You have distinguished old hotels, such as the refurbished U.S. Grant. You have upscale boutiques and the expensive shops of Horton Plaza. But turn off this main drag to the south, and the architecture becomes squat and functional. The hotels become flophouses. The shops slip downscale, their windows heavily barred.

By the time you reach Island Avenue, you've hit rock bottom. Once-grand Victorians have been turned into rooming houses and allowed to decay. Derelicts sleep in doorways. Drug addicts and dealers conduct their business in plain sight on the sidewalk. There are rescue missions, one with a sort of parking lot for shopping carts loaded with the possessions of the homeless. There are vacant lots littered with broken glass and trash. There are bars and liquor stores and hookers on the prowl. The squalor is heightened by the affluence that exists only blocks out of reach of the avenue's wretched and desperate population.

As Abrego's Dodge pulled over to the curb and stopped, John said, "Christ, I hope we still have wheels when we come out of wherever he's taking us."

"You can always stay behind and stand guard."

"No way you're leaving me here alone!"

"My stalwart protector."

"I've just decided you don't need protecting."

"About time." Then I took Pa's gun from my purse, handed it to him, and said, "Stick this in that recycling carton behind you and cover it up."

His eyes widened and he stared at it as if I'd given him a scorpion. "What're you doing with —"

"Please, John, just put it where it'll be safe."

"It's Pa's, isn't it?"

"Yes, I borrowed it."

"Well, we can't leave it here. What if somebody broke in and took —"

"It's safer leaving it here than taking it into Salazar's place. If he's as slimy as Luis says, he might search us, and then you don't know what he'd do."

John swallowed hard, nodded, and did as I told him. Then we got out and met Abrego on the sidewalk. He flashed us a reassuring grin and said, "Don't let the neighborhood fool you."

Luis led us to an alley entrance between a defunct market and a thrift shop. The alley was dark, blocked by a steel mesh gate.

226

Abrego pushed a button on the gate and a male voice spoke in Spanish through the intercom; Luis answered it, and the gate swung open.

As we started along the alley, I braced myself for the usual smells found in such places, but breathed in a sweet fragrance instead. Star jasmine. Now that my eyes were more accustomed to the darkness, I saw that flowers bloomed in profusion on the walls on either side of us. We walked the length of the buildings in single file to an ornate wrought-iron gate built into an archway. Through its scrollwork I saw a floodlit patio where plants grew in tubs and hanging baskets.

I glanced questioningly at Abrego. He grinned again, said, "Salazar keeps a low profile." Then he thumbed another button and a bell rang somewhere inside.

Heavy footsteps sounded on the terra-cotta tiles. Abrego cocked his head, listening. "That'll be Jaime, one of Marty's people."

"People?" I asked.

"That's what he calls 'em. I call 'em thugs — and worse."

A very large man loomed before us, peering through the gate. He had an odd bushy haircut and close-set eyes, and his shoulders bulged under his dark suit coat. *"Qué?"* he asked.

Luis spoke rapidly in Spanish, something

about an appointment. The man unlocked the gate and let us into the patio. After motioning toward its center, where a scattering of white wicker furniture stood inside a ring of potted palms, he left us.

Wordlessly Abrego led John and me over there. They both sat, but I remained standing, looking the way the big man — Jaime, Luis had called him — had gone. French doors opened onto the patio from the building behind it; as Jaime went through them I glimpsed dark heavy furnishings and an Oriental carpet.

"Strange setup," I commented.

Luis shrugged. "Like I said, Salazar don't want anybody to know how good he's doing." There was scorn in the words — anger, too.

"This patio reminds me of something out of Old Mexico."

"Even slime get homesick, I guess."

"Salazar's a Mexican national?"

He nodded. "Was born in Oaxaca, but he's been here even longer than I have. Spent most of his miserable life right in this area. Worst thing the INS ever did, giving him his permanent green card."

I glanced at John; he seemed poised to leap off the chair. "The guy that let us in," he said, "I think he was wearing a shoulder holster."

Luis was about to reply when the French

doors opened and a slender figure stepped out. "Salazar," Luis said.

Marty Salazar moved toward us in a languid, fluid gait. As he came closer I saw that his slenderness was deceiving; under his light summer suit, muscles rippled. His face was a narrow oval, cheeks sunken, eyes hooded. An odd triangular scar on his forehead made me think of the plates on the head of a rattlesnake; Abrego's earlier comparison had been right on the mark.

Although neither Luis nor John stood to greet him, Salazar motioned for us all to be seated. I sank into the chair next to John's. Salazar turned to Luis and spoke in Spanish — something about interrupting his evening. Abrego replied in a sarcastic tone I hadn't heard him use before. Whatever he said made Salazar's lips pull into a thin line. He sat down at some distance from us, took a cigarette pack from his jacket pocket, and lit one with a silver lighter. Through the smoke he said to Luis, "Someday you'll go too far, man."

"Someday we'll both go too far — all the way to the grave."

Salazar looked away; he didn't want to be reminded of that.

Abrego added, "These're the people I told you about. You answer the lady's questions, we'll go away."

Salazar's eyes studied John and me from under their heavy lids. After a moment he said to me, "Go ahead and ask."

"Luis tells me he saw you on Monument Road around eleven Sunday night."

"If Luis says so, of course it must be true." He shot a mocking glance at Abrego.

"A man was waiting there," I went on. "Near the road that climbs the mesa. A Jeep stopped for him, then drove up top. You followed it."

"So far I have not heard a question."

"Here's one: where did the Jeep go?"

"How would I know?"

Abrego started to say something, but I spoke first. "I'm not here to play games, Mr. Salazar. Where did the Jeep go?"

He dropped his cigarette to the tiles, ground it out with his foot. "The Jeep," he said in measured tones, "went up the road to the mesa."

"And when it got there?"

"You know the burned adobe? The Jeep went to it."

"Who was in the Jeep?"

"Just the two men."

"And then?"

"Then?"

"What did the two men do?"

Salazar's gaze became remote. "I don't

know. I left then. It is dangerous up there — the bandits, *la migra*."

That's the first recognizable lie, I thought. The border patrol can't be bothered with the mesa at night, and I'd give odds on you against any bandit in creation.

I said, "The truth, Mr. Salazar."

His eyes flicked to his right, and I followed their direction. Jaime, the bodyguard, had come up and was standing quietly beyond the circle of palms.

John had noticed too, and it brought out the street fighter in him. He tensed, ready to spring off his chair into a full-blown and potentially fatal brawl. I touched his arm to calm him, heard Luis say, "Don't even think about it, Marty."

Salazar's fingers clamped tightly on the arms of his chair. He looked hotly at Abrego, then seemed to remind himself of something, and waved Jaime off. I realized that whatever Luis had on him must be very damning indeed.

After a moment Salazar's eyes regained their remoteness. He looked at a point beyond me and spoke slowly. "It is said that someone was shot up there that night. It is said that there was a body left in the adobe."

A coldness began to creep through me. "Whose body?"

"I did not see it, of course. But it is said he was an Anglo."

"What did this Anglo look like?"

"I did not see the body."

"What happened to it?"

He shrugged. "It is no longer there."

"Did the police remove it?"

Another shrug.

"I'll ask you one more time, Salazar: what did the dead man look like?" Now my voice shook with anger.

Abrego spoke in Spanish, softly and swiftly. I understood none of it, but the words made Salazar go white around the mouth. He turned hard eyes on Luis for a long time before he spoke. "I have heard that the man was tall and thin. His hair was not blond, but not dark either. He had a mustache and a face like the falcon's."

The coldness now touched my bones. "Anything else?"

Salazar was watching me intently. Like a predator alerted to weakness in his quarry, he'd heard something in my voice, read something on my face. "There was a ring."

"What kind?"

"A heavy gold one with a blue stone carved like a bird."

Hy's ring — the one with the gull-shaped stone that matched the airborne bird on the Citabria.

For a moment I was isolated by the extreme cold. Sounds dimmed, colors faded, the faces and palm trees and floodlights blurred. Then I heard the beating of my own heart — strong and steady. Odd how it could go on doing that when everything else had shut down. . . .

"Sharon?" John and Luis spoke in unison. John reached for me, and I pushed his hand away.

Now everything came back into focus — hard, bright, sharp-edged. I saw Salazar's knowing eyes watching me, his lips drawn into a cruel smile.

"You killed him," I said. "You killed him and got rid of the body."

He continued to smile, spread his arms wide to profess innocence.

I clamped my hands onto my thighs, gripped them until they hurt. Bit my lip, drawing blood. Tried to bring my rage under control. Fatal to give vent to it now; Salazar's bodyguard had not moved far away. And I had more than my own life to think of.

After a moment I stood. Took a step toward Salazar. Jaime moved closer, stopped when I did.

I asked, "What happened to the body, Salazar?"

He shrugged, still smiling.

Luis and John stood at the same time, moved

to either side of me. Luis's restraining hand gripped my elbow.

Very softly I said, "Salazar, I know you killed him. I'm going to prove it. And when I do, I'm going to bring you down. Remember that."

Salazar's expression didn't change. The bodyguard didn't move. Luis and John seemed frozen.

I wrenched my elbow from Luis's grasp and hurried through the encircling palms to the gate.

Fifteen

I ran down the sidewalk toward the Scout, John and Luis behind me. When I reached it, I leaned against the door, my forehead pressed against the cool window glass.

"You okay, kid?" John asked.

I didn't reply. Turned to Luis and said, "He told some lies, but most of that was the truth."

". . . Yes."

"Even what he left out — that he killed my friend and got rid of the body — was obvious."

Luis nodded, face drawn with sorrow.

There it was, then: the reason I'd failed every time I'd tried for a connection to Hy. He was dead. I'd traced his every move for three days now, and all that time he'd been dead. Fatally shot on an isolated mesa, his body somewhere in a shallow grave.

Tears stung my eyes. I blinked them away. Not now.

What about the other man in the Jeep? I wondered. Dead, too? No, Salazar wouldn't have bothered to conceal that. A confederate of his? Probably. For all I knew, Salazar could have been involved in the Mourning kidnapping. And Timothy Mourning? Renshaw was right about his fate: lying in a ditch somewhere with a bullet in his brain. The two-million-dollar letter of credit? Somehow it didn't matter anymore.

I said to Luis, "I want to go to that mesa."

"There's nothing to see," he said gently. "Salazar'll have made sure of that."

"I don't care. I want to see where it happened."

"It's dark. It's too dangerous."

"First thing tomorrow, then."

Abrego and John exchanged glances.

"I'll go, regardless."

Luis said, "I got a last-minute job to drive some people north. I'll leave before it gets light. Wait till I get back, then I'll take you."

"I need to do this right away."

"I'll go with you," John said.

"No." I didn't want my brother there. Didn't want him to see me grieve. I needed to make my pilgrimage in private.

Luis seemed to understand. "I'll get somebody who knows the place to guide you. Andrés, my neighbor. You meet him in front of my building at first light, he'll take you there."

"Are you sure?"

"Just be there." Abrego turned and walked toward his Dodge, raising a hand in sad farewell.

"I'll drive," I said to John and held out my hand for the keys.

"You sure you want to?"

"Yes."

He nodded, gave them to me, and went around to the passenger's side.

I drove carefully, concentrating on each movement, keeping my mind off anything else. If I could deliver him to Lemon Grove and get to the privacy of my father's house, I'd be all right. When I let him off in his driveway, he hesitated, then came around to my window. Leaned in and kissed me on the forehead — a gesture rarely offered in my family.

"You need anything at all, call me."

"Okay."

"Call me tomorrow anyway."

"Okay."

"Kid . . ." He paused, face twisting with effort.

"What?"

"I love you. Don't forget that." Then he hurried off, hunched with embarrassment.

"I love you too, big brother," I whispered.

I turned the Scout and headed for Mission Hills.

The big house had never seemed so empty. I moved through its dust-dulled rooms, touching well-remembered objects and thinking of happier, more simple times. As I wandered, the atmosphere became oppressive; now I had to deal not only with my memories but also with my ghosts. Ghosts of Hy and me.

The first time I met him, when he told me his somewhat peculiar name: "Heino Ripinsky," he said, and I started to smile. "Don't laugh," he told me, leveling his index finger like a gun. "Don't you *dare* laugh!"

A night last fall when we drifted in a rowboat on Tufa Lake and I confided fears and dark urges that I'd never so much as hinted at to a single living person. He understood and didn't condemn me, because he had often fallen victim to them himself.

A morning when we parted in silence at Oakland Airport. I thought our fragile rapport had been destroyed, but he called after me as I walked away. "Glad you didn't say good-bye," he told me, "because it hasn't even begun for us yet."

Now it had ended for good. I wondered how long it would be before someone told the florist to quit delivering my weekly rose.

Stop it, I told myself. *Stop it!* You can't afford this kind of self-indulgence.

I went to the family room, threw the sliding door open, and went outside. The sky was overcast again, filmy clouds backlit by the moon. Quiet in the canyon, quiet in the surrounding houses. Quiet as death.

I crossed to the fence at the canyon's edge, pushed through the creaky gate, felt with my foot for the first of the stone steps built into the slope. Climbed down slowly, bracing myself with my hand on the sturdy vegetation. At the bottom I paused, peering through the darkness until I spotted the oak that held the remains of our treehouse. I groped toward it, stumbling over rocks and logs.

The platform of the house was still there, and I was now tall enough to climb up without the aid of the long-gone rope ladder. I grabbed a limb, swung my legs onto it, then scooted over to the platform. It was just large enough for me to lie on my back, staring through the spreading branches at the sky.

And more ghosts crowded into my mind. . . .

The look on Hy's face when I stepped into his house the night I finally returned to Tufa Lake: incredulity, dissolving to delight, turning to a smug I-always-knew-you-would.

We'd made love for the first time that night

— Hy's voice so rough, his hands so gentle, his body —

No! I couldn't afford that particular ghost.

Better to remember some of the bad times: My frustration and anger at his closed-face refusal to discuss his past. The way he would spot the slightest trace of phoniness or pretense in me and tease me mercilessly until I owned up to it. The time he went too far with it and I threw a pan of cooked spinach at the kitchen wall.

But we'd laughed together as it dribbled down like some science-fiction ooze.

We'd laughed a lot, and stretched our horizons, quite literally. I could still feel the heart-pounding thrill of the first time I'd piloted the Citabria. And there was the perfect three-point landing I'd accidentally made, surprising a seasoned flyer like Hy. Only a week ago we'd flown high into the White Mountains. I could still see the golden eagles, the wild mustangs, the bristlecone pines. . . .

Bristlecone pines are the oldest living things on earth — some over four thousand years. Hy had been forty-one.

I was crying now, lying on my back with tears washing across my temples and into my hair. Crying when I didn't want to and couldn't afford to because I had to do something about this terrible wrong that had been done both to Hy and to me. Crying, and I couldn't stop. I . . . just . . . couldn't . . . stop. . . .

In the course of the past three days, everything that counted for anything in my life had changed. My past was remote, no longer accessible. My present lay shattered. The future was unimaginable.

Nothing would ever be the same again.

Sixteen

Thursday, June 10

The mesa was the most desolate place I'd ever seen.

I climbed out of the Scout and followed my guide across rock-strewn ground where nothing but mesquite and spiny cholla cactus grew. The morning was overcast, the air saturated with salt-laden moisture — spitty weather, we used to call it. The wind blew sharp and icy off the flat gray sea.

Ahead of us where the ground dropped off to distant ranchland stood the tumbledown adobe hut. My guide, Andrés, stopped several yards from it and waited for me to join him. "There is where it happened," he said in a hushed voice.

I looked at the hut, felt nothing. It was simply a relic of a bygone time, crumbling now into the earth that had formed it. I started toward it, then glanced back at my companion. He stood, arms folded, staring resolutely at the Pacific. Superstitious, I thought, and kept going.

The hut had no roof, and two of the walls leaned in on each other at abnormal angles. I stepped through an opening where a door once had been onto a packed dirt floor. Loose bricks were scattered underfoot, and trash drifted into the corners; fire had blackened the pale clay.

I still didn't feel anything. No more loss or grief, no sense of horror — none of the emotional shock waves that surge through me at the scene of a violent death, even though the death that had happened here should have touched me more deeply than any.

What's *wrong* with you? I asked myself. You can't have used up all your tears in one night.

For a few minutes I stood still, looking for something — anything — and willing my emotions to come alive. But there was nothing here, so I turned and went back outside. I felt a tug at the leg of my jeans and glanced down: a little tree, dead now. Poor thing hadn't stood a chance in this inhospitable ground. A few crumpled papers were caught in its brittle branches; I brushed them away. Rest in peace.

One of the scraps caught my eye, and I picked it up and smoothed it out: U.S. Department of Justice, Immigration and Naturalization Service, Notice and Request for Deposition. The form the border patrol issues to illegal aliens when they pick them up, carelessly discarded here because it didn't matter anyway. One trip over the border fence and through the wild canyons — infested with rattlers, scorpions, and bandits — had been aborted, but that made no difference. Soon the illegal — in this case, the form showed, one Maria Torres — would be back, and others would follow in a never-ending stream. I let the paper drift from my fingers.

Then I walked away from the hut where so much had come to an end and stood at the very edge of the headland. To my right lay the distant towers of San Diego and, closer in, the vast Tijuana riverbed. The river itself had long ago been diverted from its original course; it meandered westward, its waters made toxic by Mexico's raw sewage. Straight ahead was its destination, the leaden gray Pacific. And to my left, Baja California. A border patrol helicopter flapped overhead.

I turned and faced south. Cars moved on the toll road leading away from the border; beyond it sprawled the pastel houses and iron and red-tiled roofs of Tijuana. The famed bullring — like a giant satellite TV dish that could service all of Baja — stood alone at the edge of town. I stared at the black steel-paneled boundary fence that lay across the ridge of rugged hills, and thought of satin funeral ribbons.

For a long time I stood there, thoughts and impressions trickling randomly through my mind. I recalled the words "You keep what you can use, throw the rest away." And then the sluggish flow began to rush in an unstemmable torrent toward the obvious conclusion. When I finally began to feel, the emotions were not the ones I'd anticipated. I turned and ran back to where Andrés still contemplated the sea.

I'd come here this morning on a pilgrimage, thinking that everything was over, finished. Now I realized my search was only beginning.

Lieutenant Gary Viner of SDPD Homicide had been in the same high-school class with my older brother Joey. I remembered him vaguely as an undistinguished member of a pack of boys who used to hang out in front of our house peering into the engines of various decrepit cars. He was still undistinguished, with thinning sandy hair, gray eyes that were mild to the point of vacuousness, and a wispy mustache that turned down, as if in disappointment at being the best he could grow. But when Viner spoke, I realized that behind his very ordinary facade he had not only a sharp mind but also a rapierlike memory.

"Never figured to see *you* in my office," he said, motioning for me to sit. "You haven't changed all that much. Still eat tons of chocolate?"

"Not like I used to."

Viner patted the beginnings of a beer belly. "Just as well. You could really suck it up, be fat as a hog if you didn't cut back some. That's what we were all waiting for, but you just stayed slim as ever. I take it you didn't marry that bozo who was captain of the swim team. What was his name?"

"Bobby Ellis." As I said it, I felt an irrational flash of resentment. Bobby had taken my fragile early love and virginity, then dumped me for someone more socially acceptable to his upwardly mobile parents. I realized now that I was *glad* I'd tossed his class ring off the Coronado ferry. "He married somebody with a lot of money, who proceeded to make his life hell," I added with some relish. "They're divorced now."

"Isn't everybody? What's Joey doing these days?"

"Living up in McMinnville, Oregon."

"Doing what?"

I shrugged. "Working in a restaurant — at least that's what he was doing last week."

Viner shook his head. "Joey's a good guy, but . . . You think he'll ever find himself?"

"Joey doesn't have the sense to know he's lost."

He smiled at that, then sobered. "So what can I do for you?"

I took out my identification and passed it across the desk to him. His eyes widened slightly as he examined it. "What do you know? From cheerleader to private investigator. You have your own office or work for somebody else?"

"Somebody else, a San Francisco law firm." I said it reflexively, then remembered it was no longer true. "I'm here on a routine missing-person investigation, and I came across some information that might interest you. What do you know about a shooting that occurred in a burned-out adobe on the mesa above Monument Road in San Ysidro Sunday night? Victim was a male Caucasian."

"Why do you want to know?"

"I heard about it from some Hispanics I was interviewing in the South Bay."

"So you rushed up here to report it, like a good citizen."

"No, I came up here because I think the victim may be the man I'm trying to locate."

"His name?" He picked up a pen and drew a scratch pad closer.

"I can't say. It's a routine case, no crime involved, and the family doesn't want publicity." I felt uncomfortable lying so badly, especially to an old friend of my brother, but this was a situation where I couldn't be straightforward.

Viner sighed and tossed his pen on the desk, then turned to his computer terminal. He typed, stared at the screen, then brought up some more information. "Male Caucasian. Six foot three, medium build, brown hair, no identifying marks. Shot in the gut with a forty-four Magnum. Anonymous tip was phoned in to south station — in case you aren't aware of it, San Ysidro's part of the city, which is why we've got jurisdiction — at two fifty-one Monday morning. Body's in the morgue. No I.D. on him. We're trying to get a print match, but you know how that goes."

At first I didn't speak, afraid my voice would betray my agitation. The description could fit Hy — or Timothy Mourning. Finally I asked, "Anything about a ring on the body?"

Viner stared at the screen, then shook his head. "Could've been stolen before we got to the scene. What the hell he was doing down there at that time of night . . ." He sighed again. "Beaners, that's who shot him, and odds're we'll never get the perp. If they stuck up something like the Berlin Wall at the border, it'd make my job a hundred percent easier."

I ignored that, merely said, "I'd be glad to try to make an I.D."

"Okay, you go on up there to the county center. I'll call and let them know you're on the way. Report back to me afterward."

I stood and started for the door.

"McCone," he called after me.

"Yes?"

"Can you still turn a cartwheel?"

"What?"

"A cartwheel, like you girls did every time the team scored." His smile was tinged with both nostalgia and lustfulness. "God, I used to wait for those touchdowns! You wore the prettiest little bikini pants of anybody on the squad."

Amazed, I just stared at him for a moment. Then I turned and headed for the county morgue.

The day had warmed fast, and the air conditioning at the severely functional County Operations Center up north near NAS Miramar wasn't working worth a damn. In spite of how cold such places usually feel, it was warm even in Building 14, which housed the medical examiner's office — formerly the coroner's office, a sign on the street had told me as I'd turned off Overland Avenue.

I waited in the viewing room for the un-identified man's body to appear on the TV screen, glad that I didn't need to look at it up close in the cold room, my stomach knotted tight enough as it was, my breath coming shallow. Even at such a remove the sight of the dead is unsettling, more so if the person is someone dear to you.

"Ready, Ms. McCone?" the attendant asked.

I nodded, realizing I held the arm of the chair in a steely grip.

The man appeared on the screen then: surreally bluish green, through some flaw in the transmission. He was tall, slender. Had dark blond hair, a droopy mustache, razor-sharp features. In death he looked peaceful, almost serene.

He wasn't Hy.

He wasn't Timothy Mourning.

I'd never seen him before.

I used the attendant's phone to call Gary Viner. "It's not my clients' son. I have no idea who he is."

"You sure you're not holding anything back, McCone?"

Only the killer's name, a kidnapping, a botched two-million-dollar ransom payment, and a disappearance. "I'm sure. The people

I talked with misled me."

"Beaners." Viner sighed. "Fuckin' stupid beaners. Well, thanks for trying."

"*De nada,*" I said ironically, and hung up.

Back at my father's house, I sat down at the little desk in the family room, where my mother used to pay the bills. Found a scratch pad in the center drawer and began to doodle as I thought.

No ideas came, and my mind drifted to the previous night and my confrontation with Marty Salazar. Salazar had lied, of course, giving me a description that was a composite of Hy and the man in the morgue. Which proved one thing: he'd gotten a good look at both of them before committing the murder.

I wished I could feel certain Hy was alive, but I knew that wasn't necessarily the case. Salazar might have killed him too, disposed of his body but been prevented from removing the other man's by the arrival of the police. Or Hy could have escaped wounded and by now be dead or dying. In truth, the only thing my trip to the morgue had given me was a faint hope coupled with a sense of extreme urgency. I had to move on this investigation, move fast.

My fingers were gripping the pencil I'd been doodling with; now it snapped in two. I threw the pieces into the wastebasket so hard that one bounced out again. I was angry, and not just with Salazar. I was angry at myself for not heeding what Abrego had said before we met with the man he quite rightfully described as slime.

"Part of it'll be true, part'll be lies. You keep what you can use, throw the rest away." But I hadn't done that. I'd kept it all, failed to listen critically. I'd allowed my emotions to overrule my professionalism.

Well, my emotions were stabilized now, and it was time to proceed. From here on out, I'd rely on logic. Another indulgence I wouldn't permit myself was trying for a connection to Hy. My previous failures to achieve one meant absolutely nothing; sometimes, for whatever reasons, the best of connections aren't in service.

So get started. Start with a name — no, two names. Brockowitz and Ann Navarro.

Not much to go on with either. Navarro was a fairly common surname. Brockowitz wasn't, but the person to whom it belonged could be male or female. I dug out the phone directories for both city and county from the desk drawer and hunted through them. No Brockowitzes. One A. C. Navarro. I called the number; the man who answered said nobody named Ann lived there. I checked Information for new listings. None.

After eating a sandwich made from fixings I'd bought on the way back here, I drove back to the county center and spent several tedious hours exploring their various records. I found a birth certificate for an Edward Brockowitz, but a further check revealed a death certificate as well. An Analisa Navarro had been born at Balboa Naval Hospital in 1961, but the records contained no further trace of her. No one of either name had ever registered to vote, filed a fictitious business name statement, applied for a business license or other permit, or paid property taxes.

I left the center deeply discouraged. Navarro and Brockowitz didn't have to be from San Diego County or even from California. Normally I would have carried my line of inquiry to other counties, state agencies, federal agencies, but not in this case. That process was slow, time-consuming, and guaranteed nothing.

I'd thought of one person who might be able to help me, but for safety's sake I wanted to limit my contact with her to one call. Tired as I was, I might forget to ask something, overlook the obvious question. My reactions were slowing; if I went on this way, I'd be in danger of making a potentially fatal mistake. Even though it was only four in the afternoon, I decided to go back to my father's house and sleep on the problem. Maybe my ever over-active subconscious would provide a solution.

An unidentifiable sound woke me. I sat upright on the family room sofa, saw it was full dark. The temperature had dropped markedly; a cold breeze rustled the draperies next to the patio door. I got up and went over there, looked out and saw nothing. Then I felt my way to the desk and peered at the clock. Nearly half past eleven. I'd slept over six hours.

The sound came again — somewhere out back. An animal creeping up from the canyon? Or a human creeping up on the house?

I moved to the door again and felt to make sure the screen was latched — not that it would present much of an obstacle for someone determined to get inside. Then I stood very still, scarcely breathing, and studied the patterns of light and shadow.

Another sound, and now I saw some motion — far to the right, opposite the kitchen. Just a dark ripple against the foliage, and then it went away. But not before I could tell it was a human figure. For five minutes more I waited there; then I slid the inner glass door shut and moved the security bar into place. I'd check the kitchen door next —

The phone shrilled.

Don't answer it, I thought. But what if it was important? No, that couldn't be. John was the only person who knew I was here. I'd let it ring to give whoever was outside the impression the house was unoccupied, then call him back.

After eight rings it stopped. I crossed to the desk and punched out John's number. He answered immediately. "So you *are* there. You okay?"

"Yes. What's up?"

"Your Mr. Renshaw just paid me a visit. He said —"

I cut him off. "Hang up. Get out of there and go to a pay phone. Call me back."

Without a word he did as I told him. I locked the kitchen door, checked windows, waited. When the phone rang fifteen minutes later, I snatched up the receiver.

John's voice spoke over a babble of background music. "Okay, I'm at a place called Pinky's. Somebody followed me, but they haven't come inside yet. I don't see how they could've tapped my phone when Renshaw just —"

"We don't know how long they've known about you; they could have been watching the house all day. We'd better talk fast. What did Renshaw say?"

"Gave me a message for you. If you go in to their La Jolla office and turn over the money he paid you, plus whatever information you've got on Ripinsky, they'll call it a wash."

Sure they would. "That's all?"

"That's all I let him say. I told him you and I haven't spoken in years and threw him out."

"Did he believe you?"

"Couldn't tell. But I don't think he knows about . . . where you are. Under his tough-guy act he seemed kind of desperate."

That was good on one level, disconcerting on another. If the person I'd glimpsed outside wasn't an RKI operative, who *could* he or she be? One of the kidnappers? One of Salazar's "people"? Someone whose existence I wasn't yet aware of?

"Shar," John said, "if they can find me, they can find —"

"I know. I'm going to get out of here. I need a favor, though. I'll put the key to my room at the Bali Kai in the mail to you. Go there and collect the stuff I left. Leave the room key in the express checkout and then take the rental car — the key's in the room — back to the airport. Just keep my stuff at your house."

"Will do."

"Thanks. I'll call you when this is over."

There was a long pause. Then he said, "Okay, you bitch. You don't want to meet me for a drink, screw you," and hung up. The tail had come close enough to overhear his end of the conversation.

For a moment I fretted, then reminded myself that my brother could take care of himself. Besides, Gage Renshaw knew that leaning on John wouldn't get them what they wanted — namely me.

I got up, took Pa's .45 from the end table where I'd placed it before going to sleep that afternoon, and began to prowl through the house, looking out the windows. From the empty, echoing living room I spotted a car parked down the street that hadn't been there the past two nights — an old dark-colored Datsun, shabbier than what most of the neighbors drove. The license plate was unreadable, and a big pepper tree cast confusing shadows. I crouched on the floor by the front window for quite some time before I felt reasonably certain the car was unoccupied.

That didn't reassure me much, though. After a few hours of tossing and turning, I gave up on further sleep. Got dressed and packed my things, plus the clothing of Karen's that I'd borrowed, in a bag I found in the closet of Charlene and Patsy's old room. Then I finished off the sandwich fixings and huddled in the quilts on the family room couch, waiting for the windows to grow light, for the coo of mourning doves in the canyon, for the faint hum of freeway traffic that would tell me the exodus of commuters from the neighborhood was about to begin.

Insulated as I was by thick walls and darkness, the now familiar feeling of being spied on returned. Threads of a story began to drift through my mind — one of the nightmare-provoking bedtime tales often told us by our creepy aunt Clarisse. Little remained of it except the repeated warning, echoing yet in my aunt's dramatically pitched voice: "Beware of the wolf in the shadows. He is watchful and patient, and when he catches you he will eat you up — skin and bones and heart."

I'd thought I was done with such stories — had found real life ultimately more scary — but now I realized their atavistic fears still had power over me. Well, we all harbored wolves in the shadows of our psyches, didn't we? And mine were bound to be fiercer, more bloodthirsty than most. But what happened when one's wolf assumed human form?

Maybe when I had the answer to that question, I'd be done with stories for good.

Part
Two

Monday, June 14
4:54 A.M.

*Gray dawn was breaking as I reached the top
of the high embankment. The shapes of the rocks
and scrub vegetation on the other side had begun
to take on definition. The cold sea wind blew
more strongly in this unsheltered place. I lay flat
on my stomach, then slowly raised my head and
looked around.*

*Things moved down below: they could have
been animals,* pollos, *human coyotes — or merely
branches stirring in the wind. Like the phantom
wolves of my childhood bedtime stories, they
slipped in and out of the shadows, eluding identification. For a moment my calm deserted me;
I wanted to scramble back down the embankment
and run as blindly as I had from the wolves in
my long-ago nightmares.*

*Then the calm reasserted itself, and I knew
I was done with stories for good.*

I took out my father's .45 and braced it ex-

261

perimentally on the mound of earth in front of me. Checked my watch again. Nearly five minutes had gone by. I scanned the surrounding terrain, saw no one. Listened. Waited.

Then there were sounds below, echoing in the drainage pipe. I tensed, peering through the half-light. Sniper's light, they call it —

And there was a sniper.

Seventeen

Friday, June 11

The best hiding places, I thought as I carried my bag into the bungalow, are often so blatantly obvious that no one would bother to look there.

The little motel sat on one of La Jolla's narrow streets — only miles from the newish office park that housed RKI's headquarters. Stucco with a red tile roof overgrown by gnarled wisteria vines, it was an old auto court dating from the forties and had been the scene of many a tryst — including a few of mine. Only two blocks from Prospect, the main street of La Jolla's commercial district, the real estate was prime, pricey eateries and shops encroaching on either side. The only reason the motel hadn't been torn down or tricked up was that the old woman who owned it stubbornly refused to entertain offers. Her similar refusal to upgrade its appointments had kept rates at a level I could afford.

I'd had my choice of bungalows, since only a few of the dozen were occupied, and opted for one at the rear of the court, screened by a big jacaranda tree whose fernlike branches brushed my head as I walked by. When I stepped inside, my breath caught; as I'd thought, this was the same unit where, during one magical summer home from college, I'd spent nights with a much older man, a staff member at nearby Scripps Institute, for whom I'd entertained a brief but wild passion. The terra-cotta floor, unadorned whitewashed walls, tiny primitive kitchen, and equally ancient bath looked the same; only the jacaranda tree had grown and changed. The jacaranda and me.

I shut the door and set my bag on a luggage rack at the foot of the lumpy bed, then went into the kitchen and looked out the window. It opened onto the alley where I'd parked my rental car; a back door gave access. I tested its lock, noted the window was painted shut, tested the front door and other windows. Reasonably certain the bungalow was secure, I went to the small desk and rooted through its drawer, looking for an envelope.

I'd escaped Mission Hills that morning in the flow of commuter traffic, but spotted a tail as I drove toward downtown. Once there, I turned into the garage of Horton Plaza, parked the Scout on one of the lower levels, and left by a side exit. In a nearby restaurant I forced myself to choke down breakfast and drink several cups of coffee while pretending to study the *Union-Tribune* but actually studying the other patrons and people outside the windows. A man in a Padres cap who loitered for half an hour on the sidewalk looked suspect, so I whiled away the time until ten, then walked down Broadway toward Huston's department store, where I used to work in security. The man followed.

To a shopper, a department store's layout may seem straightforward enough, although the rest rooms are usually in a baffling and barely accessible location. But an employee — particularly one who's worked security — knows dozens of hidey-holes, indirect routes, and alternative exits that aren't necessarily off limits to the general public. I made use of all of them, thanking God that Huston's hadn't done any renovations in the years since my tenure there; when I stepped onto a side street some ten minutes later, my tail was no longer with me. I then merged into the crowd of early shoppers and walked several blocks before boarding the first of three buses that took me on a circuitous route to Imperial Beach.

On Wednesday morning I'd noticed an establishment on Palm Avenue called Clunkers 'n' Junkers Rent-All. The sign spoke the truth. The blue Buick Skylark that I rented for a nominal daily fee wasn't all that old but had been ill-used: there was a dent in the driver's side; the upholstery was torn; the windshield had a jagged crack; rust showed in the seams of the metal. The clerk hastened to assure me that everything worked mechanically and none of the car's more obvious defects would get me stopped by the Highway Patrol, so I left the remainder of the money John had advanced me as a deposit, then drove to Coronado and withdrew most of RKI's advance from my checking account at Bank of America. On my way to La Jolla, I stopped by the Horton Plaza parking garage and picked up my suitcase from the Scout.

Now I located a rumpled envelope in the desk drawer, smiling when I saw it wasn't printed with the motel's name — La Encantadora — but apparently had been pilfered from the Hotel del Coronado. I sealed my room key from the Bali Kai and the key and claim check for the Scout into it. Three stamps from the compartment in my wallet where I keep extra postage, and it was ready to go.

I felt a fiendish pleasure as I envisioned the flurry of activity that particular envelope might set in motion. If RKI's operatives decided to intercept John's mail in their attempt to trace me — an easy enough task, since the box was at the foot of his long, steep driveway — they probably wouldn't believe I was stupid enough to use an envelope from a place where I was actually staying, but as a matter of routine they'd have to check it out. Especially if they had a contact who could monitor my account at B of A or had somehow managed to tap into the bank's computer network. Then my transaction at the Coronado branch would send them scurrying to Hotel Del. Still smiling, I stuffed the stamped envelope into my purse and sat down cross-legged on the bed with the phone in front of me. Then I sobered; time to get to work.

The answering machine at Anne-Marie Altman's flat in San Francisco said she could be reached at the Sacramento office of the California Coalition for Environmental Preservation. I didn't leave a message. Anne-Marie and Hank are a couple who can't live together but love each other enough to want to remain married; they occupy separate flats in a building they own in Noe Valley, but when Anne-Marie's away, Hank's in and out of her place to water plants and monitor faxes and the answering machine. For his safety, I didn't want him to have a clue to my whereabouts or what I was involved in. I would tell Anne-Marie as little as possible.

When I phoned Sacramento, though, I learned she was in a meeting. I asked when it would be over, said I'd call back then. What to do now? I wondered. Well, I knew one thing that needed attending to, but I wasn't sure I could face it just yet.

Finally I got off the bed and looked myself over critically in the mirror above the bureau. I was wearing Karen's jeans — a baggy loose-fitting type that she favored — and a pink blouse that I definitely wouldn't have bought. The differences in our personal styles were to my advantage, however: Gage Renshaw had seen me when I was wearing the slim-legged jeans and loose type of sweater that I prefer; he would have had that image of me fixed in his mind when he described me to his operatives. As for the man in the Padres cap who had followed me that morning, I doubted he was from RKI, and he hadn't gotten that good a look at me, anyway. The clothes in the suitcase were almost as good as a disguise. The real problem was my hair.

I leaned in toward the mirror and studied my image. In past years I'd changed my hairstyle very little except for — vainly, I thought when I was in a self-critical mood — dying the gray streak that had been there since my teens. My hair was black and thick and very long; I wore it free or bound into a ponytail for casual occasions, knotted or piled high when I wanted to look like a grown-up. It was probably my most recognizable feature, and I'd always been proud of it.

But now as I stared into the mirror, I saw it for what it was and wondered why I'd kept it this way. With it flowing down my back, I looked like one of those people who are trying to make time stand still. Worse than that, I looked like a caricature that was about to take its place next to the leftover hippie.

Strange, I reflected. I'd never considered myself one who hung on to the past. I thought I'd let go of it repeatedly, so many times in so many ways. Apparently not so.

I'd let go of it two nights before, though, in the ruins of my childhood treehouse. Finding out that the man Salazar had shot on the mesa wasn't Hy had given me hope, but it hadn't substantially altered any of the things I'd realized during those bleak hours. After all this was over, no matter what the outcome, my life *wouldn't* ever be the same. I could cherish the past — both remote and immediate — but the conditions that had existed then simply no longer applied. I would have to create a new present, one that would lead to a different future than I'd previously imagined. All of which boiled down to an inescapable conclusion: my hair had to go.

I grinned at myself in the mirror, marveling at the workings of the female mind. We make sweeping links between the philosophical and the mundane and think absolutely nothing of those logical — or illogical — leaps. Haircutting translates to destiny — and why not? Those of us who — as a gender — have spent the ages dreaming our dreams while our hands prepared food and cared for children and cleansed our surroundings instinctively know that everything is bound into one great whole.

That issue settled, I put aside the philosophical and went about the mundane task of locating a nearby stylist.

It was, of course, a hideous experience. For openers, the place was called Shear Mania. Secondly, the stylist, Becky, had an orange-and-green parrot's crown. Before I could run screaming into the street, she sat me down and began whacking off great hanks of my hair. I closed my eyes. Kept them closed until I got up to go to the shampoo basin. Then I glanced down and saw my former mane lying on the floor like a dead animal. I shuddered and looked away from the carnage while Becky swept it up. She shampooed what was left on my head, then took me back to her work station for final shaping. Grimly I shut my eyes again. Over the hum of the blow-dryer she said, "This is a great style for you. Take a look."

"Not until it's done."

Finally she turned off the dryer, combed, sprayed, made little adjustments here and there. Then she stuck a mirror in my hand. "Now look."

I looked. My hair fell to my shoulders, glossy and full, turning under slightly at the ends. Nothing fussy, but not too severe. Perfect.

"My God," I said.

Becky frowned, not knowing whether I was pleased or displeased.

"It *is* great," I added, mentally upping her tip. "Am I going to be able to fix it this way by myself?"

She nodded. "You've got terrific hair. It wants to fall that way all on its own. Not like mine. It's mouse-colored and wants to stick up. Finally I just said what the hell." Then she proceeded to sell me shampoo, conditioner, spray, and a diffuser-type dryer. I left there over two hundred dollars poorer but confident that no one, not even my own brother, would immediately recognize me if I bumped into him on the street.

This time when I called Sacramento, I reached Anne-Marie. "Are you all right?" she asked. "Hank told me they offered you a totally unsuitable promotion. In my opinion, it was also insulting, and I don't blame you for skipping out without telling anybody."

"I can't talk about that now."

"If it's any consolation, Hank feels terrible. As well he should. Where are you?"

"I can't talk about that, either. I'll explain it all soon, I promise, but in the meantime I need some information."

"Sure. But, Sharon —"

"When I get home we'll discuss it. Right now . . . What do you know about an organization called Terramarine?"

"They're eco-terrorists of the worst sort."

"How far would they go?"

"A few years ago it was suspected that they killed somebody — the captain of a tuna seiner whose fleet was circumventing net inspections by reregistering in a foreign port — but it could never be proven."

"I don't understand — about the foreign registry, I mean."

"The old-style deep-sea nets that most of the purse seiners use trap dolphins along with the tuna, and the dolphins are crushed or drowned. After the Marine Mammal Protection Act was passed, seiners were forced to begin using a new kind of net with a device that allows the dolphins to escape. Our fleet

272

is one of the most closely observed in the world, but foreign registry exempts a boat from inspection. The nonresponsive sector of the fishing industry simply reregistered."

"And Terramarine murdered this captain as an example?"

"We think so. At first they claimed responsibility, but when an investigation got under way and the authorities started looking closely at them, they all of a sudden had alibis."

"So they commit acts of terrorism to make a statement. How about to make a profit? Would they kidnap someone for ransom?"

She hesitated. "They might kidnap someone, but I think it would be more for the high-visibility factor than for money."

That didn't fit with the Mourning kidnapping. "What do you know about a Mexican environmentalist named Emanuel Fontes?"

"Very dedicated, very highly respected."

And that didn't fit with Fontes's company being the agency through which the kidnappers had intended to collect the ransom.

"Interesting you should mention Fontes," Anne-Marie added. "That tuna-seiner captain whom Terramarine claimed credit for murdering? He worked for Emanuel Fontes's brother, Gilbert. Gilbert owns the Corona Fleet. It used to be home-ported in San Diego, but when Fontes bought it, he moved it to Mexico."

I recalled Gage Renshaw mentioning that there was bad blood between the brothers. "In your opinion, would Emanuel Fontes have dealings with Terramarine?"

"Definitely not."

"Not even if Terramarine's purpose was to discredit his brother, or perhaps get back at him for his anti-environmental policies?"

"No. Under no circumstances would Emanuel cater to their brand of terrorism. I know, because I met him at the Rio conference last year. We spoke at length on ethical considerations."

I sighed; for a moment it had seemed I was on to a good lead. "Only a couple more questions and I'll let you go. Have you ever heard of someone named Brockowitz in connection with Terramarine?"

"Stan?" She sounded surprised. "I've heard of him, but not in connection with that group."

"Who is he?"

"Stan Brockowitz is a total asshole. A fundraiser for anti-environmental causes. You've heard of Wise Use? Alliance for America?"

"Isn't Wise Use the group that held its anti-environmental summit at the same time the Rio conference was going on?"

"Uh-huh. Got a lot of press because of that,

too. Their agenda is destructive: to open federal parkland to logging and mining. They want to get rid of all federal regulation of the environment. Alliance for America is a coalition of groups representing mining, timber, ranching, and other business interests — sort of the flip side of my organization. Then there's the Center for the Defense of Free Enterprise, a nonprofit outfit that raises money for groups fighting environmentalists. Big business contributes heavily. Needless to say, I don't like any of them, but their tactics are legitimate and I suppose in their way they're sincere. Brockowitz, on the other hand . . . His firm is called Facilitators, Incorporated — a nice catchall name for anything that benefits Stan Brockowitz."

"Where's it located?"

"San Clemente."

"Perfect place," I commented, thinking back to the days of Nixon's western White House. "Who do they raise funds for?"

"Pretty much the same groups as the Center for the Defense of Free Enterprise. But there's a difference." Anne-Marie paused briefly. "Look, can you hang on a minute? I have to take another call."

"Sure." I waited on hold, mulling over this new information. When Anne-Marie came back on the line, I said, "Before we go on

275

about Brockowitz, do you recognize the name Ann Navarro?"

"Navarro's Brockowitz's wife."

"Okay, as you were saying . . ."

"Brockowitz is a former Greenpeace member, was fairly high-placed. Around six or seven years ago he made a big power play and was forced out. He got his revenge by establishing his fund-raising firm and courting big business. His methods . . . I call them Green Peril tactics. He portrays major figures in the environmental movement as Fu Manchus and the rest of us as their dacoits, scurrying around to carry out their evil schemes."

"Clever," I said. "The specter of an evil empire is a great scare tactic — and a great way to raise money."

"Right. And Brockowitz raises a lot of it. What his contributors don't realize is that he'd turn on their causes in an instant if he saw greater profit potential elsewhere, and that his administrative costs are padded. A good deal of the money he raises gets siphoned off into his own Swiss bank account."

"Is that fact or just speculation?"

"Pretty solid speculation. One of my good friends, believe it or not, is an IRS auditor in Orange County. She goes after big-time defrauders, and for years she's been obsessed with nailing Brockowitz. She's come close, too, and that's gotten her slashed tires and a fire in her house that the arson squad labeled suspicious in origin."

"Brockowitz sounds like a sweetie. Anne-Marie, do you suppose Hy knows him?"

She laughed wryly. "You bet he does. Remember when Hy was arrested at that anti-logging demonstration in Siskiyou County last March? It was Brockowitz who set him off, taunting him from behind the picket line. The bad blood between the two of them goes way back to when Stan was still active in Greenpeace."

Interesting — very. "Okay," I said, "how would I go about getting to know Brockowitz? Or Ann Navarro?"

"Well, I'm not too sure about Stan. People with so many enemies tend to be wary about letting strangers get too close. But Navarro . . . They haven't been married more than a year, so she probably hasn't had time to get into quite as paranoid a state. As I recall . . . Hold on a minute and let me double-check this."

Again I waited. Anne-Marie returned quickly. "I remembered correctly," she said. "Navarro owns a store called the Swallow's Nest in San Juan Capistrano."

"What kind of store is it?"

"I'm not sure, but from the name I'd say

it sells tourist crap."

"Thanks, Anne-Marie. This has really helped."

"Shar, when're you coming home? Hank needs to talk with you. He's been —"

"I know he feels bad about everything, but I'll try to make it up to him. Tell him . . ." I paused, unsure what I wanted to say. Finally I finished somewhat lamely. "Tell him I'll see him soon."

Eighteen

To get to San Juan Capistrano, sixty-some miles north of San Diego, I had to pass through the San Onofre checkpoint. The distant nuclear reactor, its cones like dormant volcanoes against the sparkling sea, filled me as always with a dull foreboding; the caution signs beside the freeway that displayed the silhouettes of a fleeing family deepened my gloom. No illegals were attempting to cross the eight lanes of pavement now, and the immigration people looked bored as they waved cars through. But under cover of darkness, the illegals and their coyotes would begin to move; tensions would rise among the checkpoint personnel. Night was the bad time here, when nerves frayed and desperate people risked, and often lost, everything.

When I drove into San Juan Capistrano ten minutes later I was pleasantly surprised. It had been fifteen years since I'd last visited the mission town that had always reminded me of a sleepy Mexican village, but while it had grown, it also retained its old-fashioned flavor. There was a new restaurant at the train station and a lot more antique shops and other stores, but the mission looked as peaceful as ever. No wonder the swallows kept returning on schedule from their annual pilgrimage to Argentina.

I parked on what looked to be the main commercial street, went directly to a phone booth outside a small deli, and started to look up the address for the Swallow's Nest. Then I noticed it was right next door. What had drawn my attention was the window full of silk birds that sat on perches or suspended from near-invisible threads as if in flight. Below them a two-foot-tall peacock preened its opalescent silken feathers.

How on earth, I wondered as I crossed the sidewalk, did such a specialty shop stay in business?

Inside were more fantastical birds, so beautifully fashioned that each seemed to possess its own individuality. A brilliant macaw winked slyly from one corner; a raven's expression revealed a philosophical bent; a crow leered evilly; a cockateel looked too damn smug for its own good. I'd never been overly fond of birds — at one time, in fact, I was pathologically afraid of them — but now I found myself completely smitten with a crochety old parrot. If I had to buy something in order to strike up a rapport with Ann Navarro, that's what it would be.

I went over to it and found a price tag pinned discreetly under one wing. "Ninety dollars!"

"But handcrafted by fine artists," a husky voice behind me said.

I turned. The woman was tall and coppery-haired with large silver-framed glasses. Either this wasn't Ann Navarro or Hy had never met Stan Brockowitz's wife and had approached Ana Orozco because he expected Ann to look Hispanic.

"It *is* wonderful," I said of the parrot.

"We have smaller ones that cost less."

"No." I shook my head regretfully. "It's his personality that drew me."

"Cranky, isn't he? I call him W.C. Fields."

"Where do you get your merchandise?"

"Mostly Mexico. There's a firm that we order from that employs a stable of talented folk artists." She hesitated, studying the parrot. "Look, I think we can make you a deal on W.C. He's been on inventory for a while. What do you say to seventy-five dollars?"

I glanced at the bird. "I'm not sure. It's still a lot of money. If you have a card, I'll let you know."

"Of course." She went to the sales desk and

produced a rectangle of brightly colored card-board: "The Swallow's Nest, Exotic Birds That Don't Talk Back, Ann Navarro."

"This is you?"

She shook her head. "Ann's the owner."

I frowned, staring at the card. "Ann Navarro. Is she married to a man named Stan Brockowitz?"

"Uh-huh. Do you know him?"

"Sure I do. This is quite a coincidence. I'm on my way to San Clemente to talk with him about . . . a book I'm writing on the backlash against the environmental movement."

"Well," the woman said stiffly, "you'll be talking with the right person." She moved away and straightened W.C., who slumped disconsolately on his perch.

I said, "I take it you don't agree with Brockowitz's stance."

"Let's just say that I work here because I like real birds, all of them. Stan has raised a lot of money to oppose legislation that would regulate the oil companies more stringently. If you've ever seen what an oil spill does to bird life . . ." She shrugged.

"I'm glad you told me that. You see, Brockowitz doesn't know it, but the approach I plan to take in my book is critical of people like him. He may have sensed that, though, because he was very difficult to line up for the interview — wouldn't let me come to his house, just said I'd have to catch him at the office during working hours and he'd see if he could spare the time. I have visions of waiting around San Clemente for so long that I miss my deadline."

"That's Stan. When he's unsure of a situation, he tries to avoid it entirely." The woman gave W.C. a final pat and moved back to the sales desk.

"I don't suppose *you* could help me with his home address," I said. "I know it's a lot to ask, but it's for a good cause."

She examined me thoughtfully through her glasses. "Why do you really want to see Stan?"

I was silent, trying to come up with a believable explanation.

"Look," she added, "I don't like Stan one bit. Don't like Ann much, either. They're both opportunists without any real ethical base, so I don't feel bound to treat them in an ethical manner. But I would like to know what I'd be getting myself into."

I took out my wallet and showed my identification. "Stan's connected with a missing-person case I'm investigating."

"Oh." She seemed disappointed that the reasons for my interest in her employer's husband weren't more damning. "Well, I'm not supposed to give the address out, but I guess

283

nobody will ever need to know where you got it."

"Of course not."

Her fingers tapped against the desk and frown lines appeared above the nosepiece of her glasses. "All right," she said, "I'll give you the address on one condition."

"Yes?"

"Buy W.C. from me. I work on commission, and if I don't make a substantial sale today, Ann'll dock my weekly draw."

I glanced at the cranky old parrot, who had slumped on his perch once again; it was the best trade I'd ever been asked to make for information. "Wrap him up and write down the address," I told her.

Navarro and Brockowitz lived not in San Clemente but in a rural area to the east near the Riverside County line. It was citrus country, and the gently rolling hills were covered with acre after acre of orange, lime, grapefruit, and avocado trees. As I drove through it I reflected that this was the way the whole of Orange County had once been, before oil pumping stations reared their bobbing heads and the developers arrived to pump their own riches from the burgeoning economy. There wasn't nearly so much money to be had from tending groves of shiny-leafed trees, but to my mind they were far more scenic than the housing tracts that sold out before their rafters rose or the condominium complexes that stretched for miles of pseudo-mission sameness.

The woman at the Swallow's Nest had given me explicit directions, and I soon reached a little town called Blossom Hill. It wasn't really a town at all, just a post office, grocery, and gas station. I paused at its four-way stop, circumvented a mongrel that was lying in the middle of the intersection, and continued until I came to the first road on the right. It took me deeper into the groves, about a mile, and then I spotted a white Victorian on a hill.

It was one of the big country-style Victorians — totally different from the narrow citified houses of San Francisco. Wraparound porch, three stories, square and substantial. A drive wound up through the trees and bisected a spacious lawn. Roses bloomed along the house's walls — ancient ramblers. A maroon Volvo stood at the top of the drive, and in the old-fashioned porch swing sat a dark-haired woman in a flowered dress.

I kept driving, then pulled over when I was sure the trees and slope of the hill concealed me. Navarro's clerk had told me that her employer and her husband owned seven acres, most of it in groves that a caretaker looked after. She'd visited the property only once and said she'd found the lack of fencing and other security precautions strange for a man of Brockowitz's paranoia. I looked around, then got out of the car and moved into the shelter of the grove. The trees hung heavy with oranges; their leaves brushed against me as I climbed.

The grove ended where the lawn began. A rose arbor, overgrown by gnarled vines, stood between me and the house. I inched forward and peered through it. The woman was still in the porch swing — not doing anything, just sitting with her hands clasped in her lap. Waiting?

I'd asked the clerk to describe Navarro, and this woman fit what she'd told me: around thirty-five, short and plump, with a cap of straight black hair and prominent Hispanic features. I wondered if she might not have some Indian blood; something in the shape of her nose and jaw put me in mind of an old Paipai woman who had run a campground where my parents used to take us on the coast of Baja.

The woman — Navarro — continued to sit quietly. A car drove along the road, and her posture stiffened, then relaxed as it went by. I sank down on my haunches, balancing myself with one hand against the rose arbor. Fifteen minutes passed. Twenty. It was hot here on the edge of the grove, and my shirt clung damply to my back. I pulled it loose, lifted my hair from my neck, and was momentarily surprised by its shortness.

The sound of a car engine approached. Navarro rose this time and went to stand at the edge of the porch, leaning forward over the rail. A BMW came up the driveway — a BMW in an odd teal blue with a mobile-phone antenna on its trunk. I'd seen a similar one recently. . . .

Navarro went down the porch steps and moved toward the car. It stopped; then its door opened and another woman got out. A thin woman with chin-length blond curls, wearing a long blue summer dress that accentuated her slenderness.

Diane Mourning.

The two greeted each other, shaking hands not as if they were friends but with a certain wary reserve. For about a minute they remained beside the car, talking. Then Mourning opened the back door of the BMW and removed a suitcase. She carried it over to the Volvo, where Navarro was raising the trunk lid, and set it inside. After that they went into the house.

Going away together?

I began to backtrack through the grove,

heading for my car. As I went downhill, I spied a windfall orange and picked it up — sustenance, in case this proved to be a long stakeout. I got the car turned around and into a position where I could see the driveway. Then I waited.

One hour. One and a half. One and thirty-eight minutes —

The Volvo came out of the driveway and turned toward town. I gave it a good lead, then started my clunker and followed. The Volvo went through Blossom Hill's one intersection without pausing, took county roads to California 74, and picked up I-5 at San Juan Capistrano. I followed it south, past San Onofre and Oceanside, past Carlsbad and the state parks and little beach communities, past Del Mar and the racetrack, and on into San Diego. Dusk fell; I switched on my lights and closed the gap between us. By the time we reached Chula Vista, I suspected the Volvo was headed for the border. I closed the gap a little more so I could check out its occupants, recognized Navarro and Mourning by the shape of their heads.

At San Ysidro caution signs appeared, the same kind I'd seen at San Onofre. A high chain-link fence separated the freeway from the frontage road, but its top was bent and broken down by frequent climbing. In the drainage ditch between it and the pavement I spotted six Hispanic men running in single file toward the north. The evening's influx of illegals had already begun.

The Volvo sped past the last U.S. exit. The port of entry loomed ahead, "Mexico" emblazoned in blue on the roof over the six auto gates. Four lanes narrowed to two, then fanned out again; traffic was light, and there wasn't much of a slowdown. I gave the Volvo three car lengths and edged in behind a camper. The Mexican guards were glancing casually at the vehicles and waving them through —

And then I realized I had to turn off.

Taking the car across the border would pose no problem. Mexican immigration doesn't care who you are or what you're driving; no tourist card is required for short trips to Baja. But coming back through U.S. Customs in a rental car whose papers were clearly stamped "This vehicle not to be taken into Mexico" would cause me all sorts of problems — and the words were there in big red letters across the top of the contract.

"Dammit!" I smacked the steering wheel in frustration. Ahead, the Volvo was passing through the gate. I signaled and began edging into the left lane where there was an exit marked "U-turn to U.S." An angry driver behind me leaned on his horn; I ignored him and moved over, glanced again at the Volvo, which had picked up speed on the other side of the border control. Then I swung onto the exit, passed over the freeway on San Ysidro Boulevard, and took the northbound ramp.

So Diane Mourning and Ann Navarro were going to Baja together. Why? What was the relationship between them? Not close, that much I could tell. But I hadn't sensed hostility, just a mutual wariness —

The blast of a horn interrupted my thoughts. A Porsche that I'd cut off roared around me, its driver flipping me the bird. I gripped the wheel and concentrated on the road all the way to La Jolla, using the mechanical activity to calm my anger at losing the best lead I'd had all day. Before I went to La Encantadora, I stopped at a shopping center and bought coffee, more sandwich fixings, a deli salad, and a bottle of chilled white wine.

The bungalow had trapped the day's heat. I opened a couple of the windows to let in the cool breeze that blew up from the cove. Still too tense to eat, I poured some wine and sat down at the little desk. There were a few sheets of stationery in its drawer, also pilfered from Hotel Del. I pulled them out and began scribbling.

"What relationship betw. Navarro & D. Mourning? Husbands? Why Baja? Where Brockowitz? Who man in morgue? Where his Jeep? Where Hy's rental? Call Avis. H's credit card used since Bali Kai? Call Kate."

Now I drew a diagram with the names Brockowitz, Navarro, T. Mourning, D. Mourning, and Hy inside circles and linked by dotted lines and arrows. Around its periphery I added Marty Salazar, Terramarine, RKI, Phoenix Labs, and Colores Internacional. Under Colores, I drew another arrow and inked in the name E. Fontes. Added that of his brother, Gilbert, for good measure.

All of it was intermeshed. None of it made any sense.

I pulled the phone toward me and tried to call Kate Malloy. The Spaulding Foundation offices were closed, and Information had no listing of a home number for her. Then I tried to call Gary Viner to see if he'd gotten an I.D. on the body in the morgue. Viner was off duty, his home number unlisted. I phoned the nearest Avis office, but they couldn't give me any information on Hy's rental car. Yes, the man said, their cars could be taken into Baja. I reserved one for the next morning, just in case.

Finally I went to the kitchenette, found a fork, and wolfed down my salad, barely tasting it. Made a sandwich and poured another glass of wine. Wolfed that down and went back for seconds. And decided to call it a day and see if there was anything worth watching on TV. Maybe tomorrow things would seem clearer. . . .

But what was that big pink plastic bag on the bed? Oh, my God — W.C. I'd totally forgotten about my seventy-five-bucks-plus-tax silk parrot! I pulled him out of the sack, glared into his eyes as grumpily as he glared into mine. "You cost me a bundle, fellow," I told him, "and my cats are going to hate you."

Then I set him on the bed, leaning against one of the pillows. Stripped off my clothes and switched on the old TV. A rerun of "Cheers" was on — one of the wonderful old episodes with Shelley Long. During a commercial break I picked up W.C. and checked under his wing to see if the saleswoman had removed the price tag. She had, but there was another tag attached near the seam where the wing joined the body. I flipped the feathers up and leaned toward the dim bedside lamp to read it.

Colores Internacional, Mexico City.

The firm owned by Emanuel Fontes, environmentalist. The firm to which the Mourning kidnap letter of credit was drawn.

I clutched W.C. in a stranglehold. Flopped back against my pillow. Coincidence? I doubted that.

At first the kidnapping had appeared to have been engineered by its victim. Then a photograph of him that radiated terror had erased that suspicion. Now his wife had traveled to Baja with a woman who bought merchandise for her store from the firm to whom the L.C. had been drawn. A woman who supposedly had made contact with Hy the day he disappeared. A woman whose husband was involved in the kidnapping . . .

But why had Mourning and Navarro gone to Baja? If their journey had to do with the missing L.C., why hadn't they gone to Mexico City?

On the TV screen, Ted Danson was tossing Shelley Long's collection of stuffed animals out the window. I looked at W.C. and considered giving him the same treatment. The damned parrot had provided a clue, but I didn't know what to make of it. Now I'd probably be awake all night.

I closed my eyes, willing sleep to come, as it usually did when I watched late reruns. Images of the past few days played against my eyelids. When I opened them again, a Sea World commercial was on, showing bottle-nosed dolphins frolicking in the petting pool as kids fed them sardines. I stared at it for a moment, then smiled.

The creatures of the air and the sea were certainly being good to me tonight.

Nineteen

Saturdays can be damned discouraging from an investigative standpoint. Offices are closed, sources of information are unavailable, informants are off at the beach. I got up early anyway, made some coffee in the little percolator in the kitchenette, and crawled back into bed to contemplate my options. Almost immediately I got up again and checked the phone book for a couple of names; one I found, one I didn't.

The idea I'd had the night before while watching the Sea World commercial seemed farfetched — perhaps wine-induced — in the light of morning. I told myself I'd be better off trying to get a lead on Hy's recent activities. Trouble was, I needed Kate Malloy's help to access transactions on the foundation's American Express account, but even if I could reach her, the billing office at Am Ex would be closed for the weekend. Ron Chan at Pacific

295

Bell might be able to find out if there had been any activity on the foundation's calling card, however. I looked at my watch, decided eight-thirty was too early on a Saturday morning to bother an acquaintance from whom I was requesting a favor. As it was, I'd be stretching Chan's and my Christmas-party rapport pretty thin.

I finished my coffee, showered, and with some trepidation faced the task of fixing my newly shorn hair. The stylist's prediction proved correct, though; with little encouragement from me it fell perfectly, as if it had been wanting to do so for years. Relieved, I dressed in another shirt and pair of jeans belonging to my former sister-in-law and set out for Imperial Beach to return my rental car to Clunkers 'n' Junkers. I wasn't certain I'd again need to cross into Baja, but it struck me as foolish to be driving a vehicle that I couldn't take there.

From Clunkers 'n' Junkers I walked five blocks along Palm Avenue to the Holiday Market. Even so near the beach the sun bore down relentlessly — another unseasonably warm day, part of the screwy weather patterns that seemed to be developing all over the country. Of course, the climate has always been changeable in my old hometown, which boasts of four weather reports a day ranging from damp and foggy to cold and windy to hot and dry. Growing up there had fully prepared me for life in my new hometown, where the climate is equally schizoid.

This morning few men loitered in the drive-by hiring lot, and those who did were just there to pass the time, getting started early on bottles in paper bags. Inside the market Vic stood behind the checkout counter, rolling a cold can of Pepsi against his sweaty forehead. After an initial hesitation, he recognized me and flashed a gapped-tooth smile.

"Still *no tengas inglés?*" I asked, smiling back.

"Nah, *tengo*. Sorry about the other day, but you know how it goes. *La migra*, they got people all over, lookin' like you or anybody else."

"That's okay. After I was in here that morning, did you say anything to anybody about me and what I was asking?"

"Well, sure, some of the guys outside. I warned 'em you might be trouble. But don't worry none about them. Those guys, they don't call 'em *pollos* for nothin', you know what I mean? Chickens. Scared, they don't want to make waves. You try to help 'em, they're so goddamn grateful, after a while you want to slap 'em around."

A sailor with a bag of chips came up to the counter. I stepped back and waited until Vic had completed the transaction before I asked,

"Do you know Marty Salazar?"

His eyes narrowed, hard little points of light flashing in their depths. "Yeah."

"He ever come in here?"

"He tried, I'd cut his *cojones* off, and he knows it. Salazar keeps his distance."

"What about the men who hang around in the parking lot? Would they deal with him?"

"If they get hungry enough — and most of 'em do. Why?"

"Somebody's been following me, probably since the morning I came in here. If one of the men told Salazar about me —"

Vic shook his head. "Don't make no sense. I warned 'em about you after you left. Nobody could've followed you. And like I said, Salazar don't hang around . . . Ah, shit!"

"What?"

"That goddamn Pete!"

"Pete who works for my brother?"

"Yeah." Vic's expression soured. "Pete's my cousin's kid, and he's okay, but he's one of these guys who, you know, plays the angles. He does things for Salazar — I don't even wanna know what. I bet he's the one put him onto you."

"You mean after John asked him to find out what you knew about the Anglo who came in here?"

"Uh-huh. Pete came around with his picture

— same picture you showed me — and I told him what'd gone down. Then I gave Ana Orozco a call, and Pete took down her address to pass on to you. He probably peddled the info to Salazar."

"But why would he think Salazar'd be interested in me — or in what I was investigating?"

Vic shrugged. "Salazar's interested in everything that goes on in the South Bay. And he pays good."

So it probably had been one of Salazar's people watching me later that afternoon as I sat in the Scout outside Luis Abrego's building. Which meant Salazar had been more or less prepared for the questions I'd asked him that night. Those were Salazar's people outside my father's house, too. The man in the Padres cap whom I'd lost in the maze of Huston's department store? And what about right now?

I frowned and glanced through the barred window at the parking lot. Vic noticed my discomfort and muttered, "I'd like to bust Pete's face!"

"We'll let my brother take care of him," I said. "In the meantime, can I ask a favor of you?"

"I figure I owe you one. What d'you need?"

"A ride to the Avis rental car office downtown."

"*No problema*. And I know how to do it so if anybody's watching, they'll never suspect a thing. I'll just have my stock boy take you out of here like a sack of potatoes in my delivery van."

I wasn't sure I cared for the comparison, but I went along without complaint.

While I was waiting for my latest rental car to be brought around, I called Ron Chan's number from a pay phone in the office. No answer. Next I dropped more coins in the slot and punched out the number I'd found earlier in the directory. Professor Emeritus Harold Haslett of U.C. San Diego wasn't at his Point Loma residence, but a pleasant-voiced woman who said she was his housekeeper told me I could find him down at the harbor. When I asked where, she replied vaguely, "Oh, anywhere near the G Street Mole." G Street Mole is what old-timers call the area that's been renamed Tuna Harbor, and as I hung up I wondered why Professor Haslett — a friend of Melvin Hunt, whom I'd met at the buffet supper he and my mother had given on Christmas Eve — was spending his Saturday in what was basically a tourist trap.

My transportation, a perky white Toyota Tercel that I rented with a cash deposit, arrived just then. After I got in and familiarized myself with it, I set off to follow the lead that had seemed so promising the night before.

San Diego Bay once harbored the nation's largest tuna fleet, as well as many other types of commercial fishing vessels. I can remember going to the piers as a child to see my uncle Ed, whose frequent gifts of the daily catch helped to make the McCone food budget more manageable. Back then the waterfront was a bustling, exciting place lined with seamen's cafés and taverns, surplus stores, tattoo parlors, marine outfitters, rescue missions, cheap hotels and rooming houses, and the inevitable pawnshops. Packs of sailors roamed the area at all hours, congregating in front of poolrooms and hiring halls, drinking beer or fresh-roasted coffee, checking out the pretty girls. Vessels of all types and sizes surged gently beside the docks. I was particularly fascinated by the purse seiners, their nets piled on the pier alongside the boats while crewmen, who by and large still spoke the Portuguese and Italian of their forebears, mended them.

Today the waterfront has lost most of its flavor. The tuna trade is all but extinct, due to the closing of the city's two remaining canneries in the early eighties. Although some fish are still trucked up the coast to a cannery near L.A., very few seiners put into port at San Diego, and most commercial fishing is done by pole from smaller bait boats. The old tuna piers sit blocked off and decaying. The tattoo parlors and taverns have been razed to make way for steel-and-glass high-rises that dwarf the older structures. Ships containing museums — the *Star of India* and the steamer *Berkeley* — draw tourists; restaurants have proliferated. Farther south, Seaport Village offers theme-park dining and shopping.

Still, it's a pretty harbor, one of the prettiest in the world, and after I parked and began strolling along the Embarcadero, I felt a pang of regret for having left my native city. I found that if I looked toward the bay, I could call up some of the feel of childhood. The smells were right — fish and creosote and brine — and so was the warmth of the sun and brush of sea air against my skin. I ignored the throng of other strollers, tuned out their voices, and for a moment pretended I could hear the lilting Portuguese and Italian of the fishermen as they bent over their nets. But then a kid with an ice-cream cone slammed into me, nearly leaving a slick of chocolate on my jeans, and I was right back in the present.

By then I'd reached the area known as Tuna Harbor. A huge restaurant complex and parking lot sat at the edge of the water, and then the land curved inward, sheltering what was left of the fleet — bait boats berthed in their slips. There were benches along the sidewalk, many of them occupied by derelicts. I slowed, looking around for Professor Haslett. When I spotted him on the southernmost bench, I felt something of a shock; he barely resembled the distinguished, impeccably attired gentleman I'd conversed with at the Christmas Eve gathering.

Today the professor looked like one of those eccentric characters you often see along waterfronts: white-bearded, his thick mane protected by a shabby seaman's cap, wearing old khaki pants and a threadbare blue-and-white striped shirt. An old-fashioned black lunch box, like the one I remembered my uncle Ed carrying, sat open beside him, and he'd set out a little picnic: sandwich, chips, bottle of Guinness stout. His keen blue eyes surveyed the boats with a touch of bewilderment, as if he wondered how our tuna fleet had come to this.

I went up to him and said, "Professor Haslett, do you remember me? Sharon McCone. We met last Christmas Eve."

He looked up, squinting into the sun. "Of course, you're Kay McCone's girl."

"Yes." It still sounded strange to hear my mother called Kay. When she met Melvin — while doing her wash in one of the self-service laundries he owned, of all things — she'd introduced herself by the diminutive of Kathryn that she favored, rather than as Katie, which was what my father had always called her. Most of the people in her new life knew her only as Kay, and sometimes hearing the new name made me feel — quite irrationally — that in choosing it she'd rejected everything that had gone before, including me and my siblings. Hearing the professor speak it now brought to my mind a fragment of an old song — something about being out of step, out of time — and in keeping with my resolve to let go of things past, I shook off the last of my resentment. If my mother wanted to be called Kay, that was her business; it had nothing at all to do with me.

Professor Haslett was studying me. "You look different. Is it that you've cut your hair?"

"Yes."

"Very becoming." He motioned for me to share his bench, offered half of the sandwich. I accepted the former, declined the latter. "Strange," he added. "I spoke with Melvin last night and he didn't mention you were visiting."

"I'm not. This is a business trip, and I haven't called them because time is short and my mother would be disappointed that we can't have a real visit."

"And of course she would worry. Kay frets

because your work is so dangerous."

"Normally it isn't; she magnifies the danger. Actually, Professor Haslett, I was hoping you could give me some information. I called your home, and your housekeeper told me I could find you here."

His smile became edged with melancholy. "I suppose you find my behavior strange, perhaps even pathetic. An old man who should possess more dignity, aping the attire of his boyhood heroes, sitting on a bench beside his beloved harbor and mourning the past."

Haslett was a historian who had written a definitive history of San Diego Bay; if he mourned the past, he had more right than most of us because he knew it so intimately. I said, "I see a man who's wearing the clothes he's comfortable in and enjoying a place that's still lovely. I wish I could spend my Saturday that way."

"If you can enjoy merely sitting quietly and looking at the harbor, you're as unusual a young woman as your mother claims," he told me. "People today don't possess the capacity for contemplation; they want to be entertained. And they don't honor the past, quite frankly don't have any interest in it. My former students are good examples: most of them elected to take history merely to satisfy a requirement; they wanted to be fed the facts and have them interpreted for them, so they could spit them back during their exams and scratch off yet another item on their educational shopping list. I was quite happy to retire from active scholarship."

"How long ago was that?"

"Five years now. Not that I've retired mentally, mind you. I may appear to be merely another eccentric old man taking the sun, but actually I am conducting research for what will be my final long work — an analysis of the reasons for our port's decline."

"I'll look forward to it."

"Not with bated breath, I hope." He winked. "I am approaching seventy-eight and find myself enjoying the research far more than the writing."

I smiled and for a moment we watched a fisherman struggling along the dock with a heavy bucket. Then I said, "It's your expertise on maritime matters that I hope to tap into. What can you tell me about a Mexican tuna fishing fleet owner named Gilbert Fontes?"

Haslett pursed his lips — more belligerently than thoughtfully. "Fontes is a good example of the forces that have destroyed our port. The Corona Fleet was once the largest in our harbor. Fontes bought it in 'seventy-two. His first act was to reregister the vessels in Mexico — his method of evading the U.S. inspections mandated by the new Marine Mammal Protection Act. When they found out, local environmentalists . . . I believe you're an environmentalist? Didn't we talk at Christmas of that dreadful business you were involved in up at Tufa Lake?"

I nodded. "I don't belong to any of the organizations, although I contribute money when I can. Organizations and I don't get on too well."

"I'm not a fan of them myself. To get back to Fontes, in the mid-seventies local environmentalists staged protests at his home on Point Loma. The situation got out of hand. Fontes had . . . what shall I call them? Bodyguards?"

"I know a man who calls them his 'people.' The right word is 'thugs.' "

"Yes. Fontes had thugs, and they beat some of the protesters quite badly. The violence escalated. A neighborhood group got up in arms — not against the protesters, but against Fontes. Do you know what his response was?"

I shook my head.

"He moved the fleet to Ensenada, nearly bankrupting one of our canneries. And he closed up the house on Point Loma and moved his household to Baja. He still owns the place, but never uses it himself; strange people come and go there, however, making the neighbors — myself included — extremely nervous. A few years ago a number of us got together and made an offer on it, but Fontes turned it down. It's his way of striking back."

"Where does Fontes live now, Ensenada?"

"No, in a village on the coast, where the local authorities will protect him from protests. The Mexican environmentalists are thoroughly sick of his business practices, too. As you probably know, Mexico was signatory to last year's international accord to reduce the dolphin kill by eighty percent, but that hasn't stopped Fontes."

"Fontes has a brother who's an environmentalist, right?"

"Yes. The two don't speak, and the brother, Emanuel, bought out Gilbert's share of the family business — some sort of manufacturing concern — many years ago. Still, Emanuel has never dared use his connections to mount a protest against Gilbert." The professor's smile was pained. "Freedom of speech and assembly are not held in high regard by the Mexican Federal Police."

"Where in Baja is this village?"

"South of Ensenada. It's called El Sueño — 'the dream,' it translates. Many wealthy people, both Mexican and American, have homes there."

"And the house on Point Loma?"

"On Sunset Cliffs Boulevard." Professor

Haslett glanced curiously at me. "You seem very much interested in Gilbert Fontes. Is he part of the business that brings you here?"

"He may be. Since you're knowledgeable about environmental organizations, what do you know of a group called Terramarine?"

He made a disgusted sound with his lips. "They're extremists and fools who put the movement to shame. They remind me of small children huddling in a cardboard-box clubhouse in a vacant lot, making their war plans. They light matches and talk of how they'll set the world on fire, but in the end all that gets burned is the box, with them inside. Unfortunately, innocent bystanders often get hurt as well."

"Let me ask you this: Can you imagine them pulling off a successful act of terrorism? Say, a kidnapping where they collected a large ransom?"

He considered. "They would bungle it deplorably. And I would pity their victim, because he or she would not survive."

Now his gaze became assessing, concerned. I avoided his eyes by looking at the harbor. The air had grown hot and turgid; my forehead and scalp were damp.

"Sharon," the professor said after a moment, "I feel I should stress that even though the Terramarine people are fools, their very foolishness makes them dangerous."

I nodded.

"I'm beginning to believe that your mother is right to worry about you. Are you in some sort of trouble? Is there any way I can help?"

I pressed my lips together, oddly reminded of my last visit to the confessional: Father Halloran's kind, concerned voice offering the solace of faith; my refusal to accept it because deep down I didn't believe anymore — and that made my sins unpardonable, my soul irredeemable in his eyes. I hadn't been Catholic for many years, but now I felt an inbred urge to make a confession of sorts. For a long time I hadn't believed anyone else could shoulder my burdens, but now I wanted to lay them at this old man's feet.

But the old man was practically a stranger, and I couldn't involve him, anyway. I said, "No, I'm not in trouble. And I thank you for the information. May I ask you not to mention you've seen me to either Melvin or my mother?"

He nodded with obvious reluctance, brow furrowed, eyes still concerned.

I got up, said an awkward good-bye, and moved quickly along the waterfront to the parking lot where I'd left the car. Once, I looked back; Professor Haslett was watching me, and he raised his hand in farewell.

Twenty

When I arrived at Sunset Cliffs Boulevard on Point Loma, I stopped a man who was walking his beagle along the sidewalk and asked him if he knew where the Fontes house was. He gave me a suspicious once-over, then apparently decided I looked okay and motioned to an imposing Mediterranean-style structure half a block away. I thanked him and drove down there, pulling over to the curb and shutting off the car's engine.

The house was well kept up, the lawn well barbered, but there was a touch of loneliness about it, in spite of its proximity to its neighbors. Loneliness and abandonment, a sense that nobody lived there anymore and hadn't for a long time. A caretaker might check it periodically; Fontes's friends might be in and out; the gardeners might come and go; automatic timers might turn on lights; automatic sprinklers might play on the lawn. But only a shadow of life went on here, and to me the house seemed more desolate than if it had been

311

allowed to fall into ruins.

The man with the beagle passed my car, giving me another wary look. I smiled at him and got out. "It's in good shape for a place that's not owner-occupied," I said, gesturing at the house. "Roof looks like it could pass inspection. Of course, you don't know about termite damage; that can be the killer. Still, I've got a client who would make an all-cash deal and waive inspections, providing I can get hold of the owner."

The man's wary look faded. "Oh, you're a real-estate agent."

"Broker. Rae Kelleher, Century Twenty-one." I offered my hand.

He shook it enthusiastically. The beagle began sniffing my shoes. "Owen Berry," he said. "I live down the block, and I'd be thrilled if that place sold."

"Why? It's not rented to undesirables, is it?"

"*Used* by undesirables is more like it."

The beagle moved from the toes of my shoes to the heels. Its leash began to wind around my calves. In the interest of preserving my newfound rapport with Mr. Berry, I ignored it.

"Now, that worries me," I said — meaning the so-called undesirables rather than the dog. "Will you explain?"

312

"Fontes is a beaner," Owen Berry said. "Very well off, but still a beaner, if you get my drift. He's got a grudge against the neighbors — something that happened before my wife and I moved here — and he takes it out on them by letting all sorts of lowlifes use the place. He keeps it up, so they can't cite him for creating a nuisance; can't condemn it, either. But you should see what goes in and out of there."

The leash was wrapped tight around my calves now; the beagle was energetically snuffling my jeans. I thought, If he pees on me or sniffs my crotch, I'll smack his inquisitive little nose — rapport with his owner be damned. "What does go in and out of there?" I asked.

"Beaners. Probably drug dealers. Women with skirts up to their asses and hair out to here." The hand that wasn't holding the leash described a big perm. "Probably call girls. The only thing he hasn't loaned the place to is a faggot, but I hear that in Mexico they don't like fags any more than we do."

Now it was Berry whom I wanted to smack. The dog didn't know his behavior was disgusting. Come to think of it, Berry probably didn't, either. I curbed the impulse to tell him what I thought of him and instead said, "Well, maybe my client and I can solve the problem.

Do you have Fontes's address in Mexico, or know anyone who does?"

"I don't have it, but my next-door neighbor might. He tried to buy the place about a year ago, had some correspondence with Fontes."

"Would you ask him for it?"

"I'd be happy to." Berry yanked on the dog's leash. It cut into my calves. The animal made a gagging sound and staggered backwards on its hind legs, leash unpeeling from me like the skin of an apple. Now my sympathies were fully on the beagle's side; if there was any justice, someday he'd rip his owner's vocal cords out.

Berry began dragging the hapless dog along the sidewalk. "You coming?" he asked me.

I'd had all of him I could take. "I don't want to intrude on your neighbor. I'll wait here, if you don't mind."

As he left, I turned and looked off at the brilliant blue water beyond the sandstone cliffs, trying to clear my head of the muddying effects of Berry's bigotry. I told myself he was essentially a small and stupid man, but that didn't help. Owen Berry was a symptom of everything that was reeling out of control in our society — everything I felt powerless against.

After a while, though, the motion of the sea off the rock-strewn shoreline calmed me.

When Berry came back, without the unfortunate beagle but with a slip of paper, I was able to be civil to him. Quickly I retreated to the Tercel, calling out my thanks; several blocks away, I pulled to the curb and looked at the paper: 117 Vía Pacífica, El Sueño, Baja.

La Encantadora's courtyard seemed an oasis after my trek from Point Loma in the unair-conditioned Tercel. I parked near the office, thinking to check out after I made a quick phone call and gathered my things. The air was hot, without a breath of breeze from the cove below, but the shade of the jacaranda trees provided a measure of relief. I walked toward my bungalow, then slowed when I saw a figure move far back under the trailing branches of the tree nearest my door. An abrupt turn took me down a path between two of the other bungalows.

The bungalow to my right was surrounded by tall camellia bushes. I slipped behind one and worked my way along the wall until I had a good vantage, then peered through the shiny leaves. The figure had moved forward and was now clearly visible: tall, very thin, craning its neck toward the path I'd just taken.

Gage Renshaw.

My breath caught and I began working my way back again. It didn't occur to me to wonder how he'd found me; given RKI's considerable resources, it probably hadn't been difficult. I didn't have to question his intent, either; I'd seen the bulge under his suit coat. Armed and dangerous.

I inched along the bungalow wall to its rear, then pressed flat against it. Now what?

Renshaw had spotted me as I walked from the car — no way he could have missed me. But something about his posture — alert but indecisive — told me he hadn't quite recognized me. New hairstyle, different type of clothing, and if he'd checked with the motel office they'd have described my Clunker 'n' Junker. He'd probably sensed something familiar, however; it might only be seconds before he made the connection.

My things didn't matter. They could stay in the bungalow — although I briefly entertained a dismaying vision of them being the first in a trail of possessions discarded from here to wherever this case took me. The car posed a problem, though; I needed to create a diversion so I could get to it.

The path onto which I'd detoured led to a side street. I moved through the bushes, looked out. Saw no one and headed for the pavement. Directly across the street was a café. I ran over there, found a pay phone, and called the motel office.

316

"Unit seven, please," I said to the desk clerk.

"One moment." She connected me and let the phone ring several times. "Sorry, she doesn't answer."

"I wonder if you could go back there and check on her. She wasn't feeling well when I left her after lunch, and I'm worried." When the woman hesitated, I added, "Please? She's a diabetic."

"All right, hold on a minute." She sighed and set the receiver down with a clunk.

I hung up, rushed out of the café and across the street. As I rounded the corner near the motel office, the clerk was heading toward the rear of the court. I crouched behind another camellia bush and watched as she went to the door of my bungalow. Renshaw came out from under the tree and spoke to her. She motioned toward the door, explaining. Then she unlocked it and stepped inside. As I'd hoped, Renshaw followed.

I ran for the Toyota, key in hand. Jumped inside and jammed it into the ignition. Got the engine started, turned the car, and was out of there, seat-belt warning signal beeping furiously. As I sped away, I tried to remember if there was anything in the room that might tip Renshaw to the lead I'd turned up. The paper I'd doodled names on last night? No,

317

the maid had gone in to clean the room when I left, and I'd seen her empty the wastebasket. W.C.? The sales slip for him was in my purse.

I smiled, trying to imagine what Renshaw would make of my crotchety old parrot.

I now had an errand to run and a call to make. First stop was Gooden's Photographic Supply on University Avenue in the city's predominantly gay Hillcrest district. Gooden's has been there since the 1920s when Hillcrest was an exclusive suburb linked to downtown by a trolley line — a lily-white suburb, thanks to pioneer developer William Wesley Whitsun's concept of "restricted" housing tracts. I've often wondered what the bigoted old boy would think of the lesbians and gays who have renovated the charming cottages he built; given the way upscale boutiques and restaurants have driven out many of the old-time merchants, I've also wondered how Gooden's has survived. But that afternoon it was doing a turnaway business in its vintage building half a block from the huge arch that marks the beginning of the Hillcrest shopping district at Fifth Avenue and University.

Inside, the store was as I remembered it: a photographer's dream, with case after case full of the widest variety of cameras, lenses, supplies, and darkroom equipment I'd ever seen. Back in the days when I considered my-self a budding professional photographer — before I discovered that I had absolutely no eye or originality when it came to taking pic-tures — I would spend a good deal of every visit home in Gooden's, composing mental shopping lists. Now I recalled exactly where the telephoto lenses were kept and headed straight there.

It took me about twenty minutes to deter-mine that the lens that best suited my purposes was a Meade 1000 that converted to a long-distance spotting scope, with eyepieces that would magnify up to eighty-three times. Light and portable, it would give me great resolu-tion, even when photographing in substandard light. Not that I expected to take many pic-tures; I wanted the lens more for its spying capabilities, and when mounted on a camera it would lend me the protective coloration of your basic overequipped tourist.

The young clerk with the neo-Nazi haircut who was helping me seemed to sense an easy sale to an ignorant but affluent customer. He said enthusiastically, "With that lens, ma'am, you'll be able to count the pinfeathers on a baby bird's head at two hundred yards."

Baby birds and their pinfeathers were the last thing on my mind. Perplexed, I stared at him.

He colored. "I just assumed you wanted it for bird-watching."

"Do I look like a bird-watcher?"

"I didn't mean any offense."

"No, I want your opinion. Do I?"

"Well . . . no. Whale-watcher, maybe."

I had to smile at his pathetic effort to extract his foot from his mouth. "Okay, I'll take the lens. I'll need a camera and some film, too."

He beamed, then began steering me toward the new-camera department. Firmly I shook my head and pointed him toward the used equipment. My own camera is a twenty-three-year-old Nikkormat that I bought used; I like a single-lens reflex with as few automatic options as possible. The Canon that I selected was even more primitive than my Nikkormat and cost less than a quarter of what I paid for the lens and all its attachments.

"I don't know," the clerk muttered as he carried my merchandise toward the film counter. "It's like dressing up a warthog in a diamond necklace."

I didn't reply; I was wondering how the hell I'd pay back the cash advance I'd taken from RKI, knowing I'd have no job when I returned home.

I'd forgotten to eat lunch, so I stopped at a restaurant a few blocks away, had a quick sandwich, and used the phone to call Gary Viner at the SDPD. Viner didn't sound surprised to hear from me; I suspected there was very little that did surprise him.

"Have you gotten an I.D. on that body that was found on the mesa?" I asked.

"We have."

"And?"

He was silent.

"Are you going to make me guess?"

"That's not a bad idea."

"Stanley Brockowitz, late of San Clemente and Blossom Hill."

Now his silence had a different quality. He finally said, "Thought you had no idea who he was."

"I didn't — then."

"And now?"

"He may have something to do with my case after all."

"Then you better come in and make a statement."

"Can't. I'm . . . not in San Diego." My association with RKI had turned me into a paranoid and, apparently, a liar.

"Where are you?"

"South."

"The South Bay? Then you can —"

"Farther south."

"Mexico? Why're you —"

321

"I'll tell you about it when I get back. Have you notified Brockowitz's wife of his death yet?"

"McCone . . ." He sighed in defeat. "We've tried, but she's not at their home or her place of business."

"Then nothing's been released to the press?"

"Not till we get in touch with her. I don't suppose you have any idea where she might be?"

"Me? I don't even know the woman."

"Look, McCone, I want —"

"Will you be on duty all weekend?"

"Will I — No, I'm out of here in a couple of hours, and then I'm going home to paint the living room."

"Give me your home number."

"Why?"

"Because I might need it."

"McCone, you're not investigating this murder, are you? Because in this state you can't investigate a murder —"

"I'm not even in the country."

"I want you to get your ass back here and —"

"What's your home number?"

"It's unlisted."

"I *know* that. What is it?"

"McCone —"

"Please. For your favorite cheerleader?"

"Christ, you hand me a pain!" Then he sighed and recited the number. "This is emotional blackmail, you know. When you get back here, we're going to have to discuss your conduct —"

"What?"

"I said —"

"God, this is a bad connection!"

"I can hear you fine."

"Of course it's mine. I called you."

"I *know* you called me."

"*Balled* you!"

"*What?*"

"What?"

I hung up and made a run for the border.

Twenty-One

I decided to take the fast toll road to Ensenada, then pick up old Mexico 1, the highway that in the early seventies linked Tijuana with La Paz and forever changed the face of Baja California.

The 800-mile-long peninsula is a harsh, arid land, ridged by barren mountains and cut off from mainland Mexico by the Sea of Cortés. Its desert region remains pretty much the same as a century ago: peppered with cactus and hardscrabble ranches, many of which have long been abandoned. But with the advent of the highway, American tourists discovered Baja's scenic Pacific beaches and the quiet anchorages and villages along the Mar de Cortés; the 1990s have brought an increase in international trade to the peninsula's few cities.

After a brief stop at a Pemex station to buy a map, I sped along Tijuana's Calle Internacionale and turned south toward the first tollgate, noting changes. The border town's slums and shacks still existed, as did the gaudy souvenir shops and booze-and-sex traps, but mirrored-glass skyscrapers appeared on the horizon, lending the city a new sophistication. Farther south along the coast, the inevitable billboards, RV parks, condominiums, and hotels marred the beauty of some of the most breathtaking cliffs this side of Big Sur. When I reached Rosarito, which I remembered as a quiet fishing village, and found several posh-looking resort hotels, I realized that the Baja I'd loved as a child was on its way to disappearing forever.

The dry heat had pursued me from San Diego, and even in these coastal regions it didn't let up, rising with a vengeance from the dust-blown desert. It took me about an hour and a quarter to get to Ensenada. At first I thought the long arm of commercialism hadn't yet extended this far; fishing boats, a number of them bearing the insignia of Gilbert Fontes's Corona Fleet, bobbed in the harbor, and a few donkey carts crept along the streets. But then I spotted a sign in English proclaiming Ensenada the birthplace of Mexico's wine industry and offering tours and tastings; new hotels and restaurants and cantinas lined the waterfront boulevard. I got out of there as fast as I could and picked up the old highway.

About thirty minutes later I came upon a road that I thought should be the one to El

Sueño. I pulled over, consulted my map, then turned toward Punta Arrejaque, a finger of land extending northwest into the Pacific. The road was new, recently paved, running parallel to a riverbed choked with scrub vegetation. Down in it, I thought, was probably an older road; the dry riverbeds had for centuries been routes to the fishing villages that perched beside their mouths at the edge of the sea.

After several miles I noticed that the weather had changed; afternoon clouds stood on the horizon above the slate-gray sea, and the air was cooler. The road wound past ramshackle stands laden with produce and jars of olives and chili peppers; past a campground and a lookout point; past an airfield where small planes were tethered. Then it topped a rise, and I saw houses — some traditional white stucco and red tile, others of outlandish modern design — rambling over the gently sloping terrain. Pelicans wheeled above the sea as I coasted into the small commercial district of El Sueño — the dream.

The place *did* have a dreamlike quality: in the buildings' raw newness, in the smell of cooking oil and spices that drifted on the air, in the welcome cool breeze that played on my bare arms. The streets of the village were narrow but, like the road, recently paved; expensive cars crowded their curbs. The shops looked equally expensive: a jeweler, a sports outfitter, a florist, a wine broker, several galleries. A small professional complex held the offices of attorneys, doctors, and dentists. A branch of an American stock-brokerage had a sign that flashed the Dow-Jones average. People wandered along the sidewalks and in and out of the shops, stopping at produce stands heaped with corn, tomatoes, lettuce, and chilies. The majority were Americans, and all were well dressed, mostly in golf or tennis attire. No one hurried; no one seemed to have a care.

The town made me somewhat twitchy. I didn't dislike it, didn't like it, either. Its edges were simply too rounded, its ambience too manufactured for my taste. I felt as if I'd stepped onto a stage set for a drawing-room comedy that had absolutely no connection to the often grim realities of life in Baja.

I found a space to leave the car and went into a grocery that mainly stocked imported wines and gourmet items. The Mexican woman whom I asked for directions to Vía Pacífica spoke better English than some members of my family. She hesitated, then shrugged and drew me a little map, showing a winding road that branched off near the far end of town. Said "It's a fancy place, big villas. No trespassing," and looked askance at my rumpled clothing. I'd planned to buy some mineral water from her, but got my revenge by walking down the block for it. At a produce stand I allowed myself to be tempted by some cantaloupe slices. As in the shops of Tijuana, U.S. money was cheerfully accepted.

According to the woman's map Vía Pacífica looped off the main road toward the sea, then rejoined it at the base of the point. I found the turnoff, marked by stone pillars but no security kiosk or gate, and followed the blacktop past stands of yucca and prickly pear and barrel cactus; the strange and somewhat unpleasant scent of Indian tobacco traveled on the breeze. Houses in widely divergent architectural styles began to appear: pueblo-style with rough-hewn timbers and solar panels on the roofs; a steel-and-glass structure that put me in mind of the starship *Enterprise*; traditional weathered-wood beach houses like the ones you find up and down the entire Pacific coast; something that looked to be a cross between an Aztec pyramid and a bomb shelter. They clustered to the right of the pavement, on a small rise above a white sand beach. The sun was sinking toward the water now, its outline glaring through the layers of high-piled clouds.

Fontes's villa, number 117, turned out to be relatively conservative in appearance. Tan stucco with a muted blue tile roof, it was long and spacious; at one end stood a three-story wing resembling a church's bell tower; a one-story section connected it to a two-story wing at the opposite end. Unlike most of its neighbors, it was surrounded by a high stucco wall with jagged shards of glass embedded in its top; the upper-floor windows were secured with bars that did their best to blend with the architecture. A security-conscious man, Gilbert Fontes.

The automobile gate stood open, however. I slowed down and looked inside. The front yard held a fountain and an elaborate cactus garden bordered by a half-circular crushed-shell drive. A detached garage stood to the left. And in front of it was parked a maroon Volvo with a familiar California license plate.

I continued down the road a short distance, U-turned at a wide place, and went back to a beach access I'd noticed earlier. Several vehicles were drawn up there — not the sleek luxury cars belonging to El Sueño's affluent residents but rusted old sedans, one of which had been abandoned and cannibalized for parts. I parked the Tercel there, took my photographic equipment from the trunk, and spent about fifteen minutes assembling it and familiarizing myself with how it worked. Then I put on my jacket, shed my shoes, stuffed them into my oversized purse next to my father's .45, and carried it and the camera down to the beach. The sand was powdery soft and very clean; a few people were walking there, and others surf-fished. A young mother watched her two children as they splashed in the water, impervious to the chill on the air. I walked along looking at the houses until I spotted Fontes's.

It perched lower than its neighbors, with a walled terrace outfitted with clear glass baffles to protect it from the wind. The windows on this side were small and barred, too, but large doors opened to the terrace. No one was out there, but I saw a portable bar and moments later a man in a white waiter's jacket appeared, carrying some glasses. Preparing to entertain the guests from California?

The beach ended a hundred or more yards down from there at the mouth of the dry riverbed. The vegetation was thick: scrub cactus, yuccas, sycamores, and — farther back, straggling up the incline — greasewood. I kept walking that way, past a couple of old rotted wooden *pongas* — fishing boats — that Fontes and his neighbors probably allowed to remain there because they considered them picturesque. A few newer Fiberglas *pongas* were beached closer to the riverbed. As I neared it, I saw the outlines of buildings in among the vegetation — rough board shacks painted turquoise and lavender and pink, with rusted metal roofs and sheets for doors. Here and there a clothesline hung with bright garments stretched between the sycamore trunks, and in a clearing next to a trash dump strewn with shells and old car parts, children played. Women moved back and forth bearing baskets and buckets. I'd found the slums of El Sueño, carefully concealed so as not to mar the content of the hill dwellers.

After a while I turned and walked back toward the rotting *pongas*. Looked them over, then perched on one facing the sea, setting my bag beside me. I began to experiment with the camera, focusing on the swooping gulls and pelicans. As I homed in on them, I remembered the claim of the clerk at Gooden's: "You'll be able to count the pinfeathers on a baby bird's head at two hundred yards." How right he'd been! I swiveled, focused on the settlement in the riverbed. A woman's face confronted me unseeing, dark eyes cast down. I moved the lens to see what she was looking at; a knife slashed expertly into a plump tomato.

If I could make out that much detail at this distance, think what I might observe at Fontes's villa. The situation here was so perfect for my purposes that I crossed my fingers superstitiously against anything going wrong.

Spying on Fontes was one thing, but covertly watching this woman prepare her supper made me feel like a voyeur. I set the camera down and continued to contemplate the sea. If the people at the villa had noticed me, let them watch. Let them get used to a solitary tourist looking out at the Pacific and occasionally trying to photograph the curious muted sunset. After a while I'd become part of the landscape to them, merely another expensively equipped traveler displaying an unwarranted fascination with a phenomenon that happens every evening.

My back was turned to the villa, but my thoughts were very much on what might be happening there. First there was the Volvo, the one I'd followed last night when Ann Navarro drove Diane Mourning to the border. Ann Navarro, who in all likelihood didn't yet know she'd been a widow since Sunday night. Sunday night, when Stan Brockowitz had been shot to death on the mesa. Shot by Marty Salazar? No way to know for sure, but if Salazar hadn't personally shot Brockowitz, he knew who had.

Which brought me to an unpleasant possibility that I thought I'd better face right now: the possibility that Hy had shot Brockowitz. According to Ann-Marie, there was bad history between Brockowitz and Hy. And Hy had been on the mesa that night. While he'd never said it in so many words, I knew he'd killed at least once. He, like me, had stepped over that line because there had been no other choice.

No other choice. That was the key. If Hy had shot Brockowitz, it was because he'd been placed in an untenable situation. His motive would have had to be stronger than an old antagonism. Stronger than retaining possession of a two-million-dollar letter of credit.

Letter of credit. Who had it now? Hy? Doubtful. I'd begun to suspect that somehow it had been taken from him and he hadn't contacted RKI because he was attempting to recover it. Taken by whom? Salazar? Possibly, but if so, what did Salazar intend to do with it?

And then there was Gilbert Fontes. Fontes, whose estranged brother operated the firm the L.C. was drawn to. And Terramarine — that was the odd number in this equation. As was the apparent relationship between Fontes, Ann Navarro, and Diane Mourning. And there was Timothy Mourning, missing for twelve days now. If the body on the mesa had been Mourning's or even a Terramarine member's, this whole scenario would have made more sense. . . .

Most of the other people on the beach had departed. The young mother called to her children, and they reluctantly straggled up from the surf. She bundled them in towels, put her arms around their shoulders as they walked to the stairway to one of the villas. Dusk was falling fast. The smell of cooking fires began to drift from the riverbed; voices, too, in musical counterpoint. A white-haired man walked past along the shoreline, his Irish setter leaping joyously through the waves. The man gave me an incurious nod; the dog paid me no mind at all.

The darkness deepened. Fires danced down in the riverbed; I smelled fish and tortillas frying, heard men and women laughing. I twisted around and saw that the villas on the hill were now ablaze with light; music and cocktail-time chatter drifted down, as did smoke from mesquite barbecues. My stomach growled forlornly. The temperature had dropped; it was still comfortable, but as the night wore on it would grow cold. I had no heavy jacket or sweater; those things remained in bungalow 7 at La Encantadora.

Well, I told myself, you've endured far worse ordeals than a cold night on a beach.

I turned all the way around and studied Fontes's villa. The doors to the terrace stood open, and the white-jacketed waiter moved back and forth through them. No one else was out there; no one stood at any of the lighted windows. My eyes still on the house, I slipped down onto the sand, pulling my bag and the camera with me. There was an open space between the *pongas,* just large enough for the camera. I shoved it in there, found a piece of wood and used it as a shim to tilt the camera at a good angle. When it was full dark and no one moved on the beach, I lay down on my stomach, put my eye to the scope, and focused on the terrace.

The waiter was setting a plate of hors d'oeuvres on one of the tables. He distributed coasters, then arranged four cushioned chairs around it. After viewing his handiwork with apparent satisfaction, he went behind the bar and looked expectantly at the door. The lens's focus was so fine that I could see the web of lines around his eyes deepen as he smiled at the first arrivals.

I moved the camera slightly and focused on Diane Mourning's thin, humorless features. With her was the woman I'd identified as Ann Navarro. They got drinks, then carried them to the table and began a conversation. On Mourning's side, it was intense; her brow was drawn into worried creases and she spoke emphatically, bobbing her curly head to punctuate every three or four words. I was able

to lip-read a few: "no way, "he can't."
Navarro's heavy Indian features remained
calm; she spoke very little, but occasionally
made soothing gestures.

I studied Navarro with interest. She was
plain, almost homely, and apparently had the
sense to realize that elaborate trickery with
makeup would not enhance her looks. On the
whole, her mannerisms suggested she was
comfortable with herself; when she spoke she
displayed a certain confidence and authority.
Without knowing her, it was impossible for
me to tell if what her employee had said about
her — that she had no real ethical base —
was true. But observing her convinced me that
this was a woman who, once committed to
a plan such as the kidnapping, would carry
it through calmly, with attention to detail. If
she now had any regrets or any guilt, no sign
of either was apparent. While Mourning's face
was drawn with lines of strain, gaunt from
lack of sleep, Navarro's was smooth and
rested. While Mourning punctuated her conversation with nervous gestures, Navarro sat
still, entirely at ease.

Suddenly Mourning glanced toward the
door. Her face tightened and she reached for
her drink. Navarro looked that way, too; while
her expression didn't change, something
flashed in her eyes — anger, I thought, care-

fully checked but there nonetheless. I moved the lens and focused on a big man in a white dinner jacket who was crossing the terrace. He was Hispanic, in his sixties, with iron-gray hair and a flaccid, fleshy face; his thick features spread as if they were made of wax that had been left too long in the sun. Beneath the skin, however, was a hardness that hinted at a stubborn will; his eyes were equally hard and sunk deep in their sockets. Gilbert Fontes?

The man smiled in a way that managed to be both polite and condescending before he sat down across from Mourning. She nodded curtly and drained her glass, then set it down — hard, I thought. Immediately the waiter appeared with a drink for the man, took Mourning's glass away for a refill. Ann Navarro leaned across the table and said something to the man that ended in "Gilbert." Fontes, all right.

The three chatted idly for a while; I couldn't make out anything they said. Then their heads turned toward the door. Fontes's expression was welcoming, but with the trace of condescension I'd noticed when he greeted the women. Navarro's lips tightened. Fear showed in Mourning's eyes. I moved the camera and zoomed in on Marty Salazar.

Salazar was dressed as he'd been on Wednesday night, in a pale summer suit. The glare of the terrace's floodlights threw his sunken cheeks and the rattler-plate scar on his forehead into dramatic relief; my focus was so fine that I could make out the short lashes rimming his hooded eyes. As he crossed the terrace, he took a cigarette from his pocket and lighted it. I followed him with the lens.

Salazar joined the group, taking the chair to Mourning's right. She recrossed her legs, shifted away from him. He glanced knowingly at her and smirked. Navarro's nostrils pinched in disgust, but she moved her chair closer to the table and began talking earnestly with the two men. Again, I couldn't make out many of the words, but the conversation was definitely spirited. Salazar was doing most of the talking. After a few minutes he sat back and extended his arms, hands together, fingers pointing like the barrel of a gun. He jerked them as if firing — one, two, three times — then threw his head back and laughed uproariously.

No one else laughed. Fontes watched Salazar analytically, as if he were observing a rare type of snake. Navarro turned away, pressing her fingers to her temples. Mourning jerked in reaction, as if she herself had been shot. After a moment Fontes signaled to the waiter for another round of drinks.

I felt stunned, a little sick. Could Salazar

have been describing how he shot Stan Brockowitz? Surely he wouldn't do that in the presence of Brockowitz's widow — unless she'd been an accessory to the killing. Even then, though, would her reaction have been so restrained? Perhaps he was describing the way he'd shot Timothy Mourning. Perhaps Diane had been an accessory to her own husband's murder and now found the reality of it more than she could stomach.

Who knows? I thought. You really can't tell anymore *what* people will do.

The fresh drinks arrived; Mourning reached eagerly for hers. The conversation went on — in Spanish now, I thought — punctuated by headshakes, gestures of acceptance and protest, and some table pounding on Salazar's part. Mourning remained withdrawn from it, huddled in her chair, expression growing glassy. Navarro and Salazar appeared to be arguing bitterly; Fontes watched them with his cool, analytical stare.

My eyes ached from straining to see through the scope. I took a moment to rest them. It was cold now. I had no idea what time it was; my watch had mysteriously stopped, its luminous dial claiming it was only five-eleven. It seemed I'd been on this beach for countless hours. My back hurt from lying flat and tensed; my neck ached from craning it at an awkward angle; I was pretty sure a splinter from the *ponga* had worked its way through my jeans and into my ass. I rolled over, looked up at a brilliant scattering of stars. The sound of voices from the riverbed was now underscored by the strains of a world-weary guitar. It made me feel lonely. Lost.

In a sense I *was* lost. Had lost touch with the man I'd traveled all this way to find. Hy — his face, his body, his very essence — had become vague to me, obscured by a tangle of people and relationships and intrigues and crimes that really had very little to do with either of us. I felt as if I'd started along a straight corridor and somehow made a wrong turn into a maze. Too much more of this bumping my nose against its walls and I'd lose touch with everything that mattered. . . .

Movement up on the terrace. Doggedly I hunched over the camera again. Fontes and Salazar were standing. Salazar said something to Mourning and, when she didn't respond, reached down and jerked her to her feet. She stood, limp and spineless. Salazar took hold of her shoulders and turned her toward the door.

A man came through it, followed closely by Salazar's bodyguard, Jaime. The man was stocky and walked in a shambling gait; his clothing and mop of dark blond curls were disheveled. He wore wire-rimmed glasses, several days' growth of beard, and a numb, bewildered expression. When he saw the others on the terrace, he stopped. Jaime shoved him forward and he stumbled, then stood facing them, shaking his head.

I pressed the camera's shutter.

Ann Navarro's expression went quickly from shock to chagrin. She looked from the man to Fontes, mouth turning down. Fontes gave her a long, measured look of triumph.

Diane Mourning cried out as she recognized her husband. Timothy stumbled toward her, but she stepped back, face horror-stricken, putting out both hands, as if to fend him off.

I pressed the shutter again.

Movement behind me. A step on sand so soft that it had cushioned the others. A hand across my mouth before I could roll over or reach for the gun. A voice, low and so close to my ear that I felt moist, warm breath.

"See anything interesting, McCone?"

Shock flooded me. I wrenched away, twisted around.

Looked up into the grimly humorous eyes of my missing lover.

Twenty-Two

I stared at him in shock, unable to believe he'd turned up alive and whole on this remote strip of sand. My lips were parted, but I couldn't speak.

Hy nudged me aside, lay flat, and put his eye to the camera's viewfinder. I flopped back on the sand, landed hard, as if I'd lost my equilibrium.

"Son of a bitch!" Hy whispered.

I wasn't sure which of the things transpiring up there on the terrace so fascinated him, nor did I care. Still disoriented and struggling to comprehend this startling turn of events, I tugged at his elbow. He swatted my hand away, and I saw that the left sleeve of his dirty T-shirt had been ripped out and his upper arm sported a bandage.

"You're hurt!"

"Ssh! Flesh wound, that's all. I've got Salazar to thank for it."

Finally he turned away from the scope, and I saw he was deeply tanned and wore a short, stubbly beard. His hair curled wildly, as disheveled as Timothy Mourning's.

"What happened?"

"Tell you later. We'd better get out of here."

"We can't leave while they're —"

"Going inside, all of them." He pushed up, pulled the camera out of the hole, and hefted it. "Come on, somebody might've spotted us. You took an awful chance here, McCone."

"What about you, Ripinsky? What the hell have you been —"

"Save it." He shoved my bag toward me. "Let's go."

He was giving orders. For nearly a week I'd tracked him. With very little to go on, I'd followed only a few paces behind, then come out even — maybe ahead. And he had the nerve to give orders!

I choked back a sarcastic remark; common sense dictated we do as he said. "Keep low," I whispered, giving an order of my own, and began moving toward the beach access.

"Where're you going?"

"I've got a car up at the parking area. We'll get it, stake out the front of the house in case any of them decide to leave. While we do that, you can explain some things."

"Forget it, McCone. The local cops and a private security force patrol up there. To say nothing of Salazar and his pals. What do you think I was doing when I got this" — his hand touched the bandage — "at around four o'clock this morning?"

I hesitated. "Well, I can't leave the car there. If they find it, the rental contract'll tell them all they need to know."

"How do they know about you —"

"Save it, Ripinsky," I said in a perfect parody of him.

His lips twitched in a faint smile, and he remained crouched on the sand, eyes glittering in the lights from the villas. "Okay, you're right. We've got to get that car. We'll need it later on, anyway."

We! He could disappear for all that time and never bother to contact me. He could place me in a situation where the danger was tripled because of all I didn't know. He could sneak up on me on a deserted beach in a strange land and act as if it was perfectly normal to find me there. And then he could blithely make the assumption that we were acting in partnership. All that, with no explanations!

Suddenly I was seized by an uncharacteristic desire to swat him right smack across the bridge of his hawk nose. I restrained myself, aware on some level that my relief at finding him alive and reasonably whole — or him finding me, to put it more accurately — had given my anger release. Now I could both recognize and admit that I'd been terribly angry with him ever since this whole business began.

The realization didn't make me feel any better. I tried to speak, strangled on the words, and simply began creeping toward the beach access.

At the top of the path I paused, hand on my father's gun, scanning the parking area. A couple of the older vehicles were still there, the Tercel nestled companionably between them. Hy came up behind me, his hand moving in such a way that I knew he had a gun tucked under the T-shirt in the waistband of his jeans. In concert, our breath slowed as we watched and listened. When I was satisfied no one waited there, I touched his arm and we moved to the car.

Once inside, I asked, "Any idea where to go from here?"

"Yeah. Turn right, drive past Fontes's place, and keep going. By the riverbed there's a dirt track leading toward the beach. Take it."

I started the engine. "We're going down where the shacks are?"

"Uh-huh. People there've been letting me stay in an abandoned one since last night."

"Is that where you spotted me from?"

"Right."

I turned onto the road. "How long have you been in Baja?"

"Too damn long. And I'd feel a whole lot better talking about this after we get to the shack." Strain was eroding his speech — pain, too.

"Have you seen a doctor about that bullet wound?"

"They've got a woman down there who's better than any doctor I ever went to. I'm okay, just tired. But I'm glad to see you, even if you have done something funny to your hair." With an effort he smiled and touched my cheek.

I sped up as we passed Fontes's villa. The automobile gate was shut now, and only muted light showed in the windows.

Hy added, "You've got a lot of explaining to do, too, you know."

"That could take all night."

"McCone, we've got the rest of our lives."

The road was deserted, the gates to most of the villas closed. After a little way, the riverbed appeared — untamed nature infringing on a tenuous civilization. Hy showed me the rutted track through the sycamores and cacti; I followed it toward the firelight. He pointed to a dilapidated shack that stood some distance apart from the others, and I pulled the Tercel in next to it.

As we got out, two figures approached through the trees, a bobbing flashlight beam moving along the ground in front of them. My hand went to my gun, but Hy stayed it. He called out to them in Spanish, and they slowed their pace, their posture altering subtly. Two male voices spoke in response.

The men came up to us and stopped, rays from the flashlight reflecting upward and glinting off the rifle that the first man carried; a handgun was tucked into the belt of the second. Their faces were hard and weather-toughened, their eyes wary and knowing and as ancient as the mountains that form the peninsula's backbone. The old dangerous realities of life in Baja had been banished from outposts of high-tech civilization like El Sueño, but they'd retreated only so far as the edge of the brush.

Hy put an arm around my shoulders and drew me forward, telling them my name. To me he added, "This is Juan."

The man with the rifle nodded.

"And Tomás. Tomás didn't want me to go after you alone, but I thought two of us might attract the wrong kind of attention. He offered to fetch you for me, but I was afraid of what you might do to him." He translated the latter into Spanish, and both men laughed. Hy joined in, but unconvincingly; he'd been speaking the truth.

The three spoke for a while longer; I could follow the conversation well enough to know the men were questioning Hy about what was going on at Fontes's villa. Then Tomás asked Hy something else, and he asked me, "Have you eaten?"

"No, but I'm not hungry."

"Maybe you will be later. Tomás says his wife will bring us food; there're some people down by the fires that it's best don't see us."

"She doesn't need to —"

"She wants to. And she also wants to rebandage my arm." He spoke to the men again, thanking them for coming to greet us, and led me toward the shack.

It was a single room: rough board walls, an iron roof that in places didn't quite meet them, a packed dirt floor. A sleeping bag lay in its center, Hy's carryall beside it. He turned on a small flashlight, then dragged the bag toward the wall; stuck the carryall behind it like a bolster, removed his gun from his waistband, and tucked it underneath. "It's not much, but have a seat," he said.

I did, feeling aches in muscles that had been forced into an awkward position for hours. I looked at my watch; still stopped. I smacked it; the second hand began to move again. The flashlight's rays illuminated only the center of the claustrophobic little shack, leaving the rest in strange, angled shadows.

"These people," I said, "how come they're helping you?"

"Because they're generous, even though they have very little. They fish in ways that don't unnecessarily destroy marine life. And they hate Gilbert Fontes as much as I do. It's a bond, having that in common."

Hy seemed charged with nervous energy now. He paced back and forth, into the light, back into the shadows. "In the past dozen years, Mexico's doubled its fishing catch. There's a lot of government pressure to export more in order to bring in foreign currency; they even license the right to take the lobsters and abalones and shrimp to certain co-ops. Trawlers make big sweeps with the nets, gather everything up, pick out what they want. Then they shovel tons of dead or dying fish off the decks into the sea. *Escama,* trash fish, they call it. But it's perfectly good food that hungry people could eat."

I watched him pace, only half listening to what he was saying. I'd never seen him so hyper before. This was the Hy of the environmental protests, the man who defied and taunted the opposition, engaged in head-on confrontations with the police. There was a time after his wife, Julie, died, I'd been told, when he repeatedly hurled himself into the fray with little regard for his life or safety, but people who knew him then said he'd mellowed in recent years. Now it seemed he'd slipped back into that intense, perhaps self-destructive mode. Was it the pain from his gunshot wound that made him this way?

No, I decided, what primarily operated here was psychic pain. Exacerbated by the physical, I was sure, but deeply rooted in the years before I met him, before Julie died, even before he met her — the woman whose faith in him, he'd once told me, had kept him from destroying what little was left of his life. A week ago last Wednesday he'd reconnected with people from those nine lost years; the collision had released emotions that were eating at him in ways I couldn't begin to imagine.

Would he finally share the secrets of those years? I hoped so, but somehow I doubted it.

There was a tap on the wall next to the curtained doorway. A slender woman with heavy Indian features entered, smiling shyly. She carried a basket filled with fruit and rolled tortillas that gave off a spicy smell; a clean bandage rode incongruously on top of a melon. In her other hand she held what looked to be a jug of home-brewed wine.

Hy said, "This is Sofia." He spoke to her

350

in Spanish, thanking her for the food, and she replied, motioning for him to sit down. As she knelt beside him and began unwrapping his bandage, he said, "Sofia cleaned my wound after I staggered in here early this morning. Put a poultice on it — leaves and God knows what. Evil-smelling, but it made my arm feel better. She's been monitoring my temperature all day; it's only a hair above normal."

Sofia began swabbing the wound with liquid from a plastic bottle. Hy's lips tightened and he looked away. After a moment he said, "What I'm telling you, McCone, is that physically I'm okay. The only thing wrong with me is that I feel like an asshole."

Sofia seemed to understand that. Maybe by now the word "asshole" has — by virtue of their plenitude — achieved the status of an international password. She made soothing sounds, then smiled sympathetically at me. After all, when she was done here, she could leave; I, on the other hand, was stuck with him. Finally she departed, motioning at the basket and the jug and murmuring *"Buenas noches."*

I asked, "Why do you feel like an asshole?"

"Long story."

"I'm listening."

"What say we eat first?"

I had to admit that the smell of the food

was making me ravenous. We sat cross-legged facing each other and burrowed into the basket. The tortillas were wrapped around a fiery fish-and-vegetable mixture and fried. The melon dripped sweet juice. In contrast, the wine was raw and very, very dry. We ate with our fingers, wiping them on our jeans; we drank from a shared paper cup. When we'd eaten all the food, Hy poured another cupful of wine and we leaned against his carryall — shoulder to shoulder, arm to arm, thigh to thigh, toes touching occasionally — and told our respective stories.

I went first, since he seemed to need more time. He listened thoughtfully, asking an occasional question, making an infrequent comment. Had I met Dan Kessell? What had I thought of Gage Renshaw? Renshaw hadn't really *meant* it when he said he intended to kill him? He *had?* Well, son of a bitch!

When I got to the part about learning about the body on the mesa and thinking it was Hy who had been shot, he became very still, seemed to draw away from me, turn inward. After a moment he put his hand under my chin, tipped my face up so he could look into my eyes. "If I'd known, I'd have gotten in touch with you one way or another. You've got to believe that."

"Why *didn't* you contact me?"

352

"Same reason you haven't been in touch with your friends or family — too dangerous."

I went on with my story, speaking more swiftly now. When I finished, Hy lapsed into another withdrawn silence. Finally he said, "I've always known you're good at what you do, but I didn't realize how good. I'm not sure I would've gotten this far if our positions had been reversed."

I shrugged. "I've had a lot of practice tracing people. Your turn now."

Tension flooded his long body. He drank wine, poured some more. "Well, what you don't know starts at that clearing off Highway One-oh-one in San Benito County."

"What about —"

"It starts there," he said firmly.

So the past was still to be off limits. In spite of my pointed references to his friendship with Gage Renshaw and Dan Kessell and my stressing how Renshaw had mentioned giving him a "taste of the old action," he intended to keep the door closed on those subjects. I wasn't sure how I felt about that, how it would affect our future relationship. But I didn't want to make an issue of it now; there were too many other things I needed to know.

"Go on."

"Okay, something seemed wrong with the whole setup from the first. Diane Mourning was too unemotional, even for a basically pragmatic and unimaginative person. And Gage had told me the kidnapping might be of the husband's own manufacture. Terramarine was another thing that didn't fit: I'd never known them to keep such a low profile. And Colores, the firm the L.C. was drawn to: I know something about Emanuel Fontes, and he's not the sort to mess around with eco-terrorists, especially the ones who aren't particularly competent. So I went down there to San Benito expecting a surprise — and I got it."

"Stan Brockowitz?"

"Uh-huh. I recognized him, even though he had on this really silly disguise. He recognized me, too, started to take off. I gunned my car, thinking I could stop him, and ran into a damn rock."

"But you didn't tell Renshaw what had happened."

"No. I was starting to get a very bad hit off the situation. I doubted the kidnappers would contact RKI again if Brockowitz was sure I'd recognized him. But in case they did, I figured the less Renshaw knew, the more convincing his negotiations with the kidnappers would be. And I suppose that underneath it all I don't really trust Gage."

"Why not?"

"History," he said curtly. "Anyway, I guess

Brockowitz wasn't sure whether I'd made him or not, because the contact woman — Navarro, I found out later — called almost immediately, and I flew to San Diego. You know pretty much what went down there. Funny you getting that lead on me because I mistakenly approached the young woman at the market. I went down there, waited a long time, and was fairly pissed when I saw her crossing the parking lot. I blew it, too, used Brockowitz's name. Didn't make that mistake when Navarro finally showed."

"Hy, why do you suppose Navarro used her own name?"

"Slip of the tongue when she called me at the Bali Kai. I could tell she was rattled, wanted to take it back as soon as she said it. Anyway, when she showed up at the market, she gave me a map, told me to be at that place on Monument Road at eleven. I went down there, checked the area out, but I didn't go up on the mesa, never even noticed the road." He shook his head. "Been away from the action too long, I guess."

I ignored the questions the comment gave rise to; asking them wouldn't do me any good, anyway. "It was Brockowitz who picked you up in the Jeep?"

"Right."

"What happened on the mesa?"

He sipped wine, eyes focused at some point in the darkness — both the darkness surrounding us in the shack and, I guessed, a pocket of it within himself. After a moment he said, "Brockowitz told me he had Mourning up on the mesa. He was armed; so was I. We drove up there. It felt wrong, but I wasn't about to back out; my job was to bring Mourning home. Brockowitz suggested we leave our guns in the Jeep. I agreed; I had a backup piece. So did he, I found out later. Probably planned to kill me after I gave him the L.C. I knew too much. We went into the burned-out adobe."

I could picture the scene: darkness, except for the distant lights of Tijuana and San Diego, a few fires glowing on the hill where hundreds of Mexicans waited for their chance to make a run for it, icy wind off the sea. And the adobe: formless, black. Two men: both edgy; one orchestrating events; the other trying to stay one step ahead of him.

"Mourning wasn't there, of course," Hy went on. "No one was. Brockowitz had a torchlight. He set it on the ground, told me to hand over the L.C."

"And then he'd produce Mourning?"

"He had no intention of doing that. Mourning, he said, had planned the kidnapping; the two million was his money, and he had a right

356

to it. I asked what about Diane Mourning — wasn't it her money, too? Brockowitz seemed to find that very funny. He said Phoenix Labs was on its way to Chapter Eleven and that one of the Mournings should get clear with something. Stan was getting ready to go for his piece, I think, when Salazar came through the door." He paused. "Of course, I didn't know his name at the time. To me, he was just your run-of-the-mill bandit."

"Did Brockowitz go for his piece then?"

"Nope, he froze. I got mine out, but Salazar shot it right out of my hand, just like in the western movies." Hy's smile was pained, self-mocking. "He got me up against the wall, went through my pockets, took my cash. All the time Brockowitz stood there looking stunned. Tough guy, Stan."

I felt as if I were living the scene as he told it. I could feel the terror trapped within the adobe, smell Brockowitz's fear-sweat mixing with the sea air and cordite. . . .

Hy went on, "The L.C. was in an envelope inside my carryall." He patted our bolster. "Salazar ripped it open, found the L.C., looked at it. And then he just went crazy. Screamed, 'This is what you call a fuckin' ransom? Just a piece of *paper*, man?' He must have been outside long enough to hear everything we'd said about the Mournings and the two-mil-

357

lion-dollar payoff. Anyway, he tossed the bag at me and went for Brockowitz. And that's when Stan went for the gun in his pocket." Hy shook his head. "Dumb shit had stuck a thirty-eight in his *pocket*, for Christ's sake. It snagged. *Stupid* bastard."

"And Salazar shot him."

"Yeah. And I dove out of there, using the bag as protection. Ran like a fool expecting a bullet in my back. Salazar didn't even fire."

"Where'd you go?"

"Down the far side of the mesa, where that horse ranch is. Didn't even think about the rental car I'd left on Monument Road; somebody probably hot-wired it and drove it across the border before daybreak."

"And then what?"

"I got lucky for a change. Fell in with some illegals who were headed for a safe house in San Ysidro. They were leery of me, but those people are so afraid, and I spoke Spanish and looked like I was in more trouble than they were. They let me come along, and the next morning I started asking around. I'd gotten a good look at Salazar; he's distinctive, well known down there. By eleven I had a name and address. Got some money — Salazar didn't take my credit cards — set myself up with another car, and staked out that alley off of Island Avenue where he's got his place."

"How come those charges didn't show up on the account when Kate checked with American Express?"

He grinned wryly. "Because I actually found one of my own cards that hadn't expired. Given what had gone down, I didn't want to involve the foundation any more than I already had."

"Okay, and then?"

"Nothing until Tuesday night. Around eight Salazar and a big guy — I think the same one who was on Fontes's terrace tonight — came out in a hurry. The guy drove him to General Aviation at Lindbergh; a Cessna picked up Salazar, and the other guy left. I hung around, talked to the line people. One of them told me the Cessna belonged to Gilbert Fontes. I got him to check with Clearance Delivery; the pilot had said he was VFR for El Sueño, Baja."

"Ironic," I said. "You must have been flying out just as I was flying in. We missed each other by only that much."

"Negative. I drove. These small airfields, any stranger attracts attention. Trouble was, the car broke down north of Ensenada. I had to have it towed, notify the rental company. Then I hitched a couple of rides, didn't get here till late Wednesday night. This whole venture has turned into a black comedy of errors."

"So where did you stay? Here?"

"Not that night. There isn't even a hotel in the town, and they shut everything down at sunset. I ended up sleeping on the beach. The next morning, much the worse for wear, I went into the village, bought the sleeping bag and supplies, started asking around about Fontes. Wrong move again. There's too much money to be had here; the shopkeepers don't want to gossip or give out addresses — particularly not to a scruffy-looking gringo, even if he's buying things on a credit card. So I wandered around, pinpointed Vía Pacífica as the most likely area for a guy with a Cessna to live. Spotted these shacks and struck up an acquaintance with people who've got no stake in protecting the rich folks."

Hy's words were slurred with weariness now. He reached for the wine jug, but then let his hand fall limp to the sleeping bag. I said, "Tell me the rest of it in brief, then get some rest."

"In brief, I've been watching Fontes's place ever since. No sign of Salazar until he shot me early this morning, although Fontes's car fetched somebody from the airstrip a couple of hours before Diane Mourning and Ann Navarro showed up last night. The way I figure it, Salazar made a quick return trip to San Diego on Tuesday night or sometime before you saw him on Wednesday, then came

360

back late on Friday."

"Why, I wonder?"

Hy shrugged.

"He shot you because he caught you prowling around there?"

"Caught and recognized me. Brave fellow that I am, I ran like hell again. He fired three times, the second shot winged me."

"I'll bet that was the shooting incident he was acting out tonight for Mourning and Navarro's benefit."

"Probably. Don't know why he's so proud of it; he has to realize he didn't kill me."

"I think the purpose of telling about it was to intimidate the women."

"He succeed?"

"Scared Mourning. Navarro just seemed disgusted."

"Huh. Well, McCone, that's my story. Today I just hung around the riverbed, letting Sofia doctor me and . . . oh, hell, probably feeling sorry for myself. And then I looked down the beach and saw you, sitting there on that *ponga,* so nonchalant and confident."

"I'm not at all sure about the nonchalant and confident part," I said, "but obviously you were surprised."

"You know, I should've been, but I really wasn't. Maybe I knew you'd be along sooner or later." He placed his hand high up on my thigh, fingers taut, almost hurting me. "Jesus, I've missed you."

"Missed you, too. When I thought you were dead . . . I don't want to remember that." I turned my head, pressed my lips against his neck, desire flooding my body.

He said, "D'you understand why I feel like an asshole, McCone?"

"You shouldn't. What went wrong wasn't anything you could control. And any intelligent person would've turned tail and run from Salazar."

"I don't know." He pulled me down until we were lying flat. "I don't know, McCone," he repeated, "I'm just not the man I used to be." Then his head flopped onto my shoulder, his breath deepened and slowed, and he fell asleep.

I lay holding him, my cheek against his shaggy hair, tamping down desire. His heart beat strong and steady, his breath came regularly, but every now and then he'd moan softly or twitch.

I tightened my arms around him. Silently told him, You're twice the man I thought you were. It takes one hell of a man to admit his mistakes, an even better one not to make excuses for them.

All of which led me to suspect that what had happened in the nine years he refused to share with me was very bad indeed.

Twenty-Three

Sunday, June 13

Hy tossed and mumbled most of the night, but he slept on. My own rest was fitful. A couple of times I got up to use the facilities — as my mother would say, even in a situation like this when the facilities were a clump of Indian tobacco a few yards from the shack. The second time, at around five in the morning, I couldn't bring myself to go back inside right away and went to sit on the hood of the Tercel, breathing the cold sea air and listening to the silence.

That was one thing I owed Hy: my newfound ability to listen to the silence. Before our trip to the White Mountains — God, had it been only two weeks ago? — I'd found the echoing quiet of vast open spaces oppressive and lonesome. But in a very few days he'd shown me how to be at peace with it; tonight, with only the faint sound of surf to break the stillness, I felt comforted.

Not that I felt at peace. Overwhelmed was more like it. Again there had been too many changes with too little time to absorb them. Hy was alive; that was a gift. But he seemed far more damaged by the past week's events than was justified. And he was as determined as ever to keep his past walled away from me. I wasn't yet sure how I would deal with either of those things, wasn't sure how they would affect us in the future. And then there was my own future — the one I needed to re-create. What would that be? And what part would Hy play in it?

I just didn't know.

To keep from brooding, I forced my attention to the situation at Fontes's villa. Posed some questions, came to a few tentative conclusions. Posed some more questions to ask Hy when he woke. And finally returned to the shack.

Hy was awake. I saw his eyes glitter in the faint light from my flash, and then his hand snaked under the carryall for his gun.

"It's me," I said quickly.

He let out a long breath, withdrew his hand. "Jesus, McCone!"

"Sorry."

As I came closer, he reached up and grasped my wrist. Pulled me down, rolled my body against his, hands moving under the back of my shirt. His palms were like fine sandpaper, his fingernails jagged. I winced as one scraped my skin. Our lips touched, cracked and dry; his skin felt parched and fiery. Our bodies didn't mesh as usual; limbs tangled, joints banged together. We took each other with most of our clothes on.

I couldn't stay with it; the discomfort kept getting in the way of pleasure. It was like having sex with a stranger — one whose need was overpowering, one in whom violence was only loosely leashed. As we finished, I felt a step removed. He seemed to experience no pleasure, only release. We rolled away from each other, lay silent in the graying light. It was the first time that sex had created a barrier between us.

A tap on the wall outside. Hy stirred first, pulled his clothing together, went to see who it was. A voice spoke softly, swiftly, in Spanish. Hy stepped outside, then returned.

"That was Tomás," he said. "We have to get out of here."

I'd already been dressing. Now I stood. "What's wrong?"

"Trouble at Fontes's villa. Nobody knows what, but it looks bad. Cops all over the place, an ambulance, and now they're evacuating somebody by helicopter."

I listened, heard distant flapping. "A shooting, do you think?"

"Maybe." Hy was rolling up the sleeping bag. "Tomás is afraid the cops'll canvass the area. When there's a crime, they always come here, use it as an excuse to push people around. It'll only make it worse for them if the Federales find out they have a couple of gringos staying with them."

"Where should we go?"

"South, to a lookout point Tomás told me about. He'll come there later, after he finds out what went down."

I grabbed my oversized purse. "Let's go."

The lookout was on the tip of a smaller point some ten miles south. Beyond its rock wall, the Pacific lay flat and gray; salt air misted the car's windshield. The only other vehicle in the graveled parking area was an ancient VW bus with California plates, dented and painted in faded rainbow colors. A bumper sticker commanded us to Question Authority, and a line of empty beer cans and a wine jug sat on the ground below it. I was sure that eventually at least one unreconstructed hippie would emerge from the bus, probably with a bad hangover.

Hy and I sat in the car, staring moodily at the sea. After a while he touched my hair, pushing a lock of it behind my ear.

366

I asked, "So you really think I've done something funny to it, huh?"

"Actually I like it. It's you. Kind of a shock, though, to see somebody's gone and changed on you in such a short time."

"I could say the same."

He sighed. "I know. Let's you and me just get through this shit, okay? Maybe things still won't be the same, but who knows? They might even be better."

Slowly I nodded.

"So what d'you think went down at Fontes's place, McCone?"

I'd been puzzling about that all the way here. "A medical emergency or a shooting. Knowing who his houseguests were, I'd opt for a shooting."

"Which guest was it?"

"The shooter or the victim?" I shrugged, thinking back to my predawn speculations. "Hy, Salazar waited till Tuesday before he flew down here?"

"Uh-huh. Tuesday night around eight."

"Why wait all that time? Why not bring the L.C. to Fontes as soon as he took it off you? I presume he brought it because it was drawn to a company owned by Fontes's family."

"Maybe he didn't know what he had at first, or what to do with it. He was one disappointed dude when he saw he'd held Brockowitz and me up for a piece of paper."

"So it took him till Tuesday to figure that out, and then he contacted the wrong Fontes."

"Salazar probably knew Emanuel wouldn't deal with a punk like him. And he's probably known Gilbert for a long time. I've heard that when the Corona Fleet puts into San Diego, there's more being taken off those seiners than tuna."

"Drugs?"

He shrugged. "That's what they say."

"Okay, Gilbert sent his plane for Salazar. Salazar came down here and did what? Offered to sell the L.C. to Fontes, I'll bet."

"Sounds like the way he'd operate."

"But Gilbert couldn't put the L.C. through; he holds no interest in Colores."

"So what would you do in Fontes's place?"

I thought. "I'd resell the L.C. to the company whose account it's drawn on. He contacted Diane Mourning, who by all rights should have gone straight to RKI."

"But she didn't."

"No, instead she went to Ann Navarro. Why?"

"You say Navarro buys her merchandise from Colores. That probably means she's the one with the contact at Colores — somebody who can activate the L.C."

"How would Diane know that? How would she know her husband set up his kidnapping in collusion with Navarro and Brockowitz?"

He frowned; then his eyes grew thoughtful.

I said, "Last night, just before you came up to me on the beach, I watched Salazar's bodyguard bring Timothy out onto the terrace. Mourning looked bad, worse than in the photo that was sent to RKI. He was stumbling, obviously disoriented. He saw Diane and started toward her. Natural: his wife, safety. But what did Diane do?"

Hy raised an eyebrow.

"She threw up her arms," I said, "as if to fend him off. As if she was afraid he meant to harm her."

"And that means . . . ?"

"There's only one thing it could mean: Timothy didn't arrange for the kidnapping. Diane did. And she was afraid he'd figured that out."

Hy considered.

I went on, "Diane had two reasons for doing so. One Brockowitz told you: Phoenix Labs is about to go into Chapter Eleven. Quite a different picture than their chief financial officer presented to me when I talked with her on Tuesday. The second Gage Renshaw told me: he sensed Timothy was going to move on and not take Diane with him. Pretty soon he wouldn't be any good to her alive, so why not cash in on his death?"

"Insurance?"

I shook my head. "Renshaw says Timothy didn't believe in it, either keyman or anti-terrorist. A ransom that would bleed away whatever cash was left in Phoenix's accounts was how Diane chose to go. She probably had to give Brockowitz a hefty cut of the two million for his part in the kidnapping, but what was left would still have been better than nothing."

"How did she know Stan would arrange something like that, though? As far as I know, he's always stuck to white-collar crime."

"When this is all over, maybe we'll know. Tell me about Brockowitz," I added. "What was he like?"

"Out to get whatever he could for himself. At first he wanted to be a star in the environmental movement. When that didn't work out, he got petulant and said fuck the environment. Founded his firm to get back at the people who'd ousted him. Along the way he discovered he liked money. Not what it could buy, from what people tell me, although he lived well. But the real appeal was money for its own sake, piling up numbers. He was one of those guys who would've been happy to do anything for money — didn't matter what, or on whose side."

"And Navarro?"

"She's a little harder to figure out. Has never been allied with any cause except furthering her own interests. Her people are poor, live somewhere in southern Baja, but they managed to scrape up the money to send her to school in California. She never finished, married a U.S. citizen, got her green card, then divorced him. In the years before she met Brockowitz, she developed three successful retail operations. She and Stan got together, I'm told, when he wandered into her shop in San Juan Capistrano a couple of years ago. They must've recognized a mutual acquisitiveness and lack of scruples. One guy I know calls their marriage 'an unholy little alliance.' "

"Not too well liked, huh?"

"Not by environmentalists *or* anti-environmentalists. So far as I know, neither had a friend in the world except each other."

"And now he's dead, and she's alone."

"Or she may be dead, too, if that's who was shot at Fontes's place."

We were silent for a moment. The antiquated VW bus began to rock; a big guy with a beard halfway down his chest and practically no hair on his head stumbled out. He wore a rumpled tie-dyed shirt and jeans and a pained scowl. Genus, hippie; species, unreconstructed. He shambled over to the edge of the lookout, unzipped, and urinated.

Turned while zipping up and nodded casually to us, then climbed back into the bus.

Hy and I exchanged wry smiles. I asked, "How does all this sound to you so far?"

"Pretty solid. The Terramarine thing was just a cover, because Brockowitz knew they were one group that wouldn't deny it if the press got hold of the kidnapping story. Where d'you suppose they've been keeping Tim all this time?"

"Well, Brockowitz and Navarro have a big isolated house in eastern Orange County."

"Why keep him alive at all?"

"I suppose they thought they needed to be able to produce him for RKI until they collected the ransom. Navarro probably didn't know *what* to do with him when Stan didn't show up again."

"She doesn't know Stan's dead?"

"I doubt it. By the time they got an I.D. on the body, Navarro'd already come to Baja. And when I spoke with the detective in charge of the case yesterday afternoon, he said they were withholding Brockowitz's name from the press pending notification of next of kin."

Hy nodded. "Okay, another question: who decided to bring Tim Mourning down here, and why?"

That was one of the things I'd considered as I sat outside the shack before dawn. "Fontes and Salazar probably figured out where Mourning was — after all, Salazar must've taken Brockowitz's I.D. off his body after he shot him — and sent Jaime to Blossom Hill for him once Navarro was down here. As for why they all came here, I think they gathered at the villa to bargain. Fontes has the L.C. Navarro has the contact who can put it through. Mourning wants her cut. Salazar's either got a stake in it or is working for Fontes."

"You know all that for sure?"

"I don't *know* anything, but it's the feeling I got from watching them on the terrace last night. It reminded me of a plea-bargaining session. Navarro acted forceful, as if she had all the evidence on her side — the defense attorney. Mourning seemed frightened, but stubborn — the defendant. The men played good prosecutor–bad prosecutor. Salazar's function was to intimidate, and his tactics weakened Diane. Fontes — he stayed cool, said very little, but exerted a strong presence. And then they dropped their bomb."

"Timothy."

"Right. When Timothy stumbled out there, Diane panicked. And Navarro was shocked, kind of chagrined. She knew their grabbing him had tipped the scales."

"And that brings us to the big question:

what happened there this morning?"

"A question we can't answer until Tomás shows up." I looked at my watch. Amazingly, it was only quarter to nine. Had I reset it since I got it going again? Yes, last night while we talked.

The door to the VW bus opened again and a woman with long, matted hair lurched out, took off at a run toward the edge of the parking area, and knelt, vomiting into the brush. After a while she dragged herself back to the bus, paying us no notice.

Hy said, "I'm just as glad that decade's over."

"*They* don't know it ended."

"Now that I think of the seventies and eighties, maybe they're not so bad off."

"What about the nineties?" I asked lightly.

"Too early to tell. You hold any hope for them?"

Our eyes met; I felt a stirring of our old wordless communication. "Some parts of them I do," I said, entwining my fingers with his.

Tomás didn't arrive until after ten. As he got out of an old pickup with a winch for hoisting a boat on its bed, he looked grave. Hy unlocked the back door of the rental car; Tomás got in, cupping his hands and lighting a cigarette in an odd furtive manner. As he spoke with Hy, I was able to follow most of what he said; when I couldn't, Hy interjected a translation.

The police had come to the riverbed and questioned everyone about a drifter who had been seen on the beach and in the village — a tall, thin man with a craggy face and a stubbly beard. They were also interested in an American woman who had been sitting on the beach with an expensive camera around sunset the previous evening. The police wanted to talk with them about a shooting that had occurred outside Fontes's villa at about five that morning.

Hy asked, *"Que?"*

A young blond woman, Tomás told him. She had been shot in the back on the beach and sustained a punctured kidney. The helicopter had taken her to the trauma unit at Ensenada.

Diane Mourning.

I told Hy to ask if anyone had gone with her.

No, Tomás replied. He'd been curious about the situation at Fontes's house himself, so he'd gone into the village and asked around. The woman had gone alone, and no one else had left there since. The automobile gate was locked, and no one intended to fly anywhere; Fontes's pilot had been given the day off.

Hy continued talking with Tomás, but I lost the thread of the conversation, thinking back instead to around five that morning, when I'd been outside the shack. Mourning could not have been shot on the beach; it was a place where sound carried, and I'd heard nothing. Why had the people at the villa lied to the police? To shift attention away from themselves? Perhaps they'd seen it as a convenient opportunity to focus suspicion on Hy and me? But that didn't feel right. The last thing they would want was for Hy to tell his story to the authorities. And so far as I knew, they weren't aware I was in El Sueño.

Tomás was shaking Hy's hand. He nodded to me, then slipped out of the backseat and walked toward his truck. "Where's he going?" I asked.

"Home. He's lost his morning's fishing as is."

"What about us?"

"We can't go back there."

"I know. But now what?"

"Good question."

We were silent for a while, watching the gray of the sea pale as the sun silvered the cloud cover. The VW bus started with a puff of dark exhaust, lurched into reverse, then drove toward the road. As it passed us, its driver waved jauntily.

I said, "Mourning wasn't shot on the beach, you know," and explained.

"You think she was shot inside the villa, then."

"Probably."

"By whom?"

"Salazar?"

"Guy's got to be the world's worst shot, then. And why'd he let her live?"

"I suppose it could have been an accident."

"So they moved her to the beach and tried to throw suspicion on us."

I shook my head. "They may have moved her, but I don't think they were the ones who alerted the police to us. What probably happened was that the Federales canvassed the neighbors and came up with our descriptions."

"Huh." He was silent for a moment. "Back to the immediate question: what do we do now? We can't stay around here."

"Go back to San Diego?"

"And do what? Besides, look at us. You're grubby, and I've seen spiffier guys than me being brought into detox. You really want to brave the border control in this condition, when the Federales may have requested them to pick up and hold?"

"No, but I suppose appearances can be improved."

Again we fell silent. I knew his objection

to returning to San Diego wasn't based on a fear of being held by the border control; he just plain wasn't willing to give this thing up yet.

After a bit I said, "Okay, Ripinsky, if you had a choice, what would you do?"

He answered without hesitation. "Snatch Mourning and the L.C. Take them both across the border and turn them over to RKI. Clear my name with the people who —" Abruptly he stopped speaking.

"The people who what?"

"Give it a rest, McCone. Let's just say they're the people I knew when I was a better man than I am now. The people I knew when things like a good name still mattered."

And that was all I'd get on the subject for now. "Okay, how do you propose to do that?"

"Damned if I know."

I bit my lip, thought for a while. There were a few possibilities, but I wasn't sure they were good enough to stake my freedom — maybe my life — on.

I got out of the car and walked over to the wall by the sea. Waves smashed against rocks far below, their spray spurting up, then cascading down the cliffs. For a moment I tried to calculate risks, weigh odds, estimate my margin of error. Then gave it up because I knew — finally, once and for all — that I wasn't the kind of woman who hedged her bets.

Hy came up behind me, put his hands on my shoulders, his body warm against my back. "It's not your job, McCone," he told me.

He'd said something similar to me on a moonlit night several months before when we'd driven into a place called Stone Valley. "This isn't your fight, McCone," he'd told me then. And I'd replied, "In some ways, no. But in another, it is."

Now I thought of Timothy Mourning's horror-stricken face in the photo that had been sent to RKI. Of his numb bewilderment as he'd stumbled onto the terrace last night. And I thought of the promise I'd made myself when I set out to find Hy.

I repeated my words of months ago. "In some ways, no. But in another, it is. Besides, I know you won't go back to the States, and I'm not leaving without you."

His hands tightened on my shoulders. I sensed him struggling to speak.

I added, "So how about it, Ripinsky? Let's take Tim Mourning and his two million dollars home."

Twenty-Four

The first thing we needed to do was make ourselves more presentable. We washed in ice-cold sea water. Hy shaved off his stubbly beard and changed to a rumpled but clean set of clothing; I made what improvements I could with a comb and some makeup. Then we drove north toward Ensenada.

We encountered no police patrols, no roadblocks. Fontes, a wealthy and influential citizen, had probably convinced — or more likely bribed — the authorities not to put themselves out investigating a crime that seemed to be the end result of a dispute among Americans. At most they might circulate the descriptions of the man seen on the beach and the woman with the camera to the U.S. Border Control stations and ask for cooperation, but that would be about it.

As I drove, we discussed how to proceed. I'd pinpointed something that might conceivably be used as leverage with Navarro, but that would bear further checking. My main concern was how long everyone would remain at the villa. Diane Mourning was temporarily out of the picture, but the others couldn't be sure what she might eventually tell the authorities — or what she might do when she recovered. My take on the situation was that Fontes and Navarro would strike a quick deal and put the letter of credit through as soon as possible. As for Tim Mourning, his wife's shooting had in effect guaranteed his safety for a little while longer; a second casualty at the villa would pose more of a problem than even cops who were conditioned to look the other way could ignore. Of course, Salazar or one of his people could take Mourning to the desert, kill him, and dump him there, but I doubted they'd try that on a day when the household had come under police scrutiny.

One factor working in Hy's and my favor was that it was Sunday; nothing could be done about the L.C. until the next morning. Possibly one of them would fly to Mexico City with it today, but maybe not, and the L.C. was of secondary importance, anyway. The prime objective had always been to rescue Tim, and to do that we'd have to move fast.

Before we arrived in Ensenada, we'd figured out the details. So many to be arranged, and so carefully. Omit even one, and we'd condemn Mourning to a certain death. Tacitly we agreed not to discuss what we might condemn ourselves to if the plan failed.

In Ensenada we stopped at a phone booth and Hy called the trauma unit where Tomás had said Diane Mourning was taken. They told him that she'd been stabilized and flown at the request of her personal physician to Cabrillo Hospital in San Diego. No, the police had not questioned Señora Mourning; she was in critical condition.

Again we drove north, this time to Tijuana's Avenida Revolución, the gaudy tourist shopping area. While Hy waited in the car, I hurried along the crowded sidewalk, avoiding peddlers hawking jewelry and ignoring the entreaties of shopkeepers who stood outside like barkers at sleazy sex shows. In a clothing store I bought a colorful embroidered dress and sandals; a few doors down I stopped at another shop and bought typical tourist things — a serape, marionettes, a piñata, a sombrero, some wood carvings. Laden with them, I hurried back through the carnival atmosphere to the car and piled them on the backseat. It was after two when we finally checked into Hotel Fiesta Americana Tijuana on Boulevard Agua Caliente.

Initially Hy objected to my choice of hotel; it went against his Spartan grain to spend so much money for a place to stay. But he consented when I pointed out that in case the federal police actually were looking for us, they wouldn't be likely to check the best lodgings in town for a drifter who'd been seen sleeping on the beach down south. He stuck to his principles, though, by making me put it on my credit card.

As soon as the bellhop left our room on the nineteenth story of one of the hotel's twin towers, I dug through my bag and found the fax of Phoenix Labs's letter of credit that Renshaw had sent to me at the Bali Kai. My four-digit RKI security code was noted at its top. I dialed their La Jolla number, was told that the offices were closed but in case of emergency I should press 1, enter my code, and stay on the line. I pressed, entered, stayed. A man came on. I identified myself and said I wanted to talk with Gage Renshaw.

After the most brief of hesitations, the man said, "Give me your number, Ms. McCone, and I'll have Mr. Renshaw return your call within fifteen minutes."

"No," I told him, "get him into the office, and I'll call back."

Another pause. "I'm paging him."

And trying to trace my call. "Have him there in fifteen minutes," I said and hung up.

Hy was watching me, a faint smile on his

lips. "You've learned to play in the majors, McCone."

"Hardly. It may look that way, but inside I feel like a little kid who doesn't even know which direction to run around the bases."

He shrugged disbelievingly and went to see what was in the mini-bar. In principle he might disapprove of such luxuries, but he was demonstrating remarkable adaptability.

Fifteen minutes later I dialed the La Jolla number again. "Renshaw here," the familiar voice said.

"Don't try to trace this call," I told him.

"Ms. McCone, why don't you give it up? Come in to the office, we'll talk."

"Yes, we have to talk, but we'll do it my way. I want to meet with you — just you, none of your other people, and with no surveillance. In a public place."

". . . All right. Where and when?"

"Hotel del Coronado. The terrace bar by the beach, south end. Five o'clock this afternoon. I'll be alone, unarmed. You should be, too. They don't tolerate disturbances at Hotel Del, and if you try to have me followed after I leave, you'll never see Ripinsky, Tim Mourning, or Phoenix Labs's letter of credit again."

Total silence.

"Agreed, Mr. Renshaw?"

384

"Agreed, Ms. McCone." Damned if he didn't sound surprised.

I hung up, turned to Hy. He was grinning. "Way to kick ass, McCone."

"You think that was long enough for them to trace the call?"

"No, and I'll bet they didn't even try. Gage isn't stupid, and he doesn't underestimate other people, either."

I got my bag, took my father's gun out, and set it on the small table by the window. After removing the roll of film from the camera, I set it there, too. Then I stuck the film in my bag, slung the bag over my shoulder, and gave Hy what I hoped was a confident smile. "I'd better get going."

He stepped forward, put his hands on my shoulders. "You'll be okay, and I'll handle what I have to on this end."

"I'm not worried," I lied.

"I am," he said, proving he'd lied, too. "Don't know what I'd do if I lost you."

"You won't." I went up on tiptoe, touched my lips to his. "By this time tomorrow, it'll all be behind us." Then I hurried out of the room before all the bad, scary possibilities that lay unsaid between us could grow into even scarier probabilities.

As we'd driven toward Tijuana, the sky had

cleared and the heat had intensified. It grew stifling as I waited in the Sunday afternoon traffic jam at the border control. The U.S. Customs officials seemed to be questioning returning Americans with more than the usual thoroughness; as I inched toward the gate, refusing the overtures of peddlers who hawked flowers and jewelry and soft drinks between the cars, I saw several vehicles being turned aside for searching. When the car ahead of mine cleared, I put on my best tourist smile.

The man in uniform leaned down to my window, studying my face unsmilingly. His eyes moved over my colorful, flowing clothing to the souvenir-laden backseat. "How long have you been in Baja, ma'am?"

"Just the day, for a little shopping." I motioned at the piñata — in the shape of an exceedingly stupid-looking donkey — that now rode in the passenger seat.

"And where've you been?"

"Avenida Revolución."

"No farther south than T.J.?"

"No, sir."

"Do you own this car?"

"It's a rental."

"May I see your contract?"

I handed it to him.

"Is this San Francisco address correct?"

"Yes. I'm down visiting my brother in Lemon Grove."

The customs man handed the contract back to me. "You have a nice day, ma'am," he said as he waved me through.

I waited until I'd passed under the flashing sign that said "Watch for pedestrians crossing freeway" before I let out an explosive sigh of relief at crossing this first hurdle. My next stop would be Gooden's Photographic, which operated a one-hour developing service even on Sunday. After that I'd head for nearby Cabrillo Hospital.

It was a small private facility on a quiet side street off Sixth Avenue across from the southwestern edge of Balboa Park: three nondescript stories of beige stucco with beds of long-stemmed purple agapanthus bordering the path to the lobby entrance. Its sign said that it was a care provider for Marin County–based Sequoia Health Plan, probably the reason Mourning's personal physician had selected it. I parked in the lot beside it and got out of the car, looking around for a police cruiser. There wasn't any, and that didn't surprise me. While California law requires hospitals to report gunshot wounds to the police, this one had been sustained in Mexico; they might eventually question Mourning, but they weren't likely to devote too many valuable man-hours to a shooting that had occurred in a jurisdiction where they'd get little or no co-operation from their counterparts.

The lobby was empty except for a nurse who leaned against the information desk talking with an older woman in a volunteer's pink uniform. When I asked about Diane Mourning, the two exchanged guarded looks. "I'm sorry," the volunteer said, "she's not allowed any visitors."

"I'd like to speak with the attending physician, then. It's important; I have a message for her from Mr. Mourning."

The volunteer glanced hesitantly at the nurse, who said, "That'd be Dr. Henderson. I believe he's making rounds now."

"I'll be glad to wait."

She considered, then told me, "Go to the second-floor nurses' station. They'll page him."

"Thanks."

As I moved toward the elevator, the women were silent. I glanced back after I pressed the up button and saw them staring at me with frank curiosity.

Dr. Henderson was standing at the nurses' station when I arrived there. A heavy, balding man with a fringe of gray hair, he scrutinized both me and my identification carefully, then led me to a lounge area.

"You say you have a message from Mrs. Mourning's husband?"

"Yes. He asked me to deliver it to her personally."

"Just where *is* the husband?"

"Baja."

Henderson frowned. "He remained there, in spite of his wife being shot?"

"He was unavoidably detained," I said vaguely. "Has Diane asked for him?"

"When she was first brought in, she seemed concerned as to his whereabouts. You understand, she's been drugged for pain. She's quite restless, keeps mumbling his name, among other things."

"Other things?"

"Something about a letter and being inside a house."

"I see. What's her condition?"

"Critical, but stable. Gunshot wound with questionable kidney compromise."

"Were the police notified?"

He nodded.

"Have they talked with her?"

"Not yet. As I said, she's in considerable pain and has to be drugged."

"Would she be able to understand the message from her husband?"

"Probably."

"May I see her?"

Henderson rubbed his chin thoughtfully. "It might reassure her. Five minutes, though, no more."

He had a nurse take me to Diane's private room. She lay on a bed by the window, an I.V. inserted in her arm. The high hospital bed diminished her; she looked even smaller, paler, more fragile. As the nurse left us and shut the door behind her, I approached and touched Mourning's arm.

She opened her eyes groggily; their pupils were dilated, her gaze unfocused.

"Diane," I said, "it's Sharon McCone, from RKI."

"No." The word came out a whisper, tinged with fear.

"It's all right. I'm not here to hurt you. What happened at Fontes's villa?"

She shut her eyes again.

"Who shot you?"

No reply.

"Were you shot in the house?"

After a moment she nodded.

"Who did it? Salazar?"

". . . don't know. Didn't see . . ."

"Where in the house were you?"

"Living room."

"And who told the police you were shot on the beach?"

". . . Don't know. Blacked out . . ."

"Was Timothy there?"

Her eyes opened again, fear glazing them now. "Timothy . . ." She pressed her lips together, shook her head from side to side.

"Diane, this next question is important. Does Ann know her husband is dead?"

"Stan? Not dead. In Mexico City."

"Who told you that?"

She closed her eyes again.

"Diane, who said so?"

". . . Gilbert . . . said . . ." She was fading — or pretending to.

"Diane, *what* did Gilbert say?"

No reply. Her lips were white-edged now, and her breathing was faster and shallower; perspiration beaded her forehead. I looked for the call button and rang. The nurse bustled in and took charge.

"Doctor's an idiot for letting her have a visitor," she told me. "And if you see him on your way out, you can tell him I said so."

As I left the hospital I felt a certain amount of guilt about my insistent questioning of a critically injured woman, but I banished it by reminding myself that said woman had arranged the kidnapping of her own husband. Besides, the information I'd gleaned — that Fontes had lied to Navarro, telling her

Brockowitz was in Mexico City when he was actually in the San Diego County morgue — gave me even more leverage than I'd hoped for with Navarro. If I could get to her, I was sure I could convince her . . .

All the way to my next stop, I puzzled over Mourning's shooting. An accident? Perhaps someone had mistaken her for a burglar. The early hours of the morning were a bad time to be wandering through the home of someone as security-conscious as Fontes. Well, I told myself, no amount of worrying at the question would provide an answer now. My immediate business deserved my undivided attention.

When I got to Gooden's, I found the pictures were ready early, thanks to a slack Sunday business. They'd also turned out focused and clear. Next I went to a nearby branch of Bank of America and drew out the maximum — two hundred dollars — on my automatic teller card. That, coupled with what was left from the check I'd cashed in Coronado on Friday, came to a little over six hundred dollars; I hoped I wouldn't have to use it all.

No one was home at Luis Abrego's apartment in National City, but I wasn't too concerned. If I didn't find him waiting to arrange one of his coyote jobs at the Tradewinds, I could always contact Vic at the Holiday Market. I left the car in front of the apartment building and walked the few blocks to the bar. The streets were pretty much deserted; even on Highland traffic was so light that I could hear the rattle and hum of the Tradewinds' air conditioners at a fair distance. Inside, the bar was as dark and smoky and crowded as it had been the last time I was there; Abrego sat on the same stool, idly watching a Padres game on the big-screen TV. Again a hush fell over the room as I entered; Luis looked around to see what had caused it, saw me, and got up, grinning. Immediately the rest of the patrons lost interest and resumed their conversations.

I took the stool next to him; he offered to buy me a drink, and I asked for a club soda. When it came I drank half of it down, feeling a rush of cold as it hit my empty stomach. If I was to get through the rest of the day, I'd have to eat sometime. Maybe some fast food on my way back to Tijuana.

Abrego said, "You cut your hair since last week. You're looking better, too."

"That's because I found my friend. He's not dead, after all."

He raised an eyebrow. "So who's the guy Salazar shot?"

"I'll tell you the whole story someday. Right now I need some information from you —

the name of somebody in Colonia Libertad."
It was the poorest section of Tijuana, where
things and people were bought and sold cheap.

"Why?"

"I need somebody to help some people get
where they need to go."

"Your friend?"

"And two others, maybe three."

He seemed to understand that one of the
others would be me. "You're Americans. You
should be able to clear the border control. Or
are you bringing in something illegal?"

"Nothing illegal. It's not Customs I'm worried about. There may be somebody waiting
for us on the T.J. side."

"That's bad."

"Yes, you know how it is there. You're in
a car, standing in gridlock; a person with a
rifle on the other side of the fence in Colonia
Libertad can pick you off easily. If you're on
foot, it's even more dangerous: you're closer
to the fence, funneled through that outdoor
corridor before the customs building. Then
there's that long inside corridor before you
come to the officials; anybody can slip inside,
fire a round, run back out."

"You really think somebody's gonna go
after you?"

"Yes."

"Why?"

"I can't go into it now."

He considered. "So why don't you just cross at Tecate or Calexico? Or fly?"

"If they have somebody at San Ysidro, they'll cover those places and the airport, too. And we'd be in even more danger then, because I don't know the territory."

Luis was silent, sipping beer. "This have to do with Salazar?"

"Among others."

Again he considered for a moment. "You know, I don't like to cross over, even though I got my permanent green card. Man with my sideline — well, you know how that goes. But this time I could see my way to it. I owe you."

"Why?"

"Ana. She went to that doctor John gave me the name of. Remember I said something was wrong with the pregnancy? Well, there was. Female stuff, I don't understand it, don't want to, but the doctor said if she hadn't've come in when she did, she'd've been bad off. The doctor, that Gina, she kept Ana there in the clinic a couple of days, took care of her real good. Charged just what Ana had, two hundred ninety-five bucks. She's on her way home now."

Immediately I realized that John had taken care of any fees over and above that. What a good guy, my big brother.

"So I owe you," Luis added. "I'll bring you and your friends through."

I couldn't let him do it. "No, you don't owe me that much. We'll be even if you give me a name."

"You'd be better off with me."

"But you wouldn't be better off getting involved in this. I want you here, for the people you help. And it'll be easier for me down there if it's strictly a business proposition."

He thought for a moment, staring unseeingly at the TV. Then he said, "Okay," and pulled a cocktail napkin toward him. "You got a pen?"

I nodded and fished one from my bag.

Luis wrote two names and an address and phone number for each. "This first guy I trust, but the only reason you should go to him is if you can't get hold of the other. He's not really what you're looking for — not tough or smart enough. This other guy, he's sly, he'll steal you blind if you don't watch him, but I think you got what it takes to control him. If you can, he'll get you through."

I took the napkin and tucked it into my bag. "How much will he charge?"

"How many of you did you say?"

"Three, maybe four."

"He'll start out asking a lot, because he'll

know you're in trouble. But he'll settle for five, six hundred American."

"Thanks, Luis. I appreciate this."

"You really have to do it that way?"

"I think so." I consulted my watch: four thirty-three. "I've got to go see somebody now who might help me, but I doubt he will."

"Why not?"

I hesitated; in Luis's world, RKI's policy of not going into Mexico wouldn't make a bit of sense, and I didn't have time to explain. "He just won't, that's all," I said, slipping off the barstool.

"Guy's an asshole, then." Luis got up too and followed me to the door. "Where's your car?"

"In front of your apartment building."

"I'll walk with you. I sit around this place too damn much."

We walked in comfortable silence. Luis didn't press me for more information about what I was involved in, and for that I was grateful. When we got to where I'd parked the Tercel in the shade of an old pepper tree, I shook his hand, then unlocked the door and climbed in. Looked up to see him staring, perplexed, at the donkey piñata. His eyes moved to the backseat and he frowned.

"What's all this?"

"I bought it to make myself look like a tourist when I crossed the border. Do you know anybody who would like it?"

". . . Uh, sure, but —"

"Then will you take it, please? I don't have any use for it."

"Okay. I know some people who're real homesick. Maybe this stuff'll cheer them up."

As he removed the donkey, sombrero, wood carvings, serape, and marionettes from the car, Luis handled them gently, almost reverently. One person's tourist crap was another's treasure from home. He placed them on the steps of his apartment, then returned and leaned in my window, taking my right hand in both of his.

"Stay safe," he said, "and call me later to tell me about it."

"I will."

Then he said something softly in Spanish.

"What?"

He shrugged, looking slightly embarrassed. "Just something I tell the people I drive when I let them off."

"And it means?"

"Trust in no one but yourself and God."

Twenty-Five

I got to Hotel Del ten minutes early for my appointment with Gage Renshaw. While crossing its baronial dark-paneled lobby, I looked around for signs of RKI operatives lurking behind potted palms, but saw only well-heeled visitors and a contingent of Japanese tourists who stood near their heaped luggage, eyes glazed by jet lag. Downstairs by the ladies' room I found a pay phone and called Gary Viner.

"I assume you haven't been able to contact Stanley Brockowitz's widow yet," I said.

"No. We asked Orange County to send a man out to their place in Blossom Hill. Nobody home, but you know what? There'd been a break-in."

"Burglary?"

"None of the obvious things had been taken. And no vandalism."

Salazar's man, snatching Tim Mourning.

"And here's another peculiar thing," Viner added. "Looked like somebody'd been held prisoner in one of the bedrooms. Would you know anything about that, McCone?"

"How could I?" In order to derail that train of thought, I said, "I *do* know where Brockowitz's wife is, though, and I plan to see her later this evening. I'll break the news about her husband, if you like, and have her call you to verify it."

"Why don't you just tell me where she is and let us take care of it?"

"Can't. I'm . . . meeting her in a public place and don't know where she's actually staying. But I promise to have her call you right away."

"What time?"

"I'm not sure. Fairly late."

"I'm on night duty this week — ten P.M. to six A.M. So call me at the department. McCone, did the wife kill him?"

"I know for a fact she didn't."

"Then why all this . . . ? You know, I'm getting real tired of —"

"Got to go, Gary. I'll be in touch." I hung up and moved toward the exit.

Hotel Del's terrace stretches between the outdoor swimming pool and the white sand beach. On it is a bar housed in a white turreted gazebo that matches the main building's Victorian architecture, and a profusion of white umbrellaed tables. Most were occupied this afternoon, and on the beach a few sun-bathers were still soaking up the rays. I moved through the crowd, checking it out from behind my dark glasses; stopped at the bar and bought a glass of their fresh-squeezed lemonade. Kept going toward the south end until I spotted Gage Renshaw at a table wedged between the beach-side wall and a planter containing an evergreen shrub.

Renshaw slumped spinelessly in a molded plastic chair that was dwarfed by his long body, right foot propped on the chair opposite. From the way he was dressed, I assumed my earlier phone call had summoned him from the golf course — although what self-respecting course would admit someone wearing such disreputable-looking golfing clothes was something I couldn't begin to fathom. There was, however, no place under the faded yellow knit shirt and shabby madras pants for a concealed weapon. I scanned the people around him, a couple of families and a hand-holding pair who looked like honeymooners. Unless RKI's operatives went in for elaborate camouflage, Renshaw was here alone.

As I approached the table, he saw me and stood. Bowed mockingly and pulled out a chair for me. "How nice of you to favor me with your company," he said.

I set my lemonade on the table and took off my dark glasses. "How are you, Mr. Renshaw?"

"Not as well as I could be, thanks to you. Satisfy my curiosity on one point: it was you I saw change directions at La Encantadora yesterday?"

"Right."

"The haircut threw me off. As it was meant to, no doubt. You're quite skilled at evading surveillance."

"Let's not dwell on our past difficulties. I asked to meet with you to tell you that as of last night Tim Mourning was alive and reasonably well. Ripinsky's alive and reasonably well, too, and innocent of anything except, perhaps, bad judgment. He plans to deliver Mourning and possibly Phoenix Labs's letter of credit to you by daybreak tomorrow."

Renshaw shook his head. "I don't believe you."

I reached into my bag and took out the packet of photos I'd picked up at Gooden's. Removed the picture of Mourning stumbling onto Fontes's terrace and passed it to him.

He studied it for a moment, then dropped it carelessly to the table. "This could be an old picture."

"Look at the date stamped on the back."

He turned it over. "So? All this proves is

that you had it developed today."

"Now, where would I have gotten my hands on an old roll of film that just happened to have a picture of Mourning on it? I took that last night, in Baja. Mourning had just been brought there from the place where his kidnappers were holding him in eastern Orange County. As you can see, he's not in the best of shape."

Renshaw turned the photo over again and scrutinized his client.

I removed the second picture from the envelope and slid that toward him. "I took this one a few seconds later." It was of Tim stumbling toward Diane; her hands were extended to ward him off, and fear distorted her features.

Renshaw's eyes narrowed. He picked the photo up and looked closely, turned it over and checked the date. "We wondered why we hadn't been able to contact Diane."

"She's been in Baja since Friday night, at the home of a man called Gilbert Fontes. So has one of the kidnappers, the contact woman, Ann Navarro. As well as an evil man named Marty Salazar, who took the letter of credit off Ripinsky and shot the other kidnapper, Stanley Brockowitz, Navarro's husband."

"When did this happen? Sunday night?"

I nodded.

"He's had the L.C. all that time and hasn't bothered to put it through?" His tone was shaded by disbelief.

"Initially Salazar didn't know what it was or what to do with it. Then he peddled it to Fontes, whose brother owns Colores Internacional. The two are estranged, and the brother knows nothing about the kidnapping, so Gilbert can't put it through, either. Ann Navarro can — she has a contact there, I think — but she's been driving a hard bargain."

Renshaw looked at the second photograph again. "And Diane?"

"Diane is not so innocent as we thought she was." I explained about her setting up the kidnapping, about her getting shot, and about Fontes facilitating her return to the U.S. "If I read the situation correctly, they'll draw on the letter of credit sometime tomorrow."

Renshaw slumped lower in the chair, drumming his fingers on the table. "You say this Fontes is wealthy and influential?"

"Yes."

"Then we'll get no cooperation from the authorities down there. And we can't just go in and snatch Mourning; I explained about our policy vis-à-vis Mexico."

"No exceptions?"

"None. Especially in a sensitive case like this."

It was the response I'd been prepared for, but still my spirits plummeted. I thought of Fontes's well-guarded house and Salazar's fondness for killing. Of the coyote Luis Abrego had recommended, who was sly and untrustworthy. Of the border fence, the perilous canyons . . .

Renshaw was watching me, eyes narrowed. I said, "Then we'll get him out of there without your help."

"We?"

"Ripinsky and I."

"You don't really think you can manage that."

"We will. We've got some leverage with Navarro."

He nodded, his fingers toying with one of the photographs. "Let me ask you this: why are you involving yourself? Why not walk away from it, let Ripinsky handle it on his own?"

"I saw the photograph of Mourning they sent you. I saw him through my telephoto last night. I can't let him die."

He shook his head. "More to it than that."

More to it than that — yes. But it was a reason that simply wouldn't compute in a mind like Renshaw's.

Finally I said, "Money."

"Money."

"I took on this job for pay. Because I did it in my own way, it's been expensive. I've lost my regular job, and I'll need the rest of what you owe me. Which brings me to what I want from you: the balance, in cash, when we deliver Mourning."

"Where am I supposed to get that kind of cash on a Sunday?"

"You'll manage. Oh — and Ripinsky wants the balance of whatever you promised him, too."

Renshaw rolled his eyes.

"And we'll need a car."

"A car."

"We'll be crossing the border down by Monument Road, near Border Field State Park. When we arrive, we'll need transportation."

"We'll pick you up."

I shook my head. "We'll deliver Mourning to you. As well as tell you where you can find Diane. You'll give us our money, and we'll leave in the car you provide — without surveillance or tracking devices. And that, Mr. Renshaw, will be the end of our association."

"What about the letter of credit?"

"If we can get hold of it, we'll turn it over. Otherwise, all you have to do is contact Emanuel Fontes. No way he'll allow it to be put through."

"And Navarro?"

"I may be able to convince her to come back with us and give herself up. Otherwise you'll have to get Diane to open up and testify against her. I'm sure you can accomplish that easily."

"What about this Salazar?"

"I'll let the SDPD or the FBI handle him."

"If he ever returns to the U.S."

"Even if he — or Navarro — doesn't, I think you'll get cooperation out of Mexico. They're guilty of transporting a kidnap victim over an international boundary."

"We won't be able to touch Gilbert Fontes, though. Mexico fights extradition of its citizens tooth and nail."

I shrugged. "Fontes is really peripheral to the case. Accessory after the fact is all you'd have him on, and any good attorney could get the case thrown out of court."

Renshaw considered, then nodded as if he'd made a decision. "All right, you and Ripinsky will get your cash and your car. Where shall we meet you, and when?"

"Across from the old dairy on Monument Road. Do you know it?"

He nodded.

"Be there at midnight, but don't give up on us until first light."

"And if you don't show?"

Heart-stopper of a question. I forced the

obvious answer aside. "Be there the next night."

Renshaw gave me a look that said he was aware of the correct answer, but he also chose to ignore it.

"And don't forget to bring our money," I added, just to needle him.

"I'll bring it, even though I'm aware that you're not doing this for the money."

"No?"

"No. No more than you went after Ripinsky for money, or to satisfy a grudge. You may think I'm a coldhearted son of a bitch, and in most ways I am, but I harbor dim memories of what it's like to love someone so much you'd risk your life for them."

"I don't —"

"You may think you don't. Probably you've been hurt in the same ways Ripinsky has. You've backed off, refused to give your feelings that name. But you do love him."

Stunned at his invasion of my emotional privacy, I pushed back from the table.

Renshaw reached over and grasped my arm. "However," he went on, "in the extreme unlikelihood that I'm wrong, I'll tell you this: I'd give a great deal to see what you'd do for somebody when you get around to the real thing."

Twenty-Six

After I dropped the Tercel off at the downtown Avis office, I had a quick sandwich and
walked over to Eighth Street, where I caught
the southbound trolley. The bright red light-
rail car was packed with returning Mexicans,
up on a day pass to shop, play tourist, or visit
relatives. A few stared at me — a lone American in clothing of Mexican manufacture —
with frank curiosity; when I stared back, they
looked away. Forty-some minutes later the
trolley let us off in San Ysidro. Along with
the crowd, I walked across the freeway over-
pass, down the ramps, through the turnstile.
Then I caught a cab to the address Luis Abrego
had given me in Colonia Libertad.

By now, I thought as the cab sped along
the side streets, Hy would be back at the hotel,
having arranged for yet another car — a spe-
cially equipped one this time. I wouldn't need
to rely on his linguistic abilities to transact
my business with the coyote; most of the citizens of this border city spoke good English,

just as most San Diegans had picked up enough Spanish to get by. During the past twenty-four hours, I'd realized my Spanish was better than I'd suspected. The coyote and I would manage just fine.

The address turned out to be an auto-body shop sandwiched among row upon row of colorful shacks with lush gardens that made them seem all the more wretched by comparison. At a nearby food stand an elderly woman was frying tortillas on a stove made of an oil drum. Ragged children played stickball in the street, chickens strutted and scratched, and a mangy dog tethered to a fencepost barked incessantly. The cab driver didn't want to wait for me, but agreed when I gave him five dollars and promised another five later.

The auto-body shop was open, even though it was Sunday. I stepped inside the dark cavernous garage and saw that one wall was covered with the world's largest collection of banged-up hubcaps. No one was working, but toward the back two men in coveralls sat on a bench, smoking. The scent of marijuana drifted my way.

I went back there and asked, "Alfonso Mojas?"

The taller of the two — a lean, dark man with missing front teeth and acne scars on his hollow cheeks — looked up and said, "Who

410

wants him?" His English was Americanized, only lightly accented.

"Luis Abrego sent me."

The man turned to his companion and spoke softly in Spanish. The other rose, cupping the joint in his hand, and left by a side door.

"I'm Mojas," the man said. "Call me Al. What d'you need?"

"I want to hire you."

"To do what?"

"Take some people north."

"So why don't they come here theirselves?"

"I'm one of them."

Now he frowned. "Lady, maybe nobody told you, but lookin' like you do, you can just walk across."

"I've got a problem that prevents that. How much do you charge to make the trip?"

His eyes moved over me, obviously calculating the size of my bank account. "How many?"

"Myself and two others. Maybe three."

"All women?"

"No, two men. Maybe another woman."

"When?"

"Tonight."

"What time?"

"I'm not sure. Late."

He hesitated, took a joint from his coveralls pocket, and lit it. Sucked smoke down, then let it out in a long hissing breath. "Federales after you?"

"No."

"Carrying anything?"

"Drugs? No."

"So what's the problem?"

"Some people down here may not want us to cross, but they'll look for us at the border controls and the airports."

"Okay," he said, "okay. I don't want to know any more about that. You got transportation when we get there?"

"Someone will be waiting for us on Monument Road."

"Abrego?"

"No."

He shrugged. "Just so's I don't have to get somebody for you on that end."

"It's taken care of. How much?"

"Okay, here's how I work it: I'm in charge, you do what I say. No guns, no drugs. You got that?"

"How much?"

A final once-over. "Thousand American."

"Five hundred."

"Seven-fifty."

"Six hundred."

"You got it."

"And two of us will be armed."

"I said no guns."

I just looked at him.

"Okay, okay. All the money up front."

"Half now, half if we get there."

"I always get my clients through."

"Nobody *always* gets his clients through."

A moment's hesitation. "Fuck it. Gimme my three hundred."

I counted out the cash, hoping that Hy and I wouldn't run into any unforeseen expenses. Mojas set the joint down on a corner of the bench, counted the money again, and stuffed it into his pocket.

I asked, "Do we come here?"

He shook his head. "My place. Calle Solano. On the corner of Calle Guerrero. Pink house, palm tree and a statue of the Virgin out front."

"Good. Expect us anytime from midnight on."

He nodded and picked up the joint.

"Something else, Al," I said. "No dope smoking on this trip."

He frowned, clearly offended. "I finish this J, I stop smoking and drinking till I get you through. That's how it works."

"Good. One other thing."

"Jesus! What?"

"You know Luis Abrego. Do you also know a man called Marty Salazar?"

Slow reaction at first; then he stiffened. "What about him?"

"Luis Abrego's a friend of mine. If you don't play this straight with my companions and me, or if anything happens to us, Abrego'll be very angry. He's got something on Salazar; he can make him do things to people."

"Shit, you think I'm gonna —"

"I just wanted to make it clear what might happen if anything goes wrong."

Mojas ground the joint out on the bench, slipped it back into his pocket. "Nothing'll happen," he said. "I always get my clients through."

"Good. I'll see you later, then." I turned and walked away, trying to look calm and confident.

Before I went back to the hotel, I had the cab driver take me past the intersection of Calles Solano and Guerrero. The pink corner house with the palm tree and the statue of the Virgin Mary in front actually existed and that, I supposed, was as much assurance of good faith on Al Mojas's part as I was going to get.

Back at the Fiesta Americana I went straight to the room and found Hy sitting on the bed, staring at the TV with such rapt attention that he didn't notice me come in.

A news broadcast dealing with the shooting at Fontes's villa? I moved to where I could see the screen. Instead of a plastic-perfect an-chorperson, I came face-to-face with a leather-attired woman menacingly waving a whip at a bare-assed man who cowered on the floor at her feet. Hy saw me and started guiltily.

"What the hell is this?"

Hastily he got up and turned the set off. "Something called *Watch My Whip*. I thought it was a western."

"Sure you did."

"Honest to God." Hy is a western buff and will watch any film that comes along, including the ancient grade B ones.

I faced him, hands on hips. "A *western*, on the adult pay channel?"

"Shit, McCone, I don't understand how these fancy cable sets work. I tuned in by mistake."

"You don't understand how they work? You have a *satellite dish* at home. You get a *hundred and twenty channels*."

He shrugged sullenly.

"Besides," I added, "even if you turned it on by mistake, you kept watching. At a cost to *my* credit card of" — I consulted the guide on the TV — "roughly seven dollars and fifty cents."

"I'll pay you back."

"That's not the point."

"Good God! A few whips and some bare

buns don't add up to a full-blown perversion. I was curious, that's all. It's not like I rushed out and bought a whip, then limbered it up to use on *your* buns."

He looked so morally outraged that I started to laugh. Here we were in the middle of the most dangerous undertaking of our lives — well, mine, anyway — and we were arguing about him spending my seven dollars and fifty cents to watch a dirty movie. Hy stared at me as if he feared I'd cracked under the strain, then started to laugh too. Soon we were giggling and snorting and hugging each other, our laughter burning off some of the excess tension that fueled it.

"Jesus," he gasped, "don't ever bring me to a place like this again. I've already drunk three beers from the mini-bar and charged a steak to room service. To say nothing of renting a car that stops just short of being a limo."

The mention of the car sobered me. "We're all set?"

He sobered too. "Yeah."

"It's got a cellular phone?"

"Uh-huh, and they assured me that its range is wide enough. How about your end of it?"

"It's a go."

"What'd Renshaw say?"

"I'll tell you later. Right now we'd better get on with it."

Twenty-Seven

A heavy cloud cover overhung the Baja coast that night, blacking out the moon and stars. We cruised through the commercial district of El Sueño at around ten, the gray Cadillac Seville that Hy had rented riding so smoothly that we seemed to be scarcely moving at all. This car, I thought, was protective coloration in more ways than one. Not only did it look as if it belonged in this exclusive enclave, but it faded into the murky night.

I hung up the cellular phone and said, "The rental agency didn't steer you wrong; we're well within range."

He didn't reply to that, merely muttered, "Where's the goddamn turnoff for Vía Pacífica?"

I peered through the passenger-side windshield. "It's coming up pretty quick now . . . yes, here."

He negotiated the turn with the clumsiness of one not used to power steering. "Frankly," he said, "I'd rather be driving my Morgan."

I agreed, in spite of the low-slung old sports car's potential for ruining my spine. "I'd rather be driving my MG. Or taking off in the Citabria."

"Or doing anything except what we're about to."

"Right."

"Not much more to get through now, McCone."

"No, only the hard part." The dangerous part.

We passed the beach access; soon Fontes's villa appeared on our right. The auto gate was shut, but otherwise it looked much the same as it had the night before, lights blazing in all the barred windows. The Volvo still stood in front of the garage.

"Navarro's there," I said.

"Unless she's gone someplace in his plane or another car."

"Well, there's only one way to find out."

Hy kept driving until all the houses were behind us, then U-turned where the dirt track veered off into the riverbed. He retraced our route, slowing again as we passed the villa. "I don't see any guards," he said. "Wish we could've checked at the airstrip to see if Fontes's Cessna's being used."

"As you said last night, strangers attract too much attention at these little airfields."

We continued in silence to the beach access. Tonight no vehicles except the cannibalized sedan were parked there. Hy stopped next to the beach path and shut off the ignition.

"Car's going to be pretty obvious, sitting here all by itself," he said. "Security patrol'll probably check it out."

"Maybe not. It's expensive enough that they'll probably just assume it belongs to one of the residents. Given where it's parked, they might not check it out for fear of interrupting a tryst." I reached into the backseat for Hy's extra sweater — a dark blue one, fortunately — and pulled it over my head. Before we left the hotel in Tijuana, I'd changed back into jeans and athletic shoes.

Hy didn't respond to my somewhat shaky logic, just reached under the seat for his revolver. He got out, tucked it into his waistband. I slipped out my side, hefting the bag that contained my father's .45 and the camera. Then we walked down the sandy path to the beach.

Our footsteps were muffled, barely audible. We moved silently toward the rotting *pongas*. The riverbed was quiet tonight, faint firelight flickering; the fishermen got up early, their day usually done by noon. Even the villas on the hill showed few signs of life.

When we came to Fontes's property, Hy

went into a crouch and moved swiftly across the last open stretch of sand. I followed suit, stretching out flat on my stomach behind the *pongas* and reaching into the bag for the camera. After removing the lens cap, I shoved it into the empty space between the boats, where the piece of wood I'd used as a shim the night before still lay.

Lights shone in the villa and on the terrace, but no one was outside. I focused on the glass doors and saw that the drapes had been drawn across them. The lens's magnification was so great that I could make out their rough weave; I refocused for a bigger picture and saw shadows moving behind them.

"Anything?" Hy whispered.

"Not yet. The drapes're closed." I adjusted the focus some more. "Give me a minute. People are moving around in there. I'm pretty good at reading body language, and I may be able to identify who they are by the way they walk."

Hy fell silent, crouching behind me, his posture alert as he kept watch along the beach. I observed the shadow play on the hill.

I watched for about five minutes, comparing heights and nuances of movement. One figure entered carrying something, set it down, then left. A maid, perhaps, or the bartender. Another appeared to be pacing back and forth the length of the room. A third got up from a chair, crossed to the right where the maid or bartender had stopped, and after a while went back again.

"I don't think Fontes is there," I whispered to Hy. "These people are short to medium height."

"How many?"

"Three, but I think one's a servant. I'm pretty sure Salazar's there; somebody crossed the room in that languid gait he has."

"The other?"

"Pacing. Short, stocky. I'd say it's Navarro. Hard to tell, though."

"Not Mourning?"

"Uh-uh. They're probably keeping him under guard."

"So where d'you suppose Fontes is?"

I didn't reply. A heavyset figure had appeared and was standing next to the chair occupied by the person I thought was Salazar. The shadow stood there for about half a minute, then left again, walking in a heavy, rolling gait. Jaime? Shortly afterward a light flashed on in an uncurtained window in the two-story wing to the far right. I moved the lens and adjusted the focus; Jaime came into view, removing a shoulder holster.

"Salazar's bodyguard is there," I whispered, "and he's going off duty."

"So that leaves us with . . ."

"Salazar and Navarro. The servant. Whoever else Fontes employs. Maybe Fontes himself." I continued watching. The short, stocky figure quit pacing and sat down near the other person. For a long time there was no movement.

"Hy," I said, sitting up and resting my eyes, "how much do you suppose the people in the riverbed know about what goes on at those villas?"

"Probably quite a bit. I got the impression that they watch them the same way people used to watch prime-time soaps like 'Dallas' and 'Falconcrest.' Nobody I knew would admit to liking those shows, and they flat-out hated the characters, but they were hooked anyway."

"If we could ask somebody down there what kind of a staff Fontes employs, it would help. Tomás seems to watch that particular villa pretty closely; he might even know if Fontes is home tonight."

"I suppose I could walk down there. Don't like to leave you alone here, though."

More echoes of months ago, when he hadn't wanted me to go off into the darkness of Stone Valley without him. "I'll be okay. Just go."

He nodded and squeezed my shoulder, then got up and moved silently down the beach.

I fended off uneasiness and concern for him by applying my eye to the viewfinder.

Still no movement. Time passed slowly; it could have been five minutes or half an hour. I began to wonder why Hy was taking so long, then realized he probably hadn't even reached the riverbed. Finally I spotted some motion, focused on it. The figure that I thought was Salazar stood, appeared to speak to the other person, then left the room.

I scanned the windows of the villa, but couldn't tell where he'd gone. The other figure remained in the chair for a while, then resumed pacing. Up and down, up and down. Past the glass doors in short, fast steps. Then the shadow came closer to the drapes, and its outlines blurred. The drapes parted, and I stared at Ann Navarro.

Navarro stepped out onto the terrace, shutting the door behind her. She crossed to the wall where there was a space between the glass baffles and leaned forward, palms braced on top of it, head thrown back as she breathed the fresh night air. I scanned the rest of the house. Jaime's window was dark now, no one moved in the other lighted frames. Navarro remained by the wall.

It was a chance that might never present itself again.

I slid back, rolled over, reached into my

bag for the .45. Shoved it into the rear of my waistband, then went around the *pongas* on my hands and knees, heading up the beach toward the northern end of Fontes's property. When I got there, I began to angle in gradually, keeping an eye on the terrace. Navarro still stood alone by the wall, illuminated by the outdoor lights, head hanging down now.

Looking at me?

I stopped, watched. No, she was merely relaxing tense neck muscles.

Rock protruded from the sand next to the terrace's concrete foundation, and the land angled up along its side, where it was flanked by cacti. I moved slowly toward it, scanning the slope and beach, listening for the slightest sound or movement. When I reached the edge of the foundation, I glanced up at where Navarro stood. I could make out only the shape of her head, now turned toward the sea.

On hands and knees I began scaling the slope. The sand that overlaid the rock made it slow going. Hard to gain a foothold, a handhold. Hard to keep from sending a shower of telltale pebbles skittering down behind me. Finally I reached the place where the terrace wall butted into the hillside. The glass baffles didn't quite meet the house; there was a two-foot space through which I could climb onto the terrace. I covered my hands with the long sleeves of Hy's sweater, gritted my teeth, and moved into the thick stand of cactus.

Spines pierced my jeans. I covered my face with my sweater-swathed hands and peered between them. A barrel cactus took painful hold of my right arm; I moved my left hand to free it and suffered a painful swat. Finally I yanked the sleeve loose, tearing the wool and rustling the plants around me. Plunged forward and crouched by the wall.

No footsteps on the terrace. No call of inquiry.

After a bit I stood and peeked over the wall. Navarro was still looking out to sea; I was well outside her peripheral vision. I placed my hands on top of the wall and hoisted myself up. Rolled onto it and swung my legs over, ready to drop. Took the gun from my waistband. Slipped down to the terrace floor and stood with feet wide apart, gun extended in front of me.

Navarro's head jerked. She started to turn.

"Don't move," I said softly, "and don't make a sound."

She froze.

"I have a gun aimed at your back. Step to your right until you touch the side wall."

She moved as I'd told her, stiffly.

"Now step back this way."

She backed up, eyes straight ahead. A cool woman, Navarro.

"Good," I said, moving forward and patting her pockets for weapons.

"What do you want?" Her English was more heavily accented than I'd expected, although by no means broken or ungrammatical. Its strong Hispanic undertone was the reason Hy had taken her for a Mexican national when she'd called with the ransom demands.

"To give you some news — about Stan."

"Stan! What —"

"It's okay to turn around now. Do it slowly."

She did, eyes moving swiftly from my face to the gun. Now lines of strain cut furrows beside her mouth and eyes; she looked years older than she had through my telephoto lens the night before.

"Who are you?" she asked.

"I'm working for RKI."

Quick intake of breath.

"I know all about the kidnapping, how you and Stan and Diane planned it."

"I didn't —"

"I saw Diane at the hospital in San Diego this afternoon."

"Diane! That can't be. Gilbert said . . ."

"Said what?"

"She's dead."

"No, she's in critical condition, but she'll recover."

"Gilbert said she died on the way to Ensenada."

"She was stabilized at the trauma unit there and flown to San Diego. It was Fontes's efforts that made it possible for her to leave Baja without being questioned about the shooting."

"Oh, God!" Navarro put her hands over her face, fingers pressing hard against her eyes.

I asked, "Who shot Diane?"

She shook her head.

"You don't know?"

Silence.

"There's no point in concealing what went on down here."

No reply.

I said, "I saw Stan in San Diego on Thursday."

"You couldn't have. Stan's in Mexico City —" She bit her lips, pressed them together.

"Have you talked with him?"

". . . No."

"Then how do you know he's really there?"

"Gilbert said —"

"Just as he said Diane had died."

Navarro took her hands from her face and studied me. She seemed to be weighing what

I'd told her. "All right, where in San Diego did you see Stan?"

"The county morgue. He's dead. He's been dead since Sunday night when he tried to pick up the letter of credit. Marty Salazar shot him."

Twenty-Eight

Navarro's reaction wasn't what I'd expected. Just a slight hesitation before she said, "You're lying."

"I have an eyewitness to the shooting. He's down on the beach." Somewhere down there, and probably panicked at finding me gone. "And the San Diego police have made a positive I.D. on Stan's body. They've been trying to contact you since shortly after you came down here."

She studied my face, her expression giving no clue as to what she was thinking.

I reached into my pocket and took out a slip of paper on which I'd written Gary Viner's name and phone number. "This is the detective in charge of the case. He'll confirm."

"It's a setup."

"You don't really believe that."

Her eyes moved to the paper. She bit her lip again, then reached for it. "I'll call him. Wait here."

Such bravado in spite of the gun I held both

impressed and amused me. "No, that's not how it works."

"How, then?" Impatient now to get on with it.

"We'll go over the wall the way I came. Down the beach to the access point, where I have a car equipped with a cellular phone. You'll call Viner from there."

Navarro crossed her arms. "How do I know —"

"You don't. But you have no choice, do you?"

She shivered slightly, glanced at the door to the house.

"Let's go," I said.

She went ahead of me, crossing the wall clumsily, wincing when the cactus spines raked her skin. I had to give her credit: she never once cried out. When we were past them, I motioned for her to start down the slope. We descended and moved up the beach in tandem, keeping clear of what light the windows of the neighboring villas cast on the sand. Finally we reached the path to the parking area.

The Seville sat alone where Hy and I had left it. I urged Navarro toward it, then realized he had the keys. Why the hell hadn't I —

"Jesus, McCone, I can't turn my back on you for a minute!" Hy's head appeared from where he crouched on the other side of the car. Nodding, he said, "Ms. Navarro."

Navarro recognized him and stiffened.

"The eyewitness I mentioned," I told her. "I believe you've met." To him I added, "She's decided to call Lieutenant Viner."

"Smart choice." He tossed me the car keys, held open the passenger's door, and motioned her inside; shut it and leaned against it. I got into the driver's seat, flicked on the electrical system, and lowered the passenger-side window so Hy could hear. Holding the phone up so Navarro could see I was dialing the number on the paper she clutched, I made the call and handed the receiver to her.

Navarro pressed it to her ear. After a few seconds her eyes grew wide and her fingers tensed; she asked the SDPD operator for Viner's extension. Identified herself and listened.

"I see . . . Yes . . . I'll . . ." She glanced at the gun I held. "I don't know exactly when I'll return to California, but I'll be in touch with you."

Viner spoke some more.

"Yes, she's here." Navarro handed the phone to me.

"McCone, what the hell is going on?" Gary demanded.

"I told you I'd have Ms. Navarro contact you. And I —"

"I'm tired of this runaround. I want you in my office —"

"I'll see you in less than twelve hours." Saying it gave me a rush of confidence. Maybe saying it would make it so. . . .

"What time?"

"I don't know exactly."

"McCone —"

I was tired of arguing with him, so I broke the connection. When I glanced at Hy, he looked amused.

Navarro sat with her head down, hands twisted in her lap, still clutching the slip of paper. "It's true," she said, a desolate note underscoring her words.

"It's true."

She raised her head, turned to look at Hy. "You were there with him?"

"Yes."

"What happened?"

He squatted beside the car, described the scene more tersely than he had to me. Navarro listened silently, flinching when he got to the part about Stan being shot.

After Hy finished I said, "Everything's coming unraveled, Ann. You'd better cooperate with us."

No reply.

"You're in very big trouble," I added. "Kidnapping, accessory to transporting a kidnap victim over an international boundary. If Mourning dies, it's special circumstances — carries the death penalty."

When she still didn't say anything, Hy asked, "Where's Fontes?"

". . . He flew to Mexico City with the letter of credit late this afternoon. He was going to . . . He *said* he was going to meet Stan there and put the L.C. through in the morning. Then they'd come back here to divide the money. But now I know that Stan's —" She shook her head.

"What about Timothy?"

"At the villa. They've kept him doped up since . . . since this morning."

Hy said, "You know they're going to kill him."

"It wasn't supposed to be that way!"

He gave her a skeptical look, but didn't comment.

I said, "You also must realize what Fontes and Salazar plan for you."

Navarro still didn't want to believe what was happening. She put out her hands, fending off reality. "How do I know *any* of what you say is the truth?"

"You talked to Viner. That wasn't a set-up."

"But about Diane — how do I know she's really alive?"

I picked up the phone and held it out to her. "Call Cabrillo Hospital in San Diego. Ask for a report on her condition. When I saw her earlier, she was critical but stable. She was even able to talk with me for a while."

Navarro looked at the phone but didn't take it. "Okay, maybe that's so. But if Fontes is going to kill me and keep all the money, why did he send Diane back to the States? He could've just let her die."

"Her continued existence, as well as Tim's, is insurance that he'll get the money. He won't know for sure that you've been straight with him until the L.C. clears. If anything goes wrong in Mexico City, he's got the ammunition to force you to cooperate. Diane's a co-conspirator; Tim's a victim. They could testify against you."

"But he's treated me like a business associate, a guest in his home. He hasn't restricted me in any way."

"Of course not. He doesn't want you to suspect what he plans to do. He'd probably have let you go on believing you were to get your share of the money right up till the end. But finally the time would have come for him to dispose of his liabilities — namely Tim, Diane, and you. Easy to get rid of you and Tim, and

Diane wouldn't be that much of a problem. If I could get to her in the hospital, so can Salazar or one of Fontes's people."

Panic seeped into her eyes as she finally accepted reality. "I can't go back to that house!"

"Well, where do you expect to go?" Hy gestured at the darkness around us.

Her gaze moved from me to him, pleading.

"No," he said, "we're not going to help you."

"Unless you help us," I added.

Silence. Hy's eyes met mine. We waited.

"All right," Navarro said heavily. "What do you want me to do?"

"Help us get Mourning out of there."

"That's impossible. You'd have to get past Salazar, Jaime, and Gilbert's bodyguard."

"Two bodyguards," Hy corrected her. "Fontes has two." Obviously Tomás or someone else at the riverbed had been able to help him.

"One's with him in Mexico City."

"Okay," I said, "we're dealing with the one bodyguard, Salazar, and Jaime. Anybody else on the premises?"

"The cook and the maid don't live in. The maid brought some ice into the living room about half an hour before I came outside; she said they were both going home."

"What about the bartender?"

"Just somebody who comes in when Fontes has people over."

"Salazar didn't bring anybody with him but Jaime?"

She shook her head.

"Okay, give us some idea of the layout of the villa — where Mourning's being held, where everybody else is sleeping."

Navarro began to talk, describing the rooms and various locations. She and Salazar were in the wing that looked like a bell tower; the others were in the shorter wing at the opposite end of the house. Mourning's room was on the ground floor between those of the bodyguards, while Jaime slept directly upstairs.

Hy asked, "Is there a security system?"

"Not that I know of."

"And have all the others gone to bed?"

"I think so, but you never know with Salazar. He prowls."

Hy's mouth twisted wryly and he touched his left arm. "I'm painfully aware of that." He glanced across Navarro at me. "I'd better check it out with the camera."

"Okay." I watched him move toward the path to the beach.

His departure made Navarro nervous, as if she feared me more than him. She looked away to her right, shredding what remained of the slip of paper with Viner's number on it. When

I used the automatic controls to raise her window and lock her door, she started.

I asked, "Will Salazar go looking for you if he finds you're not where he left you?"

"I doubt it. So long as my car's still there, he'll think I've gone to bed."

"Will he check your room?"

"It wouldn't do him any good. I've kept it locked the whole time I've been here, even when I wasn't in there." She reached into her pocket and showed me a key.

"Just how doped up is Tim?"

She considered. "He was mobile, but pretty spaced out earlier today. They probably knocked him out for the night, though."

I tried to picture rescuing a heavily drugged man from the guarded house. A seemingly impossible task. And then there was the problem of moving him across the border once we got to Tijuana. The coyote, Al Mojas, might balk at the increased danger. I supposed we could hole up somewhere in the border city, make our move the next night when Mourning would be more alert, but I didn't like that, either. Every additional minute we spent in Baja could be fatal.

Of course, there was La Procuraduría de Protección al Turista — the Attorney General for the Protection of the Tourist. Wasn't that the agency all the guidebooks told you to contact if you had legal trouble down here? Oh, sure. La Procuraduría probably lived in Fontes's hip pocket; Gilbert would be waiting on its doorstep to welcome us. Besides, Mexico's judicial system operates on the Napoleonic Code: you're guilty until proven innocent. And we were about to be guilty as hell of breaking into Fontes's villa.

To take my mind off all the possible pitfalls, I decided to clear up some details that had been bothering me. I asked Navarro, "You were holding Tim at your house near Blossom Hill?"

". . . Yes. We didn't . . . treat him badly."

Even though you intended to kill him later. "How did Fontes figure out where he was?"

"Diane let it slip. She drinks, and when she drinks, she talks too much."

"Didn't it make you suspicious of Fontes's intentions when Jaime brought Tim here last night?"

"How do you know all this?"

"You've been under surveillance for quite some time now."

"Oh. Well . . . yes, at first I wondered, but then Gilbert took me aside and explained that he felt it'd be safer for all of us to be down here in Baja. He pays protection to the federal police, you see. It made sense, and besides, I'd been worried about Tim. He was alone with nobody to look after him. At first I planned only to stay down here the one night."

"What explanation did Fontes give you for having the L.C.?"

"He told me that a few years ago, before Stan and I were married, Stan got into big-time financial trouble and borrowed heavily from him to bail himself out. The note had come due, so Stan gave Fontes the L.C. as security against his being repaid out of our share of the proceeds. It surprised me, but I figured Stan knew what he was doing. I was the only one who could activate the process of drawing on it, through my contact at Colores."

"Had Stan ever mentioned this financial problem to you?"

"No."

"Or the outstanding loan?"

"No."

"Had he ever even mentioned knowing Gilbert Fontes?"

She shook her head, eyes turned down.

"And you — a smart businesswoman — bought the whole story, just like that?"

"Fontes had the L.C.," she said defensively. "He knew all about the kidnapping. He contacted Diane first, and she contacted me. We decided it was best to come down here and talk with him. Before we did, I spoke with Gilbert; I'd been getting panicky because I hadn't heard from Stan. He gave me the name of the hotel where Stan was supposed to be staying in Mexico City. I called there; he was registered."

"But you didn't talk with him."

"He wasn't in his room."

"You leave a message?"

"Yes."

"But he never called back."

"I left to come down here before he would have had a chance. Besides, I knew Stan would need a tourist card to register at a hotel on the mainland, and to get one, you have to show I.D."

"There was no I.D. on Stan's body. And you heard Ripinsky's account of the night of the shooting: Salazar was outside the adobe listening to what he and Stan were saying. That's how Fontes knew about the kidnapping and what kind of story to tell you."

"All right, I've been stupid! But you don't know Fontes, how convincing he can be. Besides, I wanted to believe him. Otherwise, it would have meant that Stan . . ."

"Which is exactly what it did mean."

"Stop it!" She pressed her hands to her ears.

I stopped. No matter what this woman had done, badgering her was a cheap indulgence.

She'd get plenty of that soon enough from the authorities, the prosecuting attorneys, and her own conscience — providing she had one.

But there were other things I wanted to know. "Ann, why did Diane Mourning contact you and Stan about kidnapping her husband?"

She drew her hands together in her lap, fighting to regain her composure. The question gave her focus; after a moment she replied calmly, "She contacted Stan. He'd known both Mournings well a few years before. They were heavy contributors to a fund-raising campaign Stan ran for the fishing industry. They needed a source of dolphin cartilage for that drug their company is developing, and they thought if they supported the fishing industry, they'd make contacts who would help them."

"So Stan met them at a fund-raiser?"

She nodded. "This was back before I knew him. Stan got to be friends with them; they spent a lot of time together. The Mournings were living pretty high back then. Too high, I guess, because a couple of years later they had to sell their boat and vacation home in Laguna Beach, and then their condo in San Francisco. After that, Stan said, he didn't hear much from them; it works that way when your friends slip into a lower financial bracket."

"So when did Diane reestablish contact with Stan?"

Navarro's mouth turned down. "A few months ago — March, maybe. She showed up at his office. She told him the labs were in trouble and Tim had lost interest in his work — in her, too. She'd found out he had somebody else that he was serious about, and she was afraid he was working up to leaving her. She played on Stan's sympathies."

Navarro looked down at her clenched hands. Separated them and rubbed them against her thighs, then brought them together lightly. "Stan and Diane started sleeping together. I found that out from his secretary. And next thing I knew, the kidnapping was all planned."

"Why'd you go along with it?"

She shrugged.

"You must have some idea."

"Well, the money, partly. Diane was going to split it fifty-fifty with us."

"Didn't it bother you to kidnap and kill someone?"

"We weren't going to kill him!"

"Come on, Ann. Mourning might not have known who you were, but he and Stan had been friends."

"Stan wore a disguise. And I was the one

who took food and stuff to Tim. I even wore a wig."

"Oh, Ann, Ripinsky saw through Stan's disguise right away, and from a distance. Of course Stan planned to kill Tim. And on some level you knew that."

She sighed deeply.

"How could you have believed what Stan told you, when you knew he was sleeping with Tim's wife?"

". . . I don't know. Maybe I thought if I helped him, I could hold him. Stan slept around a lot; I couldn't believe Diane was that important to him. But I don't know. My whole life before Stan, I never trusted any man, never gave in to anybody. I didn't want to be like my mother, you see — always doing for other people, always having babies, always saying yes, yes, yes. But when I married Stan . . . he was stronger than me, and I just got weaker. The worst of it is, I don't know why. And now it's too late."

I couldn't argue with that.

Hy appeared, moving swiftly. I lowered the window, and he leaned toward it. "We better move now. Salazar was out prowling, but he's gone inside again. When I left off watching him, he was upstairs."

I nodded. Hy went around to Navarro's door, gun in hand. I unlocked it, and she got out.

I started the car and turned it around so it was pointed at the road. Left it with the doors locked, pocketed the keys, and joined Hy and Navarro by the path to the beach.

"We'll go back the way we came," I told her. "Ripinsky'll be in front of you, I'll be behind. When we get to the villa, you'll take us to Mourning's room. Don't try to warn anybody. If you do, I won't hesitate to kill you."

Navarro looked more convinced by my words than I was; she compressed her lips and glanced at Hy.

He said, "Don't look at me. I won't hesitate, either."

As he spoke I caught a glimpse of the violence that simmered beneath his civilized exterior. I had no doubt he meant what he'd said. As for myself, I'd never know exactly what I was capable of until I was called to action.

Twenty-Nine

Light still glowed softly in the room off the terrace. Hy vaulted the wall, then gave Navarro a boost up. I followed.

We stood in the shadows for a moment. I could hear nothing but the surge of the tide and the pounding of my own heart, accelerated by the adrenaline flowing through me. Hy tapped Navarro's shoulder, pushed her forward to the door. She tried to open it, then turned, face set in lines of frustration.

I went over there and tried it myself. Locked. I pulled Navarro back toward the wall and whispered, "Is there any other door that might be open?"

"Maybe off the patio where the pool is."

"Let's go."

She led us across the terrace, down some steps, and along a path bordered by tall agaves. It curved into a walled courtyard with a pool and hot tub. We skirted them in the darkness, and Navarro tried a sliding door to the house. Also locked.

I put my lips close to her ear and asked, "Is that wing to the right where Mourning and the bodyguard are sleeping?"

She nodded.

"What about a window?"

"All barred."

I looked at Hy. He shrugged.

"You'll have to wake the bodyguard," I told Navarro. "Say you were walking on the beach and got locked out."

Hy was examining the door. He pointed to the side where the opening would be, then slipped behind an agave that grew next to the wall. To Navarro I added, "Ask him to let you in this way."

"How am I supposed to —"

"Ssh! Knock on his window; say you didn't want to disturb the others by ringing the bell."

"I don't know which —"

"Guess. If you get the wrong window, the only other person you'll disturb is Mourning."

She moved toward the wing at the right. I followed, covering her. She rounded the corner, began counting windows. Stopped at the third one, then stepped across a low bed of cacti and knocked. I stopped some five feet away as a man's voice called out in inquiry.

Navarro replied swiftly in Spanish. I caught enough of the words to know she hadn't given us away. The man said something else; she snapped at him. Then she turned and walked past me, going back to the door.

"Try to get him outside," I whispered, and followed. There was no sign of Hy, not even a shadow behind the agave. After a moment a clatter came from inside the house — the guard removing a security bar from the door. It slid open and a short, stocky man looked out at Navarro.

She stayed where she was, near the pool. Pointed at the water and said something that I took to mean she wanted him to have a look at something.

He frowned. *"Que?"*

"Está muerta."

The man came through the door, scowling.

Hy's arm shot from behind the agave and hooked around his neck. The man gagged. Hy dragged him farther outside, applying pressure on his carotid; the man went limp.

I looked around, spotted a big bin near the wall — the kind that's used to store swim equipment or lounge cushions. Still covering Navarro, I went over and opened it. Empty. I motioned to Hy. He dragged the bodyguard over there.

I knelt and searched him for a gun. There was a .44 Magnum in the pocket of his bathrobe. I took it over and dropped it into the pool. Hy picked the man up and dumped him inside the bin, lowered the lid and secured the latch. At the bottom was a ventilation screen to prevent mildew; the man wouldn't suffocate, but when he recovered consciousness, any sound he might make would be muffled.

Hy went to the door, stepped inside. I motioned to Navarro, and she and I followed.

We stood in a terra-cotta-tiled room with a bar and a pool table where a game had been in progress. A sconce burned faintly on the far wall. I located its switch and turned it off.

"Now," Hy whispered, "Mourning's room."

We crossed to an archway that opened into the hall. A carpeted stairway rose to the left, and then the hall continued to the right. Hy grasped Navarro's forearm. She walked a half step ahead of him, past an open door through which I could see a rumpled bed, to a closed door. Nodding, she pointed at it.

I went around them and tried the knob. Locked. I looked back at Hy and shook my head. He grimaced. Then I remembered that Navarro carried the key to her own room. Any given manufacturer's door locks are guaranteed to be fairly standardized, and in a house this size there was bound to be some duplication. I said to Navarro, "Give me your room key."

She fished it out and handed it over.

The key slipped easily into the lock, then stuck. I tried jiggling it, felt a loosening. I forced it and the tumblers started to turn, then jammed. I twisted harder. The lock popped with a crack.

I pushed the door open and waved Hy and Navarro inside. Shut the door behind us. No sounds from upstairs, no telltale creak of floorboards.

The room was dark except for a night-light plugged into a socket near the baseboard. Its bulb elongated our shadows, spread them over the ceiling. At the far side I made out a bedstead — and a figure lying on the bare mattress.

He wore badly rumpled jeans and a shirt, its tail untucked. He wasn't shackled in any way. He lay curled up in the fetal position, face pressed into the pillow. I went up to the bed and touched his shoulder. He gave a faint moan of protest.

I stuck my gun in my waistband and turned the man's face away from the pillow. It was Mourning. An unkempt beard covered his cheeks; they looked hollowed, his eyes badly underscored. As I moved him, his lips twitched and he mumbled something. I whispered his name. His eyes came open — dull and unfocused.

"Help me sit him up," I told Navarro.

She hesitated, then came forward. We got Mourning into a sitting position, his head lolling onto my shoulder. I looked at the nightstand for evidence of what drugs they'd been giving him. Saw only his glasses, both lenses shattered and one earpiece ripped off.

"What happened to his glasses?" I asked Navarro.

"Salazar broke them."

"Deliberately?"

". . . Yes. So he couldn't get away. Tim's practically blind without them."

It was the final obscene cruelty. My hands balled into fists. When I glanced up at Hy, I saw my rage reflected in the set of his jaw.

Mourning mumbled again.

I slid my arm around his slumped shoulders. "Tim," I said, "it's going to be okay now."

He started to raise his head, then let it fall forward.

"Tim, wake up." I put my hand under his chin, propped it up. "We're going to take you home."

More mumbles. Then, "Kill me."

"Nobody's going to kill you. You're safe now."

"Safe?"

"But you've got to help us. Can you walk?"

"Walk?"

"So we can take you home."

He flinched. Jerked back, sitting up under his own power. "Not home!"

"Ssh!" I glanced at Hy, who was listening at the door now.

"Diane . . ."

"It's okay. She can't hurt you anymore."

My words made no impression. Mourning shrank back on the mattress. I followed his gaze, saw he was staring at Navarro. "Get her out of here," I told Hy.

He grabbed her arm, dragged her over by the door. She pulled away and drew back into a corner between a bureau and the wall.

Mourning's eyes were wide and panicky now. He struggled to rise, gained a shaky footing. I got up fast and draped his arm over my shoulder. "You take her," I told Hy. "We've got to get out of here."

Hy motioned for Navarro to come out of the corner. When she didn't move, he went over and got her. She struggled and he pinned her arm behind her back. "Don't give us trouble now," he muttered. "We've got Mourning; you're expendable."

Instantly she stopped struggling and went with him.

Holding tight to Navarro's arm, Hy looked out into the hallway. Signaled to me and slipped through the door.

451

Mourning leaned heavily on me. I took a small step. He said, "Can't."

"Try."

He took a small step that almost matched mine.

"Good. Another."

"Dizzy."

"I've got you."

We navigated the space between the bed and the door.

Hy waited in the hall, still gripping Navarro by the arm. When we came out, he turned and moved toward the room off the patio. Navarro went quietly, all the fight gone out of her.

Mourning supported some of his own weight now. We moved as one, lurching from side to side like a large ungainly animal. Partway to the door he slipped and almost fell. I half carried, half dragged him the rest of the distance.

Through the archway. Past the wet bar. Around the pool table. Hy at the door now, checking outside. Navarro beside him, rubbing her arm.

Mourning saw her and stiffened. He made a growling sound and his feet churned against the tiles, as if he wanted to get at her. She shrank back against the wall.

Three feet to the door. Hy moving to help

us. Step . . . drag . . . stumble. My heart pounding. Mourning's breath labored. Step . . . drag . . . step . . . step . . . Hy reaching out —

Lights flashed on around us.

Mourning stumbled again, pitched forward, his arm slipping off my shoulders. As Hy tried to go for his gun, Mourning reeled into him. They went down. I whirled, trying to get at my .45.

Too late.

Jaime stood inside the archway, a .357 Magnum leveled at us. His thick lips twisted in a grotesque smile. He said, "Whatta buncha *payasos.*"

Payasos: clowns. Of all words, why the hell did I have to understand that one?

He added, "Stick your guns over there on the bar."

I glanced at Hy, who was getting up from the floor. He didn't look so much afraid as sheepish. We went to the bar, set our weapons down. I backed up, watching Jaime, until my buttocks pressed against the edge of the pool table. Hy stood midway between us.

Mourning lay on the floor, moaning. Navarro was still flattened against the wall, eyes wild. She pushed away from it, started toward Jaime, arms held out in a placating gesture.

Smiling, Jaime shot her in the head.

As the bullet smashed into Navarro's skull, I shut my eyes and whipped my head away so fast that pain shot up my neck. My stomach lurched violently. I opened my eyes and caught a glimpse of Hy's face — slack-jawed, sick. I leaned farther back against the table, hands splayed on the felt. Moved them around until I found a billiard ball.

Jaime was still smiling. He swung his gun toward Hy. "Shouldn't've come back here, asshole."

I straightened with the ball tightly gripped in my fingers. Moved my arm in a smooth, strong arc, and let the ball fly at Jaime's head. In the last second I saw it was the eight ball.

Jaime saw me move, but too late. As he started to swing his gun around, the hard ivory ball slammed into his temple with a resounding crack. His eyes rolled up; he went to his knees, losing his grip on the Magnum, then fell sideways.

Hy leaped for the bar, grabbed one of the guns; I went for the other. He picked up Mourning and slung him over his shoulder. There was noise in the other part of the house now — running footsteps. Salazar's voice called out in Spanish.

We plunged through the door, ran across

the patio and down the path. Veered off and zigzagged through the agaves toward the beach.

As we slid down the sandy slope, Hy gasped, "Jesus, McCone, not only're you playing in the majors but you throw one mean fastball!"

Thirty

Monday, June 14
12:17 A.M.

When we got to the car, all was quiet except for a dog barking somewhere down the road. Salazar hadn't followed us, and no one had come out of any of the other villas. Still, my heart beat fast and I had to fight off nausea every time I pictured the bullet shattering Navarro's skull.

Forcing the horrible image from my mind, I opened the door to the backseat of the Seville. As Hy laid Mourning on it, Tim grunted and then fell silent — in shock, I supposed. I got my jacket out of the trunk and started to hand it to Hy. "Better wrap this around him."

He didn't reach for it, just stood pressing his hand to his wounded arm. When he removed it, it was streaked with blood. "Damned thing's opened up," he said.

"Do you have anything in your bag that you can use as an extra bandage?"

He shook his head. "Don't worry — it's not that serious." He took the jacket from me and arranged it over Mourning. "You better drive, though."

I got behind the wheel, adjusted the seat and mirrors, and started the engine. Hy climbed into the passenger seat. Without lights, I coasted onto the road and turned toward the village. Hy twisted around and looked behind us. "Fontes's front yard is all lit up, but the auto gate's still closed."

I flicked on the headlights and speeded up. Soon we entered the village. No police in evidence, no other activity. Its sidewalks were deserted, the lights of the shops muted. Only the stock-brokerage's sign flashed; trading was up on the London exchange. I drove slowly, carefully, to the main highway. Turned north and pressed down on the accelerator.

Hy had turned to look at Mourning.

I asked, "How's he doing?"

"Asleep or passed out. Just as well."

"For now — but is he going to be able to make the crossing?"

"He'll make it," Hy said grimly.

For a while we drove in silence. Then he asked, "So what d'you want to do when this is over?"

"Sleep."

"No, seriously . . ."

"Climb into the Citabria and fly away."

"Where?"

"Anyplace where it's quiet and relatively deserted. And for a good long time."

"What about All Souls?"

All Souls! In our catching up, somehow I'd neglected to tell him what was going on there. "It's not an issue," I said. "I don't work there anymore."

"What?"

"Uh-huh." I nodded. "They were going to force me into a desk job — a promotion, they called it. I hated the idea, but was considering it because I didn't want to leave. Then before I could give them an answer, I took off to look for you. They found out, so here I am — unemployed."

"My fault."

"Why? I knew what I was doing. And maybe it's not such a bad thing, in the long run. Maybe it's time for a change."

"That's what I said before I went to talk with Renshaw."

Again we fell silent. The lights of Ensenada appeared, then receded in the rearview mirror. Traffic was light; I kept an eye out for a tail or a police car. Kept my speed down close to the limit.

Mourning stirred, then struggled to sit up. "Got to puke," he muttered.

I pulled the car onto the shoulder, and Hy went to help him. After a while they returned, Mourning looking better.

"Tim," I said as he settled into the backseat, "do you know what kind of drug they've been giving you?"

"Barbiturates of some sort." He massaged his eyes. "I've been sleeping so much I don't even know what day it is. And now I can't see more than a few feet in front of me. That Salazar bastard broke my glasses."

"I know. It's Sunday, June thirteenth . . . well, Monday, actually." I waited for a truck to pass, then pulled onto the highway.

"Christ," Mourning said. "Almost two weeks." He paused. "I really owe you people. RKI's one hell of an outfit."

I didn't respond to the latter comment, and neither did Hy, clearly as unwilling to go into the whole story as I was.

Hy asked, "Have the drugs pretty much worn off by now?"

"Yeah, except every move makes me feel winded and gets my heart pounding. And I've got a splitting headache."

Which meant he'd require a fair amount of assistance during our crossing. I said, "We'll get you something for your headache. Try to rest now."

"Where're you taking me?"

"Tijuana, then San Diego."

Hy glanced questioningly at me.

I shook my head. I didn't want Mourning getting anxious about the way he'd have to cross the border yet.

Tim asked, "Where's Diane?"

"In a San Diego hospital. Do you remember anything about her being shot?"

He was silent. "I don't remember much of anything," he finally said. Then he lay down and closed his eyes.

I looked at Hy. His expression was as puzzled as mine must have been. The man's wife had been shot, but he didn't ask about her condition. Granted, he had reason to hate her, but wouldn't that make him all the more anxious to know how badly she'd been injured? And why wasn't he interested in whether or not she'd been arrested?

"Still in shock?" I mouthed.

Hy shrugged and slumped against the door, his hand pressing his leaking bullet wound.

Half an hour later the lights of Tijuana formed a glowing dome in the post-midnight sky. Tourist cities — sin cities, in some people's opinion — never sleep. I said, "We'll take Tim to Al Mojas's house, get him some coffee and aspirin, maybe some food. Then one of us can return the car and take a cab back there."

"I'd better; it's rented in my name. Besides, I want to check the border control. There's still a chance we won't have to go over the fence."

"You sure you feel up to that?"

"I feel up to it."

"I don't have to tell you to be careful."

"You don't have to, but thanks, I will."

The streets of Colonia Libertad were as busy as if it were high noon. Children ran about, dogs barked, adults crowded the food stands or stood around trading shots of liquor. Many had the bundled look of would-be emigrants, wearing layer upon layer of clothing. I drove to the corner house with the palm tree and the statue of the Virgin Mary in its front yard, parked and left the keys in the ignition. Then I went to help Tim Mourning on the next step of his journey home.

2:36 A.M.

"I don' know, I just don' know." Al Mojas sat across the rickety kitchen table from Mourning and me, shaking his head. The room had a linoleum floor so worn that its original color was indiscernible; pink paint was peeling off the walls in scales. On the iron cookstove, a pot of spicy tomato sauce simmered. Mojas's wife, a heavyset woman named Nita, had been in and out of the room half a dozen times to stir it and offer us food. I'd declined because I wasn't hungry; Mourning had said he didn't feel well enough to eat. Nita fussed and kept pouring us more coffee until Al told her to get out and stay out.

"What don't you know?" I asked him.

"You got a guy here" — he gestured at Mourning — "so stoned he can't walk right. I'm all set to go when you get here, but now where's the others? I tell you, this whole thing's looking fuckin' iffy."

"The other man'll be here soon." I glanced at Mourning, who leaned heavily on the table, mug of coffee in a death grip. I wasn't sure he comprehended the situation, although I'd explained it to him after we came inside the house. "This one will make it just fine," I added with far more confidence than I felt.

"I don' know," Mojas said again. "You knocked my price way down. And now I got this dummy." He shot Mourning a disapproving glance. "I think I better renegotiate."

"Look," I said, "we have a deal."

He set his jaw stubbornly. "We got a deal, but I didn't know about him. Somebody who can't look out for hisself, it makes it more dangerous."

I'd promised him nearly all the cash I had,

and coyotes didn't honor Visa. "The deal stands," I said flatly.

Mojas folded his arms and looked at me.

Mourning didn't have any money on him. I was reasonably sure Hy had less than I did. Just how much *did* I have? I reached for my oversized purse, which Hy had retrieved from the beach in front of Fontes's villa along with the camera. The camera . . .

"Listen," I said again, "I've only got about twenty dollars, but I can give you something valuable to make up for the additional danger."

Mojas looked at the purse, licked his lips. "What?"

I opened the purse and took out the camera. "You can sell this for quite a bit — the lens and mount alone retail for over four hundred. Or you can keep it to use in your work. It's not as good as the night scopes *la migra* use, but it'll give you an edge."

Mojas reached eagerly for the camera. He put his eye to the scope, sighted around the room. "Oh, man," he said.

"Deal?" I asked.

"Deal." He got up and placed the camera on a cabinet behind him. Before he turned, I saw his hand caress it.

I glanced at Mourning. He'd raised his head, was watching Mojas. For a man whose life was on the line, he seemed curiously placid. Maybe he didn't comprehend how much danger lay before us. Or maybe the placidity was a side effect of his long confinement. Whatever the reason, this was not the man I'd read about in the newspaper and magazine profiles.

A car door slammed in the street. Footsteps came up the walk. Mojas left the room and returned shortly after, followed by Hy.

"Sorry I took so long," Hy said.

I asked, "Did you check the border control?"

"Uh-huh. I didn't see Salazar, but there's a guy hanging around near the corridor that goes into U.S. Customs; I could swear I saw him coming out of his place on Island Avenue."

I took a deep breath, exhaled slowly. On some level I'd still hoped we could just walk through the checkpoint like any returning tourists.

Mojas was looking interested, but he merely asked, "Everybody here now?"

"Yes," I said.

"What about the other woman?"

Hy and I exchanged glances. Mourning's head was bowed over his coffee mug. Hy said, "She didn't make it."

Mojas stood. "Then let's get a move on. You bring the dummy." He motioned at

Mourning. The whole time we'd been in his house, he'd never once addressed Tim directly.

Mourning didn't seem to notice what Mojas had called him. He looked at Hy, then nodded obediently. Hy went over and helped him stand.

I rose, hefting my bag.

"No." Mojas snapped his fingers, pointed at it. "Everything you need goes in your pockets. Stick the gun someplace where you won't get blown away if you fall."

I set the bag on the table and opened it. Crammed my wallet and I.D. folder into my shirt pocket under Hy's sweater. Stuck the gun in the waistband of my jeans. The rest of the contents — makeup, address book, comb — were inessential. At the last minute, though, I stuffed my Swiss Army knife and a piece of coral that I carry for good luck into the pocket of my jeans.

When I straightened, Hy and Mourning were already leaving the room. Mojas looked levelly at me, then turned. I followed him — the man who claimed he always got his people through.

Thirty-One

We huddled together on the hard rock ground, only yards from the border fence. On the barren hillside behind us, fires had hours ago been doused. It was a chill moonless night, and stone silent. No one moved, no one spoke, yet I could feel the presence of the others who waited here. Their fear and urgency created a pressure that surged against the fence like floodwaters against a dam; soon it would burst over the corrugated steel panels, and we would be carried on its tide down into the canyons — to deeper darkness, danger, and, for some, death.

In a hoarse whisper, Mojas said, "Them panels, they're easy to climb. You grab onto them posts, pull yourself up and over. You" — he pointed at Hy — "better help the dummy."

I glanced at Mourning. Tim didn't appear offended by the way Mojas spoke of him; in-

466

stead he studied the coyote coolly, a scientist observing a member of a lower and somewhat repulsive order. He seemed more alert now, although I noted that his reactions were still slow.

I asked, "Then what happens?"

"You stick close behind me. Canyon's maybe twenty feet ahead. Case you lose me, stay put; I'll find you. Keep low. Those scopes *la migra*'s got, they pick up every move you make. A guy told me we glow on them — yellow, like gold." He laughed bitterly. "Gold. That's a good one, ain't it? 'Course in a way we *are* gold to you people. You can't do without us."

Mourning was still staring at Mojas. Now he asked, "Why do you say that?"

"Hey, the dummy can talk! I'm sayin' it because it's true. We go over that fence, we work your fields, take care of your kids, do any kind of shit work you throw at us. Or you send your goods down here to our *maquiladores,* we send them back finished. Where'd you be without our cheap labor?"

"A damn sight closer to full employment for Americans." Tim was showing some spirit, thank God.

"Shit, man, don't give me that. What you people do, you build a goddamn fence to keep us out, hunt us down like dogs in the canyons, but you sure don't make any fuss when one of us buses your table in some fancy L.A. restaurant."

Mourning shrugged.

"Okay, you don't want to believe it, that's your business."

We continued squatting there in silence. A cold wind whipped across the barren hillside, and I turned up my collar. Hy was pressing his hand to his arm, face pained. Bleeding again?

Suddenly there was a stir farther down the fence line to our left. Running footsteps and then the clang of metal as dark figures scaled the panels. Mojas stood, looked. Shook his head as he squatted again. "Damn fools. *La migra*'s got a guy right over there on horseback."

"How can you see him?" I asked.

"You make this crossing as many times as I have, you know where to look, what to look for. Piece of good luck for us, though. Most nights they don't have more than eight or nine agents out here. Guys who just went over, they'll keep that one busy for a while. What we're gonna do is go the other way down the fence toward Smuggler's Gulch."

He stood and began moving in a crouch, motioning for us to follow. When we got to the fence, we turned east. I brought up the rear, reaching out to touch the steel panels; they were icy and unyielding. My fingers felt scarcely warmer. I crossed my arms and hugged myself, tucking my hands against my sides.

More activity behind us. More clashing of metal back where the others had crossed. I started to look over my shoulder, but lost my balance and almost fell on the uneven ground. After that I kept my eyes straight ahead, focused on Mourning's shoulders.

The commotion behind us escalated. Feet slapped and stumbled on the other side of the fence now. I heard someone curse, someone else cry out. There was a thud, and a child began to wail. The dam had burst; an unchecked stream of bodies spewed across the border and flooded the canyons. Propelled by fear, by need, by sheer recklessness, they surged forth and inundated the forbidden territory.

Mojas held up his hand and we stopped, squatted again. "Let's give *la migra* a chance to get real busy."

I looked at Hy; he was still pressing his wound. When he looked back at me, his smile was edged with pain. Mourning squatted to Hy's right, myopic gaze unfocused. He might have been getting his fear under control or contemplating his own mortality or merely zoning out. There was no way to tell what he might be thinking, no way to tell how he'd handle himself once we made our move.

The commotion on the hillside was dying down. Someone shouted in the nearby canyon, the unintelligible words echoing as they rose. Mojas stood.

"It's time."

I shot to my feet, adrenaline pumping. Hy rose more slowly, grasping Mourning's arm and helping him.

"Up and over," Mojas told us. "When you hit the ground, keep going downhill. You'll come to a clump of bushes. Wait there. When I know it's okay, we'll run into the canyon. It's real steep. Halfway down, there's a buncha rocks. We'll stop again, then move slower. I click my fingers, you follow. I stop, you stop. No talking till we get through to this big drainage pipe off Monument Road. Got it?"

"Got it," I said.

Hy and Mourning nodded.

"Then let's go."

Up and over: not so easy as Mojas claimed. Fence posts icy, panels slick. A foothold gained, lost, regained. Halfway up, I slipped. Slid back to the ground, wrenching the arm that grasped the post.

Mojas was already on the other side. Hy straddled the top, hauling Mourning up. I grabbed the post, started climbing again. Lost my footing and gritted my teeth in frustration.

Clinging to the post, I planted my right foot more securely. Brought the left up. Climbed carefully. Finally my fingers touched the top. I got a good hold, pulled with every bit of my strength.

Palms flat on the top now, pushing. Torso rolling forward, legs following. For a moment I teetered there, then lost my hold and plummeted downward. Onto American soil.

Home, yet not home. In a no-one's-land full of dangers both known and unknown. Bandits didn't discriminate against American citizens; neither did crooked coyotes and Tijuana cops.

I'd hit hard on all fours; now I pushed up, looking around for the others. Nothing but darkness, the night so black I couldn't see more than five feet in front of me. I ran downhill blindly, stumbling over stones, skidding on pebbles.

Shadows ahead now, the slope steeper. I fought for balance, pitched forward. Put my hands out and plunged into a stand of dry, prickly vegetation.

A hand grasped my arm, kept me from falling. Hy: I couldn't see him, identified him by the rough weave of his wool jacket. My breath came in gasps. I got it under control as I waited.

After a moment I heard Mojas snap his fingers. He moved out — a blur darting downhill. A second blur followed: Mourning. I nudged Hy; he went ahead of me.

Another stop: the rocks. Another wait. Another snap of the fingers.

We moved more slowly now, in a zigzag path. The ground got steeper, rockier; the vegetation grew thicker. The sky was an inverted black lacquer bowl above the canyon. Cactus spines pierced my clothing.

There were night creatures down here. Scorpions, coyotes — the real kind. Rattlers, too —

Don't think about them.

There were other people down here; I could sense their presence, hear small telltale noises. *Pollos,* badly frightened. Their coyotes, who had been known to turn on their own customers for a few pesos. And the bandits —

Don't think about them, either.

And *la migra* — God, I'd started to look upon our own border patrol as my enemy! But in a way, they were. If they picked us up, they'd want to know what we were doing out here. If we explained about the kidnapping, they'd want to know why the FBI hadn't been called in. Besides, hadn't I read somewhere that the border patrol had been accused by a human-rights organization of excessive abusiveness?

We were deep in the canyon now. Mojas's hand stayed me, pulled me down beside a rock pile. Mourning was breathing hard. Hy's body tensed — with pain, I thought.

As we waited there, I remembered the story Gloria Escobar had told me in my office at All Souls last Tuesday while trying to persuade me to accept the proffered promotion. Remembered her pregnant mother, who had brought her older sister through this same canyon unassisted by a coyote, separated from the others, attacked by bandits — and yet she had made the crossing and then walked some fifteen miles to the safe house, carrying both her daughter and her unborn child.

Gloria, I thought, I think I can understand what you were trying to tell me. Can grasp the full value of the life you've shaped for yourself and your daughter. I hope I get the chance to tell you that your mother's story has given me courage. . . .

We waited for ten minutes or more, Mojas watching and listening. As I knelt on the hard rock ground, I gradually felt a metamorphosis taking place inside me. My heartbeat slowed to normal; my adrenaline flow stabilized. Calm set in, and all my senses sharpened. My skin and fingertips began to tingle. I glanced at Mojas, impatient to be on with it.

I'd experienced this phenomenon before

when I'd spent my fear and come to terms with danger. Whenever that happened, I instinctively knew that I'd continue to leave myself open to danger my whole life. In a way, it was like a friendly adversary with whom I was at my best, against whom I'd often taken my measure.

Mojas stood and beckoned. We moved out. . . .

4:28 A.M.

The huge black-mouthed drainage pipe lay ahead of us. Above the embankment that it butted into — twenty or more feet high — the sky glowed from the lights of the South Bay.

Mojas stopped us a few yards away. "Pipe comes out about fifteen yards from here in a ditch. You cross it, you're on the road. *La migra* stops you, you say your car broke down and you're waiting for a ride. All they'll do is tell you you got no business being down here in the dark. I'll check things out now. Then you're on your own."

"Which way do we go to get to the old dairy?" I asked.

"Right, maybe a mile. Wait here." Mojas darted toward the pipe, stooped, and disappeared into the blackness.

I shivered as a gust of cold wind hit us. Looked up at the sky and saw hints of a gray dawn. Hy put his hands on my shoulders. "Almost there, McCone."

"Thank God. Is your arm still bleeding?"

"Uh-huh."

"Bad pain?"

"I'll live."

"You okay, Tim?"

Mourning nodded, teeth chattering.

Mojas was a long time coming back. I kept checking the luminous dial of my watch as five, then another four minutes went by. When he finally emerged from the pipe he ran toward us in a crouch. "Something funny's going on," he said. "There's nobody in the pipe."

Hy asked, "Should there be?"

"It's a regular crossing place. *La migra* was smart, they'd just stand on the other end with a net. Pipe's always full of people who've lost their nerve or're too tired to go on." He hesitated. "I could've swore a gun's been fired in there."

"Those shots we heard earlier?" I asked. They'd echoed off the canyon walls maybe fifteen minutes before we got to the pipe — the stutter of a semiautomatic weapon.

Mojas shrugged.

"Did you see anybody in the ditch or on the road?" Hy asked.

"No."

It didn't feel right to me. "Al, is there another way to get to the road?"

"We'd have to backtrack, and it'll be getting light soon."

"And you say a lot of people know about this pipe?"

"Well, people like me, who need to know."

I considered. "All right," I finally said, "we'll go through here." I felt in my pocket for the coyote's remaining three hundred dollars and extended it to him. "Thanks for guiding us."

He took it, grinning. "Sure. You got any more crazy gringo friends want to come home the hard way, you know where to find me." Then he was gone, disappearing into the shadows.

Hy began to move toward the pipe. I put a restraining hand on his arm. When he frowned, I mouthed the words, "I don't trust him. Wait awhile."

4:49 A.M.

Ten minutes passed with no further sign of Mojas. We got up from where we huddled on the ground and went over to the pipe. Hy and Mourning crouched and stepped inside.

476

I took a final look around and joined them.

Blackness enveloped me. Silt and rocks and debris lay underfoot. The slightest sound echoed off the curving concrete walls. Far ahead I could see a round opening full of gray light. There might not be any people in there now, but I could smell their leavings, feel remnants of their fear and despair.

I could also smell the faint trapped odor of cordite.

I stiffened, tugged at Hy's sleeve. "Something *is* wrong," I whispered.

"Yeah, I was afraid of that."

Quickly I thought through our options; they were few. "You and Tim stay here. I'll go back, climb the embankment, and take a look. Give me around five minutes, then move closer to the other end and make some noise. If anybody's waiting for us, that might flush him out."

"McCone, you climb up there, you're making a target of yourself. I can't let you do that."

"Yes, Ripinsky, you can and you will. You're hurting, and it's the only way to find out if it's safe to go on."

4:54 A.M.

Gray dawn was breaking as I reached the top of the high embankment. The shapes of the rocks and scrub vegetation on the other side had begun to take on definition. The cold sea wind blew more strongly in this unsheltered place. I lay flat on my stomach, then slowly raised my head and looked around.

Things moved down below: they could have been animals, *pollos,* human coyotes — or merely branches stirring in the wind. Like the phantom wolves of my childhood bedtime stories, they slipped in and out of the shadows, eluding identification. For a moment my calm deserted me; I wanted to scramble back down the embankment and run as blindly as I had from the wolves in my long-ago nightmares.

Then the calm reasserted itself, and I knew I was done with stories for good.

I took out my father's .45 and braced it experimentally on the mound of earth in front of me. Checked my watch again. Nearly five minutes had gone by. I scanned the surrounding terrain, saw no one. Listened. Waited.

Then there were sounds below, echoing in the drainage pipe. I tensed, peering through the half-light. Sniper's light, they call it —

And there *was* a sniper.

At first I thought it was only a tamarisk tree moving in the wind. Then I made out a man's figure, down on the opposite side of the ditch. I squinted, strained to identify details. Medium height and slender, holding a weapon. More noise came from the pipe, and the man slipped forward.

Marty Salazar, with a semiautomatic pistol.

He stood in a place where he wouldn't be visible from the pipe's outlet. Would only be visible if you were on his side of the ditch — or up here. He held himself ready, primed to fire, but patient. He'd wait until he identified his quarries, had them clearly in sight, then spray them with bullets. A person coming out of the pipe would never see Salazar. Would never know what hit him.

But he was clearly visible to a person up here. Only yards away — easily within range of her gun. If she was a good shot. And she was — very.

My fingers tightened convulsively on the .45. I relaxed them, steadied the weapon on the mound of earth.

Everything I believed in told me this was wrong. Everything I cared about told me this was right.

One shot, two at most. Shoot to kill. A gun has only one purpose: if you use it, be prepared to take a life.

More noise below. Salazar moved forward,

his stance steady, footing firm. He raised the pistol, ready.

I sighted on him. Waited until he was completely still.

And pulled the trigger.

Thirty-Two

"Listen, Shar, you are rich! What're you going to *do* with all that money?"

"Save it for when my unemployment runs out," I told my brother.

John, Hy, and I were sitting on the purloined park bench on John's hill, sipping beer and watching the sunset. We'd been there since four that afternoon, and by now felt mellow and a little giddy, and would probably regret our behavior in the morning. But for the time being, a spirit of good fellowship prevailed, a pizza was speeding to us from John's favorite Italian restaurant, and I'd managed to keep at bay the terrible images that threatened to invade my mind.

Images such as Ann Navarro dropping to the floor as Jaime's bullet smashed her skull. Such as the flight through Smuggler's Gulch in the moonless early morning. Such as the murder I'd committed on the embankment above Monument Road.

Well, I wasn't fending off the images any longer. . . .

The murder: it was just that, no sugarcoating the fact. Sure, the authorities considered it self-defense. Sure, Lieutenant Gary Viner had congratulated me on ridding the county of one of its more noxious vermin. But I'd shot a man in cold blood. Taken his life to get my people through.

Hy glanced at me, frowned, and touched my cheek. "Don't brood."

"I'm not."

"You are. I always can tell."

John said, "She's been a brooder her whole life."

The two of them exchanged wise looks. I sighed.

Yesterday had been taken up with getting medical attention for Hy's bullet wound and seemingly endless formalities with the local authorities, the FBI, and RKI. Then we went back to my bungalow at La Encantadora and slept nearly around the clock. After a late lunch, I brought Hy over here; John greeted him in that wary manner a big brother adopts when meeting his little sister's lover. Then they discovered a mutual fondness for Beck's dark beer, baseball, western movies, and hiking. Hy told John about his collection of Western Americana and novels; John showed Hy his sound system. The three of us had spiritedly talked about politics, sports, the illegal alien problem, the future of the planet, and why you can't get a decent chicken-fried steak anyplace in the state of California. I had to admit I was somewhat awed by how famously we all got along. Relieved, too: the kidnapping and my shooting Salazar had been widely reported in the press; I'd feared the killing would reerect the barrier between John and me. But he'd seen Salazar, seen the evil I was up against; taking him along while I'd investigated had allowed him a glimpse of the realities of my world that he would never forget, and created a stronger bond between us.

Now we fell silent as the sun sank behind the yucca trees. After a while John asked, "You're not still upset over Ma and Melvin getting pissed at you?"

I shook my head. "By now they're almost over it." My mother and Melvin Hunt had found out about the border crossing and shooting from the TV news hours before I'd been free to call them. Strangely, my mother had seemed angrier that I'd been in San Diego for days without contacting them than that I'd once again placed my life in jeopardy. Melvin had merely asked me not to provoke Ma any more; at his advanced age, he said in his wry way, his heart couldn't stand it.

John stood. "By now they're probably bragging to their friends about you. Listen, if the pizza guy comes, you pay him. You're rich now, and anyway, I gotta go shed a tear for Garfield."

I shook my head as he shambled up the hill to the house. Shedding a tear for a dead president is another of my mother's too-cute euphemisms, and John only says it because he knows it annoys me. Normally he would have announced that he had to go take a leak.

"So you're rich, huh?" Hy said. "And not only that, you now own a seventy-five-buck silk parrot."

"I can't wait to show W.C. to my cats. And I'm certainly richer than I've ever been. RKI *was* generous."

Renshaw had been waiting where I'd told him to when we arrived at the old dairy, with a company car and two fat envelopes full of cash for us. Because I'd shot Salazar, though, we weren't able to just drive away. The red tape was hideous, the conference with the FBI — to which the security firm finally reported the kidnapping — exhausting Then we'd agreed to meet with Renshaw, Dan Kessell, and a few of their operatives for a debriefing. Before we left RKI's offices, Kessell — a blond, burly man who looked like, and was, an ex-marine — presented each of us with an additional check matching the cash payment, and Renshaw said he'd be in touch. Personally, I hoped he'd leave me alone.

"Yeah, *now* they're generous," Hy said bitterly. "But a week ago Renshaw was going to shoot me on sight."

"Well, he's a violent man. You must have known that going in."

He was silent.

"Are you ever going to tell me about those years?" It was the first time I'd had the nerve to ask outright, and it was surprisingly easy.

". . . Someday, probably. I'm building up to it. Hard to talk about something you've never told a living soul."

"Not even Julie?"

"No." He shook his head. "She suspected some things, but I couldn't get into it. I loved my wife, but she was such a . . . purist. Such an idealist. Not at all like you."

"Thanks, Ripinsky."

He tipped my chin up, looked into my eyes. "Didn't mean that the way it sounded. It's supposed to be a compliment. You've got both feet on the ground, you face facts, no matter how unpleasant. You've got what it takes, in any situation." He smiled smugly. "You're like me."

Ten minutes later John still hadn't returned — giving us time alone, I supposed. The shadows of the yuccas lengthened and turned purple, bleeding into the dusk. The cars climbing the streets below began to put on their lights. One stopped at the foot of the driveway, and I heard its door open and close. I stood to see who it was; a long, lean figure started up the hill.

Gage Renshaw.

Hy stood, too. "What's that son of a bitch doing here?"

I shrugged, watching Renshaw. He came up the drive in his long, loose-limbed gait, wearing the same rumpled suit and frayed tie that he'd had on yesterday afternoon. I wondered if the man possessed any decent clothing.

Renshaw spotted us and came over. Before he could speak, Hy said, "Don't you think we've spent enough time together this week, Gage?"

"When're you going to brush that chip off your shoulder, Ripinsky?"

Hy made a disgusted sound.

I said, "Why don't we let Mr. Renshaw tell us why he's here?"

"You can call me by my first name, Sharon."

I ignored that. "Why *are* you here?"

For a moment he seemed at a loss for words

486

— surely an unusual state. Then he said, "I have some information and two offers. First, Fontes and Julio Sandoval, Navarro's contact in the comptroller's office at Colores, were picked up when they tried to draw on the L.C. at Banco Internacional in Mexico City yesterday afternoon. They're admitting nothing, of course, but I assume being held in a Mexican jail will loosen the tongue of one or the other."

When he didn't go on, I prompted him. "And second?"

"Jaime's okay. You can't seriously hurt anybody that stupid by hitting him on the head. And he's talking. You wondered how Salazar knew you'd be crossing with a coyote?"

I nodded.

"After you snatched Mourning, Salazar began phoning, tapped into his network of contacts here in the South Bay. Someone saw you talking with Luis Abrego in the Tradewinds Sunday afternoon. Salazar put it together, then got in touch with his contacts in T.J."

"Al Mojas gave us away?"

"That I don't know. But Salazar knew him, knew where he'd be likely to take you across. My guess is he paid Mojas to deliver you."

"But why did Mojas warn us about something being wrong?" Hy asked.

Renshaw shrugged.

I said, "I think in his odd way he'd come to like us. He tipped us, figuring we'd at least stand a chance." I turned to Renshaw. "Anything else?"

He smiled grimly. "The last missing piece: who shot Diane."

I raised my eyebrows.

"Her husband."

"What?" Hy and I spoke in unison.

Renshaw nodded. "Seems that a lot of drinking went on at Fontes's villa Saturday night and early Sunday morning. Security got lax. Before they doped Tim up and broke his glasses, he managed to get hold of Jaime's gun. Fool could've escaped, but instead he encountered Diane hitting up the living-room liquor cart and decided to sever his marital ties. Failed miserably."

"Good Lord," I said. "She's not going to try to press charges, is she?" If so, it would be on a par with the mugger who sued the San Francisco cab driver who pinned him to a wall with his taxi while trying to apprehend him. In a great miscarriage of justice, the mugger actually won the initial round.

"No, ma'am," Renshaw said. "Diane's not admitting to complicity in the kidnapping, of course, and Tim's willing to overlook her participation in exchange for her not going to the Mexican authorities about the shooting, a speedy divorce, and a distribution of their community property that's weighted heavily in his favor."

"*I* wouldn't be that charitable toward her," I said.

Renshaw glanced at Hy. "Don't ever marry this woman."

Hy grunted.

I said, "Okay, you've given us your information. What about the offers?"

He hesitated, then addressed Hy. "The partnership's still open, Ripinsky. We need somebody with your talents."

Hy's lips tightened. He stared straight ahead, arms folded across his chest.

"Listen, you can't hold a grudge forever because I shot off my mouth and made a stupid threat."

"Which you would have made good on if it hadn't been for McCone."

Renshaw's gaze turned inward. "Maybe, maybe not. But, Jesus, man, how would you have felt in my position?"

Hy seemed to be thinking that over. Finally he said, "About the same." And smiled wryly.

"Then you'll consider the offer?"

"I'll think on it."

Renshaw turned to me. "As for you, Sharon

— or is it still to be Ms. McCone?"

"I guess it's Sharon — Gage."

"As you must know, we're damned impressed with your work. Kessell and I doubt any of our operatives would have handled this situation better — or more, shall we say, creatively. We'd like you to come to work for us. I'm sure we could top whatever you were making at All Souls, and there's a very attractive benefits package."

The offer took me somewhat by surprise. And it struck me as an easy solution to my employment problem. Too easy, perhaps. "I'm flattered, Gage, but like Hy, I'm going to have to think on it."

"Take all the time you need, both of you. The offers will stand." He hesitated, looking at us as if he hoped we'd ask him to stay awhile. When we didn't, he nodded in farewell and walked back down the driveway.

"So," I said after he'd driven away, "are you really going to consider it?"

Hy shrugged. "Might as well. Like I told you a few weeks ago, it's time for a change. You?"

"I don't know if I could work for that kind of outfit."

"Well, give it some thought." He grinned. "Kind of charms me to think of becoming your boss."

"You'd find me unmanageable and incorrigible."

"Them's big words, but I find you that way now."

A pizza delivery van came up the hill and turned into the driveway. I glanced at the house, saw no sign of my brother.

"Go on," Hy said, "you're rich. Pay the man."

The nouveau riche McCone got up to foot the bill.

Thirty-Three

Thursday, June 17

When I arrived at Oakland Airport's north field at a little after two in the afternoon, Hy had already given the Citabria its preflight check and was leaning against it, looking bored and somewhat impatient. "What took you so long?" he asked.

"Well, first I had to talk with Ted."

"About what?"

"*Cogito, ergo doleo.*"

"What?"

"I think, therefore I'm depressed."

"Still?"

"Uh-huh. The interest in Latin was only a temporary respite; he's about to give up on it." I tossed my weekend bag into the rear of the plane.

"Wish there was something to be done for him."

"Maybe there is. He doesn't know it, but we're going to have a long talk when I get

492

back, and I think I'm going to recommend a therapist whom I went to school with. Anyway, then I had to talk with Rae."

"How's she? Any progress with Willie?" Hy found the combination of my assistant and the fence-turned-jewelry-merchant both bizarre and fascinating.

"Uh-uh. As we spoke, she was doing needlepoint — you know Rae, she's mastered every craft in existence — and guess what?"

He raised an eyebrow in question.

"It's a sampler for her office wall, and it says 'A rule with no exception: If it has tires or testicles, you're going to have trouble with it.' "

He snorted. "That's sexist as hell, but really pretty funny." Then he frowned. "You don't believe it, do you?"

"Well . . . sometimes I do, but the kind of trouble I have with the entity that doesn't have tires isn't something I'm willing to forgo."

"That's good. So then what? After Rae, I mean?"

"Then I was in conference with the partners." I'd expected to be at All Souls only long enough to speak with Hank and make arrangements to clear out my office, but had ended up closeted in the parlor with Hank, Pam, Larry, Gloria, and Mike for over two hours.

"They all get together to rake you over the coals?"

"Actually, no. They're restructuring my job to utilize what they call my 'unique abilities.' Translation: peculiarities. But the promotion — without the chore of supervising paralegals and with a minimum of desk duty — stands."

"As it should. But how the hell did they come around?"

"Seems Hank sat them all down and read them the riot act while I was gone. I don't know exactly what he said, but he convinced them that firing me would be tantamount to tossing a national treasure into the trash compactor." I started to get into the plane's rear seat.

Hy put his hand on my shoulder. "No, McCone. Today you're the pilot."

"Really?" I felt like a little kid does when the training wheels finally come off her bicycle.

"Really. You earned it."

He got in back, and then I climbed in front. Put on the seat belt and headset, fiddled with switches — fingers eager and slightly a-fumble.

Through the earphones Hy said, "So are you going to stay there?"

Confidently I flicked a switch; it did what it was supposed to. "At All Souls? I don't know. I told them I'd have to consider it."

"Thought you'd have jumped at the chance."

"Maybe, like you, I'm due for a change." My mind was more on the mechanics of take-off than on my future career. I started the engine. The propeller jerked, then whirred into silver motion.

Hy said, "You haven't turned RKI down yet, either."

"How'd you know?"

"I talked with Gage this morning."

"You're not going in with them, are you?"

"Nope. After these past couple of weeks, I've decided there's too much crap going down on this planet for me to spend the rest of my life doing the kinds of things Gage and Dan want me to. It's time for me to kick some butt, and the Spaulding Foundation's the perfect apparatus for that."

"Sounds as if you're gearing up for a fight. Just what is it you plan to do?"

"Things you wouldn't believe, McCone. Things you flat-out wouldn't believe."

"I'll watch with interest." Smiling, I thumbed the switch on the mike and said, "Oakland Ground, this is Citabria seven-seven-two-eight-niner. . . ."

Air traffic was light that afternoon. In a very few minutes I was cleared for takeoff, VFR eastbound for Tufa Lake. Runway 27R stretched before me like a long-awaited promise. When the little plane lifted off the tarmac, I felt an intense thrill of freedom — breaking loose into a world that had no bounds.

Sometimes, I thought, the worth of freedom can be measured only by the cost of what you give up to achieve it. If I chose a free path when I returned to the city, it would be valuable beyond reckoning.

I looked back at Hy, gave him a thumbs-up sign, and tipped the plane's left wing into a soaring arc above San Francisco Bay.